LUMO AND THE CIMMERIAN ORDER

Lumo and the Cimmerian Order.

ISBN: (Paperback): 9789334174090
For inquiries or permissions requests, please contact:
author.nileshprabhu@gmail.com

Dedication

For my parents, whose unwavering belief in me lit the path to this story.
For my sister, a constant source of encouragement and inspiration.
And for my friends and family, who never let me lose sight of the magic of storytelling.
This journey is as much yours as it is mine.

N
W
E
S
SLITHEVAR
OPHIDONIA
VALTARRA
ROCHFELL
ELDERINE
SKELIAN HIGHLANDS
GREENFIELD MEADOWS
AVALORA
VERIDIA
EVERGLADES
AVALORA
SERENDIA
LEAFCREST
HARBRIDGE ACADEMY

CHAPTER 1

"UNACCEPTABLE!" Lucius's voice cut through the air.

"Again, Oliver! What was that? Your strikes are pitiful, and your footwork is a mess," he barked, his voice carrying disappointment like a chilling breeze.

Oliver, with a heavy sigh, attempted to explain, "I'm trying, Lucius. It's just that today, nothing seems to be going right with this blade."

Prince Oliver stood in the castle training grounds, the faint smell of damp earth rising from the freshly watered flower beds lining the courtyard's perimeter. His dark hair fell into his face as a light breeze stirred the banners hanging from the stone battlements above.

The weight of a thousand disillusioned pixies seemed to perch on his shoulders, adding to the oppressive heat of the sun beating down on the open courtyard. Young Oliver grappled with the nuances of swordplay alongside his sparring partner, his journey through the intricacies resembling a Goblin attempting to master ballet—noble in intention, yet slightly awkward in execution.

Meanwhile, Lucius Stoneguard, the renowned knight and master swordsman, continued observing with a stern expression. A towering figure with graying hair, a neatly trimmed beard, and deep-set eyes beneath bushy eyebrows, he embodied the essence of discipline and unyielding strength. His face bore the marks of a life dedicated to honing his skills and imparting his wisdom to those under his tutelage.

"Trying is not enough. You must push through your limitations and give your best effort. We are training to protect the kingdom, and half-hearted attempts won't suffice," Lucius said, crossing his arms.

Oliver looked down at his sword. "I know, but my sword seems to have a will of its own today. Maybe I'm just not meant for this."

Oliver's shoulders slumped further under the weight of frustration and self-doubt that had gate-crashed his otherwise optimistic demeanor. *Why can't I get this right?* A trace of weariness crept into his voice, turning its usual cheer into a melancholic ballad.

Lucius's stern expression softened, and he approached Oliver, placing a firm hand on his shoulder.

"Don't sell yourself short, Oliver. You have the potential to master the sword, but it requires perseverance and resilience."

Oliver lifted his gaze to meet Lucius, a flicker of hope kindling in his eyes.

"Do you really think I can improve?"

"Of course. You do understand what you are doing wrong, don't you?"

"No," Oliver replied, shifting his weight from one foot to the other.

"You're defending too much. You can't win a fight by blocking alone." Lucius gestured emphatically.

"B—But every time I try to attack, I end up exposing myself to a counterstrike. If I stay defensive, at least I can control the fight," Oliver argued.

"Control? You're only prolonging it. A fight isn't just about waiting for your opponent to make a mistake—it's about creating those openings yourself. A shield may protect you, but it is the sword that wins the battle," Lucius advised.

"Now let's go. Let's show your opponent how it's done," Lucius declared with a condescending eye roll directed at Oliver's sparring partner.

Oliver decided to indulge in a dramatic lungful of air, as if the secrets of the universe could be found at the bottom of his lungs. Meanwhile, his gaze engaged in a staring contest with his practice partner.

His name was Lumoquin, but everyone called him Lumo. Everyone except Lucius, who refused to address him by his name and chose instead to call him "boy."

Lumo stood ready, his calm demeanor starkly contrasting Oliver's agitation. With a lean build and a face marked by both boyish charm and the beginnings of manhood, Lumo's dark brown eyes sparkled with playful competitiveness, despite his tranquil exterior.

"All right, Lumo, let's see if I can put these lessons into practice. Prepare yourself!" Oliver shouted.

"Oh, don't worry, Your Highness. I won't make it easy for you," Lumo replied.

Oliver lunged forward while Lumo deftly parried each attack, countering with his own swift moves. Each step stirred the loose sand beneath them, faint clouds of dust rising as their swords clashed. The sharp sound echoed through the courtyard, with wooden dummies as silent witnesses. Birds perched lazily on the castle's ledges, indifferent to the battle below.

As the clash of swords continued—*Unacceptable!* —Lucius's words kept reverberating in Oliver's mind. Oh, each strike, a veritable ballet of steel, wasn't just a physical maneuver. No, no, it was a nuanced response to Lucius's less-than-gentle encouragement.

Oliver's focus intensified, his movements becoming more fluid. Undeterred, Oliver transformed each sword swing into a retort, as if saying, *Oh, unacceptable? Well, watch this, Lucius!* His maneuvers became calculated, each jab and parry a witty comeback in swordplay language.

Lumo struggled to match Oliver's intensity. His movements were hesitant, his defense lacking. Each strike forced him onto the back foot as if he were performing a dance move he hadn't quite mastered—the "Barely Able to Keep Up Two-Step." Doubt cast a shadow over him, and frustration deepened the lines on his forehead.

Oliver feigned a strike, causing Lumo to momentarily raise his sword to block the anticipated blow.

"Now, Oliver! Seize the moment! Use the move!" shouted Lucius.

Lumo's eyes widened as he saw Oliver's blade ascending from a lower position. With the grace of a cat trying to walk on a frozen lake, he tried to regain his balance and lower his sword in defense. Alas, it turned out to be too late. In a fluid motion, Oliver deftly hooked his blade around Lumo's wrist, making solid contact. With a swift, practiced twist, Oliver disarmed Lumo, the sword flying from Lumo's grip.

Oliver took the opportunity to follow through, pushing Lumo's chest with his shoulders. Lumo stumbled backward, his back making a reluctant acquaintance with the wooden fence separating the open space from the surrounding garden.

Oliver, with a chest heaving like a dragon after a fierce battle, gracefully lowered his sword, his face etched with a mix of victory and concern. In a swift display of athleticism, he closed the distance between them, extending a hand to Lumo like a knight offering rescue to a fallen comrade.

"Lumo, are you all right? I didn't mean to—"

Lumo managed a strained smile, accepting Oliver's hand.

"I'm fine, Your Highness. That was a well-earned victory." He dusted himself off.

Lucius approached them, his voice firm but laced with a chilling coldness. "Excellent work, Prince. But remember, in the heat of battle, when your opponent lies vulnerable, you go for the kill. Mercy is a luxury the weak cannot afford."

Despite the praise, his words had a distinct edge, as if they were aimed at more than just Oliver's performance. The knight's subtle irritation simmered beneath the surface, his disapproval not just of the prince's mercy but of Lumo's very presence. As Oliver's attendant, Lumo's role at the prince's side was an unspoken irritation to Lucius. The knight had always envisioned one of his own knights or squires as a more fitting sparring partner for the prince, but the king had insisted on someone always in the prince's company—someone like Lumo, much to the knight's dismay.

Oliver's jovial nature broke through the tension as he grinned at Lumo. "Oh, that was a good fight, wasn't it? You gave it your best, my friend."

Lumo's lips curled upward, but his eyes lingered on the ground, the smile not quite reaching them. "Indeed, Your Highness. It was quite the exhilarating match."

"Remember, boy, your role is not to challenge the prince. You're here to serve and support him," Lucius growled, gnashing his teeth as he shot a frigid glance at Lumo.

For a split second, Lumo's smile faltered, and his hand tightened into a fist at his side before he straightened himself, offering a more controlled smile. "Of course, Sir Lucius. I'll keep that in mind."

"Come on, my friend. Let's head back to the castle. I'll treat you to some well-deserved refreshments." Oliver clapped Lumo on the back.

Lumo's steps were slightly slower than usual, his gaze drifting away from Oliver's eager chatter. "That sounds great, Your Highness," he said.

From across the training ground, Lumo caught sight of a group of squires practicing under the watchful eye of another of Lucius's knights—Eamon. His steady instructions rang clear, cutting through the clatter of wooden swords.

"Let's hurry before the food's gone!" Oliver grinned, steering Lumo away before he could dwell any longer.

***

As Oliver and Lumo left the training grounds, they walked across the castle courtyard. The courtyard was a vast open space, large enough to host a jousting tournament or perhaps a dragon-sized game of hide-and-seek. In the center, a majestic fountain proudly showcased the castle's prioritization of aesthetics over practicality, with its waters seemingly chosen to dance rather than quench any thirst.

"Did you see what I did there, Lumo? Wasn't that just perfect?" Oliver beamed.

"Indeed, Your Highness. It was a great move," Lumo replied, his lips pressed together tightly.

"The Iron Hook, Lucius calls it. It's all about timing and precision. You wait for the right moment, create an opening, then hook and twist. Simple, right?" Oliver chuckled, dramatically gesturing the move as he spoke.

Lumo felt a pang of frustration. He had tried to replicate the move several times in practice, but never quite managed to pull it off with the same finesse.

"I understand the technique, but executing it... that's the tricky part."

Oliver clapped a hand on Lumo's shoulder. "Don't worry. It took me years to perfect it. You'll get there with time and practice. Just keep at it."

Yeah, right, Lumo thought. *If only the Lord Knight wasn't present in their practice bouts, he might have had a chance at learning.* He smiled like a child who had just been scolded.

Oliver and Lumo continued their stroll into the castle corridors, each step echoing against the weathered walls, carrying the weight of centuries-old stories. The cold, sturdy stones spoke of a history etched in time, where battles were relics and the only foes were the occasional dust mites. Arched doorways led to chambers with heavy wooden doors, giving the corridor an extra dash of castle couture. The occasional suit of armor stood sentinel, not in defense but as a testament to the castle's commitment to outdated aesthetics.

"But honestly, I don't know why I have to practice swordplay every day." Oliver dragged his feet, the clinking of armor punctuating his slow pace as they walked through the stone corridors. "There barely seems to be any conflict around here."

Lumo chuckled. "Well, Your Highness, it's better to be over-prepared for peace than under-prepared for war. Besides, it adds a certain flair to your princely image."

"Flair, huh? Maybe I should take up juggling instead. At least that would be entertaining."

"Your juggling skills might not strike fear into the hearts of invaders, my prince," Lumo smirked.

"Who needs fear when you have charm?" Oliver grinned, casting a playful glance at Lumo.

Just as their banter hit a comedic high note, Amelia—one of the many maidservants of the castle—glided into view.

"Forgive the interruption, your Highness," she said with a curtsy. "But the king requests your presence in his court."

Lumo and Oliver shared a conspiratorial glance.

Oliver, adopting a posture fit for royal drama, traded his playful demeanor for a cloak of responsibility. "Thank you, Amelia. I'll make my way to the king's court immediately."

Oliver turned to Lumo, his eyes wide. "Lumo, did I forget a royal decree, break any ancient traditions, or accidentally insult a visiting dignitary?"

"Not that I'm aware of," Lumo said, maintaining his calm demeanor. "Take a deep breath, Oliver. I'm sure it's nothing too bad."

"You're right, you're right—" Oliver took a deep, exaggerated breath, puffing out his chest as if preparing for an impending disaster. "I'm probably just about to be scolded for another obscure royal etiquette I didn't even know existed. I mean, how was I supposed to know I needed to keep my head up while descending the stairs? Seems like a bit of a safety hazard to me."

Lumo chuckled, shaking his head. "Trust me, Oliver, you'll survive this. Just remember, the king is much more forgiving than the stairs."

Oliver cracked a small smile at that. "Point taken. Let's go then, shall we?"

As they neared the grand doors of the king's court, guarded by sentinels, Oliver decided it was time for another deep breath.

Oliver pushed open the grand doors, fully aware that the kingdom's fate, or at least the next royal spectacle, awaited just beyond the threshold.

As Oliver and Lumo meandered into the throne room, sunlight poured through the high windows, illuminating gilded arches and intricate frescoes.

Velvet banners, proudly bearing the Avaloran crest of a majestic eagle with wings outstretched, clung to the walls. Meanwhile, the chandeliers above, the attention seekers of the architectural world, dangled precariously, screaming for the spotlight. The marble floor beneath them, a canvas of craftsmanship, played host to an intricate dance of patterns, an ode to the artisanal perfectionism that apparently ran in the kingdom. A long red carpet, guided the way with a soft, "This way to his majesty."

The courtiers, an ensemble cast of nobility, shifted their gaze toward the prince as he entered.

At the far end of the room, elevated on a majestic dais, sat King Reginald, a man in his early forties with the regal bearing befitting his station. King Reginald had all the features that suited a king, dark black hair and a prominent jawline, framed by a neatly groomed beard.

"Welcome, my son," the king proclaimed, his voice echoing through the hall.

Oliver approached the dais with the measured elegance of a young prince who, despite his tender years, had already mastered the art of royal theatrics.

"You summoned, uh, father me—oh, um, sorry."

A subtle muttered, "Oops," escaped Oliver's lips, his eyes briefly widening with realization before he smoothly corrected the verbal hiccup. "You summoned me, father."

Lumo, standing nearby, couldn't help but stifle a quiet giggle.

The king, who had witnessed the slip-up firsthand, decided to dismiss it with a sheepish grin and continued, his words carefully measured, "You were summoned, Oliver. There are matters we must discuss."

Prince Oliver, though maintaining the facade of royal composure, couldn't shake off a subtle unease. "Of course, Father. I am at your disposal."

King Reginald's gaze was fixed on the grandeur beyond the throne room. "Oliver, as your sixteenth birthday approaches, the kingdom anticipates the celebration of your coming of age."

"I understand, Father. It is a significant event."

"Indeed, it is. Hence, I must announce the initiation of our traditional ceremony that accompanies this milestone."

"What ceremony do you speak of?" Prince Oliver replied, maintaining his princely poise.

"The Ceremony of Ascendance. It marks a prince's transition into his true responsibilities. You understand this, don't you?"

Shit, Oliver thought to himself. Oliver had forgotten that being sixteen meant he was technically fit to rule, not that he would get to rule right away.

"Yes, Father, do let me know what is needed of me," he calmly recovered.

"If I may, your Majesty," a voice spoke behind them.

Turning, they faced Archibald, the royal advisor. His salt-and-pepper hair, neatly groomed, framed a face marked by time and experience. His attire, a blend of regal elegance and scholarly precision, suggested a man who could seamlessly transition from advising the king on matters of state to correcting the grammar of a royal proclamation.

"Ah, Archibald, yes. Please, continue," King Reginald proclaimed.

"The ceremony, Your Highness, is slated to unfold as a grand spectacle on the day of your birthday, captivating the

gaze of both nobles and commoners alike," Archibald elucidated with a sagely nod. "The rituals themselves would be steeped in tradition. From the anointing with sacred oils to the symbolic gestures that forge a connection between the ruler and the realm; it's a majestic display that binds the sovereign and the kingdom in a sacred covenant."

Oliver's mind meanwhile sprinted like a caffeinated squirrel, trying to grasp the weightiness of what awaited him.

"Rest assured, my prince, you won't be alone in this endeavor," Archibald assured him. "The kingdom stands with you, and as your advisors, we are here to guide you through the nuances of this traditional ceremony."

"However, your Highness, there is a matter of diplomatic delicacy we must address. With the attendance of dignitaries from Veridia and Ophidonia, the ceremony extends beyond our borders. It becomes a statement of unity and goodwill. King Valdorix of Veridia is expected to dispatch his cousin, Duke Thornbriar, and King Caelumyth of Ophidonia may honor us with the presence of Count Calindor," Archibald continued, his gaze shifting between the king and the prince, like a wise owl surveying its nest.

Oh, those guys, Oliver thought to himself.

Oliver couldn't help but be reminded that ruling the kingdom of Avalora wasn't his only royal duty. There were also the less-than-delightful alliances with the neighboring kingdoms of Veridia and Ophidonia. Faces of princes and princesses from those lands flashed in his mind, their names resembling an elaborate puzzle he hadn't quite mastered. In the grand chessboard of diplomacy, remembering names seemed to be the most challenging move for a young prince.

Oliver nodded thoughtfully. "I understand, Archibald. The alliances with our neighboring kingdoms are crucial."

"Indeed, my prince, and as part of this ceremony, diplomatic exchanges will unfold. It's an opportunity to strengthen ties, foster camaraderie, and build a network that transcends borders."

The king, observing the exchange, added, "Your role in these interactions is vital, Oliver. It's a chance to showcase the diplomatic finesse that befits a future king."

Oliver, though inwardly hoped that the crown came with an instruction manual, responded with regal resolve, "I shall do my best, Father."

As the discussion delved into the intricacies of diplomatic protocols, Oliver's mind wandered. He found himself contemplating not only the responsibilities of the ceremony but also the future that awaited him.

Archibald, wrapping up the diplomatic details, stated, "Your Majesty, your Highness, if there are no further matters to discuss, I shall make preparations for the forthcoming events."

"Very well, Archibald. We trust your expertise in these affairs," King Reginald said, inclining his head slightly.

As Archibald excused himself from the royal court, Oliver turned to his father, "I appreciate your guidance, Father. I shall prepare for the responsibilities that lie ahead."

King Reginald, with a restrained smile, replied, "I have faith in you, Oliver."

With that, Oliver, flanked by Lumo, exited the throne room, leaving behind the weighty discussions and stepping back once again into the corridor.

Oliver stood there, absorbing the weight of the king's words. "An ascension ceremony... on my sixteenth birthday," he mused aloud. "That's just a few days away."

Lumo shifted his weight, his arms crossing in mock contemplation as he watched Oliver. "Well, looks like you'll finally have to start acting your age, Your Highness."

"And here I thought you were going to tell me how proud you are," Oliver shot him a playful glare.

"Oh, I'm definitely proud. Proud that you'll be the youngest monarch with a knack for losing things. Remember the time you lost your royal ring in the stables?" Lumo smirked.

"You're never going to let that go, are you?" Oliver laughed.

"Not a chance," Lumo replied with a grin. "Besides, it's part of my royal duties to remind you of your humble beginnings."

"Well, I'll just have to make sure you're always around to keep me grounded."

"That's the spirit," Lumo said, giving him a reassuring pat on the back. "And don't worry, you've got this. Just try not to trip on your robes during the ceremony."

Oliver chuckled. "I'll do my best, Lumo. I'll do my best. Now come on. I'm hungry."

***

As the evening sun reluctantly dipped below the horizon, throwing an amber glow over the kingdom of Avalora, the Thistle & Thorn, a small, lively tavern nestled in a corner of the town, came alive with merriment. Laughter hung in the air like confetti amidst the clinking of glasses. The soft melodies of a minstrel's song serenaded the patrons.

The bartender, Bart, a jovial man with a bushy mustache, regaled the patrons with his quick wit and humorous anecdotes. It was a performance that walked the fine line between entertainment and a desperate cry for a better minstrel.

"So, did ya hear the latest rumor from the castle?" Bart exclaimed, a mischievous twinkle in his eyes.

The laughter dissipated, and everyone looked curiously at him.

"What is it, Bart?" shouted Sam, one of the patrons.

"Well," Bart began, leaning in closer to the group. "They say that Sir Archibald's prized parrot has learned to mimic the king's voice and has been giving orders to the guards!"

Laughter erupted from the crowd, punctuated by snorts and chuckles.

"You're pulling our leg, Bart!" exclaimed another patron, wiping tears of laughter from his eyes.

"I swear on me barmaid's honor, it's true!" Bart insisted, feigning seriousness. "The parrot has become the true ruler of the kingdom!"

"And what are these orders, pray tell? More crackers for everyone?" jested another patron.

The bar erupted in raucous laughter once again, as if the gods of humor themselves had orchestrated a chorus of hilarity.

As the laughter subsided, Lily, the barmaid, chimed in, a mischievous grin on her face. "If the parrot is in charge, maybe it can order us another round of drinks, eh?"

The suggestion was met with cheers and applause, and Bart playfully nodded. "Consider it done! To Sir Archibald's parrot and its rule over our merriment!"

Amidst the clinking of glasses and occasional bursts of laughter, a hushed conversation emerged between two patrons.

"I heard from my cousin who works in the castle," one whispered, casting a cautious glance around. "They say the prince's sixteenth birthday is approaching, and the king has something significant planned."

The other patron leaned in, his eyes wide with curiosity. "Significant? What do you mean? Is it a grand celebration?"

"Not sure, but they said something big is being planned. I heard they bade the cooks to prepare the Skelian pigs for slaughter. Must be an extravagant affair."

"Ah, the Skelian pigs, you say? Those creatures are legendary," the other patron exclaimed, a tinge of disbelief in his voice.

"Indeed, they really are going all out."

Lily, who had overheard the conversation, couldn't contain her excitement. She banged her mug on the counter, catching Bart's attention.

"What's all this fuss about, Lily?" Bart asked, wiping down a glass with a cloth.

"Bart, did you know about this? What's the buzz about this colossal feast? Enlighten me, will you?"

Bart scratched his head, a perplexed expression settling on his face like a puzzle piece struggling to fit. "Where'd you hear this wee bit of news?"

"From those two saps over there!" Lily exclaimed.

Bart narrowed his eyes with a touch of mock suspicion and scurried over to the two men, his imposing stature making them rethink the wisdom of shrinking in their seats.

"All right, you two, spill yer guts... or no more coming into this here establishment."

The men exchanged nervous glances before one of them stammered out whatever little details he had overheard from his cousin.

Bart leaned back, crossing his arms over his chest. A mischievous grin spread across his face like a cat caught with cream on its whiskers.

Turning to face the rest of the patrons, Bart announced, "Well, well, well... it seems our prince is turning sixteen, and there's goin' ta be a feast!"

After a moment of hush, the crowd exploded into cheers and applause, as if the kingdom had just discovered the secret to unlimited pudding.

The bar buzzed with the thrill of impending gossip. Because who doesn't love a good game of make-believe in a tavern?

Bart chuckled, his voice cutting through the lively atmosphere. "Easy, folks. Wild tales won't fill yer tankards. Feast, yes. Roy'al? Let me ask around."

Most patrons probably hadn't noticed Bart's words at this point, too engrossed in their own revelries to care about the nuances of royal intrigue. The real business, it seemed, was happening at the bottom of their tankards.

Meanwhile, a shadowy figure clad in dark hooded attire sat tucked away in the corner of the lively bar, his presence unnoticed by the revelers. His brooding gaze swept across the room, observing the lively interactions and absorbing the snippets of conversations.

As the night wore on, the figure signaled for his tab.

"That'll be two silver coins and four copper pennies," Lily said as she collected the mugs from his table.

The stranger reached into his purse, the dim light catching the glint of a few coins. As he counted out the silver and copper, Lily couldn't help but notice the large scar that marred his face, much like the craggy contours of a mountain range.

"Haven't seen you here before," Lily remarked as she collected the coins.

The stranger's eyes met Lily's briefly. With a swift movement, he pulled the hood further over his face.

With a slight nod, he sorted himself, careful not to draw further attention. He rose from his seat, his movements purposeful yet unassuming, and made his way toward the exit.

***

Back at the castle, the prince prepared to settle into his chambers as night fell. Lumo was busy lighting the candles and tidying up.

“Anything else, Oliver?” Lumo asked as he finished arranging a stack of books.

Prince Oliver surveyed the room, noting the orderliness Lumo had restored. He turned to his attendant with a small, appreciative smile.

“Thank you, Lumo. You've done a splendid job, as always.”

Lumo bowed his head slightly, his voice quiet, worn from the day's work. “It's my pleasure, Oliver. Just doing my duty.”

Lumo moved toward the door, his hand already on the handle, but before he could leave, Oliver’s voice stopped him, soft and hesitant. “Are you leaving already?”

Lumo paused, looking back over his shoulder. “Do you need anything else, my lord?”

Oliver let out a long, soft sigh, his gaze drifting toward the portrait of his mother hanging on the wall. Queen Lavinia’s image stared down from the frame—flowing auburn hair and luminous brown eyes, a portrait of grace and kindness. Her untimely death had cast a shadow over the castle, and Oliver felt that absence as deeply as if it had been a wound never fully healed.

He spoke quietly, almost to himself. "Sometimes, I wish... I wish I had known my mother. It's a strange thing, isn't it? To miss someone you've never truly met."

Lumo shifted his weight, his heart tight in his chest. He couldn't name the feeling, but he knew what it was like to live with an emptiness that never fully faded. His response was a quiet one, born from years of watching Oliver wrestle with this unspoken grief. "I'm sure she would be proud of the person you've become, my lord."

Oliver didn't meet his eyes immediately, his thoughts tangled in that old sorrow. But when Oliver finally turned back to him, the faintest twitch of a smile pulled at his lips, bittersweet and fleeting. "That means more than you know."

Lumo drew a quiet breath and let a wry smile play on his lips.

"Oh! I know," Lumo added quickly, shifting his stance. "Knock, knock."

Oliver blinked in confusion, pulled from his thoughts. "What? Oh, who goes there?"

Lumo straightened and grinned. "Arthur."

"Arthur who?"

Lumo swept his arm wide, as though presenting a grand stage. "Arthur any dragons that need slaying around here?"

For a moment, Oliver stared, then broke into laughter, the sound filling the room and shattering the heaviness in the air.

"Not bad, Lumo," Oliver said, the corners of his lips turning upwards.

"All right, my lord, I'll leave you to your thoughts now," Lumo said, his grin fading but his eyes warm. "But do try not to think too much."

Oliver chuckled softly. "I'll try."

With a final glance around the room, Lumo stepped out of the chamber, gently closing the door behind him. He paused in the hallway for a moment, the sound of his footsteps echoing against the stone walls. The laughter still lingered in his ears, and for a brief instant, it almost felt like a weight had been lifted.

As he made his way down the castle's familiar halls, Lumo found a quiet comfort in the stillness of the night. He soon reached his own quarters—modest and tucked away in a quieter corner of the castle. The room itself was small, with stone walls that had witnessed the passing of countless years. A worn wooden bed occupied one side, adorned with a simple quilt that had seen better days. A small wooden table stood against the opposite wall, playing host to a guttering candle, a worn book, and a handful of cherished mementos.

Lumo crossed the room, pulling the curtains back slightly to let the moonlight filter in through the narrow window. The castle's spires stretched toward the heavens, their dark shapes outlined against the star-filled sky. A faint hint of lavender from a sachet on the wall hung in the air, a touch of softness in the otherwise plain surroundings.

Though it lacked the opulence of Oliver's chambers, Lumo's quarters held a simple peace, a place where he could breathe and think. The hum of the castle's busy corridors seemed to fade away in here, and for a moment, he allowed himself to rest in solitude.

With a final glance around his quarters, Lumo let out a contented sigh. He settled into his humble bed, ready to rest and gather strength for the adventures that awaited him on the morrow.

***

CHAPTER 2

As the first rays of sunlight painted the sky in hues of gold, Lumo breezed into Oliver's quarters with a tray of breakfast fit for royalty. The tantalizing aroma of warm pastries and freshly brewed tea wafted through the air.

"Good morning, Oliver," Lumo greeted, setting the tray on a nearby table. "I've brought your breakfast. I trust you had a restful night?"

Oliver, still caught in the clutches of morning stiffness, stretched his arms above his head, feeling the satisfying pull in his muscles.

"Good morning, Lumo. I slept like a log. Ready to tackle the day!"

"That's good to hear." Lumo chuckled. "A hearty breakfast awaits you. Enjoy."

Oliver settled himself at the table, savoring the delicious flavors that danced upon his taste buds. As he indulged in the mouthwatering treats, Lumo took a moment to straighten the room and ensure everything was in its proper place.

Once Oliver had shoveled in a princely portion of his meal, he looked up at Lumo.

"Sho, wha'sh on the agenda for today, my friend?" His words were slightly muffled by a cheeky mouthful of breakfast.

Lumo grinned. "Well, my lord, they are eagerly waiting for you downstairs. It appears the royal seamstress is bursting with excitement, insisting you grace her masterpiece for the upcoming ceremony."

"A new attire, you say?" Oliver exclaimed, between hearty gulps of grape juice, a splash of the rich liquid threatening to escape with each enthusiastic swig. He quickly wiped his chin with the back of his hand.

"Yep, they weren't kidding about the 'traditional' part, it seems. And between you and me, I think you'll be surprised."

"Is it that bad?" Oliver grumbled, setting the cup down with a soft thud.

Lumo leaned in conspiratorially, "I wouldn't call it bad, my lord. Let's just say, the royal seamstress has a flair for the dramatic. Your wardrobe is about to get a lot more... regal." He waggled his eyebrows for effect.

"Regal or regrettably experimental?" Oliver arched an eyebrow.

"Oh, it's a masterpiece in its own unique way. I don't want to spoil it anymore for you; might as well see it yourself."

"Well, let's not keep the royal attire awaiting then," Oliver said, pushing back from the table with a smirk.

Together, they descended the winding staircase, leading to the lower levels of the castle. Upon reaching the lower level, a buzz of activity greeted them. Castle staff scurried about, attending to various tasks, and the air hummed with an electric energy.

In a cozy nook, a woman of petite stature stood with the authority of a ruler in her own realm of fabrics. Her gaze, sharp as the needles she wielded, surveyed the room. Various fabrics adorned her surroundings like loyal subjects vying for her attention. She sported a tape measure around her neck like a prized medal and a pair of scissors tucked into a pocket, ready for sartorial battle.

Her name was Madame Tissuré, the royal seamstress with a reputation as illustrious as the garments she crafted. Legend had it that she once sewed an entire ball gown during a particularly long-winded royal speech, and the gown turned out more eloquent than the orator.

"Not like that, darlings! A royal garment should murmur poetry, not scream it. And, please, we're not preparing a peacock for a parade; subtlety is the gateway to regal elegance," Madame Tissuré chided with an air of exasperated grandeur. Her own attire, a beacon of subtlety, whispered elegance in the most deafening tones.

Her attendants nodded fervently, some taking mental notes while others frantically adjusted their own attire as if fearing Madame Tissuré's discerning eye.

As Oliver and Lumo approached, the royal seamstress turned her attention to them, her eyes gleaming with the anticipation of a sculptor about to mold a masterpiece.

"Ah, Prince Oliver!"

Oliver inclined his head. "Madame Tissuré, I am honored to be in the presence of someone whose mastery in the art of attire is as renowned as your own."

Lumo suppressed a smirk, knowing that Oliver's diplomatic charm was a delicate dance between courtesy and concealed amusement.

"The honor is mine, Your Highness. I've prepared something truly extraordinary for the occasion." The seamstress curtsied theatrically.

Madame Tissuré led them to a secluded area where her latest creation awaited its debut. Metaphorical drumrolls seemed to play in the background as she dramatically unveiled the garment.

"Behold, the regal masterpiece for the upcoming ceremony!"

Oliver blinked, momentarily taken aback. The attire was indeed regal, but not in the way he had imagined. It featured an abundance of frills, glittering sequins, and an assortment of vibrant colors that clashed rather than complemented. It was a fashion extravaganza of excess.

Lumo discreetly coughed to suppress a laugh, while Madame Tissuré beamed with pride.

"Isn't it exquisite, Your Highness? A true reflection of the grandeur befitting your status."

Oliver, caught between politeness and disbelief, managed a tight-lipped smile. "It's... certainly unique, Madame Tissuré. I appreciate your effort."

The seamstress, seemingly oblivious to any potential dismay, continued, "I knew you'd appreciate the avant-garde touch. It's a departure from the mundane, a celebration of the extraordinary!"

Unable to contain himself any longer, Lumo burst into laughter. Oliver looked at Lumo and couldn't help but join in. Madame Tissuré, however, mistook their laughter for appreciation.

"I'm delighted you love it, Your Highness! Now, let's get you properly fitted, and you'll be the talk of the kingdom!"

As Madame Tissuré ushered Oliver toward a makeshift dressing area, Oliver whispered, "Regal, indeed. I never knew the kingdom needed a walking carnival."

Lumo chuckled. "Sometimes, a ruler must endure the quirks of fashion for the sake of diplomacy."

Boy, was Lumo glad he wasn't in the prince's shoes or robes for that matter.

"All right then, Prince, why don't you try on the robe first?" Madame Tissuré suggested with a knowing grin.

Just then a distant commotion erupted outside. The trio exchanged puzzled glances as the sounds of raised voices and hurried footsteps reached their ears. Lumo, a furrow forming on his forehead, moved toward the nearest window.

The once peaceful view of the castle grounds was now marred by a sense of urgency as maidservants scurried about, some clutching bundles of clothing, while others hastily closed shutters and doors.

"What do you think is happening outside?" Lumo quizzed, his tone shifting from amusement to concern.

Oliver joined Lumo at the window, peering out at the castle courtyard. Chaos, it seemed, had taken up residence in the castle grounds, albeit in an almost organized manner.

Lumo turned to Oliver, his furrowed brow mirroring the prince's growing unease. "My lord, it seems there's a disturbance outside. We should find out what's happening."

Oliver bobbed his head silently.

They made their way back to Madame Tissuré, who was still engrossed in her preparations. Oliver cleared his throat, gaining the seamstress's attention. "Madame Tissuré, it appears there's some commotion outside. We need to investigate. We'll return shortly."

Madame Tissuré, preoccupied with the regal masterpiece, nodded absentmindedly. "Very well, Your Highness. I'll continue with the preparations."

As Oliver and Lumo exited the room, the sense of urgency grew stronger. The distant commotion intensified, and the castle seemed to hum with an unspoken tension.

They navigated the winding corridors, making their way toward the source of the disturbance. As they reached the castle courtyard, they spotted Lucius barking orders to the assembled guards. The courtyard had transformed into a beehive of commotion, soldiers buzzing around like diligent soldier bees in the face of an unknown threat.

Lucius continued to bark orders, motioning to the drawbridge, ensuring its proper fortification. The drawbridge separated the castle's inner sanctum from the outer world, while a protective moat—wide and imposing—encircled the fortress.

"Men, ensure the drawbridge is raised and fortified! Keep a watchful eye on the surroundings. If it approaches, raise the drawbridge immediately!"

As the soldiers scattered to carry out Lucius's commands, Oliver and Lumo approached him. Lucius, noticing their arrival, turned to acknowledge them.

"My lord, you should get inside," he said, as hastily as possible.

"What's happening, Lucius?" Oliver countered.

Lucius glanced around quickly, ensuring that the immediate area was secure before addressing Oliver.

"Perhaps now is not the time, Your Highness."

But Oliver, undeterred, pressed on with concern etched across his face. "Lucius, we need to know... What's going on here? Why is the castle in such turmoil?"

Lucius took a deep breath. "The Bonnacon, my lord. It's become agitated, and it's rampaging through the fields. We're doing everything we can to protect the castle and its residents."

Oliver and Lumo exchanged puzzled glances, their lack of familiarity with the creature evident.

Bonna-what?

Lucius, sensing their confusion, added, "It's a rare beast, not seen often. It's unusual for it to be so agitated... I, uh, don't understand. But we are doing our best, and for now, you need to take shelter inside until I send word, my prince."

"Boy, take the prince inside and do your job for once," Lucius admonished, addressing Lumo with disdain.

Lumo, maintaining a composed demeanor, nodded in acknowledgment of Lucius's command. Despite the disapproval in Lucius's tone, Lumo knew better than to challenge the knight openly. With a subtle glance at Oliver, he conveyed reassurance before gently guiding him toward the safety of the castle's interior.

As they moved deeper into the castle, Lumo sensed Oliver lagging behind.

"Oliver, we should get inside quickly," Lumo urged.

"Wait, I need to see what's happening. We should find an elevated position to get a better view."

Lumo hesitated, a subtle frown creasing his forehead. "Oliver, we don't know what we're dealing with. It could be dangerous. Taking unnecessary risks—"

"Come on, Lumo. Aren't you even a little curious about what this thing looks like? We'll stay out of harm's way, I promise," Oliver interrupted.

Lumo sighed, realizing that Oliver's adventurous spirit was one not easily tamed. "Fine, but we stay back, and at the first sign of danger, we retreat. Agreed?"

Oliver grinned. "Agreed."

With that, they ascended a nearby tower for a vantage point, Lumo still harboring reservations about the unforeseen danger that lurked outside the castle walls.

"I think I see something..." Oliver said, peering cautiously out of the tower.

"What is it? Do you recognize anything?"

Oliver squinted at the distant commotion, trying to make sense of the chaotic scene. "It's hard to tell from here..."

"Oliver, maybe it's best not to get too close. We don't know what we're dealing with."

Oliver, however, couldn't resist the pull of curiosity. With a determined glint in his eye, he muttered, "If only I could move a little... closer."

As he inched toward the edge of the tower, the stone beneath his feet gave way. The world seemed to slow for a moment as Oliver desperately grasped at the air, but the inevitable happened. With a dramatic yell, he plummeted into the castle's moat, creating a splash that echoed the unexpected turn of events.

"Oliver!" Lumo exclaimed, rushing to the edge and peering down.

A surge of panic gripped Lumo's chest. He frantically scanned the water, but Oliver's figure remained submerged, obscured by the murky depths.

For a moment, time hung suspended, and uncertainty clenched at Lumo's gut. Then, just as fear threatened to fully take hold, Oliver emerged, gasping for breath. He wasn't anywhere near the tower where he fell; instead, he appeared closer to the other side of the moat. Oliver, with determined strokes, swam toward the opposite bank.

As the waterlogged prince reached the shore, Lumo, still perched on the tower, exhaled sharply, his body relaxing as the tension eased. But the relief was fleeting—Oliver, dripping wet and slightly disoriented, turned and looked back up at the tower.

"Oliver, wait for me," Lumo shouted.

Lumo's gaze shifted toward the distant main gate. It loomed impossibly far, a journey too long with too much at stake. He could almost picture a satisfied Lucius, happily letting him go out there alone to face the creature without a second thought, but that wasn't the real problem. His heart thudded at the idea of Oliver getting there first.

The water shimmered below, dark and unwelcoming. Lumo clenched his fists, his breath catching in his throat as he glanced nervously over his shoulder, half-expecting someone to call him back. The walls were silent.

Swallowing hard, he inhaled the cool air, steeling his resolve. Then, with a final, fleeting glance around, he took a running start and flung himself from the tower, his body slicing through the air as he plunged after Oliver into the waiting depths of the moat.

SPLASH!

The water enveloped him in a chilling embrace, and for a moment, the world above became a blur. As Lumo surfaced, he spotted Oliver on the shore. Without wasting any time, Lumo swam toward Oliver. As he emerged from the water, dripping and breathless, he heard Oliver's voice.

"Here, take my hand," Oliver offered, reaching out to help Lumo out of the moat. The two friends stood side by side, both in disbelief at what had just transpired.

"We should find a way to get back in safely," Lumo said.

Oliver scratched his head, surveying the chaos around them.

"Well, we are definitely not going back the way we came. Let's take the scenic route, shall we? Along the moat, my friend."

Lumo shot him a bemused look. "Scenic route? We're not on a leisurely stroll. There's a creature out there with a penchant for destruction."

"Details, details," Oliver waved off, leading the way along the castle's moat.

As they trod cautiously, Oliver couldn't help but marvel at the surreal scene. "You know, Lumo, this would make for a great story one day. 'How I Survived a Castle Creature Rampage.'"

"Let's survive first, then you can pitch your epic tale," Lumo rolled his eyes.

As they moved along the water's edge, the sounds of turmoil became louder and clearer in the distance, and the castle's massive form cast eerie shadows over the moat. Suddenly, a deafening roar echoed through the air, sending shivers down their spines.

Lumo's eyes widened, and he instinctively grabbed Oliver's arm, halting their progress.

"Do you hear that?"

Oliver's expression shifted from curiosity to concern. "Yeah, I hear it. Is that... the creature?"

A monstrous silhouette emerged from the chaos, its massive form creating ripples in the air. The creature, known as the Bonnacon, revealed itself with a roar that seemed to shake the very foundation of the castle.

"By the gods, what is that?" Lumo muttered.

Oliver, wide-eyed, stammered, "I didn't expect it to be... that big."

The Bonnacon loomed on four massive, sinewy legs, each step sending tremors through the ground beneath. Its hulking frame was wrapped in coarse, matted fur, tangled and wild, giving the creature an air of primal ferocity. Its glowing eyes pierced through the chaos, fixated on everything in its path. Its most threatening feature was the bull-like horn, curving menacingly backward, poised to batter anything unfortunate enough to be in its way.

As the creature advanced, a group of castle guards, led by Sir Eamon—one of Lucius's knights—moved forward with shields raised to confront it. Lumo and Oliver, hidden in the shadows, watched the dramatic encounter unfold.

The Bonnacon, sensing the approaching threat, turned its attention to the guards. With a low, rumbling growl, it lowered its head, ready to charge. The guards braced themselves, shields raised in a unified front.

But just as the clash seemed imminent, the Bonnacon executed a surprising maneuver. With a swift and unexpected turn, it faced the other way. In an astonishing display, the creature expelled a fiery stream of burning substance from its rear end, creating a scorching arc that sizzled through the air.

The guards instinctively huddled behind their shields, creating a makeshift barrier against the fiery onslaught. The burning substance splattered against the shields, sizzling and hissing as it met the protective metal.

Lumo and Oliver watched in a mix of awe and disbelief as the guards, though faced with the bizarre and unexpected, managed to shield themselves from the creature's potent attack.

"I—Is it spraying poop?" Oliver exclaimed.

Lumo, still standing in disbelief, could say nothing. His drooping jaw said it all.

As the guards faced the unexpected onslaught of the Bonnacon's fiery expulsion, their formation broke, and panic spread among their ranks.

"Retreat! Fall back!" shouted Sir Eamon, his voice strained with urgency. The guards, their shields still sizzling from the bizarre attack, hastily retreated from the creature's vicinity.

Lumo and Oliver, observing from their concealed position, exchanged a worried glance. The chaos around them intensified, and the looming threat of the creature turned their previous fascination into genuine fear.

"We need to find cover," Lumo urged, pulling Oliver away from the edge of the moat. "That thing is unpredictable."

Oliver gave a quick, determined look.

As they tried to hurriedly seek refuge among the castle's architecture, the distant roars of the Bonnacon echoed, signaling its relentless pursuit of the guards. However, amidst the turmoil, the creature's gaze shifted, locking onto the hidden duo.

Lumo's eyes went round, "Oliver, it sees us!"

The Bonnacon, as if guided by some unseen force, diverted its course toward the two friends. Panic set in as they realized the looming danger.

The air crackled with tension as the Bonnacon prepared to charge, its massive form poised for a destructive onslaught. Lumo and Oliver froze in dread.

In an ominous turn, the creature pivoted, and time seemed to slow to a crawl. Oliver and Lumo could only watch, helpless, as the colossal beast readied itself for a dire assault.

Was this their end? Destroyed by a deluge of burning feces?

Just as the terrifying possibility loomed, the Bonnacon unleashed its fiery assault. Lumo and Oliver, well, pretty much screwed without armor or weapons, cowered instinctively, arms raised to shield themselves. In a desperate embrace, they huddled together, eyes tightly shut, awaiting the impending deluge of burning excrement.

In that heart-stopping moment, a surge of magical energy erupted, and a shimmering barrier sprang to life around Lumo and Oliver. The luminous shield flickered like starlight.

Brilliant sparks erupted like fireworks as the fiery stream collided with the shield. The protective barrier held firm, deflecting the flames away from the helpless duo. The air crackled with the clash of magical and primal forces, and for a moment, time seemed suspended in the balance between destruction and salvation. Frustrated by the unexpected resistance, the Bonnacon let out a roar of defiance.

As time seemed to catch up to the speed of the intense moment, Lumo cautiously cracked open one eye. The relief that flooded him was indescribable.

Realization dawned upon him, and in an instant, joy surged through his veins. With newfound excitement, he opened his other eye, eagerly confirming their safety.

“We made it, Oliver! We're alive!” Lumo exclaimed, unable to believe that they were. “Open your eyes, we're in one piece!”

Oliver, disoriented but catching on to Lumo's enthusiasm, slowly opened his eyes. He watched wide-eyed as the shimmering barrier held firm.

Lumo and Oliver exchanged a bewildered glance. The castle grounds, once a chaotic battleground, now bore an eerie calm as the Bonnacon paced back and forth, unable to breach the enchanted barrier.

“Are you all right?” a voice, calm yet powerful, erupted from nowhere.

The source of the voice revealed herself—an enigmatic figure draped in robes of flowing azure, her eyes a vibrant shade of indigo. A delicate circlet, adorned with gleaming gemstones, rested upon her brow.

“Serena,” Oliver stammered, still recovering from the shock.

“Serena!” he exclaimed again, this time with a joy that seemed to overshadow any lingering shock. In that moment, he couldn't have been happier to see anyone else in the world.

Lumo couldn't help but smile. Serena Starwhisper, the Imperial Sorceress, radiated an aura of strength and wisdom that brought a surge of hope in their moment of despair. High cheekbones framed a face that was both regal and approachable, while a cascade of silvery hair fell in soft waves around her shoulders. Her lips, a soft shade of rose, curved into a calm yet resolute expression.

"Serena," Lumo muttered, respect evident in his tone. The sorceress had an all-knowing smile plastered on her face.

Oliver, shaking off the initial shock, added, "Thank you, Serena. We owe you our lives."

Serena raised her hands, and a soothing energy emanated from her staff. Her voice carried a quiet authority as she recited an incantation, the words rippling softly through the air.

Hush now, racing heart, and calm thy beat,
Let tranquility rise from head to feet.
Whispers of peace, like a gentle stream,
Flow through the soul like a peaceful dream.

The melodious chant filled the space around them and the ambient tension seemed to yield to the rhythmic cadence of her spell. The once-agitated Bonnacon, its fiery rage momentarily quelled, appeared to be entranced by the sorceress's mystical command.

As she concluded, her staff traced graceful arcs in the air, directing the flow of magic. The last syllable left her lips, and a serene calm settled over the creature. The fiery gaze of the Bonnacon softened into a more tranquil state, and the magical barrier, still standing strong, now seemed to exist in harmony with the subdued beast. Serena's ancient and potent incantation had achieved a delicate balance, and the once-menacing creature stood subdued as if lulled into a peaceful slumber.

"You are welcome," she said, turning back to the duo. "Now let's get you boys back into the castle."

As the echoes of Serena's incantation lingered in the air, a sudden commotion erupted. The castle guards, led by Lucius, rushed onto the scene with urgency etched on their faces. Lucius, his eyes scanning the surroundings, locked onto the unexpected gathering near the moat.

"What in the blazes is going on here?" Lucius bellowed, his voice a thunderous proclamation of authority. The guards, forming a protective perimeter, awaited his command.

Serena turned to Lucius, her chin held high and her shoulders relaxed. Oliver and Lumo, still under the lingering effects of her calming spell, observed quietly.

"Lucius," Serena greeted. "A minor disturbance with the Bonnacon, but all is under control now."

"Under control, you say? Nothing has been under control since he arrived." He scowled, pointing a finger at Lumo.

Aware of Lucius's disapproval, Lumo maintained his composure, but nothing he could say at the moment would make anything better. All he could do was lower his gaze to not enrage the knight any further.

"What in the realms is the prince doing out here? Didn't I explicitly instruct you to fulfill your duty and safeguard his Highness's interests?" Lucius's scowl deepened.

Serena stepped forward. "Lucius, the Bonnacon posed a threat, and I took the necessary steps to ensure the safety of the castle and its residents. Is that not an integral part of your duty as captain?"

Lucius hesitated for a moment. “T—The safety of the castle is my concern, and it's the prince's responsibility to stay within its walls.”

Serena's expression remained steady. “Sometimes, Lucius, the safety of the castle requires us to venture beyond its walls. Your duty and mine are intertwined in preserving the well-being of this realm, not just the castle.”

Lucius, though visibly conflicted, couldn't argue with the logic presented. He cast a stern gaze toward Lumo, who met it with a mixture of remorse and defiance. At that moment, Oliver, who had been observing the exchange with a growing sense of responsibility, stepped forward.

“Sir Lucius,” Oliver interjected, his voice carrying a tone of earnestness. “It wasn't Lumo's fault. I—I fell into the moat, and he came after me. We didn't mean to cause trouble.”

Lucius's gaze shifted to Oliver, and for a moment, his stern expression softened. However, the knight's disapproval lingered.

“I shall escort the boys back to the castle,” Serena declared, breaking the deadlock between Lucius and Lumo.

Lucius, still discontent but recognizing the futility of further argument, nodded reluctantly. “See that you do. And, Prince Oliver, please see that such incidents are avoided in the future. Your safety is paramount, and the fate of the kingdom relies on your responsible actions. Choose your companions wisely.”

With a final disdainful look, Lucius turned on his heel, barking orders to the guards to resume their duties. Serena, with a graceful yet firm demeanor, gestured for Oliver and Lumo to follow her.

"You have a knack for getting into trouble, don't you, prince?" Serena asked as they walked away from the commotion.

"Yeah, sorry about that." Oliver scratched his head, sheepishly. "I really did fall into the moat, you know."

"I can see that," Serena said, observing Oliver's wet clothes.

"So, when did you get back?" Oliver asked.

"Just now."

"Oh, that's nice. So how was it at Harbridge?"

"Still the same," Serena replied.

Harbridge was the largest magic academy in the realm. Situated on an island to the southeast, it was a difficult place to get to. The academy was a sanctuary for those gifted with essence. The island's isolation provided the perfect environment for focus and growth, away from the distractions of the mainland, making Harbridge Academy a beacon of learning and a crucible for the next generation of powerful mages. Serena, who had studied at the academy, would occasionally visit Harbridge to meet her mentors and inspire the new generation of mages.

"Well, it's good to have you back," Oliver grinned.

"Likewise. Now, I suggest you two change out of those wet clothes, lest you catch a fever."

Lumo gave a sympathetic nod. "I'll help the prince get changed."

The trio disappeared within the castle.

***

Somewhere in the countryside, John, a farmer, trudged across the field, sweat beading on his forehead as the farmhouse came into view. He spotted Mary, his wife, working in the garden, her hands deep in the soil, her wide-brimmed hat casting a shadow over her face.

“Working your magic again?” he called, leaning against the fence.

Mary glanced up, smiling. “Just trying to bring a little nature’s charm to the place.”

John wiped his forehead with the back of his hand. “Well, you certainly make it look like home.”

Their eyes met, a silent understanding passing between them, but the moment was broken by Rusty's bark from the corner of the yard. John turned to see the dog acting strange, his ears perked, his tail stiff.

“What’s got you all worked up, boy?”

Mary joined him, wiping her hands on her apron. “What is it, Rusty? Did you spot another squirrel?”

The dog was focused on the grazing cattle, and John followed his gaze. Something was wrong.

John's heart sank. “Mary, come here.”

She dropped her tools, hurrying to his side. Her face went pale as she saw what he saw—one of their cows lying lifeless, its body sprawled unnaturally across the earth. The animal's skin had an unnatural pallor, and strange markings crisscrossed its hide, like scars carved by an unseen hand.

Mary's voice was tight with disbelief. “How could this happen?”

John shook his head, kneeling to inspect the body. “I don’t know.” He ran a hand over the soil nearby, noticing deep gouges. Unease crept up his spine.

“We need to tell the neighbors,” he said, his voice hardening. “Something’s not right.”

***

Back at the castle, King Reginald sat on his imposing throne, his usually warm eyes now burning with fury as he addressed the two figures before him. Oliver stood as still as stone, his head lowered, staring at the ground. Lumo maintained a stoic exterior, though his tense stance betrayed a mixture of guilt and apprehension.

The sorceress observed the proceedings with an air of detached interest. Lucius remained at his post, arms crossed, his mouth tightening as he watched, a glint of contempt in his expression. Archibald positioned himself discreetly, prepared to offer counsel if needed.

King Reginald's fingers drummed an impatient rhythm on the armrest.

"Explain yourselves," King Reginald's voice rumbled through the hall. "How is it that my own son and his attendant managed to venture outside the castle walls amidst the chaos of the Bonnacon threat?"

Oliver cleared his throat, summoning the courage to respond. "Father, it was an accident. We were in the tower, and—"

King Reginald's hand slammed onto the armrest of his throne, cutting off Oliver's words. "Silence! I do not want excuses. The peril you exposed yourself to is a direct threat to the very core of our kingdom."

Lucius, unable to contain himself, interjected, "It was the attendant's negligence, Your Majesty. He should have been more vigilant, especially in times like these."

The king's expression softened, just barely, as he turned his focus on Lumo. "Is this true, Lumo? Were you negligent in your duty?"

Lumo's gaze dropped, his shoulders heavy, as though bearing an invisible weight. The memory of the prince's near brush with danger clawed at him. Usually, Lumo would dismiss Lucius's animosity, well aware of the hostility Lucius harbored toward him. But this time, it was different. They could have died. The gravity of the situation magnified Lucius's accusations, making Lumo acutely aware of the consequences of his lapse in judgment.

Lumo took a steadying breath, his voice firm but burdened. “Your Majesty, I take full accountability for the lapse in judgment. It was my mistake, and I deeply regret the consequences.”

Oliver shifted beside him, glancing at his friend before stepping forward. “Father, it wasn't Lumo's fault. I—was curious, and I insisted on exploring. He tried to dissuade me, but I was adamant.”

King Reginald's gaze briefly shifted to Oliver.

“You don’t have to take all the blame, Lumo,” Oliver said, turning to Lumo.

Lumo remained silent.

Lucius, sensing an opportunity, took a step forward. “Your Majesty, I had instructed the boy to take the prince to safety within the castle walls; it’s obvious this is all his fault. Perhaps a lesson is in order. Locking him in the dungeon for a week might teach him the gravity of his responsibilities.”

Oliver swallowed hard, his heart racing as he locked eyes with his father. His voice, barely steady, broke through the tension. “Father, I—”

“Silence!” the king bellowed, cutting off Oliver once again.

The room plunged into an eerie silence, the weight of the king's words settling like a heavy shroud. The atmosphere grew taut; every breath felt like an intrusion into the quiet tension. King Reginald, in that pregnant pause, seemed immersed in profound contemplation. Oliver found his mind in a whirlwind of uncertainty. *Was his father actually contemplating Lucius's suggestion?*

Breaking the quietude, the king reluctantly unfurled his words after a lingering moment.

"Lumo... you will be confined to the dungeon for a week as punishment for your negligence. Perhaps this will serve as a reminder of the importance of your duties."

"What?" Oliver screamed, disbelief painted across his face like a vivid brushstroke. The decision his father had just pronounced felt surreal, as if it had been pulled from a nightmare. King Reginald had always shown kindness to Lumo—perhaps even more than to Oliver himself. *What could he possibly be thinking?*

"Enough! My decision is final," the king declared, his tone cutting through the air with unwavering authority. A pointed glance toward Oliver silently conveyed that further protests would not be tolerated.

Lumo swiftly grasped Oliver's hand, offering a reassuring squeeze to convey that everything would be fine and urging him to remain silent.

"Yes, Your Majesty." Lumo bowed.

Lucius, a satisfied smirk playing on his lips, stood with an air of triumph, relishing the outcome as if it were a personal victory.

"Oliver, you will be confined to your chambers until further notice. We cannot afford any more reckless behavior till the ceremony," the king decreed.

The king's words hung in the air, a heavy decree that cast a shadow over the young prince and his attendant. The sorceress observed silently, her face unreadable, as the royal court grappled with the consequences of an unintended escapade.

As Lumo was escorted to the dungeon and Oliver to his chambers, the king concluded discussions with Lucius and the sorceress, ensuring that all was well within the castle walls.

***

CHAPTER 3

"HEAR YE, HEAR YE!"

"Gather 'round, good folk of Avalora! A proclamation of such gravitas awaits your delicate eardrums, you might want to reinforce them with royal-grade cotton!" The royal scout announced with a flourish, stepping onto the proverbial stage of the town square.

A band of scouts followed suit, some beating drums with more enthusiasm than rhythm, others sounding trumpets that seemed to be in a heated argument with each other. The kingdom, in its infinite wisdom, spared no expense in ensuring the people of Avalora were not left to their imaginations—they preferred drumrolls and trumpets, apparently.

The proclamation echoed through the town square, and the citizens of Avalora, accustomed to the occasional royal spectacle, gathered in anticipation. Whispers and hushed conversations spread like wildfire among the crowd.

"Another royal decree? I hope it's not about the proper way to eat soup. Last time, I spilled it all over myself trying to impress the king's envoy," a townsman said, trying to mock the scouts.

The royal scout, undeterred by the undercurrent of sarcasm, cleared his throat.

"Fear not, good people! This proclamation is of utmost importance. Drumroll, please!" said the royal scout cheerfully as he gestured to the enthusiastic yet uncoordinated drummers.

The drums beat erratically, more chaotic than a henhouse during a fox visit. Most of the townspeople had already gathered in the square. Among them were two faces well-acquainted with the general population: Bart, the proprietor of Thistle & Thorn, and his ever-charming barmaid, Lily. Known for bringing immeasurable joy and happiness to the lives of Avalora's denizens—or, at the very least, a good buzz—this dynamic duo had a way of turning any occasion into a spirited celebration. After all, who wouldn't find joy in a mug of T&T's finest ale or a glass of Lily's specially mixed concoctions?

"If only the royal budget included music lessons for the scouts," Bart muttered.

Lily shot him a sideways glance, her expression unamused, as if Bart's comment was the last thing she needed. A subtle roll of her eyes indicated that she was far too accustomed to Bart's repertoire of stupid jokes.

"Well, what is it then?" Lily asked the royal scout, her tone curt and direct, throwing the scout slightly off his usual charm. He paused, as if recalibrating, and then cleared his throat.

"Ahem... yes!" The royal scout started, his gaze momentarily drifting toward the erratic drummers. "People of Avalora, behold! The kingdom will be celebrating the ascension ceremony of the sole heir to the throne, His Highness Prince Oliver!"

Hushed whispers spread amongst the gathered crowd.

"We know that, get to the juicy part!" Lily exclaimed with a playful smirk.

"Wait... what? Oh, right, yes! The grand event will take place three days from now. There will be feasts, festivities, and a chance for all of Avalora to bask in the glory of our future king!" The scout delivered, his enthusiasm rekindled as he dished out the details that even Bart and Lily found intriguing.

"Is there goin' to be free ale?" Bart inquired, his tone laced with slyness, almost hoping the scout would deny it. After all, it would mean more opportunities for him to draw in customers. If the customers couldn't make it to the bar, well, the bar would just have to find its way to the customers.

"Let's see now? Yes! There will indeed be free ale at the feast!" The scout confirmed, quickly consulting his written itinerary.

"Fr—Free Ale??" said a gruff voice from the back.

As Lily turned around to see who it was, there was no mistaking the person who said it. A large man, rotund and imposing, stood there with a contented grin, his round face adorned with a thick beard that seemed to have crumbs of the last meal still lingering. His belly, round enough to double as a dinner table, proudly led the way into the gathering. It was a marvel how a man with such an unusually spherical physique could navigate through life with such gusto. It seemed that, for the man, the circumference of his waist was directly proportional to the joy in his heart.

"Well, hello there, handsome. What's your name? Never seen you around here," Lily flirted.

The man, his eyes twinkling, grinned wider, revealing a gap between his teeth. "Me? I'm Gus! Gus... the Glutton, they call me."

"And why do they call you that, sweetie?"

Gus took a pause. "Oh! I don't know... Maybe because I love to eat... I think." He scratched his head, his sincerity and simplicity shining through despite the verbal struggle.

Lily let out a playful laugh. "Gus the Glutton, eh? I'm Lily. If you're as good with a mug as you are with words, you might just be the life of the upcoming festivities."

"F—Festivities? Ah, well... if there's food and drink, Gus is in!" It was obvious Gus didn't understand fancy words. The head-scratching continued.

"Well, at least someone 'round here is straightforward," Bart chuckled.

As Lily continued to banter with Gus, the town square buzzed with excitement. The royal scout continued his proclamation, detailing the upcoming celebrations.

"Shriek!"

Just then, a woman screamed in the distance, her cry echoing through the town square with a high-pitched, sharp sound.

The crowd's attention shifted as the woman's scream pierced the air, causing heads to turn in the direction of the commotion.

Bart, sensing trouble, moved closer to the disturbance. Gus, oblivious to the unfolding situation, scratched his head and glanced around, still trying to make sense of the word 'festivities.'

Amidst the curious and concerned crowd, a scene of distress unfolded. The source of the disturbance became clear: a woman, visibly distressed, was being harassed by a menacing figure. The groper, a burly thug with a sinister grin, seemed to revel in causing fear.

As the onlookers gasped at the unfolding situation, Bart's protective instincts kicked in.

"Hey, you there! Enuf of that. Leave the lady alone," Bart asserted, approaching the thug.

Lily, busy with Gus, paused mid-laugh, tilting her head to peer past him. Her brow creased as she caught Bart's voice, a tone that didn't match the usual banter.

"Mind your own business, mustache. This has nothing to do with you." The thug smirked.

"It becomes me business when ye're causing trouble in me town. Step away from the lady, or things will get unpleasant for ya."

"Unpleasant, you say? I'd like to see you try, old man," the thug laughed mockingly.

As the tension escalated between Bart and the thug, Lily's eyes widened, and she leaned closer to Gus. "Gus, that guy is huge! He'll tear Bart apart." She paused, sizing up the thug before looking back at Gus. "You're about his size, maybe even bigger. Can you go intimidate him?"

Gus blinked. "In—timmy—date?"

Lily sighed. "I mean, scare him a bit. Make him think twice about messing with us. Look, just go there and ask the guy to stop. Please?"

Gus, a genuine and kind soul, frowned at the idea of confrontation. He looked down with a visible unease. "Okay, Lily. I'll try."

As the argument between Bart and the thug reached a boiling point, Gus entered the scene with an air of gentleness.

"Err... Excuse me... Mr. Huge sir, can you stop, please?" Gus stammered as he stepped next to Bart. He shuffled his feet, glancing nervously at the ground before forcing himself to meet the thug's gaze, his hands twitching at his sides.

The thug, taken aback for a brief second, stared intently at Gus. Perhaps he had never seen a guy bigger than him. But it wasn't just his height; his girth was equally frightening.

The atmosphere in the square grew thick with tension as the two giants stood face to face, so palpable that it seemed one could cut through it with a knife.

"Who are you?" said the thug, feigning seriousness.

"I—I'm Gus. Gus... the Glutton, they call me," Gus replied.

The thug couldn't help but smirk, a hint of amusement flashing in his eyes. "Gus the Glutton, did you say? What are you going to do, eat me to death?" he chuckled, taunting Gus.

Gus shifted uncomfortably on his feet, clearly out of his element. The thug, reveling in the discomfort he was causing, took a step closer to Gus, sneering, "Come on, tubby, say something impressive."

Gus stammered, "I—I don't want trouble."

"If you didn't want trouble, you shouldn't have come here, big guy," the thug retorted, clenching his fist, his confidence swelling like a balloon.

Growing concerned for Gus, Lily stepped forward. "Hey, we're all reasonable people here. No need for a fight. Just go on your way, and we'll forget about this."

"Move, woman," the thug sneered. With a sinister grin, he shoved Lily aside, causing her to stumble and fall.

"Lily!" Gus exclaimed in a mix of concern and anger as he watched her fall.

Fueled by a surge of anger, Gus charged toward the big guy with a determined "Arghhh!" However, the thug, anticipating the move, sidestepped with ease, and Gus tumbled forward, landing face-first on the ground.

The bad guy, finding amusement in the situation, burst into laughter.

"Well, well, looks like tubby can't even walk straight! What were you thinking, challenging me?"

"Lily, are ya okay?" Bart said, helping her to her feet. "Hold on, I'll go fetch the guards."

"No, wait!" Lily replied as she continued staring at Gus.

Gus had slowly hoisted himself up from the ground, his eyes gleaming with a quiet intensity. In a swift motion, he reached into the folds of his attire, revealing a small flask of alcohol. The square fell into a hushed expectancy as Gus, undeterred by the escalating tension, took a resolute swig. But Gus didn't stop there. Ignoring the bewildered glances from the onlookers, he continued to chug the contents of the flask.

The thug, initially smirking in amusement, couldn't hide the confusion creeping into his expression.

"What's this guy up to? Trying to drown his sorrows before I make him cry?"

But Gus, seemingly oblivious to the thug's commentary, kept chugging until the flask was empty. The tension in the square reached a peak. And then, with a sudden and unexpected release, a thunderous sound echoed through the air.

"BURRPPP...!"

As Gus let out a thunderous "BURP!" that reverberated through the square, shimmering bubbles floated gracefully from his mouth. The thug, initially taken aback, watched with a mix of confusion and amusement as the bubbles surrounded him.

The bubbles popped near the thug, and the effect was almost instantaneous. Laughter erupted from him, starting as a chuckle and escalating into uncontrollable fits of mirth.

Unable to comprehend the sudden burst of hilarity, he doubled over, clutching his stomach.

The thug, amid his laughter, managed to gasp out bewildered words, "What's happening... hahaha... Why is this so damn funny… hahahaha."

Each attempt to speak was interrupted by renewed peals of laughter, as if the very air around him had become an endless source of amusement.

Gus, still riding the wave of unexpected power, burped once again. This time, a new set of bubbles emerged, dancing in the air before converging near the thug. As the bubbles popped, a profound sadness overcame the once-laughing thug. Tears streamed down his face, his laughter replaced by heart-wrenching sobs.

"Why... why am I crying… I can't... stop… crying... What kind of trickery is this?"

Bart, Lily, and the crowd watched in astonishment as Gus, with nothing more than belches and bubbles, manipulated the emotions of the menacing thug.

With another determined burp, Gus conjured a third set of bubbles that erupted with a lively tune. The thug, caught in this bizarre spectacle, found himself moving awkwardly to the invisible rhythm. His tough facade crumbled as he shuffled and twirled, limbs betraying him in a clumsy dance. The crowd, initially stunned, burst into laughter and applause, their disbelief quickly giving way to amusement.

"What is this nonsense? I can't... stop dancing! Make it stop!"

His futile attempts to regain control only intensified the comical nature of his movements. The thug, once a menacing presence, now resembled a marionette under the influence of an unseen puppeteer, his every step and gesture dictated by the playful tune.

"All right, all right! I'm sorry... please... just make it stop," the thug pleaded, his tough facade completely shattered.

Gus, with a subtle smirk, burped once more, and the bubbles dissipated. The thug, now free from the enchanting effects, stumbled to a stop, panting and disoriented. He looked at Gus with a mix of bewilderment and exhaustion. The once-menacing figure now resembled a disoriented and defeated man, his tough exterior shattered by Gus's unconventional powers.

With a final desperate glance at Gus, the thug turned and fled from the town square, his retreat marked by a comically uncoordinated sprint. The onlookers burst into laughter at the sight of the thug's dramatic escape.

Lily, shaking her head in disbelief, glanced at Gus. "Well, I'll be darned."

Bart, joining in the laughter, clapped Gus on the back. "I've witnessed me fair share of scuffles, but that, me friend, was a masterpiece. Who'd have thought belchin' could be so potent?"

"I just... didn't want anyone to get hurt," Gus replied, scratching his head with a sheepish smile.

The crowd, now buzzing with chatter and laughter, dispersed, leaving behind a town square that had witnessed one of the most unconventional confrontations in its history.

***

Oliver gazed out of the window at the stone walls that seemed to enclose him in a gilded cage. The air hung heavy with the scent of polished wood and flickering candlelight. A soft knock on his door drew his attention, and he turned to see Amelia entering with a tray in hand.

"Good evening, Your Highness. Is there anything you require?"

"Amelia, have you heard anything about Lumo? Is he all right?" Oliver said, almost jumping out of his seat.

"I'm afraid not, Your Highness. The dungeon is heavily guarded, and... I couldn't get any information," Amelia answered, looking down at the tray in her hand.

"This is absurd. Lumo is my best friend; he shouldn't be treated like a criminal."

"I understand, Your Highness. If there's anything specific you need, please let me know. I'll do my best to assist you," Amelia said as she placed the tray on the table.

Oliver's thoughts lingered on Lumo as Amelia left the room.

***

Meanwhile, Lumo's boots scuffed against the uneven stone floor as he paced his cell. The air was heavy and stale. His hands clenched and unclenched at his sides, the faint chill seeping up through his fingertips, a reminder of how little warmth the cell allowed.

The events of the past day replayed in his mind like a haunting specter. The daring climb into the tower, Oliver's fall into the moat, the harrowing encounter with the mysterious creature—it all felt like a series of ill-fated choices that had led him to the cold embrace of the dungeon.

He couldn't shake the nagging question: *How could he have approached the situation differently?*

Lumo pondered the choices he had made, each one a stepping stone leading to this confinement. His mind wrestled with the what-ifs, wondering if a different path could have spared him this fate as he paced back and forth.

Amidst the oppressive silence, a troubling realization dawned upon him, a revelation that lingered in the damp air like a subtle poison.

"Why would the king imprison me for an entire week? Oliver's ascension ceremony is days away," he mumbled to himself as he stopped pacing.

"This has to be an error in judgment, right?" he wondered aloud, the questions echoing in the cold confines of his cell.

Lumo was lost in his thoughts, the questions circling his mind like restless birds. He couldn't help but think that his current predicament had all the logic of a fish attending a swordsmanship class.

"You must be special..." a voice broke Lumo's train of thought.

Lumo's attention snapped toward the speaker, a shadowy figure observing him with a sly grin. Despite the dire circumstances, the stranger possessed an air of mystery, and there was a certain confidence in the way she carried herself.

"Why do you say that?" Lumo inquired.

"Take a good look around, friend. Notice anything different about our... accommodations?" the girl chuckled mischievously.

Lumo glanced around, realizing that, indeed, the quality of his cell was notably better than hers.

"I've been in and out of this place more times than I can count," the girl continued explaining, leaning against the cell bars. "And trust me, they don't usually provide such luxurious lodgings; seems like the king has a special interest in you."

"And to whom am I speaking, may I ask?" Lumo said, trying to understand the enigmatic stranger.

"What are you, a noble or something? Who talks this way?" the girl replied, crossing her arms and rolling her eyes, dismissing Lumo's question altogether.

"I—I'm the prince's attendant," Lumo replied, momentarily forgetting the girl had still not answered his own question.

"Well… that makes sense. So, what'd you do? Steal the silverware?"

Lumo's face flushed as he stammered, "I… do not steal…" He took a breath, straightening his posture. "Who are you?"

"Me? Oh, just a humble guest of the kingdom. A master thief, if you will," grinned the girl.

"Well, if you are a master thief, then how did you end up in the dungeon?" Lumo asked, narrowing his eyes.

The girl leaned closer to the cell bars, her eyes gleaming with amusement. "Call it an occupational hazard. Even the best get caught when the loot's too good to resist."

As the wavering torchlight cast shadows on her face, Lumo discerned more details. The girl moved with a nimbleness that suggested a life spent in the shadows. Her mysterious green eyes sparkled with intelligence, and her dark burgundy hair fell in unruly waves around her shoulders, framing her face in wild defiance. A few damp strands clung to her forehead, and her olive skin, marked by faint smudges of dirt, hinted at a heritage from sunlit landscapes.

"But enough about me. What about you, prince's attendant? What grave crime landed you in this charming establishment?"

Lumo hesitated, unsure of how much to reveal.

"I—I made a mistake. This is my punishment."

The girl leaned back, her grin fading into a more thoughtful expression. "Mistake, huh? We've all made our fair share."

"It wasn't just any mistake. It could have gotten ugly."

"Ugly, how?"

"Err… I don't know if I—"

"Say no more... I get it. Well, we all have our demons and sometimes it's best to leave them right there in the closet."

A subtle change swept across the girl's face. She looked down, her playful demeanor completely gone.

Lumo, noticing the shift, continued, "What's your name, by the way? I'm Lumo."

"Meera. I'm going to take a nap now. Bye," she said as she quietly retreated to her less-than-comfortable bed.

***

Mary and John fidgeted, exchanging worried glances, as they watched their neighbors slowly traverse the field.

John cleared his throat, "Thank you all for coming on such short notice…"

Mary gestured toward the cattle. "Something's happened, and, well... we didn't know who else to turn to."

A tense silence hung in the air as the villagers gathered around.

Robert, an older gentleman with a graying beard, squinted at the strange markings on the cow. "I've never seen the likes of this. What could've caused it?"

George, a stout man known for running the village's primary grain mill and often being skeptical of anything out of the ordinary, grumbled, "Probably some kids playing a prank, thinking it's funny to scare us all."

Emma, a young mother, looked around nervously. "But who would do such a thing? My Timothy wouldn't dream of it, nor would any of his friends. It doesn't sit right."

Robert's astute wife, Helen—a known scholar in the village with a penchant for history and folklore—leaned in for a closer look, "It seems a bit elaborate for a prank, George. These aren't random scratches. They're deliberate, almost... ritualistic."

George snorted. "Ritualistic? Next, you'll have us looking for witches in the woods."

"It's not just mischief, though," John said, his expression grave. "There's something else. Look here." He lifted the cow's neck slightly, revealing a puncture wound. "The blood's been drained."

"Oh gosh!" Emma gasped, covering her mouth.

"This is most bizarre," Robert agreed.

Helen's expression turned thoughtful. "I wonder if there might be something in the village records, something that could explain this."

George rubbed the back of his neck, reluctantly nodding. "Alright, Helen. You dig through those dusty books. But what do the rest of us do in the meantime?"

"We keep watch," John said firmly. "If anything like this happens again, we'll be ready."

The villagers exchanged uneasy glances before slowly dispersing, their minds heavy with more questions than answers.

***

The torchlight cast wavering shadows along the dimly lit corridors of the castle. Amelia expertly went about her evening chores, the soft rustle of her apron mingling with the distant echoes of the castle settling for the night. As she approached a concealed corner, a flicker of movement caught her keen eye.

"Who could it be at this hour?" she pondered, her breath hitching slightly as her curiosity beckoned her forward.

Intrigued, she edged closer, the muffled hum of whispered exchanges now evident in her ears. The interplay of shadows unveiled two figures locked in a covert conversation, their words weaving through the hidden recesses of the castle.

Amelia instinctively pressed herself against the wall, eavesdropping on the exchange. The mysterious figure, obscured by the darkness, spoke in hushed tones.

"I trust you've ensured that everything is proceeding as planned?" the man said.

"Yes. All preparations are in order," said a voice. A low cadence bore the weight of a connection to the inner workings of the castle.

"We must proceed with caution. The timing is crucial, and we cannot afford any missteps."

Suddenly, a shocking revelation escaped the lips of the unseen confidant, causing Amelia to gasp involuntarily. In her surprise, she bumped into a nearby suit of armor. Her heart pounded as she fumbled to steady the clanking pieces. Desperately, she leaned closer to the wall, pressing herself into the shadows in an attempt to conceal her presence. Her breath came in shallow, quiet gasps as she strained to hear the conversation, praying that the noise had gone unnoticed.

"What was that? Did you hear something?"

"Keep your voice down. We can't risk being discovered."

The duo, alerted by the unexpected disturbance, exchanged hurried words.

"We should disperse for now. We'll reconvene later."

In the blink of an eye, the shadows disappeared, leaving Amelia alone in the now silent corridor. With a furrowed brow, she cautiously checked the surroundings but found no trace of anyone. The mystery hung in the air as Amelia struggled with the weight of what she had uncovered in the hidden corners of the castle.

***

CHAPTER 4

The castle courtyard, bathed in the soft glow of the morning sun, served as the regal stage for the awaited arrival of the Veridian dignitaries. Lucius, clad in his knightly attire, stood with an air of stoic authority, flanked by Archibald, his eyes alight with a subtle excitement.

"Lucius, any sign of their approach?" Archibald inquired; his gaze fixed on the horizon. He shifted his weight from one foot to the other.

"They should have passed the Avaloran border a while ago. They should be here any minute," Lucius replied, tapping his fingers against the hilt of his sword, a habit that betrayed his anticipation.

"All right, that's good to hear," Archibald acknowledged, straightening the crease on his robes with a quick flick of his wrist, his posture relaxing slightly.

As the welcoming party eagerly awaited the arrival of the Veridian envoys, a distant rumble echoed through the air.

"I think that's them," Lucius announced.

As the source of the sound drew nearer, the silhouette of the Veridian party became clear against the backdrop of the midday sun. The air seemed to shimmer with anticipation as the magnificent Equinox Stallions, draped in black and white, came into view, pulling a resplendent carriage adorned with the colors of Veridia. Hooves and wheels clattered in unison.

"No guards?" queried Archibald, shifting his weight ever so slightly toward Lucius.

"Oh, there are guards," Lucius smirked.

The Equinox Stallions, previously in seamless motion, gracefully came to a standstill. The carriage halted as swiftly as it had arrived.

Suddenly, as if caught in a delicate ballet, the bodies of the majestic stallions shifted and contoured, a magical metamorphosis unfurling before the mesmerized onlookers. Their sleek bodies shifted and reshaped, with magical energy guiding the change. As the equine features faded away, human traits emerged. Muzzles turned into strong jaws, manes flowed into hair, and hooves became agile feet. Neighs transformed into resonant human voices, and the rhythmic beating of hooves became the measured footfalls of armored warriors. The once-hooved creatures now stood as imposing human guards.

The carriage doors swung open, revealing Duke Thornbriar, who stepped out with regal grace. His attire blended noble elegance with a subtle hint of authority. With a sharp and discerning gaze, he surveyed the courtyard. Duke Alaric Thornbriar proudly bore the insignia of Veridia—a magnificent stag—symbolizing his lineage and responsibilities. His dark, tousled hair framed a chiseled face marked by distinguished crinkles at the corners of his piercing green eyes, reminiscent of the lush Veridian landscapes.

Adorned in attire befitting his noble station, the duke wore a cloak that cascaded in deep hues of forest green and midnight blue. A pendant, an heirloom passed down through generations (or so the family lore insisted), dangled nonchalantly from his neck.

With a respectful nod, Lucius stepped forward to welcome the distinguished guest.

"Duke Thornbriar, it is an honor to welcome you to the kingdom of Avalora. Trust you had an eventful journey."

The duke, his eyes glinting with a hint of mischief, replied, "Ah, ze roads were paved with excitement and surprises, as one would expect in zis lands, mon ami."

As the duke continued, he greeted Lucius with a warm handshake.

Archibald, joining the conversation with a bow, added, "Duke Thornbriar, your presence graces our humble kingdom. We trust your visit brings prosperity and joy."

"Archibald! Zis is so good to finally meet you again," the duke exclaimed, almost leaping forward with exuberance, the greeting almost catching Archibald off guard.

"I 'ope zis time you remember ze name, non?" he added, playfully raising an eyebrow.

"Why, yes, yes! Of course," Archibald replied, attempting to reassure the duke, recalling the one time he had mistakenly called him Duke Thornberry.

Archibald's sweeping gestures signaled the maids within the castle to approach, bearing trays adorned with goblets of the finest Avaloran wine and delicate refreshments.

As Archibald, Lucius, and the duke were engaged in pleasant conversations, one figure stood out in silent distress—Amelia, who was amongst the maidservants attending to the refreshments. Amidst the vibrant atmosphere, her eyes darted nervously.

Spotting a brief lull in the conversation, Amelia mustered the courage to approach Lucius.

"Sir Lucius, may I have a moment," she whispered.

"What is it?" Lucius replied, his demeanor shifting ever so slightly.

"May we speak in private?"

Just then, the duke turned to Lucius with a raised eyebrow.

"Sir Lucius, I trust ze preparations for ze ceremony are proceeding smoothly?"

Amelia hesitated for a moment, standing on the precipice of intrusion. Lucius, sensing her persistence, swiftly brushed her off with a curt, "Now is not a good time. We can talk later."

"Indeed, Your Grace. The diligent efforts of our team ensure that everything is proceeding according to plan," Lucius replied.

"Zhat is good," the duke responded, sipping a goblet of wine.

"So where is ze prince?" the duke asked, as he glanced around.

"Oh, Prince Oliver is—" Lucius began.

"Prince Oliver is resting in his chambers," Archibald interrupted firmly but respectfully.

"Good, good..." Duke Thornbriar swirled the wine in his goblet. "I can't wait to meet ze future king. And how'z King Reginald, still hearty and hale, I 'ope?"

"His Majesty has eagerly awaited your arrival, Your Grace." Archibald gestured toward the main entrance. "Why don't I show you to your chambers where you can rest for a while? Sir Lucius will attend to any further arrangements, and His Majesty will meet you soon."

Duke Thornbriar accepted Archibald's proposal gracefully, allowing himself to be led toward the chambers awaiting him. The regal procession moved through the castle halls, leaving the courtyard momentarily silent, save for the distant murmur of conversations within.

As the duke disappeared behind the grand doors, Lucius turned his attention back to the courtyard, his eyes scanning the surroundings for any signs of disturbance. Satisfied, he resumed making arrangements for the Veridian guards.

***

A few hours passed, the sun casting long shadows across the stones. As Archibald rejoined Lucius in the courtyard, a hushed expectancy lingered in the air. The moment had come for the Ophidonian dignitaries to arrive. The sky above the courtyard shimmered as a colossal serpent-shaped vessel was spotted in the distant sky. The serpent ship approached with a grace that seemed to defy the laws of mortal aviation.

As it descended, the ship coiled in mid-air before finally landing in a coiled serpent-like pose. The courtyard fell into a reverent hush as the ship's mouth opened slowly and its serpent's tongue-shaped ramp slid out.

From within the vessel, a group of guards clad in pitch-black scaly armor stepped out. Silently and with practiced precision, they scanned the surroundings. One of them, a stern-faced captain, declared, "All clear!" The soldiers quickly huddled into a single-line formation on both sides of the ramp.

Following this assurance, a figure emerged from the depths of the ship. Count Calindor, a dignified representative of Ophidonia, slowly descended the ramp.

Lucius, poised to extend his greeting to Count Calindor, found his attention abruptly diverted as a shadow behind him materialized into a familiar figure—a presence both known and unexpected: the Princess of Ophidonia.

In a moment that caught the assembly by surprise, the princess revealed herself, her silhouette gracefully taking form behind Count Calindor. The courtyard, already enchanted by the grand spectacle, now held an added air of intrigue as Princess Seraphina stepped into the midst of the gathering.

Lucius and Archibald exchanged a glance. Swiftly, Archibald assumed the role of welcoming the royal party, taking a quick step forward like a cat pouncing on an unsuspecting mouse.

"Princess Seraphina! This is indeed a surprise!" he exclaimed, extending a warm welcome. Not forgetting the count, he added, "Count Calindor, welcome! Your presence graces our humble kingdom."

Princess Seraphina acknowledged him with a slight incline of her head. "Thank you, Lord Archibald. Calindor and I bring regards of Ophidonia to the Kingdom of Avalora."

The princess, it seemed, had been well-trained in the diplomatic arts despite her young age.

As Archibald offered a courteous bow, Lucius stepped forward, joining in the reception. "Princess Seraphina, Count Calindor, Avalora is honored by your visit."

Count Calindor, with a slight lift of his chin, replied, "The honor is ours, Sir Lucius." His voice, smooth and cold, echoed through the courtyard, carrying with it an undercurrent of calculated diplomacy.

Count Calindor, a man of enigmatic demeanor, stood tall and lean; his features bore a certain smoothness. His eyes, a shade of deep black, betrayed little emotion, giving away nothing of the thoughts that lay beneath the surface.

Princess Seraphina moved with ethereal grace, her midnight hair framing a face as serene as moonlight on still waters. Eyes of deep sapphire held a quiet wisdom, and her robe—dark and shimmering like serpent scales—offset her pale skin with striking elegance.

"Did you journey well?" Archibald asked as he quietly gestured to the maidservants again for refreshments.

"The journey was..." Count Calindor began, his tone carrying a hint of dissatisfaction.

"Yes, of course," Seraphina interjected, her voice cool and dismissive, brushing aside the count's sentiment.

"I am really sorry to come unannounced, Sir Archibald. You see, I insisted to my father that I should be present at this ceremony. I wish I could have sent word ahead, but it was a... last-minute decision."

"Oh, that's quite all right, Your Highness. We couldn't be happier."

As Archibald continued his diplomatic exchanges with the princess and the count, a messenger hurried into the courtyard, whispering urgently into Lucius's ear. His expression darkened, and he excused himself discreetly.

"Lord Archibald, Princess Seraphina, Count Calindor, forgive my abrupt departure. There's a matter that requires my immediate attention. Sir Marcus will accompany you and ensure your comfort," Lucius explained with a curt nod toward a capable knight standing nearby.

Lucius quickly made his exit toward the drawbridge, signaling something outside the castle needed his urgent attention.

"Well then, shall we head into the castle? It's almost lunchtime. His Majesty King Reginald will be eager to meet you both," Archibald said.

Princess Seraphina inclined her head in acknowledgment, and the procession, led by Archibald, started its graceful movement toward the castle. As the royal procession entered the heart of the castle, the grand doors closed behind them, shutting out the courtyard's golden glow and leaving it in a quiet, anticipatory silence.

***

"Helen," Robert began, his deep voice carrying the weight of news, "I heard from old Tom down by the castle. Seems a Bonnacon went wild. Unusual business, I reckon."

The musty scent of ancient parchments hung in the air, adding a sense of nostalgia to the room. Helen, seated at a worn wooden table cluttered with parchments and quills, looked up from her research notes. Her scraggly silver hair cascaded in uneven waves. Her eyes, however, still held a spark of intellectual curiosity, glinting behind the slightly fogged lenses of her glasses.

"The Bonnacon?" Helen asked curiously, pulling aside her glasses. "When did this happen?"

"Tom said it happened a few days ago… created quite a ruckus, apparently," Robert replied, pulling out a chair and taking a seat across from Helen, setting his hat on the table and smoothing his hair back.

"Was anyone hurt? That thing can be… dangerous," Helen said, her fingers idly tracing the lines of an old leather-bound tome.

"I don't think so. Seems the sorceress subdued the beast," Robert replied, leaning back in his chair. The worn wood creaked slightly, and he crossed his arms, a thoughtful expression on his face.

"Oh, okay, that's good. So, did they say what started it?" Helen's hand stilled.

"Nope." Robert scratched his chin.

"Do you think it's connected to the... dead cow?" Helen inquired, her gaze shifting from the book to the scratch marks on the wooden table.

"I'm not sure, but it surely isn't a daily occurrence, is it now? I wonder what could drive such a creature to act out of its nature," Robert tilted his head, studying her. "Do you think you can check if those books of yours say something about this as well?"

"Umm... sure," Helen muttered as she put her glasses back on.

"What about the other thing... did you find anything yet?"

"I'm not sure yet, Robert, but look here... does this symbol look like one of the symbols on the corpse?" Helen delicately pointed to the intricate markings in the book.

Robert squinted, his eyes narrowing in an attempt to identify the faded symbols. "Umm... I'm not sure. Why, what is it about?"

"The book is kind of old; I found it in the back, and most of the pages are tattered. So, I can't tell for sure, but I think this symbol was surely present on the dead cow back at John's," Helen explained.

"What's the book called?"

"Tales of the Hidden Light," Helen said, looking directly at Robert.

"Sounds serious. What does it say?" Robert leaned forward; his hands clasped together.

"Like I said, the book is quite old. I wish I had a better version. It's so hard to make out anything from it, but something here did interest me. The mentions go as far back as a millennium ago," Helen confessed, her eyes squinting in concentration.

"What's that?"

"It says something about the... Cimmerian Order," Helen disclosed, her words hanging in the air like a ghostly echo from the past.

"The Cimmerian Order?"

"Yeah, I think they were a secret cult or something."

"A cult? This is getting too strange, Helen."

"I agree, but I'm pretty sure this marking is the same as the one on the corpse," Helen insisted.

Robert paused for a moment before breaking the silence. "Ok, let's agree for a minute that it is the same symbol... but this cult, the Cimmerian Order you say, it makes no sense. There are—were no secret cults in Avalora."

"Well, if we all knew about it, it wouldn't be a secret now, would it?" Helen quipped.

"Helen, I suggest you look into something else; we would be better off without conspiracy theories," Robert advised, his concern etched in the lines of his face.

"Um, you're right... I guess. I'll look at something else," Helen conceded.

Helen sighed, her gaze reluctantly leaving the worn pages of the ancient tome she had been deciphering. As Helen shifted her attention, the room settled into a quiet rhythm, the only sound the soft rustling of parchment and the occasional crackle of the aging fireplace.

"Anyone in there?" a voice said as the couple heard a knock on their door.

Robert promptly opened the door to find George standing there with a sack on his shoulders and a casual smile on his face.

"Oh, hello, George," Robert greeted.

"Robert, hello. You all set?"

"Yeah, give me a minute," Robert replied.

"Hey, Helen! George's here; it's time. You sure you're not coming?" Robert turned toward the interior of the cottage, raising his voice.

Helen walked up to the door.

"Remember to get those buns from the market, hon," Helen said as she gave a peck to Robert on his cheeks. She handed him his bag for the trip.

"All right then, we're off. Take care, Helen," Robert said as he followed George to the caravan.

As Robert settled onto the front of the caravan, George promptly took the reins. The back of the caravan was laden with produce from the grain mill and empty containers to bring goods back from the kingdom.

"Okay, so the castle should be a day's ride. Hope you got everything you need," George recounted.

Robert looked back, ensuring all was in order before signaling the go-ahead. He waved a final goodbye to Helen, still standing at the door.

"Don't drink too much…" Helen shouted after them.

The door creaked shut, leaving behind the quiet hum of a village afternoon, punctuated by the distant clip-clop of hooves fading into the horizon.

***

The grand luncheon hall echoed with the clinking of silverware and hushed conversations as the esteemed guests indulged in the lavish spread. King Reginald, seated at the head of the ornate table, observed the lively exchanges around him.

Calindor engaged the king in discussions about the recent trade agreements, his deep voice carrying authority. Archibald, sitting beside the king, interjected with strategic insights. Duke Thornbriar sat across from the count, his piercing gaze surveying the room. He occasionally exchanged polite nods with the others. A few other nobles from Avalora graced the table, none related to the king by blood, but still necessary considering the vastness of the kingdom and its various political affairs.

As the din of conversations continued, the fragrance of exotic dishes wafted through the air, adding to the opulence of the scene. The chandeliers above cast a warm glow over the hall.

Princess Seraphina sat beside Count Calindor, appearing visibly bored as her eyes kept scanning for Oliver.

"Will Oliver not be joining us?" Princess Seraphina grumbled.

"Ah, yes. Oliver should be here momentarily. What is taking the boy so long?" The king silently motioned for one of the servants to fetch him.

"Princess Seraphina, you are the spitting image of your mother, aren't you?" the king attempted to engage her.

"Thank you, Your Majesty," Seraphina responded with a slight bow of her head, evidently pleased that the king mentioned her mother rather than her father.

Calindor continued discussing trade agreements with King Reginald. "Your Majesty, the Ophidonian vineyards have produced an exceptional vintage this year. Perhaps a trade agreement could see your royal cellar graced with our finest wines?"

"An excellent proposal, Count. We shall discuss the details further after the ascension ceremony," King Reginald arched his back slightly in satisfaction.

Amidst the exchange, Duke Thornbriar leaned in with a tone of curiosity. “Count Calindor, I 'ave 'eard whispers of a new alliance in ze eastern provinces. Any truth to zese murmurs?”

“Rumors, my lord. The winds of gossip are often unpredictable. However, I assure you, Veridia remains a valued ally,” Calindor replied.

Growing more impatient, Seraphina tapped her fingers lightly on the table. “I hope Oliver is not making a spectacle of himself again. We have important matters to discuss.”

The king chuckled, attempting to lighten the mood. “Young Oliver always has a flair for the dramatic. I'm sure he'll arrive in due time, my dear.”

Before Seraphina could respond, the king shifted the topic. “Speaking of youth, Calindor, I trust your son is adjusting well to his studies at the academy?”

“Indeed, Your Majesty. Young Sebastian is proving to be a diligent student,” Calindor's expression softened with paternal pride.

As the conversations flowed, the servants discreetly circulated the room, offering refills and ensuring the guests lacked for nothing.

A few moments later, the grand doors creaked open, and Oliver made his entrance. His presence, though delayed, brought a momentary pause to the conversations as all eyes turned toward the heir to the throne.

“Ah, there he is,” the king announced with pride.

“What took you so long? Everyone has been waiting for you,” the king clapped his hands over Oliver’s shoulders. A subtle squeeze of the shoulders indicated he was not to make any mentions of earlier incidents.

"I'm sorry, I was detained… with arrangements, father," Oliver said, his eyes locking onto the king's without wavering.

The king, trying his best to pretend to ignore Oliver's remarks, gestured toward the guests. "You remember Count Calindor and Duke Thornbriar, and of course, Princess Seraphina."

Oliver nodded politely to the guests, his gaze briefly drifting toward Seraphina.

"Oliver, why don't you take a seat beside Princess Seraphina," the king pointed to an empty seat beside her.

Oliver, a pawn in the kingdom's chessboard of diplomacy, promptly took a step forward and took the seat. As he sat, he couldn't help but notice the overpowering scent of jasmine emanating from her.

"Nice perfume, Seraphina," he spoke softly.

"Jasmine. Is that your preferred scent, Oliver?" Seraphina raised an eyebrow.

Oliver, now noticeably flustered, stammered for a moment before managing to reply, "I, um, well... I just happened to notice it. Not that I... I mean, it suits you."

A soft laugh escaped Seraphina's lips, and she leaned in slightly. "Tell me, do you often notice details like scents, or is it just when you're in the company of a certain princess?"

Oliver shifted uncomfortably in his seat. He cleared his throat, his cheeks turning a subtle shade of pink. "Well, you see, Princess, a prince's attention is often divided among many matters, and... um, scents just happened to be one of those details that caught my notice today."

"Caught your notice, did it?" she teased, her tone lightly flirtatious.

"These trade agreements seem mighty interesting, don't they?" Oliver said, taking a gulp from a chalice in front of him.

"Trade agreements can wait. We were discussing scents, remember? I'm curious to know what else catches your notice when you're not immersed in the intricacies of royal affairs," Seraphina chuckled.

Oliver, now more flustered than ever, managed a nervous laugh. "Well, there are plenty of things, I suppose. The chandeliers, the tapestries, the intricate details of the hall... I'm not always preoccupied with, uh, scents."

Seraphina, enjoying Oliver's unease, continued to playfully press. "So, you're saying the grandeur of the hall distracts you from the finer details?"

"Exactly! The grandeur, the discussions, the upcoming ceremony... it's all quite overwhelming, you know." Oliver snapped his fingers.

Seraphina leaned in a bit closer, her hand delicately tracing the rim of her chalice. "Overwhelming, you say? Perhaps you need a moment of respite, Prince. A distraction from the grandeur and intricacies."

"A moment of respite sounds... quite appealing, actually."

Seraphina's fingers grazed the edge of Oliver's hand on the table, a subtle and intentional gesture. "Sometimes, amidst all the royal duties, one must find solace in the little things. Don't you agree?"

"Y—Yes, I mean, absolutely. Solace is... crucial."

Seraphina's lips curled up, and she continued to playfully trace her fingers across Oliver's hand.

"Perhaps a stroll through the palace gardens could offer such solace? Away from the bustling hall, just the two of us..."

"A stroll? In the gardens?" Oliver blinked in surprise.

“Why not, Prince Oliver? Sometimes, the fragrances there are equally captivating, and who knows what other details might catch your notice.”

Oliver felt his cheeks grow warmer, his attempts to conceal his flustered state faltering. Before he could formulate a response to Seraphina's suggestive proposal, their conversation was interrupted by the commanding voice of the king.

“Ladies and gentlemen, esteemed guests, if I may have your attention,” he announced, rising from his seat.

Oliver, largely relieved by the diversion, shifted his focus to the king, the blush on his cheeks beginning to subside. Seraphina withdrew her hand gracefully, and both turned their attention to the monarch.

“The time has come for us to discuss the impending ascension ceremony,” King Reginald continued. “As you all know, tomorrow is the day when our prince will begin his journey into adulthood, and this ascension ceremony marks his rightful place as heir to the throne. It is a momentous occasion, and much is to be discussed about the intricacies.”

King Reginald then gestured toward Archibald, indicating that it was time for him to contribute to the discussions about the upcoming event.

Archibald, accustomed to the subtle cues of the royal court, rose from his seat and bowed.

“Thank you, Your Majesty. The ascension ceremony is a moment of great importance for our kingdom. Beyond the symbolic aspects, we must consider the practicalities of the event. Security measures need to be at their utmost, ensuring the safety of all attendees. Rest assured, Sir Lucius has taken care of it,” Archibald announced, glancing around for the missing knight. “The ceremony will be a public spectacle and the perception matters greatly. A well-crafted message from Prince Oliver can shape how the citizens view his reign."

Archibald turned toward Prince Oliver, a gesture not lost on those in attendance. There was an unspoken understanding that the responsibility of crafting this crucial message rested upon his shoulders. Oliver, though still a bit flustered from the earlier exchange with Seraphina, quietly dipped his chin.

"Perhaps, a toast?" Seraphina interjected. "I can help Prince Oliver craft a well-worded toast." Turning to Oliver with a flirtatious smile, she added, "After all, a memorable toast can make a lasting impression on the people, don't you think, Prince Oliver?"

"Excellent suggestion, Princess Seraphina," King Reginald acknowledged, raising a hand in approval. "A well-crafted toast can indeed set the tone for the entire ceremony."

"In Veridia, our toasts, zey are not just words; zey are poetry, each one, 'ow you say, a masterpiece in celebration," Duke Thornbriar spoke, ensuring his voice carried weight in the ongoing discussions, unwilling to be overlooked.

Count Calindor, sensing the importance of his contribution, added, "A carefully crafted message should also highlight our commitment to stability and prosperity. I must say though, I have my apprehensions about inviting commoners to the ceremony."

"Ah, but a public ceremony, it is crucial for highlighting ze prince's stature, n'est-ce pas?"

"These are all excellent suggestions, Your Graces," Archibald said, gathering the table's attention. "I'm sure Prince Oliver will consider all your contributions. As for your suggestion about keeping it a private affair, Count Calindor, it's regrettably too late. Besides, it adheres to tradition."

Calindor, realizing that his advice might not be heeded, chose to yield the floor.

"Furthermore, esteemed guests, let us not overlook the significance of attire and public appearances during the ascension ceremony. While I'm confident that each of you has given due consideration to your ensembles, just in case there are any last-minute adjustments, Madame Tissuré, our esteemed royal seamstress, will be available this evening to ensure that every detail aligns seamlessly with the grandeur of the occasion," Archibald continued, his words carrying an air of assurance and meticulous planning.

Oliver's mind was abruptly drawn to the upcoming attire he would be wearing during the ceremony. At that moment, a subtle relief washed over him, entertained by the notion that perhaps, once Princess Seraphina witnessed the regal splendor of his ensemble, her interest in him might wane.

As the exchanges continued, Oliver's initial defiance over his best friend's imprisonment began to fade. The weight of his impending ascension ceremony loomed large, overshadowing the chaos around him. Amid the orchestrated conversations, Amelia tried to approach him, concern etched on her face. But each time she attempted to get close, Princess Seraphina hovered nearby, preventing any private conversation.

As the discussions about attire, toasts, and the upcoming ceremony continued, a subtle shift in the atmosphere hinted at the closure of the grand luncheon. The fragrance of exotic dishes still lingered in the air, and the warm glow of chandeliers above continued to cast a regal ambiance over the hall.

***

"Meera, are you awake?" Lumo asked.

A faint groan escaped Meera as she stirred in the dimly lit dungeon. She shifted, trying to find a more comfortable position on the hard, unforgiving bed.

"Awake? In this cozy dungeon? I'm living the dream," Meera replied.

Lumo chuckled, the sound echoing in the confined space.

"So, what's on your mind, criminal?" Meera continued, her voice carrying a sly edge.

Lumo sighed for a moment, but something about Meera made him feel at ease. At ease enough to continue to talk to her, despite her otherwise harsh-sounding words, not that he had a choice. Maybe it was the way she spoke, alternating between a good friend and a good fiend.

"I've been thinking about the circumstances that led us here. It's not every day one finds oneself in the company of a notorious thief," Lumo said as he tried to match Meera's attitude.

"Ah, flattery will get you everywhere, Lumo," Meera quipped, her words accompanied by the subtle shuffle of her movements. "But really, what's a charming man-servant like yourself doing in a place like this?"

"I told you, it was a mistake, but anyway, there was something else on my mind."

"What's that?" Meera said as she slowly got up from the bed and walked closer.

Lumo hesitated for a moment, then decided to take a chance. "You know, normally I am so busy with attending to Prince Oliver that I don't have a chance to think about things, but being in this cell has given me so much time to contemplate."

"I'm listening..."

"I was thinking about how I got here, you know."

"Yeah, you said it was a mistake, I know," Meera said with an eye roll.

"No, I mean, how I ended up here in the castle, with Oliver."

Meera saw where this was going and decided it was probably best to let Lumo continue.

Lumo took a deep breath.

"I remember the first time like it was yesterday. It was years ago—the first time I saw the king. I was just a child, barely old enough to understand the significance of the moment. The king arrived on this magnificent horse; there were so many guards."

Meera leaned against the cold stone wall, motioning for Lumo to continue.

"Oliver was there too. Even as a child, I could tell how different he was from me. I remember the king dismounting his horse and exchanging some words with Oliver."

Lumo paused, lost momentarily in the memories of that day, like a traveler caught in a dense fog.

"Lucius wore that shining armor he still wears, and I remember that was the first time I had ever seen a knight. Looking at him, I really wanted to be a knight too."

Lumo continued, the memories flooding back. "The king and Lucius spoke in hushed tones, their words a mystery to my young ears. Oliver stood there, his gaze meeting the king's with a strange mixture of defiance and curiosity. I remember feeling small in the presence of such power."

Meera's eyes were fixed on Lumo.

"I couldn't understand the gravity of that moment then, but now I realize it was a turning point. The king looked at me, seemingly out of nowhere. His eyes were assessing, calculating, and then he said something to Lucius. I didn't catch the words, but the next thing I knew, I was being taken away from the only home I had ever known."

Lumo's gaze drifted to the dungeon walls, as if he could still see the distant past playing out before him. "I became an attendant to Oliver, the prince. It's funny how life works, isn't it? From a humble beginning, suddenly thrust into the corridors of power."

Meera remained silent, allowing Lumo to continue his story.

"Life in the castle wasn't what I thought it would be. Instead, all these politics and unrelenting condescension made me feel smaller at times."

"Lucius hates me. I've never heard him say my name, ever. He just calls me 'boy' or whatever he fancies."

"Why?" Meera asked.

"I'm not sure. I can only assume it's because of where I came from," Lumo sighed.

"Oliver was the only real friend I had, yet the differences in our station were vast. But the king, he's always been so kind to me, like a fatherly figure."

Lumo's gaze met Meera's, a hint of vulnerability in his eyes. "I've always wondered why the king chose me, why he brought me to the castle that day. It's a question that has lingered in the back of my mind, hidden beneath the duties and expectations placed upon me."

"Did you ever ask the king?" Meera spoke slowly.

"Hah! No... I did ask Oliver this one time, though. He said he didn't remember much, but that he was quite happy with how things turned out," Lumo said. "I let the thought go after that, but being here I couldn't help but think about how things might have been different. Gosh, I don't even remember what my parents look like."

"Wait, what? Don't you have any memories with them?"

"Umm… I don't know. I can't seem to remember anything from before that point."

Meera nodded thoughtfully, her gaze meeting Lumo's. "Not remembering your parents... that's... heavy, even for someone living in a castle. Have you never tried to dig deeper, find out more about where you come from?"

Lumo sighed, a mix of frustration and resignation in his expression. "I've considered it, but every time I think about delving into my past, there's something stopping me. It's almost as if I'm meant to stay within the confines of what fate has allowed me to know."

"Sometimes… the shadows of our pasts are like locked doors, and we hesitate to turn the key," Meera said with a thoughtful voice that rarely surfaced.

Lumo looked at Meera as if she was exactly the person he needed to talk to at that very moment.

"What about you, Meera? What's your story?" Lumo inquired.

After a small pause, Meera replied, "Come now, Lumo, I don't know you well enough to share stories of my life filled with crime; besides, that would be like confessing to my deeds now, wouldn't it?" A gentle smirk left her face.

"Oh… yes, of course, you're right," Lumo said with a slightly disappointed look.

"Hey, Lumo, come here, will you?" Meera said as she motioned for Lumo to come closer to her cell.

Lumo approached, curious about what Meera had in mind. As he neared, Meera reached through the bars, attempting to grasp his hands. Lumo, thinking she was offering reassurance in her own way, allowed her to hold his hands.

"Huh, that's interesting."

Lumo, puzzled, asked, "What's interesting?"

Meera thought for a moment, examining Lumo's hands.

"Nothing... it's nothing," she said, finally releasing his hands and taking a small step back.

"What? Come on, tell me."

"Your hands are quite soft," she remarked after a brief moment of silence. "I would have expected a man doing all the chores you mentioned to have rougher hands. Interesting, don't you think?"

Lumo looked at his own hands as if seeing them for the first time. "Well, I suppose I haven't been doing much manual labor lately. It's mostly attending to Prince Oliver's needs and the likes."

"Must be a life of luxury you lead, then. Soft hands and all," Meera chuckled.

Lumo tilted his head, intrigued. "Luxury? I wouldn't call it that. Just the nature of my duties, I guess."

"Hmm," Meera mused, deflecting subtly. "Or maybe you're just not telling me everything about yourself." She let out a playful smirk.

Outside the dungeon, the air filled with tension as the echoing footsteps of guards mingled with distant voices. The clinking of armor and the murmur of urgent conversation indicated an approaching commotion.

"Hold on, you can't go in there. It's off-limits," a guard spoke.

Amelia's familiar voice cut through the air, determined and urgent. "I must see Lumo. It's important. Let me through."

"Orders are orders. No one gets in," the guard reiterated, standing firm.

"That prisoner in there is the prince's attendant. The ceremony is tomorrow and the prince's amulet has gone missing. He's the only one who knows where it was kept. Let me in, and I'll get the information from him quickly. I have a lot of other things to tend to," Amelia said, trying to ascertain her urgency.

The guard hesitated for a moment but ultimately conceded.

"Fine, but make it snappy. We're not supposed to let anyone in."

Amelia rushed into the dungeon, her eyes searching for Lumo's cell. The guards kept a watchful distance as she navigated the dimly lit space.

"Lumo, we don't have much time," Amelia said, her voice hushed as she approached him.

"Amelia, I overheard the conversation with the guard; I do not know about this amulet," Lumo confessed, scratching his head.

"No, it's not that; it's something else."

Lumo's eyes widened, sensing the gravity in her look.

"Well, what is it?"

Amelia, glancing around nervously, spotted Meera nearby. She motioned for Lumo to join her in a corner, away from prying ears.

"Amelia, what's the matter?" Lumo pressed.

"I overheard something last night, and I didn't know who else to turn to," Amelia spoke in a low tone, her voice barely audible.

"The P—Prince..." she began, her voice faltering.

"Amelia, please, tell me!" Lumo's impatience turned into a desperate plea.

"The prince is going to be... abducted."

***

CHAPTER 5

Amelia's words hung in the air like an ominous prelude, echoing through the dungeon's cold stone walls. Lumo stared into her eyes, the weight of her revelation settling heavily upon him.

"The prince is going to be abducted." Amelia's hushed words reverberated in his ears.

Lumo's mind raced, grappling with the sudden turn of events. Part of him hoped it was a joke, but Amelia wasn't the type to joke about something like this. He had to try to stay rational. He had to get to the bottom of it.

"Abducted? Why? B—By whom?" Lumo stammered.

Amelia, still casting cautious glances around and ensuring no prying ears lingered too close, leaned in. "I overheard a conversation last night. Plans, Lumo. Sinister plans to seize the prince during the ceremony. I do not know who it was or why they plan to do this, but it will happen tomorrow during the ceremony." She explained what she saw and heard the night before.

"Have you tried speaking to Lucius?" Lumo asked, still trying to maintain composure.

"I have, but things were so chaotic today. And I couldn't even spot him in the evening... Look, I don't have all the time in the world. The guards will probably ask me to leave any minute," Amelia shared, quickly gazing toward the dungeon door and back. "I know you are closer to the prince than anyone. You are the only person I could trust."

"Amelia... what do you expect me to do? I am locked up here in the dungeon."

Amelia hesitated, her face falling as she glanced down, visibly torn.

"I—I'm sorry. I wasn't thinking clearly."

"Listen to me," Lumo urged, gripping Amelia's trembling hands through the bars. "You need to speak to Lucius, Archibald, or even His Majesty if you must. If what you said is true, it's our responsibility to avert this crisis."

Their conversation was abruptly cut short by the guard's stern voice from outside.

"Hey, you! You need to leave. Haven't you got the information you need yet? What is taking so long?"

Amelia jerked back. "Yes, I have. I'm leaving now," she called out, her voice steady even as her hands shook.

"I must go now, Lumo. I'll try to speak to Lucius first thing in the morning," she said, offering a final reassuring look.

As the heavy door creaked open, swallowing Amelia's silhouette, a cold draft swept through the dungeon. The door thudded shut behind her, sealing Lumo once more in the suffocating silence of his cell. The weak light cast long shadows that danced, echoing the turmoil in Lumo's mind.

His thoughts raced, trying to make sense of the sinister plans to abduct the prince. The gravity of the situation pressed upon him, and a sense of helplessness clawed at his chest. He was locked in a dungeon at a crucial moment.

A traitor inside the castle? Who could it be? Lucius? Was this his plan all along? After all, he was responsible for suggesting Lumo's punishment. What purpose would it solve, though? There were too many unanswered questions, and Lumo just wasn't mentally equipped to deal with them.

As the seconds stretched into a heavy pause, a sudden interruption shattered the silence.

"A bit too old to be your girlfriend, isn't she?" Meera's voice cut through the quiet.

Lumo's head snapped up, startled by Meera's remark. The dim light caught the glint of curiosity in her eyes as she observed him from her neighboring cell. The gravity of the situation clashed with Meera's irreverent interruption, creating an odd moment for Lumo.

"Meera, I'm really not in the mood for chit-chat right now," Lumo said, worry evident on his brow.

Meera, perched on the edge of her bed, studied Lumo's face. "Is everything okay, Lumo?"

A heavy sigh escaped Lumo as he ran a hand through his disheveled hair. "No, it's not," he admitted, his gaze fixed on some distant point.

"Well, you want to talk about it?"

"Talk about it? You don't talk about yourself, and yet you want to know everything about me?" Lumo snapped.

A moment of uneasy silence settled between them, broken only by the low hum of the dungeon's stillness.

"Okay, then," Meera said, a subtle shrug accompanying her nonchalant response as she retreated to her bed.

"Wait... I'm sorry," Lumo's voice softened, regret coloring his words as he took a step closer to Meera.

"It's just that I'm dealing with an issue that I can't wrap my head around."

"I understand. I will leave you be," Meera said as she adjusted her position on the bed.

"She's not my girlfriend, you know."

"Oh, who is she then?" Meera said, once again getting up and sitting on the edge of her bed.

"Amelia is one of the other maids in the castle."

"Ah, I see. So, what did she want? She seemed kind of nervous, you know."

Lumo hesitated, but he had to get it off his chest. "Meera, something terrible is about to happen, and I'm stuck in here. I don't know what to do."

"Calm down, Lumo. Why don't you tell me what happened?" Meera said, slowly getting up and moving toward Lumo.

Lumo narrated the entire incident to Meera. Meera listened intently, her eyes momentarily darting to distant places and then finding themselves back to Lumo. After he was finished, Meera took a moment's thought before responding.

"This prince, is he a good fellow?" Meera asked, her gaze shifting to the floor.

"Of course, he is my best friend. Even now, I'm sure he is worried about me being here. If only I could speak to him."

"Well, why don't you?" Meera asked nonchalantly.

Lumo shrugged in disbelief. "Meera, I—"

"I mean you should escape and go to him," Meera said, cutting Lumo off.

"I... can't do that... that would be against the king's orders."

"So? You can spend another week in the dungeon after this crisis has been averted, can't you?" Meera countered.

Meera's reasoning made insane sense to Lumo. For as long as he could remember, loyalty to the king's orders had been the cornerstone of his identity. The very thought of defying a royal decree would have been unimaginable, a transgression not to be entertained.

He recalled a moment from his past. As a young boy, he had once questioned a minor order, believing a different course of action to be wiser.

Sir Eamon had pulled him aside, eyes blazing with anger. "Never forget your place, Lumo," Sir Eamon had growled, fiercely. "The king's word is law. Doubt it, and you doubt the very foundation of our realm."

Lumo had spent the night cleaning the stables, the sting of Sir Eamon's reprimand lingering long after the work was done. That lesson had stayed with him, a constant reminder of the unyielding nature of duty.

Yet, in the fading shadows of the dungeon, with the weight of an impending crisis bearing down on him, Lumo felt the foundations of his steadfast loyalty tremble. Perhaps for the first time in his life, going against orders seemed like the right thing for him to do. In that moment of contemplation, Lumo felt the weight of responsibility wrestle against the chains of tradition. The decision to escape, though fraught with peril, seemed less like an act of defiance and more like a necessary course of action.

With fierce determination, he looked at Meera. "I should escape… but how?"

"You're asking the right question now," Meera smirked mischievously.

"Okay, so what now?"

"Come closer, let me explain the plan to you."

As Lumo leaned toward Meera, she whispered her escape plan to him. Lumo's eyes widened as he absorbed the details, the weight of their impending actions settling upon him. With a nod, their eyes met again.

"And now... we wait for tomorrow. I suggest you get some sleep, Lumo. We need to be well-rested."

***

The day, like a reluctant debutante, had finally made its entrance—still in the early morning stages.

Bart, Lily, and Gus strolled just beyond the castle gates, the early morning sun casting a warm glow on the cobblestone path. A faint aroma of blooming flowers lingered in the air, mixing with the earthy scent of the stones beneath their feet. The gentle breeze carried the fragrance of the castle gardens, teasing their senses as they made their way toward the castle gate.

"C'mon, Gus, pick up the pace a bit!" Lily said as she watched Gus lag behind.

"Easy now, Lily, what's the rush?" Bart asked.

"This place is going to be packed. I want to be in the front row," Lily squealed.

"I'm coming," Gus said, picking up his pace. It was a scary sight, given a man of his size.

The trio continued their stroll until they reached the castle gates. A small crowd had already gathered at the gates, and the guards were barking orders in an attempt to avoid chaos.

"In one line, folks!" Marcus shouted above the growing murmur of the crowd.

The air buzzed with excited chatter as people adjusted their positions, waiting for their turn to pass through the gate.

"What's going on here?" Lily muttered, casting a curious glance at the guards orchestrating the queuing process.

"Isn't it obvious? Too many people," an older lady in the queue reported.

As Lily, Bart, and Gus gradually shuffled into line, the minutes ticked by like a slow march, each passing second bringing them closer to the imposing castle gate. The crowd ahead inched forward, their anticipation palpable in the hushed whispers and fidgety movements.

As they approached the gate, Marcus continued barking orders.

"Keep it moving! In one line," Marcus repeated, his authoritative tone cutting through the ambient murmur.

Finally, it was their turn. Lily, Bart, and Gus stepped forward in unison, preparing to present themselves for entry. Marcus, focused on maintaining order, mechanically glanced at the approaching trio. However, when his eyes fell upon Gus, a moment of sheer surprise disrupted his practiced composure.

"Well, I'll be," Marcus muttered, momentarily forgetting his duty as the gatekeeper. "You're a big fella, aren't you? What's your name?"

Before Gus could deliver his signature introduction, Lily cut through.

"He's Gus, this is Bart, and I'm Lily. Can we hurry this up?" Lily said, her patience waning quickly.

Marcus, recovering from his initial shock, managed a nod. "All right, move along, but watch your step."

As Lily, Bart, and Gus walked through the castle gate, the courtyard opened up before them, revealing a scene they hadn't anticipated. The once spacious area was now quickly filling up with a growing crowd of people.

Bart's eyes widened in surprise. "Blimey, this is quite the turnout. Looks like everyone had the same idea, Lily."

"You can say that again," Lily blurted.

"How are we goin' ta get a good spot at the front now?" Bart quizzed.

"I have an idea," Lily declared. Turning to Gus, she encouraged, "Gus, big guy, how about you take the lead?

Let's see if that size of yours can part this sea of people for us."

"Me?" Gus mumbled, his childlike innocence shining through.

"Yes, you," Lily said, pushing Gus as if it made a difference.

Gus slowly approached the crowd, and as he did, a large shadow seemed to engulf a row of people who looked back worriedly.

"Excuse me, please... may I get in," Gus spoke softly.

As if not needing any further encouragement, the crowd willingly parted, allowing Gus to move further along, with Lily and Bart trailing him like twin tails.

"Sorry, move aside, coming through..."

As Lily, Bart, and Gus made their way through the now somewhat parted sea of people, the grand stage where the prince would be anointed became increasingly visible in the distance. The excitement in the air mingled with the nervous energy of the crowd. Lily, eager to secure their front-row positions, urged Gus to keep forging ahead.

When they neared the stage, elegant floral arrangements and refined decorations came into view. Nobles occupied a separate, velvet-roped section, mingling in low voices. Seraphina, Calindor, and Thornbriar were already seated there, their attire reflecting the grandeur of the occasion. Seraphina's deep blue gown sparkled with silver accents, her hair adorned with a serpent-shaped brooch. Calindor's cloak, clasped with a silver serpent, matched his suit's subtle, serpentine details. Thornbriar wore a robe of earthy greens, his Veridian staff carved with patterns of trees and creatures—rumored to be a gift from the mystical dryads themselves. Groups of Ophidonian and Veridian guards stood steadfast, clearly demarcating the two sections.

"Looks like they invited everyone from the kingdom; couldn't they have been more selective?" Calindor said, glancing condescendingly at the gathered crowd.

Seraphina observed the multitude with a discerning eye. "They all seem quite happy to be here, though."

"Ugh, but look at some of these people," Calindor expressed, pointing toward a bunch of commoners in less-than-desirable clothing.

Thornbriar leaned in. "Zis reminds me of zis story of a married man who once ventured into ze Elderine forests of northern Veridia. Zere, 'e saw ze most beautiful forest nymph, or so 'e thought."

"And what fate befell this infatuated fool?" Calindor inquired.

The duke's eyes gleamed with a mysterious twinkle as he revealed, "Ze nymph turned out to be a Huldra."

Princess Seraphina leaned forward with genuine curiosity. "A Huldra? What manner of creature is that?"

"Zey are a sort of troll species."

"Trolls are hideous, Thornbriar. Are you concocting tales again?" Calindor remarked.

"I said 'sort of,' non?" Thornbriar calmly clarified. "Ze Huldra, you see, appears as a beautiful nymph in every aspect, except for one dark secret."

"What secret?" Seraphina asked, her curiosity piqued.

"On 'er back lies a massive hole, a cavernous void," Thornbriar whispered. "I suppose you can imagine what 'appened to ze enamored man."

"What happened, Thornbriar?" Seraphina jumped.

"Ze man, ensnared by ze Huldra's allure, approached 'er wiz reckless abandon. But as 'e embraced 'er, 'e was devoured by ze darkness within. Ze void on 'er back consumed 'im entirely, leaving nothing but ze echoes of regret in ze shadows of ze forest."

"How dreadful!" Princess Seraphina remarked, a shiver coursing through her.

"Which brings me to my point, Mon cher." Thornbriar directed his gaze at Calindor. "Ze truest beauty is found in ze soul, not ze silk."

"Is this some attempt at moralizing, Thornbriar? I assure you; I have little interest in cautionary tales. The realities of our world require discernment, not whimsical fables." Calindor scoffed, clearly annoyed.

As the trio stood in a rather awkward silence, the air shifted with the arrival of Archibald. He entered the noble area with an air of authority, in an elegant white suit. Serena followed closely.

"Ah, Princess Seraphina, Lord Calindor, Lord Thornbriar," Archibald greeted them, his eyes scanning the area. "Enjoying the festivities, I hope?"

"Indeed, Archibald. The turnout is most impressive," Seraphina responded politely.

Archibald stepped aside, allowing Serena to come into full view. "You remember Serena."

Serena took a gracious bow. "My apologies for my absence yesterday, Your Graces. There were some urgent matters to tend to."

"Zis is quite okay, my lady." Thornbriar took the lead as if pulled by a magnetic force. "I 'ave to say, ma chère, you are looking rather ravishing today."

Serena acknowledged Thornbriar's compliment with a graceful nod. A subtle, almost imperceptible smile played on her lips. "Your words are kind, Master Thornbriar."

Thornbriar, taking the response positively, tilted his head slightly. "Tell me, ma chère, 'ave you ever witnessed ze dance of ze Veridian fireflies?"

"I've heard of them but never seen them in person. Their dance is mesmerizing apparently," Serena replied.

"Oui, but ma chère, ze Veridian fireflies are nozing compared to you. Their luminescence is dimmed by ze radiance zat graces your every step."

"You have a poet's heart, Master Thornbriar. It seems Veridia has gifted you not only its landscapes but also its way with words," Serena replied, her demeanor unyielding.

Archibald, sensing the need to steer the conversation, interjected with a diplomatic smile. "Well, everyone, I must attend to some duties. Enjoy the festivities. The entertainment should commence shortly."

Thornbriar, extending a hand toward the sorceress, gracefully ushered her toward the vacant seat beside him. "If you 'onor zese seats, ma chère, perhaps I shall weave enchanting verses as vibrant as Veridia's blooms. What say you?"

As Archibald withdrew discreetly, he cast one final glance around, ensuring the nobles were all comfortably settled.

***

"It's almost time, Lumo," Meera said eagerly. "Hope this works; this isn't going to be easy."

"I'm ready," Lumo replied.

"There's no turning back after this… just saying."

With a nod, Lumo confirmed that he indeed was ready for whatever lay ahead.

As the appointed moment arrived, Meera recounted their daring escape plan in her mind. The strategy was simple:

incapacitate the guards and make a swift exit. However, flawless execution was as practical as teaching a cat to play the piano. Timing, it seems, played a crucial role in their plan, especially as the guards' shift approached its end, ensuring their fatigue would work in their favor. Attempting the plan at any other time risked failure, with potentially dire consequences. Meera's adept observational skills, honed from her experience, had allowed her to study the guards' routines in the preceding days.

"Well, here goes nothing," Meera spoke to herself as she set her plan in motion.

With an unnecessarily convincing display, Meera pretended to faint. As she positioned herself on the floor, Lumo took the cue to play his part in the scheme.

"Help! Guards, the girl has fainted," Lumo shouted.

One of the guards, hearing the commotion, turned to his companion. "Go check on her. I've got this area covered."

The guard shuffled toward Meera's cell with a set of keys jangling at his side. The dim light wavered weakly as he approached the seemingly unconscious Meera.

"Hey, what's going on?" the guard grumbled as he observed the situation.

Lumo seized the moment and shouted again, "Hurry! She might be seriously ill!"

The concerned guard hastily unlocked the cell door and leaned over to assess Meera's condition. "Huh, looks like she's fainted," the guard remarked.

"Is she breathing?" Lumo prodded.

The guard, momentarily taken aback, leaned in to inspect Meera more closely. The slight forward movement proved to be an unwitting opening, and with a burst of agility, Meera sprang into action. Meera swiftly pulled the guard to the floor, causing his head to bang hard against the unforgiving surface. He crumpled unconscious to the ground.

Meera quickly exited her cell, her movements fluid and silent. She positioned herself near the back of the dungeon's main door, preparing for the next phase of their escape. With a hand signal, she motioned for Lumo to initiate the next part.

“The prisoner is escaping!” Lumo shouted once again, trying to imitate the guard’s gruff voice.

The remaining guard, alarmed, rushed toward the commotion through the dungeon’s main gate. His eyes narrowed as he witnessed his companion lying unconscious on the cold stone floor.

“What the—” he muttered, baffled by the sudden turn of events.

Lumo, seizing the opportunity, couldn't resist a touch of humor. With a smug grin, he shouted, “Hey, friend, ever heard the phrase 'behind you'?”

As the guard turned around, perhaps the last thing he saw at that moment was Meera’s fist. With a thud, the guard crumbled, joining his companion in dreamland.

“Quickly, we need to get out of here,” Meera said as she freed Lumo from his cell.

Lumo grabbed the sword from one of the guards, and they made their exit toward the outside.

As Meera and Lumo cautiously moved through the dimly lit corridors, the distant echoes of approaching footsteps reached them at the crossroads. The sound of armored boots against the cold stone floor signaled the arrival of a new set of guards.

Lumo instinctively gripped the sword, a determined look on his face. Lumo’s heart started beating faster than a hare in a carrot patch. The rhythmic thumping of the footsteps echoed in his ears, and he grappled with the possibility of a head-on confrontation. As the seconds seemed to stretch into minutes, Meera quickly grabbed Lumo, pulling him to a corner.

"Wait, Lumo," she whispered.

Scanning their surroundings in the dimly lit dungeon, Meera spotted a stack of crates near the corridor entrance. She swiftly moved toward them, searching for anything that could serve their purpose. Among the discarded items, she found a small, sturdy rock with a sharp edge. With a stealthy approach, Meera retrieved the makeshift projectile, a rock that fit perfectly in her nimble hand.

"We need a distraction."

Spotting a torch on the wall at the far end of the corridor, she positioned herself to throw the projectile. Taking careful aim, Meera threw the rock. It flew across the vast length of the corridor before hitting the metal bracket supporting the torch. A feat ordinarily impossible, yet Meera had managed to accomplish it with impeccable aim. A sharp, resounding CLANG was heard as the rock hit the metal.

The guards, alerted by the unexpected sound, investigated the disturbance. Meera, seizing the opportunity, signaled for Lumo to follow as they quietly moved away from the commotion, using the diversion to their advantage.

Meera led the way, her steps swift and purposeful. Lumo followed closely, his grip tight on the sword, a silent acknowledgment of the potential dangers lurking around each corner. The air was thick with tension as they pressed forward.

As they rushed up a series of stairs, the flickering light of a torch revealed a heavy wooden door. Meera approached it cautiously, listening intently for any sounds from the other side. Satisfied that the coast was clear, she gently pushed the door ajar, allowing a beam of daylight to pierce through. Her eyes, momentarily blinded by the sudden brightness, quickly adjusted to the external world.

"Okay, I think we are in the clear," she said as she motioned for Lumo to follow.

Just as they stepped into the open, an unassuming guard came into view, his eyes widening at the sight of the escaping prisoners.

"Stop right there!" he bellowed, reaching for his weapon.

"Run!" Meera screamed.

The duo made a quick dash in an attempt to escape, but the guard's hand caught hold of Meera's cloak, bringing her to an abrupt halt.

"Lumo, run! Don't look back!" Meera shouted over the commotion; her eyes locked with his.

Lumo hesitated, torn between loyalty and self-preservation. His heart pounded, not just from the imminent threat but from the internal struggle. For a moment, he took a step away, the conflict evident in his furrowed brow and clenched jaw.

Then, he heard Meera's desperate plea, a simple yet powerful, "Let me go."

The guard's grip tightened on her, and the vulnerability in Meera's voice tugged at something deep within Lumo. It wasn't just loyalty; it was a connection built on shared hardship, trust, and a sense of partnership.

"You're in trouble now," the guard declared as he dealt with a helpless Meera squirming in his hands.

In that moment, a surge of determination and loyalty overcame Lumo's fear. Without a second thought, he turned back, sprinting toward the struggling duo.

"Let her go!" he shouted, adrenaline coursing through him. As the guard's attention turned, Lumo shoved him hard, causing the guard to stumble backward, momentarily surprised. Seizing the opportunity, Lumo quickly helped Meera to her feet. Without looking back, they sprinted together toward freedom, the groan of the fallen guard fading behind them.

Meera and Lumo burst into the open courtyard, the distant sounds of alarms echoing through the stone walls behind them. The courtyard buzzed with activity, the ceremony already underway.

"I must find Oliver," Lumo said urgently, his eyes darting through the throng of people.

Meera grabbed his arm, pulling him aside. "The other guards are looking for us now; there's no time. We need to blend in and disappear into this crowd."

Lumo hesitated, torn between the urgency of escape and concern for his comrade. Meera's grip tightened, and she locked eyes with him, conveying the gravity of the situation. The courtyard was no longer a safe haven; any delay could lead to their recapture.

Reluctantly, Lumo followed Meera as they melted into the crowd of commoners gathered for the ceremony. The vibrant mix of people provided cover, their anonymity shielded by the varied faces and attire of those attending the event.

As Meera and Lumo skillfully navigated through the crowd, the urgency of their escape weighed heavily on Lumo's mind. He couldn't shake off the awareness that every passing moment brought them closer to the impending danger involving Oliver. In the midst of the chaos, Lumo's thoughts raced, and he couldn't ignore the crucial reason behind their daring escape—the need to prevent Oliver's abduction. The realization hit him hard. If he failed to contact Oliver and thwart the plot against the prince, their entire escape would be rendered meaningless. The stakes were higher than he had initially thought, and the fate of the kingdom rested on the success of their mission.

Their mission was far from over, but for the moment, the cloak of the crowd provided a temporary sanctuary, allowing them to slip away from the clutches of the pursuing guards.

***

CHAPTER 6

As the jesters took the stage, their colorful costumes and whimsical antics brought joy to the faces of the gathered audience.

One of the jesters stepped forward with a mischievous grin. “Before we go, here's a royal jest for our distinguished audience. Why did the royal barber go to the king?”

A collective murmur of curiosity swept through the crowd.

“To check the king’s crown!” the jester concluded, pointing to his teeth and head together with a theatrical flourish.

The courtyard echoed with laughter as the jesters exited, leaving the audience in high spirits. As the jesters stepped off, a troupe of men and women clad in striped black and white attire gracefully took the stage. Their faces were painted a ghostly white, with dark, exaggerated eyebrows and lips drawn into silent expressions. Anticipation grew, but the performers remained silent, confusing the crowd. As the group commenced a series of oddly comical gestures amongst themselves, it became increasingly evident—these performers were mimes.

Through vivid, wordless expressions, they soon had the puzzled audience laughing and cheering. The mimes, in their silent and whimsical world, began a delightful comedic act. It started with one mime comically attempting to escape from another. In response, the pursuing mime, with a twinkle in his eye, pretended to lasso an invisible rope.

To the audience's amusement, the imaginary lasso found its mark, encircling the fleeing mime. With a swift and theatrical tug, the lasso-wielding mime pulled on the unseen rope, prompting the fleeing mime to comically resist, running in place against the imaginary force.

Like a chain reaction, more mimes leaped into the fray, aligning themselves on the side of either the fleeing mime or the pursuer. Before long, the entire chase sequence turned into a comical tug-of-war, with one group of mimes pulling the other group to their side, going back and forth.

"Wow, these mimes are good performers!" Seraphina exclaimed, noting their perfectly synchronized movements.

"Hmm, they aren't pretending though," Serena said, her face giving nothing away.

"What do you mean?"

"It's real. You just don't see it," Serena explained.

As the comical tug-of-war reached its peak, a brilliant idea sparked among the mimes in one group. In a synchronized moment of silent understanding, they collectively released their grip on the invisible rope. The other group stumbled backward in surprise, their antics eliciting hearty laughter from the audience.

"What do you mean it isn't real?" Seraphina asked, raising one eyebrow.

The sorceress stared intently at the group of mimes, attempting to discern something. Her gaze shifted back to Seraphina as she replied, "At least one of those mimes is conjuring real invisible constructs. The rest may be acting, but it wouldn't be too difficult, given the rope is real, now, would it?"

Wide-eyed, Seraphina scanned the mimes, attempting to discern the real performer among them.

Just then, one of the mimes pointed to a single person in the crowd—the easiest person they could find: the large and imposing Gus.

"Me?" Gus asked, pointing to himself in disbelief.

The mime on the stage bobbed his head in confirmation and gestured for Gus to come up on stage.

"Go, Gus!" Lily and Bart cheered, encouraging him to play the part of the volunteer.

Unable to refuse, Gus walked up to the stage halfheartedly. Once Gus was on stage, the mimes began their next act. Two of them skillfully mimicked the creation of an invisible wall, pretending to press against an unseen force. With overdone gestures, they extended this invisible barrier around Gus, enclosing him within an imaginary box. The mimes, with a synchronized motion, gestured for Gus to leave the invisible box they had playfully created around him.

As Gus attempted to push through the imaginary walls, he found himself in a struggle. Every attempt to find an exit was met with resistance, and the more he tried, the more the audience erupted into laughter.

Finally, when Gus had given up, one of the mimes mimicked turning a doorknob on one side of the wall. Theatrically, he then gestured for Gus to come out. Carefully pushing with his hands, Gus discovered no resistance, and to the delight of the audience, he stepped out of the imaginary box.

"There, that's the real one!" Seraphina squealed.

The mimes collectively took a bow, even as a slightly befuddled Gus walked off the stage. The audience, thoroughly entertained, erupted into applause, appreciating the spectacular performance the mimes had presented before them.

"Are you okay, Gus?" Lily inquired, as Gus rejoined them in the crowd.

"Yea… I'm okay," Gus mumbled, avoiding eye contact.

"Ah, how was that for ya, Gus? Did them mimes truly have ya trapped?" Bart asked, leaning in with a curious grin.

"Yes." Gus looked down in embarrassment, rubbing the back of his neck.

"It's okay, Gus. We'll find them later, and you can trap them in one of your bubbles," Lily winked at Gus.

On the stage, the mimes concluded their performance with a few more delightful antics, taking a final bow in perfect unison. The crowd once again erupted into applause as the mimes, still in character, walked off the stage, playfully pulling an imaginary rope that led them out of sight. As they made their exit, Archibald stepped onto the stage.

"Excuse me for a moment," Serena said, as she quickly retreated to the noble's section to be seen a moment later at the corner of the stage.

Archibald looked at Serena as he gestured something to her. Serena, taking the cue, raised her staff to discreetly cast a spell to enhance Archibald's voice.

"As we gather here today for this momentous occasion," Archibald declared, his amplified voice capturing the audience's focus, even as some were still searching for where the mimes had disappeared. "It is not just an event; it is a celebration of unity and prosperity within our kingdom."

Archibald raised his hands, commanding attention. "This ceremony, the anointing of Prince Oliver, signifies more than just a royal tradition. It is a sacred ritual that marks the transcendence of our beloved prince's journey into adulthood—a symbolic passage that reaffirms his commitment to our great kingdom."

He paused for a moment, allowing his words to resonate through the courtyard. The anticipation among the audience grew, their eyes fixed on the stage.

"As we anoint him today, we not only recognize his rightful place in the..." Archibald kept going, his speech probably longer than anything the prince had planned.

The crowd was bored already.

As the crowd fell into utter silence with Archibald continuing with his speech, a storm was brewing in one person's mind—Lumo's. A mix of urgency and concern furrowed his brow. The escape from the dungeon had been a daring endeavor, and the guards were undoubtedly searching for them. However, with the impending abduction plan hanging over his thoughts, Lumo couldn't afford to be solely focused on evading capture. Archibald's amplified voice echoed through the courtyard, making it clear that the ceremony was progressing, and time was slipping away.

With a determined expression, Lumo whispered to Meera, "We need to find a way to get closer to the stage. Follow my lead."

As Lumo inched slowly through the crowd, weaving through the sea of spectators, he felt Meera's hesitation. Turning toward her with urgency painted across his face, he started, "Meera, we need to—"

But before he could finish his sentence, Meera gently inched away. "Sorry, Lumo. I have to go my own way."

Meera slowly backed into the crowd, leaving Lumo standing alone amidst the throng of people.

"And now," Archibald announced, "I invite you to witness this sacred anointing ceremony. Behold, as Prince Oliver takes center stage."

A ceremonial hush settled over the audience. Suddenly, a soft drumroll echoed, building rhythmic suspense. Soon after, the triumphant sound of trumpets joined in, heralding the arrival of royalty.

The crowd remained focused on the stage as King Reginald and Prince Oliver emerged from the side entrance. Lucius trailed closely behind them. As they advanced into the spotlight, the drumrolls reached a crescendo, and the trumpets blared in unison. Archibald, with a twinkle in his eye, gestured toward the king and prince.

"Ladies and gentlemen," Archibald proclaimed, his voice now accompanied by the grandeur of the musical ensemble, "Behold, His Majesty, the esteemed King Reginald, ruler of our glorious kingdom, and his heir, the soon-to-be-anointed Prince Oliver!"

The crowd erupted into applause, the sound blending harmoniously with the musical fanfare. Raising his hands high in the air, King Reginald acknowledged the ovation, while Prince Oliver scanned the gathering with a nervous smile.

Oliver's mind, though initially filled with concern about the absurdity of his attire was soon replaced by a different kind of concern—stage fright. The sheer magnitude of the audience seemed to make him forget all the words he had planned to deliver in his speech.

As King Reginald and Prince Oliver took their designated places at the center of the stage, Archibald stepped back, allowing the royal duo to become the focal point of the grand ceremony. The drumrolls and trumpets gradually faded into a soft, ceremonial melody.

Archibald quietly gestured for some attendants in the back to make their entrance and they approached carrying a vessel of sacred oil and a ceremonial sword. The attendants moved with practiced precision—a performance in its own right, which Archibald had likely made them rehearse a hundred times.

In the audience, a stranded Lumo moved cautiously toward the stage, inch by inch. As he neared the front, he suddenly found his path blocked by the large and imposing figure of Gus. Before Lumo could figure out an alternative route, Lily chimed in with a playful tone, "Hey, no cutting in, friend."

"Move, please, let me get in," Lumo pleaded.

"The lady said no cutting in, didn't ya understand?" Bart sternly intervened.

Lumo, realizing he was probably causing a commotion, cast a quick glance around, contemplating his options before finally giving up—at least for the moment.

On the stage, the ceremony reached its pinnacle. King Reginald stepped forward as Prince Oliver took a knee. Placing the ceremonial sword on Prince Oliver's shoulders, he spoke words of guidance and encouragement, meant not only for his son but for the entire kingdom to hear.

"Oliver, my son, you stand on the threshold of a new era. The decisions you make and the actions you take will shape not only your destiny but the destiny of Avalora. Remember, true strength lies not in the sword you wield but in the wisdom you carry and the compassion you show. Lead them with courage and fairness, and never forget that a king's greatest duty is to serve his people. Be just, be kind, and be unwavering in your commitment to the values that make Avalora great. Rise, Prince Oliver, the future king of Avalora."

The crowd erupted into cheers.

As the anointing ceremony concluded, Archibald, with a gesture, invited the king and prince to address the assembly.

Oliver shifted nervously, trying to recollect the words he and Seraphina had discussed for his speech.

Before the king could deliver his speech, the atmosphere in the courtyard took a chilling turn. There was a sudden shift in the weather, and out of nowhere, a dense smokescreen erupted on the stage, mere feet away from Prince Oliver. The courtyard fell into a hushed silence as the smoke billowed around, obscuring the once-clear view.

From within the dissipating smoke, a figure emerged—the jester who had entertained the crowd earlier. In a dramatic revelation, he removed his mask, unveiling a menacing visage. Dark eyeshadows framed his cold, calculating eyes. His pale skin stood in stark contrast to his shoulder-length, disheveled black hair. A large scar stretched across the length of his cheek. Despite his colorful jester costume, there was nothing colorful about the man wearing it. The audience, frozen in disbelief, watched as the unexpected turn of events unfolded before them.

With a frightening display of speed, the scarred man advanced toward the prince, seizing him with a razor-sharp blade pressed against his throat.

"Stay still, or the prince meets his end," he declared, his words hanging heavy in the tension-laden air.

Lucius, the king, Archibald, and the entire assembly stood paralyzed, grappling with the surreal and perilous situation that had befallen them. Lumo, standing in the crowd, watched helplessly as his worst fears came true.

Regaining his composure in the face of the unfolding crisis, Lucius stepped forward, his hands gripping his sheathed sword. He had to be careful not to make any sudden movements that could end the situation in utter disaster. There was no way he could move fast enough to disarm the assailant and save the prince.

"Release him now, and you may yet find mercy," Lucius demanded.

The scarred assailant, unfazed by Lucius's warning, maintained his grip on Prince Oliver, his face set in a perpetually serious expression. As the standoff reached its peak, arrows sliced through the air, cutting across the courtyard. Panic seized the crowd, scattering them in chaotic disarray. Taken aback by the barrage of arrows, Lucius quickly positioned himself as a shield, guarding the king. The Veridian and Ophidonian guards quickly huddled together, protecting their own dignitaries. The courtyard echoed with the sounds of chaos—screams, shouts, and the disconcerting twang of bowstrings. The joyful celebration had given way to a scene of pandemonium.

The sorceress hurriedly held up her staff, trying to conjure a large magic barrier to shield the area.

Arcane forces, heed my call,
Within this space, erect a wall,
Unseen and potent, let it stand,
A protective veil, across this land.

The magic barrier slowly materialized, starting at the top and expanding downward, forming a dome that deflected a few arrows. But before the barrier could fully solidify, a sudden disruption startled the sorceress. She felt an unexpected tug on her staff as if an invisible force sought to wrench it from her grasp. In the corner of the courtyard, the mime from earlier emerged, wearing an ominous grin that sent shivers down the spines of those who laid eyes on him. As the sorceress grappled with the unseen force, a powerful yank resulted in the staff being forcefully torn from her grip. The barrier, which had manifested just moments ago, unraveled and dissipated, leaving the area vulnerable once more.

As the arrows continued raining down, Lily, Bart, and Gus attempted to navigate the dispersing crowd to safety. Lily's eyes caught a glimpse of Lumo, frozen amidst the tumult, his gaze locked on the stage where the scarred man held Prince Oliver at knifepoint.

Witnessing Lumo's determination to reach the stage despite the crowd moving in the opposite direction, Lily felt a surge of concern. In a moment of urgency, she shouted above the clamor, "Are you mad, kid? Gus, grab him! Let's go!"

Reacting instantly to Lily's command, Gus pivoted toward Lumo. With determined strides, he reached Lumo, his powerful grip enveloping him before he could advance any further toward the perilous stage.

"Let me go, I must save Oliver." Lumo struggled.

Gus wouldn't listen. He hoisted Lumo and carried him on his shoulders. As they retreated from the chaotic scene, Lumo couldn't shake the feeling of helplessness, his mind echoing with the haunting image of the scarred man menacingly holding the prince.

As the chaos unfolded, the masked assailant tightened his grip on Prince Oliver, maintaining his menacing stance in the midst of the disarray. Lucius, standing firm amidst the flying arrows, continued to negotiate with the scarred assailant, demanding his surrender.

The scarred man seemed undeterred by the escalating turmoil. Without any visible emotion, he uttered an incantation under his breath, weaving dark magic into the air. Amidst an unsettling aura of magic, the sorceress, still grappling with the loss of her staff, sensed a powerful spell taking form.

In an instant, a mystical portal, reminiscent of a dark void, materialized near the stage, its ethereal glow cutting through the chaos. The scarred man, still holding Prince Oliver hostage, seized the opportunity. With a swift movement, he propelled himself and the captive prince through the portal, disappearing from view in the blink of an eye. The mime followed suit, stepping into the magical gateway without uttering a single word. Before Lucius could reach them, the portal closed behind them, plunging the courtyard into an unsettling stillness.

As the assailants escaped, the barrage of arrows abruptly stopped. The air filled with the pounding of frantic footsteps, the rustling of panicked whispers, and the distant wails of distressed onlookers. Gasps and murmurs rippled through the crowd, the collective astonishment at the assailants' sudden vanishing act evident in the wide-eyed stares of those who had witnessed the escape.

Lucius had been torn between the urgent need to save the prince and the crucial task of safeguarding the king. The disappearance of Prince Oliver into the portal left him facing a difficult situation. All he could do now was ensure King Reginald's safety. Redirecting his focus, Lucius began moving swiftly toward the monarch, determined to shield him from any impending danger. Yet, just as he closed in on the king, an ominous twang echoed in the air. The deadly trajectory of an unseen arrow found its mark, striking the king with a sickening thud.

"Your Majesty!" Lucius screamed.

Without a moment's hesitation, Lucius knelt beside King Reginald, his hands urgently assessing the severity of the king's injury. The regal attire was stained red. The courtyard, now silent except for the moans of the wounded and the distant sounds of chaos, became a battlefield of its own.

"Help, Guards!" Lucius urgently called out, his eyes scanning the chaotic scene for any sign of his companions. Most of the palace guards were occupied, tending to the injured and working tirelessly to restore order. Marcus had swiftly rallied a group to search for the mystery assailants who had disrupted the celebration.

Drawn by Lucius's call, the sorceress hurriedly stepped closer. Archibald emerged from his cover in the distance, a stain on his crotch telling the story of how he felt in the moment. He quickly scanned the area for the dignitaries. Finding them nowhere in sight, he assumed they had retreated back to the castle.

"We need to get him to safety," Lucius mumbled.

A few guards quickly arrived on stage. Lucius swiftly took command, barking orders to his guards with stern authority.

"Secure the immediate area! Form a defensive perimeter around us. Where are the healers?"

"Can you save him?" Lucius anxiously looked at Serena.

"I—I'm not sure," Serena replied.

In the midst of the commotion, a few brave healers rushed to the king's side, assessing the severity of his wounds.

"Stabilize the king, and prepare him for transport to within the castle. We can't afford to lose him," Lucius instructed them.

"Men! The king's safety is our highest priority, guard him with your life!"

"Lucius, we need to tend to the other wounded as well," Serena reminded.

"Guards! Assist the healers and protect the vital areas of the castle," Lucius instructed another set of guards.

"Madam Sorceress, can you help the healers?" Archibald inquired.

"My staff... was stolen, but I can help with some lesser spells," Serena replied, her tone apologetic.

The castle staff, under the leadership of Lucius, worked cohesively to bring stability to the chaotic aftermath of the attack. Their actions would not only determine the immediate safety of the wounded king and dignitaries but also set the tone for the kingdom's response to the larger threat that now loomed over them.

***

CHAPTER 7

"Let me go!" Lumo shouted at the top of his voice, squirming in Gus's grip as he kicked his legs in protest. They had safely retreated to outside the castle grounds.

"You can put him down now, Gus," Lily said as she looked back.

Lumo winced as Gus carefully lowered him to the ground. Lily and Bart, still processing the unexpected turn of events, hovered anxiously.

"Do you know what you have done?" Lumo shouted.

"Saved your life, that's what," Lily replied. "Look, kid, we don't know you, but whatever you were planning couldn't have been good. Why don't you calm down first?"

Lumo took a minute to gather his composure. He closed his eyes, trying to breathe. Lily observed him closely, noting the tension in his shoulders.

"Oliver… I should have saved him," Lumo spoke, tears welling in his eyes.

Lily looked at him with warmth in her eyes. Here was a kid barely older than the prince, and yet she could feel the pain in his eyes.

"What's your name?" Lily said in a soft, understanding tone.

Lumo stood silent, his mind still grappling with thoughts of how he had failed to do the one thing he should have. He clenched his fists, struggling to find the words.

"I'm Lily," Lily said, trying to force a smile.

Lumo looked up at Lily, Bart, and Gus, all standing beside him. He finally calmed down enough to be able to speak. "I'm Lumoquin... Lumo. I am—was the prince's attendant." He paused, his throat tightening as he wiped the tears from his eyes. "This is all my fault; I should have saved him."

Lily exchanged a glance with Bart. After a brief moment, she took a step closer, her voice gentle yet firm. "Lumo… we don't know the full story here. But from the looks of what happened, I don't think anyone was prepared for it. I don't think you should take the blame—"

"I knew," Lumo cut her off, his fists clenching at his sides as he looked down.

As Lily and Bart continued exchanging bewildered glances, Lumo continued, disappointment lingering in his voice. "I knew about the abduction. I—I just couldn't do anything about it."

A moment of silence passed before Bart spoke up.

"Lumo, I'm Bart. Look, we know we just met ya and all, but we're sound people, and if ya spill yer story with us, I'm sure we can help or at least make sense of the whole shebang."

Lumo's shoulders tensed as Lily and Bart continued staring at him.

"I... I don't know if I can," Lumo admitted, his voice wavering. He avoided making eye contact, his gaze fixed on the ground as he struggled to find the right words.

Seeing Lumo hesitate, Lily leaned in slightly. "Lumo, we might be strangers, but we're here to help. Sometimes, sharing the burden makes it a bit lighter. Whatever it is, we can figure it out together."

Lumo glanced up, meeting Lily's empathetic gaze. The sincerity in her eyes offered a glimmer of trust, but the fear of judgment lingered. After a deep breath, he spoke, choosing his words carefully as he unraveled the secrets he had carried.

Lily and Bart listened in stunned silence, their expressions shifting from curiosity to deep concern.

"So, yer tellin' me there was a plan brewin' from within the castle, and they actually went through with it?" Bart's voice held a solemn note, his usually jovial expression darkened. "This is more than just an attack. It's a downright betrayal!"

Lily's gaze shifted towards Bart. "I need to tell you something," she murmured. "That man... the one with the scar. I had seen him a few nights ago."

"What?" Bart gasped.

Lily locked eyes with Bart. "In the tavern, a few nights ago. I spotted him, and I knew something felt off about him."

"Well, did he tell ya his name? Or where he came from?"

Lily shook her head. After a brief pause, she spoke up.

"There was something, though... when he was handing me the coins. I noticed this tattoo on his wrist... It kind of looked like an eye; there were some runic symbols too that didn't make any sense to me."

Lumo, who had been quietly absorbing the information, furrowed his brow. "We need to inform Lucius and His Majesty. I need to get back in the castle," he said, hurriedly looking back at the castle gates.

"Wait," Bart said, raising a hand to stop him. "Are ya sure, kid? I got a bad feelin' about all this. I don't trust this

Lucius fella. Ya did mention someone from the castle was involved. How do ya know whom to trust?"

"Bart's right," Lily said. "Besides, I'm sure they've got the castle on lockdown now. And if you did try to enter, they might just end up imprisoning you again. I think it's best you stay put for now."

"The king… I trust him. He needs to know everything if there's a chance to save Oliver," Lumo said, with a deep stare.

A pause settled over the group, the weight of their predicament sinking in. Lily broke the silence, "All right, maybe you are right, but how are you going to get in without getting caught?"

Lily was right; there was no way for Lumo to get in without risking getting caught. In fact, there was no chance he could enter without the guards recognizing him, or so he thought. As Lumo stood in silence without answers, Gus's gentle voice broke the tense atmosphere.

"I can help," Gus said.

"How?" Lumo, Bart, and Lily all jumped at Gus.

"I'll need a few things," Gus said nervously. He scratched his head, trying to recall. "Uh, so I need some cha-mo-mile tea and, uh, also some Bubblegum syrup. Do you guys know where I can get some?"

The trio looked at Gus puzzled but realized soon that he wasn't joking about it.

"I'll go with Gus. Bart, you stay here with Lumo," Lily declared.

Bart grunted in agreement, keeping a watchful gaze on Lumo, while Lily and Gus hastened to the town square.

Returning in half an hour, Lily and Gus triumphantly held a bag containing chamomile tea from the local herbal store and a bottle of Bubblegum syrup from the confectionery.

"Mission accomplished." Lily grinned, holding up the bag. "Lumo, are you sure about going through with this?"

"I gave it me best shot, tried talking the lad out of it, but that young fella's got the determination of a feisty imp; he won't back down, not for the life of him," Bart explained, a sense of resignation in his voice.

"I have to do this," Lumo said with puppy dog eyes.

"Okay, then let's go over the plan. Gus will help you get up to the balcony of the king's chamber without getting caught, but once you are in the castle, it's up to you to not get caught. You need to get into the king's chamber and wait for him however long it takes, got it?" Lily detailed.

"Got it," Lumo said enthusiastically.

"Here, put on this cloak, so the guards don't recognize you," Lily said, handing him a fresh cloak.

"Okay then, Gus, you're up," Lily said, turning to Gus.

Gus shuffled nervously, glancing between the flasks of chamomile tea and Bubblegum syrup in his hands. His voice, low and unsure, piped up, "Uh, so, um, you see... my GranGran taught me this—Cham-omile tea and Bubblegum sweet, together they fly, oh such a treat."

Lumo exchanged a bemused glance with Lily, who in exchange reassured him with a gentle clap on the shoulder that Gus wasn't insane. It was just the way he was and Lumo would soon find out.

Gus took a deep breath, his hands trembling slightly as he alternately sipped the chamomile tea and Bubblegum syrup. He hesitated for a moment, glancing around as if making sure everything was in place. Then, with childlike enthusiasm, he began jumping up and down.

And then, in the midst of his jumps, Gus let out a hearty burp. It wasn't a sound of embarrassment; rather, it was the release of something magical. As he opened his mouth wide, a large bubble began emerging, growing with each passing second. The bubble, slightly larger than Lumo's size, floated around gently after fully forming.

Gus, wide-eyed and proud, extended his hands toward the floating bubble as if guiding its path. The bubble, glistening with a soft pink glow, seemed to respond to his whims.

Lumo's skepticism turned to wonder as he found himself entranced by the magical display. The bubble, seemingly under Gus's control, gently glided toward Lumo.

With a wide grin, Gus gestured toward the bubble, inviting Lumo to step in.

"Go."

Lumo exchanged a glance with Lily, who nodded with an encouraging smile. Taking a leap of faith, Lumo pushed himself into the shimmering bubble. It yielded like thick, elastic gel, stretching around him as he pushed through. The surface of the bubble resisted his movement at first, then yielded and enveloped him with gentle resistance, as if he were being swallowed by a semi-solid substance. Inside, the air felt slightly thicker, and a faint tingling sensation spread across his skin, like static electricity dancing over his nerves.

As the bubble, with Lumo inside, floated gently into the air, Gus continued to guide it with a sense of pride.

"Remember not to get caught!" Lily shouted as the bubble carried Lumo upwards toward the castle.

Lumo looked down at the trio below, completely unaware of their shouts, seemingly in his own bubble.

***

The day had been chaotic thus far. No one had anticipated it would come to this. The entire kingdom had witnessed how lapse their security was, how unprepared they were, how weak they were.

As the chambermaids drew the curtain, the king's chamber was filled with a warm glow, belying the chaos that had unfolded in the courtyard a few hours ago. The atmosphere in the chamber was heavy with the scent of medicinal herbs and the lingering tension from the earlier events. The candlelight, now struggling against the persistent daylight, danced lazily on the walls.

Lucius, Serena, and Archibald, having weathered the storm of the morning, gathered around the bed where King Reginald lay. The king, weakened and pale, appeared to be in a moment of respite, though the uncertainty of his condition persisted. The healers had managed to seal the king's wounds, yet what lingered underneath worried everyone immensely.

"I hope the healers can counteract the poison." Lucius sighed.

He dared not speak of what would happen if they were unsuccessful. With the only heir to the throne gone, the fate of the kingdom hung in the balance.

"I've never seen anything like this. It's... it's dark magic," Serena said. The subtle quiver in her voice betrayed the unease that simmered beneath her calm exterior.

"Any news of the assailants?" Archibald asked.

Lucius shook his head with more disappointment.

"You know how bad this makes us look? Especially when the other kingdoms were watching so closely. I shudder at what is going to happen next on the political front," Archibald spoke grimly.

The trio stood in a brief moment of silence.

"So, you're telling me you had no clue this was going to happen? This is unbelievable," Archibald complained, his question pointed directly at Lucius.

Lucius furrowed his brows. He took a moment to choose his words carefully.

"Archibald, believe me, this was as much a shock to me as it was to you. The security breach was unprecedented. We had no intelligence, no warnings. It was a calculated strike, and we were blindsided."

He glanced around the room, meeting the eyes of both Serena and Archibald. "We'll launch a thorough investigation, and heads will roll for this. I give you my word."

"What about the princess and the others? Have they left already?" Serena asked calmly.

"They should have left already," Archibald confirmed.

"What about the casualties? Do you have a count yet, Lucius?"

"Eleven dead, a few injured," Lucius replied, his voice heavy with sorrow for the lives lost under his watch.

As the room fell into silence once more, a faint groan escaped the king's lips.

"We should let him rest," Lucius said.

The trio departed the king's chamber, a solitary breeze slipping through the partially opened window, carrying with it a whisper of the outside world as if seeking to dispel the tension within.

"No one but the healers are to get in or out." Lucius scowled at the guards stationed outside as they made their way through the once-vibrant corridors.

***

As the sun continued its ascent, the magic bubble carrying Lumo glided with a whispering touch onto the balcony of the king's chamber. Stepping out from the cocoon of quiet solace, the sounds of the outside world rushed back to greet him. The scent of bubblegum lingered in the air. With a soft pop, the bubble dissipated, leaving Lumo standing alone on the balcony.

Lumo hesitated on the balcony, casting a cautious glance around. His eyes darted from side to side, searching for any sign of intrusion or unwanted presence beyond the window that separated him from the king's chamber. Satisfied that the chamber seemed quiet, he carefully pushed aside the large window to enter. The room welcomed him like a silent ally, and he closed the window behind him with a gentle click, shutting out the distant clamor of the kingdom beyond.

Now inside, Lumo trod lightly over the chamber's rich carpets, almost tiptoeing to avoid making a sound. His gaze shifted to the still form of King Reginald, pale and vulnerable on the bed.

"What in tarnation?" Lumo mumbled.

The king's face, usually adorned with the vigor of health, was now marked by a sickly pallor. Dark veins traced a sinister path along his skin, a visible manifestation of the poison's cruel grip. Lumo's breath hitched as he took in the frailty of the once-mighty ruler, a stark contrast to the regal figure Lumo had known.

The air in the chamber seemed to thicken with a silent gravity. Lumo's mind raced to comprehend the situation before him. He hadn't anticipated finding the king in such a dire state. Confusion clouded his face as he struggled to grasp how the mighty king had fallen into such vulnerability.

A torrent of emotions cascaded through Lumo—disbelief, concern, and a profound sense of responsibility. The image of Oliver disappearing into the portal flashed before his eyes, and a knot tightened in his stomach. *How could this have happened? Was Oliver's capture somehow connected to the king's condition?* But he couldn't afford to dwell on the unanswered questions now. If he didn't share everything he knew with the king now, there might not be another opportunity. Time was a precious commodity, and every passing moment increased the stakes.

Lumo approached the bed with cautious steps. As Lumo neared, King Reginald stirred, his eyes fluttering open as if responding to the presence in the room. His eyes widened at the sight of Lumo.

"Lumo?" he murmured, his lips twitching in pain.

The king's gaze, weakened but focused, met Lumo's. He struggled to form words. Lumo leaned in to catch the feeble whispers that escaped the king's lips.

"Lumo," the king's voice was a mere breath. "Oliver... is..."

Lumo gently clasped the king's feeble hand, as if trying to urge him to preserve his strength. "I know. I saw it happen."

King Reginald shook his head, too weak to respond. He struggled with his breathing. He took shallow breaths, each one seemingly more difficult than the last.

"Your Majesty, someone has betrayed us, someone from within the castle. I do not know who it is, but I assure you my loyalty lies with you and the prince," Lumo continued, still clutching the king's hand.

King Reginald, whose gaze had momentarily turned away, refocused his gaze on Lumo, his eyes clouded with pain.

"Lumo, I..."

Lumo kept his gaze locked with the king's, searching for meaning in the unspoken. Yet, the message remained indecipherable, the king's dwindling strength rendering it inscrutable.

The weight of unspoken truths hung heavy in the air. Lumo had carried the burden of information, thinking it would be the key to finding Oliver. Yet, faced with the king's frailty, he realized that his revelations would be of no use. In the silence of the chamber, Lumo's thoughts raced, grappling with the futility of his prepared words. The king, once a pillar of strength, lay before him in a state of vulnerability that rendered information impotent.

As he continued to hold the king's hand, a blend of frustration and helplessness shrouded Lumo's eyes. There was a chasm between what he wanted to say and what the king could comprehend in his weakened state.

In that moment, Lumo's mind drifted back to a time when the roles were reversed. He was only ten, bedridden with a high fever, the world around him a blur of pain and delirium. Yet, through the haze, he remembered the cool touch of a damp cloth on his forehead, the gentle murmur of voices—Oliver's and the king's.

"He'll be all right, won't he, Father?" Oliver's young voice had trembled with concern.

"Lumo's strong," King Reginald had reassured him. "But he needs rest, Oliver. He'll need you to be strong for him, too. Just as he'll be strong for you, through the good times and the bad."

Lumo had felt Oliver's small hand gripping his, a gesture of solidarity that had given him comfort. The memory now burned in his mind; a reminder of the bond that had been forged in that moment of vulnerability.

Pulling himself back to the present, Lumo's helplessness transformed into resolve. Faced with the reality that there was no one else to trust, he steeled himself for the daunting task ahead. If he couldn't rely on others, he would have to navigate the treacherous path alone and do whatever it took to find Oliver.

A spark ignited in Lumo's resolve. Despite the futility, he spoke with determination, "Your Majesty, I will find Prince Oliver, I promise."

Lumo's words did not fall on deaf ears. Almost instinctively, the king's eyes widened, and he reciprocated by clutching Lumo's hand, his grip as tight as his fading strength would allow.

"Lumo... please."

The room felt colder, the air heavier, as if the very walls were holding their breath.

"You must..." The king's voice was barely more than a rasp, but it carried the weight of his last reserves of authority and desperation. "You... must save the bloodline..."

Violent coughs racked the king's frail form as he attempted to speak, the sound echoing through the chamber. He withdrew his hand, a sign of his weakened state.

Lumo turned his head toward the chamber entrance, panic settling in his eyes. Outside, the guards, alerted by the disturbance, hastily approached.

Sensing the impending commotion, Lumo swiftly moved toward the window to retreat.

"Goodbye, Your Majesty," he mumbled to himself as he slipped onto the balcony.

Outside, on the balcony, a new challenge awaited Lumo—one he hadn't anticipated: how he would get out. His initial hope, that conveying vital information to the king would lead to a just reinstatement, now lay in shambles.

The king's chambers were perched on the fourth floor of the castle, and as Lumo peered down, he could see the murky moat below. While he had leaped into its depths before to rescue Oliver, this time, the situation was different. Jumping from this height was dangerous, but what choice did he have?

"I can do this, I can do this," Lumo kept mumbling to himself.

As Lumo steadied himself to execute his next move, a familiar voice erupted from nearby.

"You're going to break a few bones if you jump, criminal."

Lumo recognized Meera's voice instantly, yet he couldn't spot her. He looked around to discern where it came from. Suddenly, Meera descended from above, jumping down gracefully and landing on her feet.

Lumo, surprised, could only manage, "Meera? How did you...?"

"You want all the details now, or do you want to get out?" Meera quipped.

"How do we get out?" Lumo asked, a smile tugging at his lips.

Meera grabbed the piece of rope dangling from her waist and tied one end to the railing. She unfurled the rope and it fell down.

"Let's go," Meera said.

Meera secured the rope tightly and gestured for Lumo to go first.

The climb down was swift but nerve-wracking. As Lumo reached the bottom, he landed with a controlled splash. He quickly swam to the edge. Meera followed suit, displaying agility and finesse in her descent.

The rope, now hanging above the water, swayed gently. Lumo and Meera, water dripping from their clothes, moved away from the castle.

Lumo, still catching his breath, turned to Meera. “How did you know I was here?”

“Trade secrets, my friend. Let's focus on getting as far away from here as possible first.” Meera smirked.

“I thought you left.”

“I did… I did. But I have a knack for showing up at just the right time,” she replied. “Now, let’s go. I don’t want to get caught again.”

***

CHAPTER 8

Where do we go from here? Lumo thought as he walked out of the castle with Meera by his side, still drying himself off from his unwanted swim earlier.

"You're falling behind again," Meera said, her voice breaking through his thoughts.

"Meera..." Lumo paused.

"What's the matter?" Meera questioned, glancing back at him.

"I don't know where to go now."

It was true. In the past few days, the world had changed for him. He was abruptly yanked out of his monotonous life, which was all Lumo had known. To top it all, he knew that by now news of his escape had reached Lucius, and he was sure that he was now branded a criminal, at least back at the castle. But worst of all, he was lost. He had lost his only home with nowhere to go.

Meera's face softened. She placed a reassuring hand on his shoulder.

"It'll be okay, Lumo. I've been out on my own for the longest time now. You know what I've learned?"

"What?" Lumo asked eagerly.

"Sometimes, losing what we thought was everything opens the door to something better. I've been in tight spots before, and every time, it led to unexpected opportunities. So you need to buckle up and pick up the pace."

Lumo pondered her words. It made sense, but it still didn't answer his question.

"So, where do you think we should go?" he asked.

"Where I always go when I'm wanted—a new location," Meera smirked as she started walking slowly.

"Wait… I can't just leave everything; I still need to find Oliver," Lumo insisted, standing his ground.

"You're still on that?"

"Well, yes, of course. I need to save him," Lumo said. "Meera, come with me, help me. You've got skills. I know with your help I can surely find and save Oliver."

"Why would I do that, Lumo? What's in it for me?" Meera asked, her expression slightly serious.

After a small pause, Lumo replied.

"You said it yourself; you've been in tight spots and it's led you to unexpected opportunities. Maybe this is your chance."

Meera scoffed, but her raised eyebrow hinted at a hidden interest in Lumo's proposal.

"If we can save the prince, you don't ever have to run anymore. This is your opportunity," Lumo said. "You will no longer be a thief; you will be a hero."

"Master thief," Meera corrected, with an eye roll, her smirk betraying a hint of pride.

"C'mon, you know what I say is true." Lumo took a step closer.

"Hmm… I don't know, it seems dangerous."

"You're right, it probably is. I won't lie. Look, come with me, and I'll leave it to you to choose not to continue the moment it gets dangerous. And when I save Oliver, I promise you, you will still be cleared of all your wrongdoings in the past and get the credit you need. Oliver is the future king, and he is my best friend," Lumo said, laying his cards on the table.

Meera narrowed her eyes, assessing Lumo's sincerity. The promise of redemption was a tempting offer, but she was not one to trust easily.

"You sure about that? You don't even know what I have done."

"You've not killed anyone, have you?" Lumo said with a slightly panicked expression.

"Well, of course not. What do you think I am, a heathen?" Meera retorted.

Lumo let out a nervous laugh, relieved by her response.

"Well then, I'm sure you'll be okay. So, deal? You help me find Oliver, and that's all I ask," Lumo said, holding out his hand for Meera to shake.

A pause filled the air as Meera made a decision.

"Deal," Meera said as she shook Lumo's hand.

Lumo and Meera walked side by side, the uncertain path stretching out before them. The sun had almost dipped below the horizon, casting long shadows across the landscape. The last hues of twilight painted the sky, giving way to the emerging stars as the moon peeked its head.

"Those friends of yours seem like nice people," she remarked casually, her tone breaking the quietude.

"Friends, who?"

"That big guy and the lady with the sharp tongue."

Lumo pondered for a moment, his thoughts quickly aligning. He shot Meera a wry glance, squinting his eyes at her description of Lily. Then he realized something.

"Wait, Gus and Lily? I never told you about them."

"Yeah, but I overheard them at the town square. It's how I was able to find you in the first place."

"Oh, yes, they are the ones who helped me get into the castle. That big guy has magical powers," Lumo explained.

Meera's eyebrows lifted in curiosity as Lumo narrated the incident. Her gaze was intent, absorbing every detail.

"I see. Maybe they can help us get some refuge for the night? Unless you want to camp it out in the woods." Meera crossed her arms, tilting her head as she regarded Lumo.

"That's a great idea!" Lumo exclaimed. "The Thistle & Thorn, that's where they'll probably be. Lily is the barmaid there, and Bart, the owner, is also a good guy."

"The tavern? No way, the guards will likely be searching the area." Meera shook her head.

"At night?" Lumo raised an eyebrow.

"Well, if it's late enough, then maybe not," Meera replied.

"Okay, so we wait for nightfall and see if we can get some help from them. Plan B: we camp it out in the woods. Sound right?"

"I guess…" Meera said, hesitantly.

***

A few hours later, the sky had fully succumbed to the night, casting a blanket of darkness over the land. Lumo and Meera found themselves on the outskirts of the town, shadows playing tricks as they hid in a cluster of bushes, waiting for the opportune moment to approach the Thistle & Thorn.

The usual vibrant atmosphere surrounding the tavern had dulled, the aftermath of the attack on the castle leaving an indelible mark. The air was tinged with an uneasy stillness, and the distant sounds of the night were muted by an unspoken tension.

As Lumo and Meera observed from their concealed vantage point, a few guards patrolled the area. The Thistle & Thorn, normally bustling with activity, now stood under the watchful eye of wary sentinels, still searching for clues about the assailants and the missing heir.

Meera leaned in closer to Lumo. “We need to wait for the guards to pass. This might be a long night, Lumo. I propose we set a time limit, a threshold after which we might need to resort to Plan B.”

“Alright. By the way, you’ve camped in the woods before, haven’t you?” Lumo asked.

A ghost of a smile played on Meera's lips. “Lots of times. It’s quite fun, actually. Haven’t you?”

“A few times, but never without an army of guards and rather extravagant tents to protect us from the snakes.”

“Snakes? You’ve got a lot more to worry about than a few slithering friends. You’ve forgotten about those nasty howling wolves, those rustlings in the shadows, and those nasty eyes peering from the darkness,” Meera said, making gestures with her hands.

Lumo's eyes went round at Meera's vivid description. He glanced nervously into the dark expanse beyond their hiding spot, half-expecting the imagined creatures to materialize.

“Let’s make sure we set a longer time limit before we execute Plan B then?” Lumo said, sheepishly.

Meera couldn't help but chuckle at Lumo's reaction. Lumo joined in with a shared laugh.

As the guards completed their patrol and disappeared into the night, Lumo and Meera exchanged a knowing glance. The opportune moment had arrived. They emerged from their hiding place, pulling the hoods of their cloaks over their heads. The night air carried the subtle scent of damp earth and the distant sounds of nocturnal creatures.

The door to the Thistle & Thorn creaked open as they cautiously entered, greeted by the muted ambiance of the tavern. The usual lively chatter had been replaced by hushed conversations, and the air held a somber undertone.

The patrons who had gathered were not there for revelry but rather seeking solace in the company of others who shared the weight of the day's losses. Faces were etched with grief and concern, and the clinking of glasses was replaced by the muffled sounds of shared condolences.

Lumo and Meera moved further into the tavern, their eyes adjusting to the dim light. They found an empty corner where they could observe without drawing too much attention. Lily was busy serving a few patrons, her usual vibrant demeanor replaced by a more solemn expression. Bart moved among the tables, offering comforting words to those in need.

As Lumo and Meera listened, fragments of conversations reached their ears. Talk of the attack on the castle, the missing prince, and the lives lost filled the air. The atmosphere was heavy with the collective sorrow of the townsfolk.

Lumo leaned toward Meera, his voice barely audible over the subdued murmur of the tavern. "This might not be the best time to ask for help. We should wait for the right moment."

Meera's eyes flicked around the room, noting the crowd that filled nearly every corner of the tavern. After a moment, she leaned closer to Lumo and whispered, "Hey, Lumo. Do you have coin to pay these people? With this many customers, I doubt they'd let us stay here for free."

"Um, no. But I don't think they would mind. We can always pay them later."

"Nonsense. Let me quickly go steal some silver from some drunk saps," Meera replied, getting up.

"Oh no, you don't." Lumo caught her hand. "No more stealing, Meera."

"Running a tab is never good, Lumo."

"And stealing is?" Lumo shot Meera a look.

"You sure you don't have any silver?" Meera sighed, sitting back down. "Didn't you work for the prince?"

"We were never paid with coin. The rest of the staff and I sort of worked for keeps. But they've taken good care of us. It's been a fairly comfortable life."

"Oh, that reminds me! Did you find out where Amelia went?"

Lumo stared into space as he realized he had completely forgotten about her. He wondered what had happened to her, whether she was successful in relaying the information at all, and if she had been, then how could the disaster still have unfolded so perfectly.

"No," he replied, with a serious expression.

"I think we should be careful, Lumo. There are so many missing pieces here."

Lumo nodded. "Yes."

A few minutes later, as they continued to wait in the dimly lit corner, Lily approached their table, ready to take their order. The soft glow of the lanterns revealed her wearied expression. Lumo and Meera pulled down their hoods, revealing their faces, and Lily's eyes lit up as she recognized Lumo.

"Lumo? You made it! So, how'd it go?" Lily exclaimed with a hint of surprise.

"Shhh!" Lumo asked her to lower her tone. "Yes, but all didn't go as per plan, I'm afraid."

"Oh, I see. Well, if you're already out here, then I suppose it'll be okay," Lily said, her gaze shifting naturally to Meera. "I see you're making friends at the tavern already."

"Ah, right! Lily, meet Meera, she's my friend. You know—the one who helped me back in the..."

"Got it." Lily winked. "Hey, Bart, come over here when you can," she shouted toward Bart.

"Nice to meet you, Meera. I'm Lily. You can relax; you are safe here," Lily said reassuringly.

Meera watched as Bart slowly crept up behind Lily.

Lumo and Meera greeted Bart as Lily filled in the other details.

"Well, all right, you two, enjoy yourselves here for the moment. We will talk later," Lily said as she continued her rounds at the other tables for orders.

As the night wore on, the patrons gradually dispersed, heading back to their homes, leaving the Thistle & Thorn with a more deserted feel. The once-crowded tables now stood empty, save a few patrons who were probably staying the night in the rooms above, and the murmurs of conversations dwindled to an occasional whisper.

Lumo and Meera noticed the diminishing crowd and seized the opportunity. They approached Lily, who was now wiping down the bar, and Bart, who stood with a thoughtful expression. The air in the tavern had shifted from mourning to a reflective calm, providing a more suitable environment for a conversation that required discretion.

Lumo leaned in and spoke to Lily and Bart, recounting his tense meeting with the king and his dire condition. Lily listened attentively, her eyes widening at the tale. Bart, too, expressed concern, realizing the gravity of the situation.

Bart spoke in a low voice. "Lumo, this is a grave situation. I suggest ya do not go blabbering about this to anyone, at all."

Lumo gave a slow, almost imperceptible dip of his head.

"So, what's yer plan now?" Bart asked.

"We need to find more information about the assailant, the one with the scar," Lumo replied.

"And the tattoo…" Lily added.

"Ah, yes, Lily, can ya draw this tattoo, or try yer best to replicate it? I'm sure that can help us get some more information," Bart suggested, handing Lily a parchment and a quill from behind the counter.

Lily took a moment, pondering as she recalled the image of the mark in her head.

"Okay," she sketched on the parchment, describing each detail as she went. "So there was this eye, and it was inside a triangle, like this, and then there were some runic symbols, maybe something like these, but I could be wrong."

Meera, intrigued by Lily's sketch, held up the parchment against the light, examining the details more closely.

"I've seen this before… I can't remember where," Meera said as she put the parchment back on the table.

Unbeknownst to the group, a figure had eavesdropped on their conversation. The man, an elderly figure with weathered features, approached the group, clearing his throat to pardon himself.

The atmosphere shifted from a calm discussion to a subtle tension, wary of the newcomer who had approached them. Lily instinctively held the parchment close, concealing the drawn symbols, while Bart's eyes narrowed slightly, gauging the stranger's intent. Lumo and Meera exchanged a quick, questioning glance, uncertain of the figure's motives.

The elderly man, sensing the tension, offered a tentative smile and spoke, “Pardon me for overhearing, but I couldn't help but catch a glimpse of that drawing. It reminded me of something I've seen before, not too long back.”

The group's guarded expressions relaxed slightly, curiosity replacing suspicion.

“If I may,” the man continued, “I'm Robert. I run a bee farm over at Greenfield Meadows. We had a peculiar incident a few days ago. Thought it might be of interest.”

“Go on, then,” Bart said.

Robert went on to describe the incident, narrating how they had stumbled upon a dead cow bearing similar markings to the ones Lily had just sketched, back at John's farm.

“...And so, we thought there might be more to such an incident. My wife, Helen, has been searching for clues ever since. She's quite clever in uncovering mysteries,” Robert said, finishing his drink as he gently placed the mug on the table.

“Did she find out anything yet?” Lumo inquired, clearly intrigued. His eyes gleamed with curiosity.

“Well, sort of. She did say something... uh, but I shot it down. Sometimes, she gets carried away with wild theories,” Robert replied. He recalled the conversation with Helen, the raised eyebrows, and the disbelief at a seemingly far-fetched idea.

Bart leaned forward. “Were ya at the castle earlier, Mister?”

“Yes, I was.” Robert nodded.

“Then ya know that there's no such thing as too wild after what happened now, is there?”

The gravity of the situation had shifted perspectives, making even the most improbable theories worth considering in the search for answers.

“Ah, I suppose you’re right. Well, Helen found something in an old book; she mentioned something about a cult… Let’s see, the Chimerian Order, was it?”

“The Cimmerian Order. Now, I remember!” Meera shouted, her sudden outburst catching the attention of the group. Quickly sensing the need for discretion, she lowered her voice. “This isn’t good, Lumo.”

Meera's gaze bore into Lumo's. The corners of her lips tightened, suppressing the anxiety that threatened to surface.

“Wait, they’re real? Helen said she found mentions of them from over a millennium ago,” Robert gasped.

Meera nodded slowly, the fear still clinging to her eyes like an unshakeable specter.

“So, they still exist?” Lily questioned.

Meera stood in silence. Her silence said it all.

“Meera, how—what do you know about them?” Lumo stammered, his eyes searching hers.

“T—They, uhmm…” Meera began, in visible unease. “They’re a shadow cult. I’ve heard of them from my time underground.”

Lumo’s eyes widened, his pupils dilating in surprise.

“Meera, what do they want with Oliver?” Lumo said, gripping Meera’s shoulders as if trying to steady her.

“I don’t know, Lumo. But I can tell you this: these people aren’t to be trifled with. They're everywhere, and the power wielded by some of the sorcerers and assassins in their ranks... you can't even imagine.”

A silence settled in the tavern as each person absorbed the revelation.

"How… is this possible? I've heard me fair share of rumors in this bar, and not once have I heard of such a cult," Bart said, breaking the quietude.

"I assure you, they exist. You've not heard of them because they don't want you to," Meera insisted.

"But then why would they publicly abduct the prince? Wouldn't they rather do it in secret?" Robert, injecting a dose of logic, questioned.

"They wanted everyone to see it." Lumo stared into space, wide-eyed, as if uncovering the answer. "They could have abducted him anytime, but they chose this moment because they knew everyone was watching. It's no coincidence."

As the truth dawned on them, a pensive hush enveloped the group. The wavering candlelight painted shifting contours on their faces, underscoring the seriousness of the situation. Bart broke the quietude with a heavy sigh.

"Well, I reckon we're in a spot of trouble, aren't we now?"

"Meera, you spoke of this underground…" Lumo started.

"Under—Oh, yeah, it's a network, mostly thieves and rogues. Every major city has some sort of network that operates beneath the law," Meera continued.

"Do you think we can learn more about this cult from there?"

"I think it's our best chance," Meera confirmed.

"Bart, do you know how to get into this network?" Lumo asked.

"I'm a straight-up righteous business owner, lad. No clue."

"Lumo, we need to tread carefully. It's not a place you can just stroll into. Not easy to get into, not at all," Meera cautioned.

"Meera, please. You know I'm not going to back out now. Are you?" Lumo pressed.

A flicker of hesitation crossed Meera's eyes before she sank into her seat. "There is a way, but it'll need some coordinated efforts and a clever ruse. We're going to need all the help we can get."

The group leaned in, intrigued by Meera's scheme.

"All right, we have to play it smart. These guys usually operate in the shadows, hence the 'underground'," Meera explained with air quotes. "We need to pique their interest. As long as we can pretend to offer something of their interest, we can gain their attention enough to get an entry into their world."

"How do we do that?" Lumo asked.

"We need a cover story, something that would explain why we're poking around without raising eyebrows."

"And..." Lumo prodded, leaning forward.

Meera paused, drumming her fingers thoughtfully on the table. "Well, usually it's something our friends might be particularly interested in—mystical artifacts, rare herbs, potions, that sort of thing," she continued. "So, I propose we act as a group of traders looking for such."

"You think it'll work? We both appear rather young to be traders, don't we?" Lumo tilted his head.

Meera shrugged. "Hmm... perhaps Bart or Lily can join us?"

"That wouldn't work. We've been here too long. They likely know us already." Lily shook her head, crossing her arms.

"That's true," Meera agreed, her eyes narrowing in thought. "What about that big guy, Gus? I think he looks old enough. You think he can join us? Where is he anyway?"

"Gus had a bit of indigestion, apparently," Lily chimed in. "But he's a kind soul. I'm sure I can convince him to help you two," she winked.

"Okay, so it's settled then." Meera clasped her hands together. "Gus will be the trader, and you and I can be his apprentices. We need to start subtly making inquiries, dropping hints in the right places, and, hopefully, someone will reach out to us."

Lumo cracked his knuckles with enthusiasm, a determined grin spreading across his face. "All right!"

"Oh! One more thing. We'll probably need a cart or something. Can't be merchants without a cart," Meera said sheepishly.

The duo turned to Bart, their gazes hopeful, expecting him to provide a solution.

"Don't be lookin' at me; we have our ale delivered to us, we do," Bart said, a bemused expression on his face.

A hint of disappointment spread across Lumo and Meera's faces.

Just then, Robert stepped in with a generous smile. "I might have a caravan for you. It's my mate George's, but I suppose we could lend it to you young'uns for a few days," he offered.

Meera's eyes lit up with a spark of gratitude, and she shot a quick, appreciative glance at Robert.

As the group finalized their plan, Bart grinned, a mischievous glint in his eye. "Looks like quite a plan now, doesn't it? To celebrate our ingenious scheme, how 'bout a round of drinks on the house, eh?"

The proposition was met with cheers and laughter, a momentary release of tension. As the drinks were distributed, Bart raised his mug high. "To Gus, the trader, and his apprentices."

The group clinked their mugs together, a united front against the looming darkness. The taste of ale lingered on their lips as Bart, with a sly grin, declared, "Now, me friends, enjoy the merriment, but we'll have to close the bar soon. We've got vacant rooms upstairs. Best you make yourselves comfortable for the night, so ye do."

As the group dispersed eventually, seeking refuge in the vacant rooms of the Thistle & Thorn, a sense of quietude settled over the tavern. Amidst the quivering candlelight, Lily and Bart found themselves alone, the only occupants of the now-hushed establishment.

Lily, with a cloth in hand, meticulously wiped down the worn wooden surface of the bar, her movements rhythmic and familiar. Bart, ever the meticulous proprietor, took care to stow away bottles, lock cabinets, and ensure the hearth's dying embers were tended to.

"You think it'll work?" Lily quizzed.

"I reckon they'll be grand, they will."

With a final extinguishing of the last candle, the tavern succumbed to darkness, leaving only the echo of footsteps as Lily and Bart ascended the creaking stairs to their living quarters.

***

CHAPTER 9

The following day dawned with an eerie stillness that hung over the castle grounds like a heavy shroud. Lucius addressed a group of guards in the war room, frantically trying to formulate a plan for the search of Prince Oliver. The war room, usually silent and deserted, was now abuzz with meticulous planning. A map of the kingdom sprawled across the table, displaying marked points at strategic locations. The scent of aged parchments mingled with the aroma of candle wax, filling the room.

As the heavy wooden door creaked open, Archibald and Serena entered the war room. Lucius, deep in conversation with the guards, looked up as they entered, his eyes revealing the weariness that had settled upon him.

"The boy has escaped." Lucius scowled. "Marcus says the guards chased him, but he disappeared into the crowd. He has got to have some hand in this, I just know it."

"Who, the attendant?" Archibald inquired.

Lucius nodded, anger simmering in his eyes.

"You're not thinking clearly, Lucius. He's just a boy," Archibald reasoned.

Serena, arms crossed, added. "Archibald's right. Besides, he couldn't pull something like this off."

Lucius clenched his jaw, his eyes narrowing. "Don't underestimate him. There's more to that boy than meets the eye. I've had my suspicions, and this escape only confirms them. I'm sure he's played a part in this. We need to find him and get to the bottom of this."

Lucius wanted to say more. *How was it that a mere boy could outsmart his men and escape?* Yet, in light of the unfolding events from the previous day, he discovered his pride held in check.

"Are you hearing yourself, Lucius?" Archibald argued further.

Lucius paused, glancing around at the guards who exchanged doubtful looks. A moment of realization struck his eyes, and he sighed, "Perhaps I'm letting my frustration cloud my judgment. Still, we can't afford to dismiss anything at this point."

Shifting the focus, Archibald redirected, "What about the plans for the search? Can you fill us in?"

"Here, here, and here," Lucius pointed to marked locations on the map. "This is where my men will be searching primarily."

"All right, do you need anything from us?"

Lucius shook his head.

"I've sent messages to the neighboring kingdoms, expressing our regrets for the chaos at the castle and assuring them that we have the situation under control," Archibald reported.

Serena, stationed by the window, nodded solemnly. "Good. We need to maintain some semblance of order amidst this chaos."

With the room steeped in contemplative silence, Serena took a deep breath, her expression resolute. "There's something I need to inform you both. Since I've lost my staff in the chaos, I must leave the castle grounds to procure another."

Archibald and Lucius exchanged a worried glance.

"Now? His Majesty's condition is getting worse. We can't afford to leave the castle unprotected," Lucius said, his concern clear as day.

"Without my staff, my ability to assist with major spells is severely limited. I may be of no use to you."

Archibald and Lucius couldn't argue with her; however, there was an uneasiness in the air.

"I have another agenda; someone who can help me—us. My absence will be brief, I assure you," Serena concluded, staring at the horizon.

"Get what you need and return as soon as possible. We can't afford any more setbacks," Lucius nodded reluctantly.

As Serena left the war room, the heavy door closing behind her, Archibald turned to Lucius. "We should focus on the search for the prince. Let's hope Serena finds the help she needs quickly."

With a shared sense of determination, Archibald and Lucius resumed their planning, the war room once again becoming a hub of strategic discussions. Outside, the castle grounds remained wrapped in an eerie stillness, echoing the uncertainty that lay ahead.

***

"Is that it?" Meera said, spotting an old caravan with Robert standing next to it proudly. The horses pulling the caravan, one gray and the other brown, both mares, fidgeted in their spots, occasionally neighing and pawing at the ground with their hooves.

Lumo squinted at the caravan, sizing it up. "I think this will do the job."

Robert beamed, his weathered face breaking into a smile. "She may be old, but she's sturdy."

Meera circled around the caravan, inspecting its structure. "Sturdy is good. The last thing we need is a breakdown."

George, the owner of the caravan, struggled with unloading a few supplies from the caravan. He had a wooden cast around his leg, a reminder of events from the previous day at the castle.

"I'll help," Gus said as he picked up a large wooden crate. In his hands, it didn't seem so large.

"You know, if you're ever looking for a job, you'll be welcome at the mill, big guy," George commented as Gus carried the crate inside.

A few moments later, the caravan was ready for the trio. Robert clapped his hands together. "There you go! All set."

Bart and Lily, flanking Gus, accompanied him to the caravan.

"Gus, remember to think like a trader, okay? And if you find yourself short for words, let Meera do the talking."

As Gus struggled to climb onto the front, George hurriedly ran to him, limping on one leg. "Err… perhaps you'd best be seated in the back? Or she might tip over," he said.

Gus smiled sheepishly, muttering a "Sorry…" as he awkwardly climbed onto the back.

Lumo and Meera promptly climbed to the front, and Lumo took the reins.

"Any advice on where we should head first?" Lumo asked.

Bart scratched his head, deep in thought. "Ah, ya might want ta have a word with Old Maebh. She runs the apothecary in town, knows more about herbs than anyone else. Just be careful; she's a shrewd one, she is."

As the caravan rolled out of the Thistle & Thorn's yard and onto the road, the trio couldn't help but feel a sense of trepidation. The road stretched ahead, leading them toward the town and, potentially, the information they sought. Gus sat nervously in the back, while Lumo and Meera pulled up their cloaks, hiding their faces as they arrived in the town.

Arriving at the town, they found it bustling with activity. Market stalls lined the streets, merchants hawking their wares, and townsfolk going about their daily business. A few guards patrolled the town, but Lumo and Meera blended in seamlessly, looking the part of ordinary merchants. After a brief search, the caravan ultimately came to a stop at the entrance of a quaint apothecary, distinguished by a weathered sign that read: "Apothecary Alchemica."

Gus, once again, grappled with the challenge of disembarking from the caravan.

"You ready, Master Gus?" Meera's tone was laced with mischief.

Gus let out a shaky breath, rolling his shoulders to loosen up. The trio made their way into the shop, Gus leading the way, and Lumo and Meera following close behind. The air inside was filled with an odd scent. The scent of various herbs and medicines clashed together, creating a somewhat foul smell. Shelves lined with bottles and jars of colorful ingredients surrounded them. The room was dimly lit by the soft glow of hanging lanterns, casting an almost mystical ambiance.

A small bell chimed as they entered, drawing the attention of an elderly woman hunched over a cluttered counter. A younger attendant busied himself in the back, scribbling notes as he examined the shelves. Maebh's sharp eyes peered over a pair of spectacles as Gus entered. Meera and Lumo were almost hidden from view behind the massive Gus.

"Well, hello, welcome," Old Maebh rasped, her voice like the creaking hinges of an old door.

"H—Hello..." Gus greeted back.

"How may I help you?" Maebh responded, her gaze shifting from Gus to Lumo to Meera.

As the trio now stood in front of the counter, Gus spoke awkwardly, "I'm trader Gus... I need rare medicine and herbs."

Old Maebh, slightly taken aback, replied with a confused expression, "Trader? Where from?"

Even as Lumo restrained an exasperated sigh, Meera, sensing Gus's awkwardness, quickly stepped in.

"Excuse me, ma'am, I'm the Master's apprentice. I'm afraid Master Gus has developed a throat condition and so he refrains from speaking beyond the absolutely essential. We are traders from far-off lands. We travel across the land looking for goods to trade in."

Old Maebh raised an eyebrow, her lips twitching with a concealed amusement. "Oh, I see, I'm sorry to hear about the throat condition. Please let me know how I may be of service."

"Master Gus, would you mind if I negotiated here onwards? I could learn a thing or two," Meera said, looking up at Gus.

Gus bobbed his head.

"Thank you, Master."

"As Master Gus said, we are looking for rare medicines and herbs," Meera continued.

"Ah, any particular kind?" Maebh replied.

As Meera stood blank-faced, Maebh spoke once again.

"I mean, do you want the healing herbs, the poison ones, the purifying kind, or enhancing tonics? We have a host of remedies available."

"We want everything, as long as they are rare and difficult to obtain. You see, we profit from trading these goods to other provinces. Only the rarest kinds will do, no other."

"Oh, all right. Henry, could you get the red ledger, please?" Maebh said, directing her voice toward the attendant in the back.

The attendant quietly reached for a drawer, removed an old worn red book, and carried it over to Maebh.

"Let's see now," Maebh started, adjusting her glasses. She turned a few pages and slid her fingers across a list. "These are the rare and higher kind we have right now: Starlight Lotus—healing herb, Moonshadow Petals—healing herb, Deathshade Blossom—poisonous plant…"

Maebh seemed engrossed in reading out the entire contents of her book, one by one. Meera's patience, having quickly run out, interrupted Maebh.

"Can we just look at the list, please?" she said.

"Well, of course, here you go," Maebh said as she turned the book around, facing Meera.

Meera stepped forward to take a closer look. As Meera perused the list, she noticed that some entries were crossed out.

"Why are these crossed out?" she queried.

"Those are unavailable, dearie."

Meera looked at the list again.

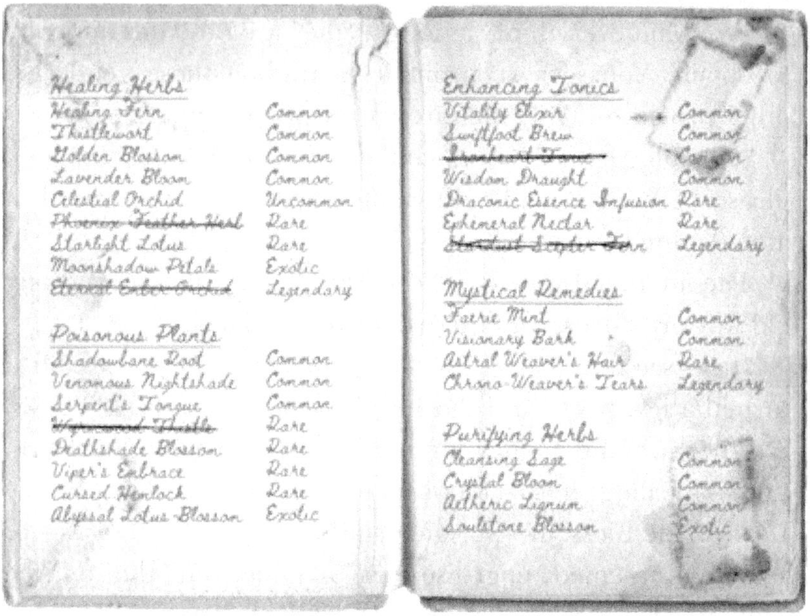

"I see, and as I noticed, the legendary ones are the highest quality then?"

"Yes, there are different grades for each ingredient, depending on their rarity. The legendary ones, I'm afraid, are almost impossible to get."

As Meera scrutinized the list once more, she realized that almost all the legendary ones were crossed out.

"Those are the ones we want then!" Meera squealed.

"Oh, dear. Let me see," Maebh said, turning the book again to review the list.

"Ah, we only have the Chrono-Weaver's tears in that category," Maebh said, re-inspecting the next few pages as well.

Just then, the quiet attendant in the back spoke up. "Maebh, that item might be unavailable as well. I was about to update that list."

"Oh, my. I'm sorry, dears. Afraid, you're out of luck."

"Well, we must have those. We are ready to pay a handsome price for them, let's say two times the market rate. Isn't that right, Master Gus?" Meera said.

Gus gave a large, sheepish grin.

"Your venture is indeed fascinating, young ones. However, obtaining such rare ingredients involves more than just a visit to my humble shop. Might I suggest you try the Merchant's Guild?" Maebh suggested.

"How about three times the market rate, then!" Meera exclaimed.

"I'm sorry, miss. I wasn't bargaining. I apologize if I came across as such."

"Okay, thank you," Meera said, pretending to be dejected. "Where is the Merchant's Guild again?"

"It's the large building down the road. They're usually interested in bulk trade, but that wouldn't be a problem for you traders." Maebh smiled bemusingly. "They might even make arrangements to buy some of your own wares."

"All right then, we will try our luck there, but if you come across any of those ingredients in the meantime, please let us know. We will pay four times the market rate!" Meera said, her voice loud enough to fill the room.

"Will do, dear."

Just as Meera, Lumo, and Gus turned around to leave the shop, Maebh spoke once again.

"I almost forgot, here's something for your throat condition, Master Gus. It's a special tonic made from Mandragora root. Should clear that throat condition in no time. Only four silver coins," she said, extending her hand.

Meera, Lumo, and Gus exchanged surprised glances as Maebh presented the item to them. Meera nodded quietly to Lumo, a sign that it was probably best not to decline, given how they had bragged about paying heavily for the other items.

"I don't have any coin, you know that," Lumo whispered, a panicked look on his face.

"Well, neither do I, unless you want me to steal again," Meera whispered back, a hint of frustration in her voice.

"No, we agreed on no more stealing," Lumo replied, pouting slightly.

"Well, if neither of us have any..."

Together they turned to Gus who looked at them nervously. With a sigh, he handed his pouch to Lumo.

"Thank you," Lumo mumbled as he paid Maebh.

After collecting the tonic, the trio quietly made their way out of the shop, the door creaking slightly behind them.

"Well, that was fruitless." Lumo kicked a small stone as they walked.

"We're going to have to do that at a few more locations around town, Lumo," Meera said.

A crease formed between Gus's eyebrows as he listened, his hands nervously fidgeting at his sides. The smile faded from his face, replaced by a tense, uncertain expression. He was worried all his coins would be spent on useless things when what he really needed was just more food.

"So, she said the Merchant's Guild is down the road. Should we head there, then?" Meera suggested, looking ahead with purpose.

"Okay, Meera. But, can we walk?" Gus asked, taking a deep breath. "I—I don't want to climb up and down the cart again."

"Sure, yeah," Meera replied.

The trio walked down the bustling street, the scent of various goods wafting through the air. After an eventful walk, the Merchant's Guild loomed in the distance, its grand facade hinting at the wealth and commerce within. The exterior boasted a mix of polished wood and stone, giving it an air of prestige. The entrance featured a pair of grand doors adorned with the guild's emblem—perfectly balanced weighing scales. As they approached, the noise of the lively marketplace gradually faded, replaced by the murmurings of serious business, like the sudden hush that falls over a room when someone mentions taxes.

Upon entering, the trio found themselves in a spacious hall adorned with banners representing various trade alliances. Lumo recognized some of the banners, belonging to the other kingdoms. The Avaloran crest, a majestic eagle on an orange banner, stood out prominently. Nearby, the Veridian crest displayed a proud stag against a green background, while the Ophidonian crest featured a serpent coiled menacingly on a black banner. Inside, the atmosphere was charged with the energy of negotiation and commerce. Merchants, dressed in fine attire, moved about, discussing deals and showcasing their goods.

Meera led the way, navigating through the busy hall with confidence. Lumo and Gus followed, their eyes wide with curiosity. The trio approached a large desk where a well-dressed clerk was busy organizing scrolls and documents.

"Greetings," Meera said, addressing the clerk. "We're traders in search of rare goods. Could you direct us to someone who can assist us?"

The clerk looked up from his work, studying the trio with a discerning gaze.

"Guild card, please," he demanded with a curt tone.

Meera hesitated for a moment, her mind racing to find a solution. "Err… we don't have a guild card. We're independent traders."

"You must have a guild card to conduct business here. Please register first," the attendant insisted, handing them a form. "Please fill in all the details. The fee is seventy-three silver coins."

Gus almost had a panic attack.

"Seventy-three silver coins! Hah, no way we're paying that. C'mon, Gus—I mean, Master Gus, let's go check elsewhere," Meera declared, steering the group toward the exit. The doors swung shut behind them.

"What now? This is going to be more difficult than I imagined," Lumo voiced his concern.

As Meera paused, considering their options, Gus's stomach growled loudly.

"S—Sorry, can we get something to eat?" Gus said, stroking his stomach.

"Good idea, we can take a break and look around a bit," Lumo suggested, offering a small grin to Gus.

As they meandered through the lively marketplace, Gus noticed a quaint food stall in a corner, emanating the tempting aroma of freshly cooked fare, and his stomach rumbled once again.

"There," he suggested, pointing to the stall where a portly man expertly flipped sizzling skewers over an open flame. The enticing sizzle and the rich scent of spices drew them in.

As they savored the flavorful bites, the atmosphere was a blend of sizzling skewers, lively chatter, and the occasional haggling from nearby stalls.

Meera watched as Gus devoured the meat, with a satisfactory look on his face.

"Easy, Gus," she said.

"See why they call him Gus the Glutton," Lumo chirped.

"I see it. Has it always been Gus the Glutton?"

"Augustus. That's the—mm—name my Ma and Pa gave me," Gus replied, chomping down on the meat.

"Augustus, eh?"

"Yeah, I think he was some—mm—king or something. It was my—mm—Ma's idea to name me that. She always—mm—said I had all the qualities of a king." Gus smiled broadly, bits of food lodged between his teeth and droplets of sauce spilling from the corner of his mouth.

"But I like Gus; it's—mm—simpler."

Meera smiled awkwardly.

"Oh, we can try the potions master's shop next. I think it's around here somewhere," Meera said.

"Do you think we should try looking for other rare things? Like antiques or something? If we are going to be traders, we can trade in anything, can't we?" Lumo suggested.

"That's true. Okay, let's try the potions shop first, and then we can head to the antique store later."

"Excuse me, sir, where can we find the potions master's shop?" Lumo asked the food stall owner, who was deftly managing the skewers.

"Master Rowan's shop? It's on the other side of town, should be at least a thirty-minute walk from here," the shopkeeper replied.

"That's a long walk; best we get back to the caravan, then," Meera suggested.

Gus, having downed a decent-sized meal, seemed less concerned about the inconvenience. The group headed back, walking slowly toward the caravan, ready to visit their next potential location.

Just then, from a nearby alleyway, a voice called out to them.

"Psst! Over here."

Turning toward the sound, the trio spotted Henry, the attendant from Maebh's shop, waving them into the alley. Cautiously, they approached him.

"What's the matter?" Meera asked, eyeing Henry with suspicion.

Glancing around to ensure no one was eavesdropping, Henry spoke in a hushed tone, "I couldn't help but overhear your conversation with Old Maebh. You're looking for more than what's on the shelves, aren't you?"

Meera exchanged glances with Lumo and Gus, gauging their reactions.

"What do you mean?" she replied nonchalantly.

Henry smirked knowingly. "I've got a friend who deals in the ultra-rare stuff, things you won't find in any ledger. You interested?"

Lumo and Meera exchanged glances. They couldn't believe their search was over so quickly.

"Yes, we're interested!" Lumo exclaimed.

"Not so quickly."

Meera leaned in. "All right, what's the catch?"

"Okay, look, so this... friend of mine, he works in this shadow network, you see. But the guy is dangerous. I owe him a large debt, something that can't just be paid off. So, I need you to do me a favor first."

Lumo's eyes gleamed with excitement as he heard the words "shadow" and "network."

"Go on," Meera said.

"There's a shipment of rare gems coming in from Veridia, we know this, but we don't know when and where. The Merchant Guild has the info, but we're not able to get this information. Get it for me and I'll introduce you to my friend. Deal?"

"Merchant Guild? Oh, no, we are not registered with them, they refused to deal with us," Meera said.

"So, register with them," Henry said nonchalantly.

"We can't register with them; they are asking for—"

Lumo cut in, "We prefer to be anonymous; they are asking us to give them our whereabouts during registration."

Henry blinked rapidly, his head tilting to one side.

"Are you some sort of amateurs or something?" He shook his head in disbelief. "Look, that guy at the counter, just slip him some coins, and he'll accommodate you."

Meera hesitated, eyeing Henry warily. "Slip some coins? That seems... unconventional. What guarantee do we have that they won't betray us or report our actions?"

Henry sighed. "All right, all right. You're new in town, I get it. Let me break it down. The Merchant Guild here is not as pristine as they might appear. A few extra coins in the right hands, and you become a registered trader without all the formalities."

"So, we grease some palms and get the information for you. What's the catch beyond that?" Lumo asked.

"That's it. We need to know exactly when the shipment is arriving and where, and the sort of security measures they have in place."

Meera exchanged a glance with Lumo. "That's it? Just gather the details on the shipment?"

"Yeah, anything else? 'Cause, you know, I've got all day to just stand here and explain the whole master plan to you." Henry rolled his eyes.

A pause settled over the group as Meera and Lumo contemplated the situation. They knew getting into the underground network wouldn't be easy, but the realization that they were becoming involved in someone else's scheme made them apprehensive. They only hoped their part would end at gathering information.

"Okay, we will try to get the information you need. But if you don't hold up your part of the bargain…" Meera's voice trailed off.

Henry raised an eyebrow. "You've got guts, I'll give you that. Don't worry, you get me what I need, and you'll meet my friend. Just remember, though, crossing him is not something you'd want to do."

With the pact established, Henry provided them with a few additional pieces of information they would need about the shipment itself.

"…And, one more thing."

Lumo and Meera leaned in, anticipating.

"Just be wary of the Guildmaster—Roderick. He's sharp, and will sense right away if anything is off."

"When you're done, come see me at Maebh's and then wait for me back here, got it?"

Lumo and Meera nodded in acknowledgment.

With that, Henry quietly slipped into the shadows. As they left the dim alley, the trio couldn't shake off the feeling that they had just stepped into a world far more complex and perilous than they had initially anticipated.

The trio retraced their steps toward the bustling center of the market where the Merchant Guild held its imposing presence. As they entered, they approached the large desk where the same clerk, engrossed in his work earlier, now diligently sorted through a stack of parchment. He glanced up as they approached, his expression one of polite indifference.

"Guild card, please," he requested in the same unwavering tone as before.

Meera exchanged a quick glance with Lumo, and Gus shifted nervously from foot to foot. This was the pivotal moment, and they were about to dive into the unknown.

“Ah, about that,” Lumo began, flashing a disarming smile. “We've decided to register with the guild after all. You know, for the perks and all.”

The clerk raised an eyebrow but extended a registration form, nonetheless. “Fill this out with all the necessary details. The fee is seventy-three silver coins.”

Lumo's confident grin wavered, but he quickly regained composure as he accepted the form. While Lumo took charge of the conversation, Meera surreptitiously scanned the area. She noticed a discreet exchange of coins happening at another counter, confirming Henry's earlier advice. The guild's operations seemed more fluid than the rigid facade suggested. She quietly nodded to Lumo to proceed.

Lumo hesitated for a moment, then slipped a few silver coins into the clerk's view.

The clerk's stern facade softened, and he pocketed the extra coins with a knowing look.

“Very well, welcome to the guild,” he said as he handed them a card with details that clearly did not belong to them.

“How can I help you today?” He greeted them politely.

“We are traders, we are looking for deals on new and high-value goods,” Lumo informed.

“High-value goods, do you mean luxury goods?”

“Yes, exactly! Like rubies, emeralds, that sort.”

“So, do you wish to sell or buy these goods?”

“Buy or trade,” Lumo replied.

“I see. I would just like to remind you that the Merchant Guild doesn’t actually deal in the goods themselves, but we facilitate the trade of such goods and take a cut. Our share is ten percent. Do you agree?”

"Agreed," Lumo said.

"All right, then please wait in the waiting area and someone from the guild will approach you shortly," the clerk said, gesturing toward a designated area with plush chairs, separated from the main hall by a gilded partition.

As Lumo, Meera, and Gus settled in the waiting area, they quietly reviewed the plan and discussed the questions they needed to ask to gather the necessary information. Moments later, a well-dressed guild member approached them with a friendly smile.

"Greetings, esteemed traders. How may the Merchant Guild assist you today?"

Lumo took the lead. "We're in the market for rare gems and high-value goods."

"Well, you've come to the right place, then. We can connect you to some traders. Could you tell me more about the exact types of gems you are looking for?" the man pressed.

"We're looking for the rare kind, especially Veridian gems," Lumo replied.

"Ah, yes. We know some traders who deal in such gems. Should I get you their contacts?"

"No, wait. Let me tell you that we have already been to a few traders, and it seems that a lot of the stuff they are selling isn't Veridian at all. We can tell because the Veridian gems have magical properties, and as magic users ourselves, we can identify these goods," Lumo said, gesturing to Gus.

"I assure you, the traders we can connect you to—" the man rushed to say.

"Look, we are not taking any chances. We travel from place to place, and so we cannot afford to deal with any counterfeits. Can you tell us if there are any fresh shipments coming from Veridia? We wish to inspect it at the source before any unscrupulous traders can make any swaps," Lumo interrupted.

The man's eyes darted to the floor, his jaw working silently as if he were chewing over his next words. Finally, he spoke. "All right, just a minute, then."

He quietly slipped away to return a moment later.

"I bring good news; a shipment of Veridian gems is scheduled to arrive in Avalora in four days," the man announced.

Lumo and Meera exchanged glances.

"That's excellent. Could you provide details on where the shipment will be received?" Lumo asked.

Just then, a sudden commotion erupted nearby, distracting their attention. The guild member, with a quick apology, excused himself and hurried away.

As Lumo, Meera, and Gus waited in anticipation, a new face approached them. His attire, a rich burgundy robe embellished with intricate gold embroidery, marked him as a person of high standing within the guild.

Lumo recognized him immediately. He had seen him at the castle. There was no mistaking the thin man with the pointy chin and monocle—it was Roderick.

"Good afternoon. I'm Guildmaster Roderick. I apologize for the abrupt departure of the attendant who was assisting you. How may I further assist you?" Roderick offered.

Lumo's heart skipped a beat, a momentary worry creeping in that Roderick might also recognize him. However, Lumo swiftly regained his composure, masking any hint of recognition in his expression.

"Good afternoon," Lumo greeted. "The earlier attendant mentioned a shipment of Veridian gems arriving in four days. Could you provide additional details? We're keen on visiting the source, intending to inspect the gems firsthand and make immediate purchases."

Roderick studied Lumo for a moment, his brows furrowing as if grappling with a distant memory. "Haven't I seen you before somewhere?" he mused, adjusting his monocle.

Lumo's emotions churned beneath a veneer of composed calm.

"P—Perhaps in passing, Guildmaster," Lumo replied with a quick gulp. "We do frequent various markets and events."

A silent pause hung in the air as Lumo anxiously awaited Roderick's response, uncertain if his explanation had convinced the Guildmaster.

"Ah, well, I suppose the faces do start to blur after a while. Now, about the Veridian shipment," Roderick continued, "It will be arriving at the Southern Docks on the morning of the fourth day. A reputable trader named Edmond will be handling the reception."

Lumo's shoulders relaxed as he let out a soft, shaky breath. He shared a brief, knowing glance with Meera. Their mission was nearly complete; the only remaining task was to uncover the details of the security measures.

"I will send a pigeon right away, informing him of your arrival. I hope the other attendants have informed you of the guild's commission?" Roderick spoke once more.

"Yes, they have," Lumo replied.

"Anything else, then?"

Lumo, maintaining his composed facade, decided to approach the topic of security cautiously. "Guildmaster Roderick, we appreciate the information on the shipment's arrival. However, considering the nature of the goods, we find ourselves concerned about security. Could you enlighten us on the measures in place for the protection of such valuable cargo?"

"Of course, we understand the sensitivity of the matter. We simply want to ensure that the shipments are in capable hands. We would hate to waste our time, only to find out that the goods had been compromised along the way," Meera chimed in.

Lumo and Meera exchanged subtle glances, hoping their inquiry appeared more as a responsible concern than a probing question.

Roderick, maintaining his affable demeanor, flashed a smile. "I hope you understand that I cannot disclose the specifics, but I assure you there are stringent measures in place. One can never be too careful, especially with valuable cargo."

Roderick stood there, his smile fixed in place.

"All right then, thank you," Lumo said. He wanted to press further, but something about the way Roderick stared didn't sit well with him.

"Oh, by the way. Whom should I say is visiting? I need to inform Edmond, but I didn't quite catch your names."

Caught off guard, Lumo stammered, "Uh, I'm Lu...ther and this is... Mirabell and...Gu—"

"Gundolf," Meera interjected.

Roderick's expression didn't shift, though his gaze lingered on Lumo with a subtle intensity.

"Luther, Mirabell, and Gun...dolf," Roderick repeated, as though committing the names to memory. "Very well. I'll ensure Edmond is informed of your impending visit. If there's anything else you require, don't hesitate to let me know."

Lumo and Meera expressed their gratitude, and as Roderick excused himself to attend to other matters, the trio decided to leave the Merchant Guild.

"Gundolf? Really?" Lumo asked, raising an eyebrow.

"Well, at least I came up with something," Meera pouted.

As they exited the guild, Lumo couldn't resist the urge to glance back. Roderick was engrossed in conversation with another guild member, his amiable smile now concealed behind a mask of professionalism.

"Well, that went smoother than expected," Lumo remarked.

Meera nodded. "But there's something about Roderick. Did you see the way he looked at you?"

"Yes, but we got what we needed… almost. Anyway, let's just get this over with, then."

As the group walked back to Maebh's shop, Meera offered to enter the shop, while Lumo and Gus waited outside.

The bell chimed once again as Meera entered, and Maebh looked up again.

"Hello, dearie. Back so soon?"

"Hello, Maebh, I just wanted to pass along Master Gus's gratitude. His throat is feeling much better now," Meera replied.

"You're most welcome," Maebh beamed. "And perhaps, while you're here, you might be interested in some extraordinary tonics. They work wonders for the skin."

Meera, however, appeared preoccupied, discreetly scanning the shop for Henry. Spotting him in the back, she subtly gestured with a nod of her head, signaling that the task was accomplished.

"Oh, no. Thank you. I'll be taking your leave now," Meera said, swiftly making her exit.

"Goodbye," Maebh waved as the door closed.

"Did you see him?" Lumo inquired as Meera joined them outside.

"Yeah, I passed on the message. We'd better go wait for him at the alley."

***

As Lumo, Meera, and Gus waited in the alley for Henry's arrival, the minutes dragged on, and the air grew thick with the kind of anticipation that made even the rats consider taking a nap.

"You don't think he would stand us up, would you?" Lumo asked.

"I hope not. But if I end up in the dungeons again because of some harebrained heist scheme, I'm blaming you. And I'm going to make sure every bite of that stale dungeon bread is on your conscience, Lumo—and I'll describe each one in excruciating detail," Meera quipped, narrowing her eyes at Lumo.

Lumo gave a small, awkward laugh, scratching his head.

After what felt like an eternity, Henry finally appeared at the entrance of the alley. He moved cautiously, one foot slowly following the other, as if the ground beneath him might betray his presence. His shoulders were hunched slightly, his gaze shifting as if he were trying to avoid being watched.

"About time," Meera said, tapping her foot.

"Let's not waste any more time," Lumo added. "We've got the information you wanted."

Henry leaned in, his eyes darting between them. "Tell me everything."

Meera began recounting the details about the shipment of Veridian gems—the arrival date, the location at the

Southern Docks, and the involvement of the trader named Edmond.

After Meera was done, Lumo continued, "Now, you hold up your end of the deal. Introduce us to your friend, the one from the shadow—"

Henry, however, raised a hand in a halting gesture. "Not so soon. This information needs to be passed ahead."

"That wasn't the deal, Henry. We did our part; now it's time for you to do yours," Meera argued.

Henry leaned against the alley wall, crossing his arms. "I said I'd introduce you, and I will. But it's not like my contact is just waiting around for you. This isn't a simple rendezvous at the market. These things take time, and they need to be handled with care."

Lumo stepped forward, his tone firm. "When?"

"Patience is a virtue. I'll send word when it's time, and not a moment sooner."

Meera exchanged a glance with Lumo, both grappling with the realization that their involvement in this clandestine world meant playing by a different set of rules. The uncertainty of the situation hung in the air, leaving them with little choice but to trust Henry's word and await further instructions.

"Don't worry," Henry assured them with a sly grin. "You'll get what you came for. Just be ready when the time comes. Now, where do I reach you three?"

"You can send your message to the bartender at Thistle & Thorn. He will relay the message to us," Lumo replied, hesitantly.

"Got it. I've got to go now. Too much lingering in one place attracts unwanted attention."

As Henry melted back into the shadows of the alley, the trio was left standing there, contemplating the intricate web they had woven themselves into. The path ahead seemed murky, filled with unknown dangers and unforeseen challenges—just another day in paradise. All they could do now was wait and gear up for the next chapter in their wild adventure.

***

CHAPTER 10

"How's the leg now, George?" Bart quizzed.

"All better now, Bart, thank you for the hospitality. You've certainly made our stay here more memorable," George replied, favoring his mended leg as they gathered their belongings in preparation for the journey back to the farm.

A few days had passed since the incident at the castle. George's gait still bore traces of a limp, and the cast on his leg would linger for a few more days. Robert and George saw no point in staying at the kingdom anymore, and their lives back at the farm waited for them.

"Goodbye, Lumo, Meera," Robert greeted as he climbed onto the front of the caravan. "You are most welcome at the farm anytime."

"Bye, Robert," Meera greeted.

As the gang waved their farewells, the creaking caravan set in motion, its wheels grinding against the terrain.

***

The sorceress rode through the dense forest, her horse's hooves blending with the rustle of leaves above. Sunlight filtered through the canopy, casting dappled light on the ground. She approached a clearing where a weathered cottage stood, its timbers worn and half-swallowed by nature's slow claim.

Dismounting, she approached, scanning for any sign of life. Inside, empty rooms greeted her, save for birdsong filtering through cracks in the wood. The scent of aged wood and old memories filled the air within. Moving through the quiet space, she let her fingers graze old remnants, but nothing gave up its secrets. Even the overgrown garden outside whispered of a forgotten past, yet held its mysteries close.

Undeterred, the sorceress mounted her horse and pressed on. Soon, the forest opened to reveal a small farmhouse, standing firm amidst the trees—sturdier than the desolate cottage she'd left behind. She dismounted, approached the door, and knocked gently. A young couple answered, their eyes cautious as they took in her presence.

"Yes?" they questioned.

It was clear that they weren't used to unfamiliar faces showing up on their doorstep.

"Good day. I'm Serena. I was wondering if I could ask you a few questions," Serena said, her tone calm yet persistent.

"What about?" asked the man.

"About the cottage in the woods," Serena replied.

The woman beside the man furrowed her brows, exchanging a quick glance with her partner. "Cottage… oh, the abandoned lodging?"

"Yes. Would you mind if I came in?"

The couple hesitated. After a brief moment, they gestured her in, the creaking door revealing a modest, lived-in interior.

The man cleared his throat. "Sorry, we're not used to visitors, you see."

Serena offered a small nod, acknowledging their hesitance.

"Please, have a seat. I'll make some tea," the young woman said, gesturing toward a worn-out sofa.

As the young woman disappeared into the adjacent room, Serena took in the modest interior of the farmhouse. The light from a nearby window revealed family portraits on the walls and worn furniture that spoke of years spent in this homely abode.

The woman returned shortly, balancing a tray with a steaming teapot and a couple of mismatched cups. She placed it on the table, offering Serena a warm smile. "Tea is ready. We haven't had guests in quite some time."

"Thank you. How long have you been living here?" Serena asked.

The woman chuckled, pouring tea into the cups. "Oh, we've been here for as long as I can remember. This farmhouse has been in the family for generations."

"It's a charming place. Do you enjoy living here?"

The man, who had been quietly observing, spoke up, "It has its challenges, like any place, but we've made a good life here; quiet and away from the bustle of the kingdom."

Serena nodded, appreciating the simplicity of their life. "It is peaceful. I'm sorry for intruding, but I'm looking for information about the man, the one who lived in the cottage. Any details you can provide would be helpful."

The woman glanced at her partner, a puzzled look on her face. "The man who lived there? We didn't even know anyone still lived in that old place."

"Did you ever hear anyone else inquiring about the place?" Serena pressed.

The woman shook her head. "Not that we know of. The old cottage just became a forgotten part of the landscape."

"I see. Perhaps I should ask some of your neighbors then."

"You're welcome to try," the man said.

Just then the door at the front of the cottage swung open, and an elderly man entered the cottage. As Serena looked back, the man's gaze, seasoned with years of experience, met Serena's.

"Father," the young man said. "This is Serena; she wanted to know about the cottage in the woods."

The elderly man scrutinized Serena for a moment before offering a nod of acknowledgment.

"Serena, is it? Hello, I'm Willem."

"Good day, Sir. I apologize for the intrusion; I'm inquiring about a man who used to live in the cottage in the woods," Serena explained, her tone respectful. "His name is Sylvanus. I was hoping you might have some insights."

"Sylvanus, you say? It's been a while since someone asked about him. What do you want to know?"

Serena leaned forward slightly, her gaze intent. "I'm interested in learning about his whereabouts. Any information you could provide would be immensely helpful."

Willem took a seat on the sofa beside Serena, resting his walking stick against the frame. "Sylvanus was a recluse, kept to himself mostly. Quiet fellow. Lived in that cottage for years, him and that lad. Then, one day, he just left without a word."

"Lad?" Serena inquired, her interest piqued. "Do you remember anything about the boy?"

Willem scratched his chin. "Thin, fair haired. Looked about seven or eight. Sylvanus treated him like a son, though they weren't kin. The boy looked nothing like him. Rumor is he died of a mysterious illness. Sylvanus left shortly after that, and no one hereabouts heard much about him since."

"Do you remember when he left?" Serena pressed.

"Must have been, what, ten, twelve years ago? Don't remember much about the last few years them was here. Sylvanus was also sick apparently."

"I see."

"Verily, odd fellow, that Sylvanus was."

"Did Sylvanus have any visitors or acquaintances? Perhaps someone who might shed light on his departure?"

The elderly man's gaze drifted, as if delving into the recesses of the past. "There were whispers, rumors of hooded figures seen around the cottage. Folks said Sylvanus dabbled in things best left alone. But as for concrete answers, I'm afraid you won't find them anywhere around here."

Serena nodded, absorbing the nuances of Willem's recollections. "Thank you, Sir Willem. Your insights have been valuable."

As Serena prepared to leave, Willem spoke once more. "That pendant you wear, Sylvanus wore something like that."

"Pendant..." she repeated, her fingers tracing the outline of the pendant.

"Yes, the one with the stag on it."

"Indeed," Serena replied, clutching her pendant. Her gaze lingered on the design, lost in contemplation.

"I take it you knew him well then," Willem ventured.

"He was my mentor. Thank you. I think I know where he might have gone... Veridia."

Serena bid farewell to the farmhouse and its inhabitants. The forest embraced her once more as she mounted her horse and made her way toward the unknown, her mind buzzing with the newfound lead. The cottage, the farmhouse, and the tales woven into their walls faded into the backdrop.

***

Bart was busy tending to patrons and polishing mugs behind the counter as the day unfolded. Just before afternoon, a small beggar kid, no more than seven or eight years old, cautiously entered the tavern and approached the counter. Bart, noticing the child, grunted in disapproval.

"This is no place for the likes of ya; run along now," Bart said, shooing the kid away.

The child handed Bart a crumpled note before darting out of the tavern. Bart unfolded the note, his eyes scanning the hastily scrawled message.

To the traders looking for the Medicines.
Today evening at 07:00.
Come to the back of Hemmingsworth's.
Knock thrice and when prompted say the word Dandelions.
Don't be late.

Bart called over Lumo and Meera, informing them of the mysterious note. The duo gathered around the bar, exchanging glances as they listened to Bart's account.

"A message arrived for ya. Here," he said, as he handed the note to Lumo.

"Hemmingsworth's?"

"Yeah, a tailoring shop at the edge of town. One of the best garments one can get, I reckon," Bart said, displaying his own attire, seemingly from the same place.

"Dandelions? Do they expect us to show up dressed as a meadow?" Meera joked, looking amused.

"Well, it's certainly an upgrade from what you're wearing," Lumo smirked.

"Oh, so now I'm a fashion disaster?" Meera shot back. "Fine, I'll just make sure my meadow look pairs well with your plain old grass."

"Thank you, Bart," Lumo said, trying to stifle a grin as they prepared to leave.

***

Come evening, Lumo, Meera, and Gus navigated through the quieter evening streets, eventually reaching the edge of town. The murmur of daily life had subsided, replaced by the occasional flicker of lamplights.

"This is the spot," Meera declared, her eyes focused on the prominent sign reading 'Hemmingsworth's' in front of them. The sign proudly displayed an intricate motif, leaving little to the imagination with its depiction of crossed scissors.

"Appears to be closed," Lumo noted.

"The note said to come to the back of the shop. This way," Meera said, leading the way.

The trio moved around to the back of the shop, following the note's instructions. A small red door stood before them. Gus wondered if he could fit through the door—probably with a bit of effort.

Lumo knocked thrice on the door, and after a brief moment, a peephole on the door slid open from the inside. A pair of peering eyes scanned the area as a hoarse voice erupted from the other side of the door.

"What's your favorite dinnertime snack when the moon is your plate?" the voice echoed.

Lumo cleared his throat and responded, "Uh, dandelions?"

The peephole closed abruptly, and the door creaked open, revealing a narrow staircase descending into darkness.

Lumo and Meera exchanged uncertain glances as they descended into the depths. Gus followed, squeezing through the doorway.

As they reached the bottom, the scene unfolded into a dimly lit cellar. Reels of colored cloth were neatly stacked along the walls, interspersed with tailoring equipment and tools neatly arranged on wooden tables. The room seemed to stretch beyond what the modest building above ground could contain. The doorman motioned for them to follow him as he led the way. At the far end of the cellar stood a massive iron door.

"Through there," the doorman pointed.

As Lumo, Meera, and Gus complied, they entered a larger chamber where the atmosphere intensified. The room was alive with the rhythmic clinking of coins, the shuffling of cards, and the occasional burst of laughter. Rough-looking patrons gathered around makeshift tables, engrossed in various games of chance.

"This is…" Lumo started.

"A gambling den," Meera finished his sentence.

Amidst the thick haze of smoke from cigars and pipes, the trio struggled to look for their confidant. After a brief search, they spotted Henry, discreetly sitting at a table near the far end of the room. His eyes met theirs, and he signaled them to join him. Lumo could feel the weight of unseen eyes observing their every move, especially with the big Gus following closely behind them.

Henry rose from his seat as they approached, a faint smile playing on his lips.

"Glad you made it," he said, gesturing for them to sit.

Henry signaled for drinks, and a thin man wearing tattered rags swiftly approached, serving the trio with drinks. Lumo couldn't help but draw a stark mental contrast between the elegant service provided by the lovely Lily at the T&T and the ragged appearance of their current server.

"Nice establishment you have here," Meera remarked.

"Yeah, we call it 'The Nugget'," Henry replied. "Now, let me introduce you to Kael, the owner," Henry said, gesturing toward a dark corner of the room. "I warn you, though; he doesn't take kindly to staring, so avoid too much eye contact."

As the trio approached the darker corner of the room, their eyes fell upon a large, burly man seated between two women on either side. A smaller individual, distinctive in stature, sat next to him, accompanied by a few more women. Gus recognized the large man instantly—it was the thug he had bested earlier at the town square. His eyes widened at the sight, and as the burly man spotted Gus, his did as well.

"Y—You're Kael?" Gus stammered.

Before the man could reply, the smaller man seated next to him spoke up, his tone sharp. "No, I'm Kael. Who's asking?"

Henry hurriedly stepped forth to introduce the group.

"Hello, Boss. This is... err..." Henry paused, realizing he hadn't acquired their real names. He elbowed Meera, prompting her to continue.

"We are a trader group. This is Luther, I'm Mirabell, and this is Gulileo," Meera introduced.

Lumo almost slapped his forehead.

The thug sitting next to Kael hurriedly muttered something in Kael's ear, and Kael's eyes absorbed the details, his eyes squinting ever so slightly.

"So, Gulileo, or is that Gus, the glutton? Are any of your names true?" Kael spoke with a serious expression, his gaze piercing.

Meera, realizing that the gig was up, confessed, "Okay, fine. Those aren't our real names. What's wrong with having aliases?"

Kael looked at them sternly, a moment of silence hanging in the air.

Lumo broke the silence. "Lumo—I'm Lumo, this is Meera and Gus."

Kael's eyes continued scrutinizing the trio, and his expression transformed abruptly from seriousness to a wide, jovial smile that lingered for a moment.

"So, what do you want?" he said curtly, his expression turning serious just as abruptly.

Lumo and Meera exchanged uncertain glances as Kael's mood shifted. Henry stepped forth once more, explaining the group's intent and their role in procuring information about the shipment.

"So, these are the fellas who got the info, yeah?" Kael lit a cigar. "Well, you're a fool, Henry."

"P—Pardon me, Boss?" Henry stammered.

"I said, you're a fool. It's probably why you're still in debt. These guys are no traders," Kael stated bluntly, exhaling a plume of smoke from his mouth.

The realization hit Henry, Lumo, and Meera simultaneously, their expressions changing from confusion to concern.

"Tell me, Henry. When you are playing cards with a seasoned gambler, and he doesn't even blink when you try to palm an ace, what do you think that means?" Kael quizzed.

"Uh, I don't know, Boss."

"It's a telltale sign that he's seen your trick before..." Kael clarified, his tone serious. "Just like the Merchant Guild. They sensed the foul play and they upped the security at the docks. You're going to be paying off your debts for a long time, Henry."

"As for you three, I'm intrigued about why you are really here, so I'll hear you out before deciding what to do with you. Go on," Kael continued, punctuating his words with puffs from his cigar.

While Kael continued to smoke, Gus stared intently at him, taking note of the tiny suit on Kael's small frame. His gaze shifted and stuck onto Kael's face. Something about his eyes set deep within their sockets, his thick nose slightly upturned at the tip, and lips pressed together in a thin line intrigued Gus.

Kael, sensing Gus's gaze, spoke loudly. "Have I got something on my face, big guy?"

"N—No, sir," Gus responded, immediately averting his eyes.

"Moose, why don't you show our friend some of the festivities of the house? You two need to patch things up, anyway," Kael said casually, gesturing to the burly thug next to him.

"Yes, boss," Moose replied, getting up and leading the ladies and Gus away to another part of the den. Gus reluctantly followed, stealing a quick glance back at Lumo, who offered an assuring nod.

"Now, back to business. Tell me what you want?"

"We're looking for information," Meera said as she slid Lily's drawing in Kael's direction.

Kael's eyes narrowed as he examined the parchment, a notable crease forming on his forehead. "This is..."

"We're searching for a man with that tattoo on his wrist."

Kael's expression hardened, and he abruptly pushed the parchment back, dismissing it.

"I can't help you."

"But you know of the tattoo," Meera pressed.

Leaning in, Kael's voice dropped to a near whisper. "Look, you're getting involved in something you shouldn't. It's best you leave now; I will allow it."

"We know about the Cimmerian—" Meera started.

"Shhh..." Kael silenced her with a gesture, leaning even further. Ashes from his cigar fell like tiny embers on the table. "Lower your voice."

"You're either very brave or very foolish," he continued, all the while staring at the duo.

"Desperate... that's what we are," Lumo said. "Look, we really need your help."

A moment of silence lingered, broken only by the ambient sounds of the den. Kael appeared to be contemplating something deeply. And then, Kael broke into a sudden grin, the jovial demeanor returning.

"Desperation can be a powerful motivator. Fine, I'll help you, but not for free."

Lumo raised an eyebrow. "What's the price?"

Kael gestured to a nearby table. "Let's settle this the way we do things here: a game of chance."

"Win, and I'll give you the information you seek. Lose, and you'll work for me until your debt is paid off. A fair deal, wouldn't you say?"

Lumo's eyes narrowed, his jaw tightening as he processed Kael's proposition. The implications of losing and potentially becoming indebted to Kael were not lost on him.

"Work for you until our debt is paid off?" Lumo repeated, a hint of skepticism in his voice. "What guarantee do we have that you'll hold up your end of the bargain?"

Kael leaned back, swirling the cigar in his fingers, a sly grin playing on his lips. "My word is my bond, boy. Besides, in my line of work, reputation is everything. I don't break deals."

Lumo was uneasy about the proposition, but this was their only lead.

"Deal. We'll play your game. If we win, we get the information right away."

Meera turned to Lumo with a look of disbelief. He had not even considered her opinion on the matter.

Kael's grin widened. "Agreed."

With a wave of Kael's hand, the room sprang to life. Slaves scurried to rearrange tables and chairs, creating a makeshift gambling arena amidst the haze of smoke and swirling lamplights. The denizens gathered around, their faces hidden in the shadows, eager to witness the unfolding game of chance.

Lumo and Kael took their seats. A dealer, wearing a weathered expression and skilled hands, shuffled the deck of cards with rhythmic precision. The den fell silent as Kael explained the rules of the game.

"It's quite a simple game. For lack of better imagination, we call it 'Guess'," Kael began.

A man carrying a stack of wooden chips approached the table, placing them in front of Lumo and Kael.

Lumo counted his stack. "Twenty-six chips."

"We start the round with a one-chip bet each. You have to guess the card drawn by the dealer, suit and rank. Whoever guesses it correctly wins the pot; otherwise, the closest match wins, suit over rank. You following me?"

"Err, yes. Go on," Lumo replied.

"If no one guesses the card exactly but someone wins, they only get back the chips they bet at the start of the round, and the pot carries over."

Kael looked Lumo in the eye to make sure he followed.

"The drawn cards will be revealed and then discarded. We raise the initial bet after a while. Any questions?"

"Um, no." Lumo shook his head slightly. "Seems to be a game of chance."

"Sure," Kael grinned.

The man who had carried the chips earlier returned, carrying an orb-shaped device and placing it in the center of the table.

"What's that?" Lumo asked.

"Just some fancy lighting." Kael chuckled. "All right, let's start then, shall we? Everyone, please give a round of applause to our player."

The room erupted into claps, even as Meera and Gus watched nervously.

"You go first," Kael directed.

"All right, I pick the King of Hearts," Lumo said.

"Ace of Spades," Kael chose.

The dealer shuffled the cards promptly and placed the deck on the table. Before the dealer could pick the card, the orb in the center of the table pulsed green.

Lumo spotted a satisfactory grin on Kael's face.

The dealer then picked the card on the top and turned it over. It was the Ten of Hearts.

"Suit wins, challenger may withdraw his token," the dealer announced.

As Lumo grabbed his stray chip, Kael's chip was pushed into the pot. Meera and Gus cheered as Lumo won his first round. Kael, however, appeared visibly conflicted.

"Shuffle it properly," he directed. "Let's go, next round."

"Queen of Diamonds." Kael picked first this time.

"Um, Queen of Clubs."

The gem pulsed again and the dealer picked a Two of Clubs.

"Suit wins, challenger may withdraw his token," the dealer announced again.

"I think he understands the game; just be quiet," Kael fumed.

The dealer zipped his lips.

As the second round ended, Lumo still had his starting stack intact, while Kael had twenty-four chips left and the pot stood at two chips.

The game continued for a while, with Lumo winning most of the games. Kael was visibly frustrated. Moose hurriedly came over to Lumo's side, and Kael stopped him with a gesture of his hand.

"It seems that luck favors our friend."

"Thanks." Lumo's response was steady.

Meera and Gus had been cheering the entire time.

Fifteen rounds had passed and Lumo had won twelve of them, whereas Kael won only three. The pot stood at fifteen chips. All the discarded cards were placed in another pile. Kael's gaze wandered to the discarded cards, his mind silently calculating something.

"Let's up the ante, shall we? Three chips sound all right?"

With Lumo now taking the leading chip position at twenty-three chips and Kael at only fourteen chips, he didn't seem to mind. Kael, however, knew something that Lumo didn't. The game simply wasn't a game of chance. Kael had been counting the discarded cards. Amidst the discarded cards, there was only a single card of the spades suit, and Lumo had no clue. Kael had calculated in his mind that the odds of a spade turning up would be higher.

As Lumo pushed in his three chips, Kael picked first.

"Five of Spades."

"Let's go with the Jack of Hearts," Lumo picked.

As the dealer turned over the next card, it was the Four of Spades.

"Ah, just missed it," Kael remarked. But he smiled proudly, having bested Lumo this round. "Well, next round then."

Lumo picked the Ten of Clubs and Kael picked yet another spade, the Queen.

The dealer revealed the next card as the Five of Spades.

"If only I had stuck to my pick from the last round," Kael laughed.

Lumo was a bit disappointed having lost two games in a row. With a total of six chips lost in the two rounds, Kael had managed to close the divide between their chip counts. He couldn't be happier.

Meera leaned in closer to Lumo.

"Lumo, I think he's counting the cards."

"Wait, what?"

"There must be more spades in the draw stack," Meera shared.

"Sharp," Kael muttered. "But the advantage is gone now. It's anyone's game really."

Lumo now had seventeen chips remaining and Kael had fourteen.

"I'll let you pick first," Kael said as the next round began.

"Lumo, pick a spade," Meera said.

"Um, he said it's even now. I think I will pick the King of Hearts," Lumo decided.

"The Ace of Spades," Kael chose with a wicked grin.

The dealer drew a King of Spades.

Kael laughed again. "Sorry, I bluffed earlier. But I promise there's no advantage now."

Lumo looked onward in shock. If only he had listened to Meera and picked a spade.

Kael, having won the game, had managed to tie the chip count. Both Lumo and Kael had fourteen chips each, and the pot stood at a grand twenty-four chips.

"You're a good kid," Kael remarked. "But it's probably best you never gamble again. It's not for you."

"Let's just get on with it," Lumo replied, a bit frustrated at the consecutive losses.

"I have a proposition," Kael began. "We're both at the same chip count. Let's go all in and no smaller wins anymore. We keep going till one of us guesses exactly and the winner takes it all. What do you say?"

"Don't do it, Lumo," Meera mouthed. "He's got some trick up his sleeve."

Lumo rubbed the back of his neck, the exhaustion sinking into his bones. "Let's just finish this," he muttered. "King of Hearts."

"Ace of Spades." Kael grinned.

Darn it, another spade? Meera thought. If Kael had indeed bluffed again and if the exact card did show up by chance, all would be lost, and they would have to work for Kael for who knows how long. *How could Lumo be so careless?*

As the dealer sought to turn the card, all eyes in the room shifted simultaneously. The orb in the center pulsed green and faded.

A loud cheer erupted in the room as the dealer turned over the card. Lumo stared in disbelief as the realization hit him. He had picked the exact card: The King of Hearts. The room buzzed with excitement as patrons discussed among themselves, and Meera and Gus were ecstatic.

"Guessed," said the dealer, half-eyeing Kael's reaction nervously.

Amidst the buzz in the room, Kael's face, however, was calm and composed.

"It seems that luck indeed favors you; well done." Kael's lips twitched, a grudging respect in his tone.

A mixture of relief and triumph swept over Lumo, Meera, and Gus. Meera couldn't contain her excitement, and she jumped up with a triumphant cheer.

"We did it! We actually did it!" she exclaimed, a wide grin on her face.

"Now, you hold up your end of the deal," Lumo demanded, standing up.

"Fine, I'm a man of my word, but not here. Follow me," Kael said as he led Lumo and Meera to another chamber.

The room was dimly lit, with worn tapestries along the walls. In the center of the room, there was a large, low, wooden table surrounded by a large single sofa and two smaller, yet equally comfortable, sofas. The worn rug beneath the table, though faded, added a touch of warmth to the room. Kael gestured for Lumo and Meera to take a seat, settling himself onto the larger sofa. Lumo and Meera occupied the smaller sofas on either side of Kael.

"That man you seek, tell me, does he have a large singular scar on his face?" Kael spoke in a deep voice.

"That's him! You know him, then," Lumo exclaimed.

Kael nodded. The expression on his face showed a mix of fear and disgust.

"Malikoth," he began. "Malikoth the unbearable, they call him. He's the one you seek."

"Where do we find him?"

"You don't. I don't have all the answers, you know."

"But you know about him. Is there anything else you can tell us? Please," Lumo pleaded.

Kael looked at Lumo with a thoughtful expression.

"He is—was my son."

Lumo and Meera's eyes widened at the revelation. A distant gaze overtook Kael as he delved into memories of a forgotten time.

"My boy," he continued, his voice trembling with the weight of the past. "His name was Elion; named after the god of light."

Lumo and Meera exchanged glances, absorbing the tragedy woven into Kael's words.

"He was a child of joy, with eyes that sparkled like the morning sun..." Kael continued, his voice now a mere whisper, a lament for a time irreversibly lost.

"What happened?" Lumo muttered in a low tone.

"They took him, these cultists. Twisted his very essence, turned the laughter into anguished echoes," Kael revealed, his hands clenching into fists as if grappling with an invisible force.

"You know what it's like to be a pawn in chess? Sacrificed to the whims of the court?"

"My Elion, once so full of life, now a puppet dancing to their sinister tune," Kael muttered, his gaze fixed on a point beyond the chamber walls.

Lumo and Meera shared a moment of sadness, their eyes reflecting empathy as Kael revealed the painful truth about his lost son.

"You see why I ask you to stay away from them?" Kael continued. "I warn you. If there's darkness in your heart, these people will find a way to use it."

A wave of fear swept over Lumo as he spoke. "They've gotten Oliver. Please, we need to find them."

"I know of the prince..." Kael responded. "But you are far too young to do anything about it."

"Please..." Lumo urged. "If there's a chance we can save Oliver, don't you owe it to your son?"

Kael fell silent as his gaze wavered between Lumo and Meera. With a heavy sigh, he broke his silence.

"The shrine in Serendia. They worship their god there. Do you know the place?" Kael grunted.

Lumo shook his head.

"West of here, near the Veridian border. Should be a day's ride. I can't promise they'll be there, but that's where you start."

Lumo spoke with a newfound determination, "We'll find these cultists. We owe it to him and to you, Kael. No one else should suffer at the hands of these cultists."

"We'll leave at dawn. Every moment counts," Meera added.

Kael, though stoic, showed a hint of gratitude in his eyes. "I can't guarantee your safety, but if there's a chance to save another soul from their clutches, I won't stand in your way. Moose will accompany you. He knows the lay of the land."

"Thank you, Kael," Lumo extended a grateful nod.

"Before you go, may I ask how the three of you will be traveling?"

"Um, we will probably borrow some horses from our friend."

"What about the big guy? He'll need a sturdy horse."

They hadn't considered it. Given how Gus struggled to get on and off the caravan, they realized that Kael was right—a normal horse might not accommodate Gus's large size.

"I'll have Moose bring over one of the draft horses, the kind some knights ride with their heavy armor."

"Thank you," Lumo said. "You've been a great help."

As they prepared to leave, Kael's voice echoed in the dimly lit chamber. "Just remember, the path you tread is perilous. Darkness will test your mettle."

Lumo, Meera, and Gus left the den, making their way to the Thistle & Thorn one final time.

***

CHAPTER 11

Serena strode through the grand entrance of the castle, her new staff emanating a subtle glow. Spotting a guard nearby, she inquired, “Where can I find Archibald?”

The guard nodded and pointed toward the direction of the king's chambers. Serena made her way through the familiar corridors. Upon reaching the king's chambers, she found Archibald overseeing the attendants attending to the monarch. Archibald turned as he noticed her arrival.

“How is His Majesty?” Serena inquired.

“Serena, good, you’re back. We're doing what we can, but the poison's grip is persistent,” Archibald informed her.

“I'll see what I can do. Stand back, please,” she informed the attendants.

Serena approached the king's bedside. Archibald stepped aside, gesturing for the attendants to give her space. The subtle glow from her staff intensified as she weaved intricate gestures in the air.

In shadows deep, where poisons creep,
By mystic waters, their grasp we'll keep.
Serpent's breath, now slow your pace,
Grant this soul a guarded space.

Serena murmured the incantation, her voice steady amid the tense silence. With a sweep of her hands, wisps of magic flowed from her staff, coiling in the air. In one decisive motion, she directed the energy toward the king. A blue barrier took shape around him, its light pulsing in steady waves. Serena's forehead glistened with sweat.

Archibald observed with a furrowed brow, his gaze shifting between Serena and the king. The room fell into an anticipatory hush, broken only by the subtle crackling of magical energy. Moments later, the pulsating barrier dissipated like morning mist under the sun's rays.

"Did it work?" Archibald questioned.

Serena nodded calmly, "It will arrest the spread, but it's no cure."

Archibald's gaze lingered on the king before drifting to Serena.

"Thank you, Serena. Your talents are invaluable in these trying times. Now, about that ally you mentioned..."

Serena gestured toward the doorway. "Let's step outside; we can discuss it there."

Exiting the king's chambers, Serena turned to address Archibald. "The ally I mentioned is probably in Veridia, and I will need to travel there. My return may not be as swift this time."

"Probably? You mean you are not certain?"

Serena shook her head. "It's a calculated guess."

"Tell me, who is this ally you speak of?"

"You know him, Archibald—Sylvanus," Serena replied.

"The former royal sorcerer?" Archibald's eyes lit up.

Serena confirmed with a nod.

"But he's been gone for over a decade," Archibald spoke.

"He can help. He knows more about dark magic than anyone I know."

A crease formed on Archibald's forehead as he contemplated Serena's words. "You think he is in Veridia? Perhaps I could ask someone from Veridia to assist."

"No, I assure you, he won't be easy to find. But I know I can find him; you have to trust me."

"All right," Archibald conceded. "But Veridia is quite a journey. Perhaps it's best to discuss this with Lucius first."

"Where is Lucius?" Serena asked, her voice determined.

"The armory. I think he was preparing for an expedition himself. He was eagerly awaiting your return."

"I will speak with him, then," Serena said.

Serena made her way through the corridors of the castle until she reached the armory, Archibald following closely behind. The clanging of metal and the scent of freshly forged weapons filled the air.

As she entered, she spotted Lucius deep in conversation with Marcus, both surrounded by a flurry of activity as armorers and guards prepared for their impending expedition.

Lucius turned at the sound of Serena's footsteps, a genuine smile gracing his face. "Serena! You're back. I see you have your staff, good."

"We have matters to discuss, Lucius."

"Of course. Marcus, give us a moment," Lucius instructed, and Marcus promptly excused himself from their conversation.

Noting that Marcus was out of earshot, Serena began. "You're going somewhere…"

"Yes, I've been awaiting your arrival. It seems my men have gathered intel of disturbances in a village near the Veridian border."

"News of the assailants?"

"Not sure, but it could be connected." Lucius straightened himself. "No time to waste. I must go there immediately. With you here, now I can be at ease."

"About that..." Serena hesitated, her hand reaching up to tuck a strand of hair behind her ear.

Lucius raised an eyebrow as Serena continued. "I must depart for Veridia. I may not return for a while."

"What? But we need you here," Lucius scoffed.

"She's looking for Sylvanus, Lucius," Archibald stepped forward.

"Oh." Lucius blinked.

"I think he is in Veridia. I must find him if there's any hope of recovering the king's condition, Lucius," Serena said.

"This is... most untimely," Lucius said, concerned.

"You mentioned the village is near the border. Perhaps we can travel there together, and once we are done there, I can continue forward to Veridia," Serena said.

Lucius reluctantly agreed, shooting a glance at Archibald. "It seems we have no choice."

"It'll be all right, Lucius. Is Marcus going with you?" Archibald checked.

"That was the plan, yes."

A weighty hush settled between them.

"No matter. Marcus will remain here," Lucius said, some hesitation still lingering in his voice.

"I'll wait for you at the gate," Serena said.

Serena waited at the castle gate, her staff in hand, as the distant sounds of approaching footsteps and clinking armor grew louder.

Soon, Lucius and Marcus, accompanied by a regiment of guards, emerged into view. As they approached the castle gates, Serena's keen eyes quickly caught sight of Lucius's formidable battle armor. The armor, starkly different from the one he usually wore, signaled battle readiness. A crimson cloak billowed behind him as he walked.

"Mithril?" Serena inquired; her gaze focused on the gleaming armor.

"You've seen their power the other day. I'm not taking chances."

Serena nodded reassuringly.

With a final nod, Lucius signaled for the gates to open. The rhythmic hoofbeats of the horses echoed through the castle courtyard as Serena, Lucius, and the guards set out on their journey. Marcus watched as they disappeared, eventually signaling the guards to draw the castle gates.

***

"Here, I've packed enough food for your journey," Lily said, handing a large sack to Gus.

"Thank you, Lily." Gus smiled.

Bart, standing nearby, glanced at Lumo and Meera. "Do ya got everything ya need, kids?"

"We'll be okay. Thanks, Bart," Meera replied, adjusting the straps on her bag.

"And take care of me horses," Bart added.

"Of course," Meera said.

"Ya mentioned someone's bringing a horse, fer Gus?"

"Yeah, Moose. He should be here soon."

As Meera's words left her lips, the group turned their attention to the approaching sound of hooves, and soon Moose appeared on horseback, leading a larger horse by the reins.

"You!" Bart exclaimed as he set his eyes on Moose, recounting his earlier encounter.

"It's okay, Bart. He's Kael's accomplice. He's going to be accompanying us to Serendia," Meera said.

"Meera, that guy—"

"Yeah, we know," Meera cut him off. "Gus told us everything, but it's all okay now. Look, they're friends now," she said, pointing at Gus and Moose.

Moose had Gus in a playful headlock, his knuckles digging into Gus's scalp as he ruffled his hair with exaggerated enthusiasm. It was the kind of roughhousing friends who had known each other for a long time might engage in. The conversation shifted to an animated discussion about the horse—a large shire, which suited Gus perfectly. Despite Lily's evident irritation with Moose, Gus was busy playing the role of mediator, introducing Moose to her in a new light.

"Blimey," Bart shook his head.

Lumo approached Bart one last time, and before Bart could say anything, Lumo hugged him tightly. Bart, momentarily taken aback, quickly reciprocated.

"Thank you for everything, Bart. I don't know how to thank you and Lily," Lumo said.

"No thanks needed, lad. And please, this isn't er last meeting. Yer welcome here anytime," Bart said with a warm smile.

Lumo nodded, genuine warmth in his eyes.

Bart clapped a hand on Lumo's shoulder. "You take care, now. And watch out for each other."

As Gus climbed onto his horse with Moose's help, Meera, already mounted, chimed in, "Lumo, we should leave now."

"Right, let's go," Lumo said, tearing himself away from the moment.

Bart and Lily stood side by side, watching as the group departed on their horses.

As the riders disappeared into the distance, Bart turned to Lily with a silly grin on his face. "Well, back to our thrilling, action-packed routine of pouring drinks and washing mugs."

Lily chuckled, swatting him playfully.

Bart put an arm around Lily's shoulders as they turned to head back inside.

***

The group rode for hours, the landscape gradually shifting around them. The once familiar fields and meadows gave way to dense forests. As they continued, the forest gradually opened up to reveal a vast plain stretching to the horizon. Tall grasses swayed with the gentle breeze, and wildflowers painted the landscape with bursts of color.

Gus, usually towering over others with his exceptional height, maintained his unique perspective even on horseback, as his steed outmatched the others in size. Lumo and Moose rode at the forefront, with Meera trailing right behind, and Gus following after Meera. After a few more hours of riding at a fast pace, the group gradually eased into a more leisurely speed to allow the horses some much-needed relief.

Lumo, riding alongside Moose, broke the comfortable silence. "Have you been with Kael for a long time?"

"Been a few years now," Moose replied, turning his head. "Kael appears tough, but he's a lot softer than he looks. That's where I come in."

Lumo offered a brief smile. "Yeah, too bad about his son," he commented.

"He told you about his son? Huh, he never speaks about it to anyone... well, I guess it figures."

"What do you mean?"

Moose observed Lumo and the group, choosing his words carefully. "I mean you guys are special after all."

"How so?"

"I mean, you and Gus are magic users. Don't know about the girl," Moose said, nodding toward Meera. "It's not often that a party of magic users comes to see Kael; usually, it's degenerate gamblers."

Lumo chuckled, "I'm no magic user. I wish I were."

"You playing dumb or something?" Moose quizzed.

Lumo tried to read Moose's expression. He realized that Moose was either dead serious or largely disillusioned.

"No, really. I'm just a regular guy."

"Hah! Okay, play it that way if you want."

"I'm not playing at anything. Why do you think I've got any magic in me?" Lumo countered, puzzled by Moose's insistence.

Moose struggled to reply, and the words evaporated in the air, leaving a brief moment of silence.

"Because I saw it. We all did," Moose finally replied.

Lumo tugged at the reins of his horse, slowing down. He trailed behind briefly, then picked up the pace again, rejoining Moose.

"I have no idea what you are saying. Tell me, how exactly did you see me use magic when I'm telling you I've never used it before in my life?"

Moose took a moment again to reply. "I'm sure you noticed the glowing green gem on the table when you played with Kael."

"Yeah?" Lumo raised an eyebrow.

"What do you think it does?"

"Oh, I get it now," Lumo laughed, connecting the dots. "You think I have magic because the gem was glowing. It was obviously glowing because of Gus or someone else. I have to say, it's ingenious of Kael to have an artifact like that; after all, you don't want people to win by using magic."

"Then why didn't he stop you?" Moose asked. "And no, you're wrong; it's not a magic-sensing gem."

"Huh?"

"It's not a magic-sensing gem. It's much more than that," Moose continued. "Tell me, do you think a guy like Kael is where he is now simply by chance? Kael rarely leaves things to chance."

Lumo, clearly lost for words, waited for Moose to continue, feeling a growing sense of unease.

"The gem channels a user's magic and converts it to luck. Kael, being magically gifted himself, usually always wins... unless someone with greater magic is playing against him..." Moose clarified. "Like you."

"To be honest, I'm surprised he let the game continue."

Lumo's eyes widened as Moose revealed the information. His heart raced with disbelief. This was a revelation beyond his wildest imagination.

Thoughts raced through Lumo's mind, a whirlwind of confusion and realization. *Magic? Me? How is that even possible?* The words lingered, echoing in his thoughts, challenging the very foundation of his understanding of himself. *Was Moose messing with him? That had to be it.*

A moment of tense silence hung between them, broken by Moose's voice that brought Lumo back to the present situation.

"The bridge up ahead, need to be careful. Too rickety."

As they approached a small bridge in their path, their horses drew to a halt, and Lumo noticed the swelling current underneath. The bridge, a precarious assembly of worn wooden planks and frayed ropes, remained suspended over a tumultuous river.

"We should cross this one at a time," Moose instructed.

Getting off his horse, Lumo was the first to cross. Each step he took caused the timeworn structure to creak and sway slightly. Lumo, undeterred by the creaking planks, cautiously advanced across the bridge to the other side. Meera followed suit, leading her horse by the reins. When Moose stepped on the bridge, it protested more vehemently. As he took deliberate steps, the wooden slats grumbled and groaned like a cantankerous old man complaining about the weather. Eventually, Moose made it across, the bridge bearing the load. Finally, it was Gus's time to cross the bridge.

"Be careful, Gus!" Lumo shouted from the other end.

"Go slow!" Moose added with a shout.

As Gus placed his feet on the bridge, the creaking sound escalated, as if the old man was now in a heated argument with a stubborn door, each plank wheezing and moaning under his weight. Each step seemed to intensify the strain. The group collectively held their breath, watching as Gus navigated the unstable pathway.

Gus moved as slowly as possible, and for a moment, it seemed he would make it across. But just as Gus was nearing the end, a deafening crack echoed through the air. In a heartbeat, the timeworn structure beneath him collapsed.

SPLASH!

Gus's horse was the first to fall in.

Moose, quick on his feet, rushed forward, managing to catch hold of Gus momentarily.

"Uh, help..." Gus screamed.

The scene hung in suspended chaos as Moose strained to keep Gus from plummeting into the raging river below. Time seemed to tick faster, and with each tick, Moose's grip slipped, till he could no longer hold Gus. Gus too fell with a large splash into the river below, and Lumo and the others watched helplessly as Gus, along with his horse, were swept away by the unforgiving current.

The water, churning with rapids, carried them swiftly downstream. Gus struggled to keep himself afloat amidst the relentless force of the river.

“Hurry, this way,” Moose instructed.

Lumo and Meera followed Moose swiftly on foot. They noticed Gus’s head pop out of the water and quickly dip back in with a back-and-forth. Gus’s horse was nowhere to be seen.

Lumo's heart pounded as he watched the chaotic scene unfold. For a brief second, it reminded him of the time Oliver had fallen into the moat, except it was much more serious this time. They ran along the riverbank, desperately trying to keep pace with Gus's rapid descent.

“There’s a fall at the end. We need to be quick,” Moose said.

Lumo’s and Meera’s gazes shifted to the far edge of the river where it seemed to disappear. They caught a tiny glimpse of Gus’s horse, frightened and disoriented, desperately attempting to swim against the current, and then in an instant, it disappeared from sight.

Lumo’s gaze shifted back to the struggling Gus, who managed to grab hold of a rock before slipping back down. The river's wrath seemed indiscriminate. As the group ran along the riverbank, they were able to inch ahead of Gus, and they soon reached a point where Moose signaled a halt. The river's roar grew louder as they positioned themselves near the edge.

“Girl, cast your rope there,” Moose instructed.

Meera waited for the opportune moment for Gus to arrive at the point. She would have only one shot.

"Grab the rope, Gus," Meera shouted as she unfurled the rope hanging on her waist and cast it in one quick motion toward Gus, who managed to grab hold of it amidst the churning rapids.

Lumo and Moose rushed to anchor themselves, gripping the rope alongside Meera. The force of the river tugged relentlessly at Gus, and for a moment, it seemed they might succeed in pulling him to safety.

"Pull, everyone! Pull!" Lumo strained, muscles tense as they fought against the unyielding current.

Gus's desperate pleas echoed as the group struggled, inch by inch, to counter the river's force. The tension mounted, but just as hope kindled, the water intensified, dragging Gus dangerously close to the waterfall's edge.

"Come on, Gus! Hold tight!" Meera encouraged, her voice barely audible over the roaring water.

The rope strained under the immense pressure, each member of the group giving their all. But nature's force proved overwhelming. With a sudden, violent jerk, Gus went over the edge, the group yanked forcefully toward the precipice.

Lumo and Moose strained against the force, feet slipping on the wet ground. Lumo's grip on the rope tightened, but the combined might of water's power and gravity seemed insurmountable.

"Keep pulling!" Lumo shouted.

The group teetered on the edge, their collective strength barely holding them back. They strained against the edge, managing to pull Gus up a bit further only to have the ground betray their efforts, sending Gus sliding back toward the brink. In a cruel back-and-forth, nature played with Gus's fate.

And then, SNAP! The rope, strained to its limit, snapped with a resounding crack.

The force yanked the group backward, and they landed on the wet ground, mud clinging to their clothes. For a moment, they lay there, catching their breath, the sound of the rushing river a constant reminder of what they had just faced.

Lumo scrambled to his feet and rushed back to the edge. His heart was pounding. The frothy waterfall cascaded down the steep drop, and he strained his eyes, desperately searching for any sign of Gus. Panic and fear gripped him as he couldn't see Gus amidst the frothy mist created by the waterfall. Meera and Moose joined Lumo, their eyes scanning the pond at the base of the fall.

Just when all hope was lost, Moose shouted, “Look there!”

Lumo's gaze followed Moose's pointing finger, and amidst the chaos, he spotted Gus floating on a watery bubble at the far edge of the pond.

“How?” Meera gasped.

As Meera struggled with the thought, Lumo’s eyes widened with realization.

“It can’t be...” Lumo laughed. “I'll be damned if Gus didn't conjure up a water bubble from the water he drank. That guy never ceases to amaze me.”

“Damn,” was all Meera could muster.

The group, still processing the unexpected turn of events, watched as Gus remained buoyant on his improvised water bubble. It was a moment of awe, the realization that, against all odds, Gus had found a way to defy the river's wrath.

Relief flooded over them as they watched Gus slowly make his way to the edge of the pond.

“We have to get down there, now,” Lumo demanded.

"It's suicide if we try to get down from here," Moose cautioned. "We have to follow the path. It will lead us there."

"Gus, stay put. We are coming!" Lumo shouted at the top of his lungs, but his voice struggled to compete with the thunderous roar of the waterfall.

"Let's go, it's getting late. This way," Moose directed.

Mounted on their horses, the trio advanced. An hour passed, frustration growing in Lumo's voice.

"How much longer, Moose?"

"We're halfway there," Moose replied.

Another hour brought them to lower ground.

"Here, this way. We need to trail off this path and head into the forest. I hope Gus hasn't wandered off," Moose said, pointing to the looming trees.

As the three of them stepped into the forest, tall, venerable trees created a natural roof above them. Narrow paths woven by woodland creatures crisscrossed the forest floor, leading the group deeper into the heart of nature's sanctuary. Night fell and the owls hooted in the distance.

The trio moved in silence, only the gentle sway of branches and the horses' hooves on twigs disrupted the quiet. The murmur of falling water reached their ears, promising the pond's proximity. Emerging from the trees, the pond revealed itself. Gus was nowhere to be seen.

"Gus!" Moose shouted. "You here?"

Lumo and Meera joined the calls.

"He's not here," Moose concluded after a brief search.

"Where could he have gone?" Lumo asked, clearly worried.

"My guess is as good as yours, kid," Moose replied. "We should camp here for the night."

"But... Gus is out in the woods. We have to keep looking."

"It's late, kid. The forest is home to dangerous beasts. We can't keep creating a ruckus."

"Gus may be in danger, then," Lumo fretted.

"Look, if there's anything we've seen so far, it's that Gus is resourceful enough to handle himself. Besides, it's possible he might circle back to this point."

"Moose is right, Lumo," Meera chimed in. "Our horses need to rest too. We can start looking for him at the crack of dawn."

Lumo reluctantly conceded as the other two members began setting up camp. He stared into the forest one last time, hopeful that Gus might turn up, then rejoined the group.

Lumo and Meera found themselves sitting at the bank of the pond. Moose emerged from the trees, a bundle of twigs and kindling in his arms. He arranged the wood in a small pit and struck a few dry rocks together, igniting the dry tinder. A gentle flame blossomed, casting a warm glow over the trio and dispelling the chill of the night.

Lumo and Meera watched in silence as Moose tended to the fire, his movements deliberate and methodical. There was a sense of reassurance in the flickering flames, a reminder that even in the darkest of times, there was light to be found.

Lumo gazed into the flames, his mind swirling with worry for Gus. "Do you think he's all right out there?" he asked, his voice tinged with concern.

"Gus is resilient. I think the wild must worry about him more than he needs to worry about the wild," Meera jested.

"Yes, you're right," Lumo agreed, a slight chuckle escaping his lips. "I just hope he doesn't stray too far away."

Lumo watched the flames dance, lost in thought, before turning his attention back to the present.

"Oh! I completely forgot about what Moose was saying earlier."

Lumo turned to address Moose, only to find him already fast asleep, his head resting against a makeshift pillow of bundled clothing. Lumo blinked in surprise, a bemused smile tugging at the corners of his lips.

"Wow, he must have been really tired."

Meera stifled a giggle, "Seems like it. Such a sleeping beauty! Maybe you should kiss him, Lumo."

Lumo chuckled softly. "No, I'm good."

"So, are you going to tell me what he was saying, then?"

"Yes, he was... um, saying something about how that gem sensed magic in me," Lumo said.

Meera stared at him blankly. Lumo quickly filled her in on the earlier conversation with Moose.

"...To be honest, I have my doubts that gems like those even exist. I mean, I know some gems are used to channel magic, but for a gem to have a specific purpose; I have never heard of it before," Lumo concluded.

Meera, who had been listening intently to Lumo's words, paused for a moment, her gaze shifting to the burning flames.

"You know, Lumo. I haven't been completely honest with you," Meera finally spoke.

Lumo's eyes darted to Meera's face, trying to read her expression.

"Do you remember that night in the dungeon when I held your hand?"

"Yeah?"

"Well, for one thing, your hands aren't that soft," Meera smirked.

"Huh?"

"That night when I held your hand, I was trying to read your memories, with this," Meera said, pointing to a small gem on her ring. "It's a memory stone, quite rare. It allows me to see a glimpse of the other person's memory. Don't ask me how I got it..."

Lumo's eyes went round with the whites showing.

"Memory stone? Wait, you can use magic?"

"Um, I have the essence, but I haven't studied the art. Too much effort," Meera said. "Besides, who's going to teach a thief new tricks?"

"Oh, I see."

"I don't use it often, you know. It can be quite unsettling to see someone's memories, but you were going on about your parents and I had to see." Meera rolled her eyes.

"Meera, can you cut to the chase, please." Lumo's patience waned. "What did you see? Do you know where my parents are?"

"That's the thing. I couldn't see anything. I could see everything you told me already, but nothing of before. It's quite strange."

Lumo's eyes widened in astonishment, his breath catching in his throat as he struggled to comprehend the implications of what Meera had just disclosed.

"So, you mean to tell me that you couldn't see anything about my past? Not even a glimpse?"

Meera nodded solemnly. "That's right. It's like your past is shrouded in some sort of... I don't know, protective barrier. It's difficult to explain."

Lumo ran a hand through his hair, his mind racing with possibilities.

"The truth is, I don't know if you have any magic in you, Lumo. But clearly, something about you isn't normal... and that's part of the reason I stuck with you," Meera said with a serious expression.

Lumo fell silent, his gaze returning to the flames. Thoughts churned in his mind, questions without answers swirling around like leaves caught in a whirlwind. Lumo's heart raced in his chest, each beat echoing the urgency of his desire for answers about his past.

"I don't know what to make of all this," Lumo admitted finally, his voice barely above a whisper.

Meera reached out, placing a reassuring hand on Lumo's shoulder. "We'll figure it out. Together. But for now, we should sleep."

As Meera positioned herself to sleep, she had one final thing to say. "Gems like those do exist. That's one thing you can cross off your list."

Lumo sat by the fire, his mind still reeling from Meera's revelation. The crackling flames provided a comforting backdrop to his racing thoughts, their dance casting fleeting shadows across his troubled face. He tried to make sense of it all, but the puzzle pieces refused to fit together neatly.

As exhaustion tugged at his eyelids, Lumo reluctantly conceded to the weariness that weighed heavily upon him. He lay down beside the fire, his body sinking into the soft earth beneath him. The rhythmic crackle of the flames and the gentle bubbling of the water soothed his troubled mind.

In the quiet embrace of the night, Lumo's thoughts drifted to Gus, lost somewhere in the depths of the forest, much like Lumo himself felt lost in the labyrinth of his own thoughts.

***

CHAPTER 12

Dawn had arrived, and Lumo, exhausted from the previous day, had finally fallen into slumber after a restless spell.

"Gus!" Lumo shouted as he jolted awake. That was the last thing on his mind before he slept.

"Oh, good. You're up," Meera said, glancing at him. "It's dawn; we need to move."

Moose was already up and preparing the horses for the day.

Lumo rubbed his eyes and shook off the grogginess. "What's the plan, Moose?"

Checking the supplies, Moose responded, "I've been looking at the tracks around here. Seems Gus is headed in that direction." He pointed toward a path leading into the dense forest.

"How can you tell it's Gus?"

Moose crouched down, studying the imprints in the dirt. "Gus has a weir... err distinct way of walking. Plus, his boots are larger than ours. Look here, these imprints are broader and larger than a normal boot print."

Meera chimed in, "Impressive, Moose. How far do you think he might have gone?"

Moose straightened up. "Hard to say exactly, but he can't be too far. We need to catch up."

"And the shrine in Serendia, how far from here?" Lumo asked as he mounted his horse.

"Not too far. We'll pass through a village before reaching the shrine. It's on the way. If Gus moved this way, we might find him there," Moose replied, adjusting the reins.

Tightening the straps on her horse, Meera added, "Let's hope he's taken shelter there."

As the trio mounted their horses, they followed Moose into the depths of the forest. The path was narrow, with sunlight struggling to filter through the thick foliage overhead. Moose continued to scrutinize the ground, occasionally stopping to examine marks left on the soft earth.

"He seems to be on the right path. The imprints are fresh, not too much foliage disturbance. We're getting closer."

They rode through the forest in a somber procession, the only sounds being the hoofbeats of their horses and the occasional birdsong. After what felt like an hour, they emerged from the shadowy woods into the welcoming warmth of daylight. They finally arrived at what appeared to be a dirt road.

"Looks like Gus kept a straight course. Good thing too, else we might have lost him in these woods," Moose said, guiding his horse.

The trio rode along the path, following the trail that Moose diligently traced. As they approached, the distant signs of a village became more pronounced, but an eerie hollowness lingered in the air. The village stood in eerie silence, its cottages like empty husks lining the desolate paths.

As they entered the village, an unsettling atmosphere greeted them. The narrow, winding streets appeared deserted, devoid of the usual signs of life. The cottages stood with closed doors and shuttered windows. The bustling scenes of daily life ordinarily seen in other villages were replaced by an unsettling stillness—the market stalls stood abandoned, the blacksmith's hammers eerily silent, and the narrow streets echoed with an unnatural quiet. The village appeared frozen in time, as if it held its breath.

The group's further entrance into the village drew wary eyes. Villagers, armed with pitchforks and makeshift weapons, cautiously approached, their faces marked with fear.

"Hold on, we mean no harm. We're just passing through," Lumo called out, keeping his sword sheathed but raising his open palms in a gesture of non-aggression.

The villagers exchanged anxious glances. Just when the tension seemed unbearable, Gus's voice cut through the silence from the back of the group.

"Lumo, Meera!" he exclaimed. "Easy, everyone... These are my friends."

The village chieftain stood next to Gus—an elderly man with a hunchback. He signaled for the villagers to lower their arms, and the villagers cautiously complied.

"Gus! You're okay, thank goodness," Lumo said, spotting Gus.

They disembarked their horses and moved toward Gus.

"Yeah... I'm okay," Gus said with a sheepish smile.

Their gaze shifted toward the chieftain standing next to Gus. Beady eyes, sharp and calculating, peered out from beneath heavy brows. A long beard, streaked with threads of silver, cascaded down from his chin.

"Oh, this is Chief Vaida," Gus introduced. "Chief Vaida, these are my friends - Lumo, Meera, and Moose. I was with them before... I got lost."

“Welcome to our village, travelers,” the chief greeted, his voice gravelly yet warm. “I am Chief Vaida. It is a rare sight to see outsiders in these parts, especially during such troubled times.”

Lumo, Meera, and Moose exchanged hesitant glances. A look around the village signaled that all was not right. Something grave had befallen and perhaps their intrusion wasn’t welcome.

“We apologize for the intrusion, Chief Vaida,” Meera spoke up. “We were merely passing through when we stumbled upon your village. We mean no harm.”

Chief Vaida's gaze softened at Meera's words, a twinge of understanding crossing his weathered features.

“Please, come with me,” he urged, his voice tinged with urgency. “It is not safe to linger outside for long.”

He gestured for the group to follow him, his movements slow and deliberate as he led the way through the deserted streets of the village. Entering the house, the group settled around a table. Platters of stale baked bread, accompanied by bowls of vegetable stew, were placed on the table. Chief Vaida gestured for them to take a seat, his weathered hands pouring steaming mugs of herbal tea with practiced ease.

With a weary sigh, Chief Vaida lowered himself into a worn armchair, his gaze lingering on Gus with a mixture of fondness and sorrow.

“Your friend here, Gus,” he began. “Reminds me of my son, may he rest in peace. Such a thoughtful lad, always eager to help.”

Gus's cheeks flushed with a mixture of pride and sadness, his gaze momentarily clouded with emotion. Yet, as Chief Vaida spoke, his eyes couldn't help but dart toward the food that adorned the table.

"Tell me, travelers," he began, "Are you traveling to Veridia then?"

"No, we are... um, looking for a shrine around here. Do you know of it?" Lumo asked.

A shadow passed over Chief Vaida's weathered features; his eyes wide with a primal fear that refused to be concealed. His gaze darted nervously around the room, as if expecting some unseen horror to materialize from the very walls themselves.

"I'm afraid I know of the shrine you speak of," Chief Vaida admitted, his voice grave. "What business do you have there?"

Lumo hesitated, exchanging a cautious glance with his companions before answering Chief Vaida's question. He explained their mission to the chief as briefly as possible.

Chief Vaida's eyes widened further at Lumo's words, the fear in his expression deepening. "This is... you cannot possibly comprehend the danger you're walking into," he warned, his voice trembling with urgency. "That shrine is a place of unspeakable horrors; one we are too familiar with."

"What do you mean?" Meera asked.

Before Chief Vaida responded to Meera's inquiry, a sudden commotion erupted outside his house. The door burst open, and a distraught woman stumbled in, her eyes brimming with tears and her voice choked with anguish.

"Chief Vaida, please! When are they sending help?"

The woman's husband followed closely behind; his face flushed with worry as he tried in vain to soothe his distraught wife.

"Please, Beth, calm yourself. I'm sorry, Chief Vaida. Please excuse us," he said gently.

"But it's been two days already..." Beth cried.

Chief Vaida's expression softened with empathy as he approached the distressed couple. Placing a gentle hand on the woman's trembling shoulder, he spoke in a soothing tone, "I understand your fear and frustration, Beth. We are doing everything we can to bring your daughter back safely. Help is on its way."

The woman's husband gave an approving look. "Please, Beth, let us trust in the chief's wisdom," he implored, gently guiding her toward the door.

With a heavy heart, Chief Vaida accompanied the couple to the threshold of his home, offering words of reassurance and comfort along the way. As they stepped outside, the man cast a grateful glance back at the chief before gently pulling his wife away, their figures soon disappearing into the gloom of the village streets.

Chief Vaida closed the door behind them and turned back to face the group, his expression weighed down by the burden of their shared plight.

"That's twelve now..." he muttered under his breath.

Turning to the group, he spoke with a sense of grim resignation. "This is the reality we face, travelers. That shrine you seek; it's the cause of our misfortune."

"Please, you can trust us, Chief Vaida..." Lumo implored. "But you have to tell us everything."

Chief Vaida sighed, his gaze fixed on the floor. "It started several days ago. People started disappearing from our village without a trace—women, men, children... At first, we thought it was the work of bandits or wild beasts, but as more and more vanished, a pattern emerged."

Lumo and his companions listened intently as Chief Vaida continued. "The disappearances all led to the shrine you mentioned. We believe it to be the epicenter of these dark deeds."

"Haven't you approached this shrine yourselves?" Meera asked.

"We did, once. But we were met with horrors beyond imagining. Creatures of darkness guard that cursed place, and they do not take kindly to intruders. We've sent messages to the kingdom pleading for aid, but so far, none has come."

A heavy silence descended upon the room, suffocating in its intensity.

"The responsibilities of being a chief... You saw the woman? How could I tell her there is nothing we can do?"

Chief Vaida's hands clenched into trembling fists, his knuckles turning white with the strain of his frustration.

"Chief Vaida," Lumo spoke up. "What are these creatures you speak of?"

Chief Vaida stared deeply into Lumo's eyes as he said the words, "The Cwn Annwn."

"Koon Anoon?" Lumo repeated.

"Hounds of the dark..." Chief Vaida continued. "They roam the shadows. But it's not just their physical form that's horrifying. These hounds can sniff out the very essence of fear, and they hunt with relentless pursuit."

Lumo could fathom the fear in the chief's eyes.

"You heard them last night, didn't you?" Chief Vaida said, turning his attention to Gus.

The group collectively turned to Gus, who was busy stuffing his face with less-than-crusty bread.

"Mm—T—Those howls? But I thought they were dogs from—mm—within the village," Gus stammered, his words coming out slightly garbled as he gulped down the bread.

"You mean they roam the village streets at night too?" Meera asked.

"No. The Cwn Annwn aren't of this world. The closer their sound, the further they are."

Lumo's eyes widened with surprise.

"Encountering one of them was enough to make us retreat; nearly lost a good man too," Chief Vaida said, shaking off the memories of the encounter. "One can only imagine what other horror lurks within the shrine."

"So... these hounds are only seen at night, then?" Lumo reasoned.

"You don't understand. Whoever brought these hounds into our world is capable of doing much more. Honestly, I'm not even sure if the kingdom can deal with these people... That shrine has existed for centuries, but why now?" Chief Vaida appeared lost in thought.

"Chief, our resolve to go into the shrine is undeterred," Lumo declared with determination.

Chief Vaida's brows knit tightly. He shook his head slowly.

"Travelers, you do not understand the peril you face. Even the bravest among us have faltered in the shadow of that shrine. To willingly step into its darkness is to court death itself."

Lumo stood firm, his gaze steady. Meera, however, exchanged a nervous glance with Moose, while Gus fidgeted uncomfortably in his seat.

"Chief Vaida, could you point us—"

Before Lumo could complete his sentence, Meera interrupted, "Lumo, can I speak to you in private?"

Stepping to a corner, Meera voiced her concern, "Lumo, perhaps we should wait for reinforcements from the kingdom? Or at least..."

"Meera—If there's anything I've learned in the last few days, it's that I cannot trust anyone from the kingdom, especially not Lucius. If we wait for them, who knows what will happen to those people… and Oliver," Lumo interjected, his tone serious.

"But—"

"Look, if you think it's too dangerous, I will understand if you back out now… I'm thankful for your help, Meera, and I'll hold up my end of the deal," Lumo said, with some hesitation.

Just as Lumo turned to readdress the chief, Meera stopped him.

"Now, look here, you dolt. I know you think you are some sort of righteous hero, and granted, your intentions are noble, but that doesn't mean you shouldn't think things through."

Lumo blinked blankly, taken aback for a moment.

"I think at the very least we should gather more information about these cultists and find a way to enter the shrine without getting caught. Perhaps talk to other people in the village as well. Blindly rushing in is foolish," Meera continued.

Lumo's expression softened as he listened to Meera's words, a pang of realization hitting him square in the chest. She was right, as she often was.

"You're right, Meera," Lumo admitted, his voice tinged with a touch of humility. "I'm sorry."

Meera gave a half-smile, half-eye roll.

"I've been rushing headlong into this without really thinking things through… Oliver's in trouble, and I want to help him, but I can't risk all of us getting hurt without a plan." Lumo glanced around at his companions.

"We need to gather more information, talk to the villagers, figure out a way to enter the shrine without getting caught," he continued, his tone more measured now.

"Good." Meera's lips curled in a slight, approving expression.

"Thank you, Meera."

Turning back to face the chief, Lumo continued, carefully choosing his words, "Chief Vaida, we want to know more about these cultists. Have you or anyone else had any interactions with them in person?"

"Some, but it was many moons ago."

"I see. Well, you mentioned that the shrine has been here for a while. Surely, before recent times, someone has seen the inner workings of the shrine as well."

Chief Vaida's expression remained somber as Lumo pressed for more information, his eyes clouded with concern. He hesitated for a moment, weighing his words carefully before responding.

"There was someone from the village..." Chief Vaida began. "Joined the cult many years ago. But you won't find him now; he's gone."

"Oh, did he speak to anyone about his time there? Perhaps a friend or..."

"His wife. She's still alive. I'm not sure if she will speak to you about it though. Some memories are best forgotten."

"Do you mind if we try talking to her?" Lumo asked.

Chief Vaida shook his head ever so slightly.

"Isolde's house is the one with the green door and the Tulip Garden outside."

Lumo nodded. "Thank you, Chief Vaida. We'll approach her with discretion."

With a determined stride, Lumo motioned for Meera to follow even as Gus and Moose continued sipping on their cups of herbal tea. As the duo made their way through the village streets to find the wife of the man, an air of tension pressed down on them like a storm cloud ready to burst.

Soon enough, they arrived at the humble cottage where Isolde resided. As they knocked on the door, it creaked open slowly to reveal a woman in her late thirties. She regarded them with a mixture of curiosity and suspicion, her eyes betraying a deep sadness that seemed to linger beneath the surface.

"Yes?" she said.

Meera stepped forward. "Hello, madam. Chief Vaida granted us permission to speak with you; may we come in?"

"What is this about?" the woman asked.

"We need to speak about your husband," Meera replied.

Isolde's gaze flickered with a hint of recognition, but she remained silent as if unsure whether to trust strangers.

"We know it may be difficult, but we need to understand more about his time with the shrine," Meera said calmly.

Isolde hesitated for a moment longer before finally nodding. With a heavy sigh, she beckoned them inside.

"Gideon was a good man…" she began. "Before—"

"We understand. We don't mean to judge, but we believe your husband may hold the key to uncovering information about the shrine and the people who inhabit it. Anything you can tell us would help," Meera urged.

"It would be best not to—"

"Please, they have our friend," Lumo interrupted.

"And people from the village too," Meera added.

Isolde lowered her head. "Yes, of course. What was I thinking?"

With a nod, she led them to a modest shelf adorned with trinkets and faded photographs, where a worn journal gathered dust among the mementos of a life once lived.

"This belonged to my husband. He kept it hidden, but I found it after he... disappeared."

DAY 1

I have been initiated into the sacred order, the whispers of our forebearers guiding me to this momentous occasion.
Tonight, I witnessed the power of the leader granted by our one true god.
All hail Lord Cernunnos.

DAY 9

Tonight, as I commune with our deity in the sacred chamber, I feel the weight of destiny upon my shoulders.
The leader's words echo in my mind, reminding me of the great purpose that binds us together.
All hail Lord Cernunnos.

As Lumo skimmed through the journal, his heart sank with each entry he read. The words painted a picture of a man consumed by fervent devotion. The words spoke of a fervent dedication, a devotion that bordered on obsession. Yet, amidst the passages filled with cryptic references, there was nothing concrete Lumo could decipher.

"These entries speak of their God. Is there anything else you can tell us? Perhaps about Gideon himself," Lumo remarked.

"I remember the first day. He was so excited to have found a purpose. I tried telling him not to get too pulled into it, and it worked for a while... His visits weren't so frequent at the start, but as time passed, he started spending more time there, disappearing for days sometimes… and then he just left…" Isolde said, with a troubled look on her face.

"Did he tell you more about his time there or the people he worked with?"

"No," Isolde said, with a dejected look. "He was so secretive, especially since I told him not to indulge with them too much… If only I had stopped him…" Tears started running down Isolde's cheeks as she recounted her past.

"What about this leader? Did he speak of a name? Was it Malikoth?" Lumo pressed.

Reading Isolde's tearful expressions, Meera nudged Lumo, prompting him to give Isolde some space. A moment of silence prevailed as Lumo complied.

"Isolde, are you all right?" Meera said, clapping a hand on her shoulder.

"I'm sorry. It just hurts so much," Isolde sobbed.

At that moment, a small boy, about six years old, peeked into the room. "Mommy, why are you crying?" he asked worriedly.

Lumo quickly moved to the boy, crouching down to his level. "Hey there, champ. Your mom just got some dust in her eyes. Everything's going to be okay. What's your name?"

"Jasper," the boy replied innocently.

"That's a nice name. How about we go to the other room for a bit, Jasper?" Lumo suggested, guiding the boy away.

Once they were alone again, Meera continued, "I understand."

"Isolde, this is a memory stone. If it's all right with you, I can read your memories with this. Of course, I will understand if you don't agree," Meera said, pointing to her ring.

"Okay," Isolde said, wiping the tears off her cheek.

Managing a strained smile, Meera held onto Isolde's hands. With a deep breath, Meera closed her eyes, focusing her mind on Isolde's memories. In an instant, vivid images flashed before her mind's eye, each one a fragment of Isolde's past.

Meera found herself immersed in Isolde's memories, experiencing them as if they were her own. She saw glimpses of Gideon's joy on the day he joined the cult, his eyes alight with fervent zeal as he spoke of his newfound purpose. She saw Gideon proudly displaying the use of fire magic to light a candle. The initial excitement gradually gave way to concern and worry as Gideon's visits to the shrine became more frequent and prolonged.

Gideon's heated arguments with Isolde echoed in Meera's mind, her voice filled with desperation as she begged him to abandon his devotion to the cult. But Gideon was resolute, even when Isolde tearfully protested. In one vivid memory, Meera felt a pang as Gideon pushed Isolde away, leaving a scar on her hand—a lasting reminder of that painful encounter.

As the memories unfolded, Meera felt a deep empathy for Isolde, a woman whose life had been shattered by forces beyond her control. She saw Isolde's quiet devastation as Gideon walked away for the last time, unaware she was carrying his child. Meera experienced Isolde's struggles as a single mother, her sleepless nights, and the quiet triumphs that marked her journey, each one forging her resilience and strength.

When the memories finally came to an end, Meera opened her eyes, her heart heavy with the weight of Isolde's pain.

"Isolde," Meera said softly. "Thank you for sharing your memories with me. I know it must have been difficult, but your bravery is admirable."

Isolde nodded in response to Meera's gratitude, her eyes shimmering with unshed tears.

Lumo had re-entered the room. Observing the tender exchange, he stepped forward cautiously. "Meera, did you... see anything?" he asked, delicately.

"Yes," Meera replied, turning momentarily to Lumo.

"Isolde, I noticed the robes Gideon wore as he left for the shrine. You wouldn't happen to have more of those, would you?"

Isolde's eyes widened in surprise at Meera's question, her gaze shifting to the adjacent room.

"I think so," she murmured.

Isolde excused herself, disappearing into the adjacent room. Moments later, Isolde reappeared, clutching a bundle of fabric in her hands.

"I found them," Isolde said softly. She carefully unfolded the bundle, revealing a pair of burgundy-colored robes embroidered with the same symbols they had seen thus far.

Lumo and Meera examined the robes with fascination. The fabric felt heavy in their hands. They exchanged quick glances with each other, knowing they could now enter the shrine dressed as members of the cult.

"Thank you, Isolde," Lumo said. "You don't know how much this helps. I hope you don't mind us borrowing these?"

Isolde shook her head.

As Lumo and Meera gathered the robes, Isolde spoke up. "Do you… plan to enter the shrine?"

"Indeed."

"If… you see Gideon, could you—"

"We will try." Lumo smiled roughly.

Isolde's lips parted in a brief, grateful expression. "Thank you."

"We should get back to Gus and Moose," Meera reminded.

With a final nod of gratitude, Lumo and Meera took their leave, exiting Isolde's abode.

Arriving back at the chieftain's house, Meera and Lumo were greeted with the sight of Moose on horseback. Moose appeared to be ready to depart.

"You're going somewhere?" Lumo asked.

"I'm heading back. Kael asked me to get you guys this far, and now I need to head back," Moose replied.

"But we could use your help, Moose."

"I'm sorry, I've done as asked. I need to get back to my life now."

"It's all right, Lumo," Meera encouraged.

"Take care," Moose said as he tugged at the reins of his horse.

The horse galloped away with Moose's silhouette fading in the distance.

***

CHAPTER 13

Gus shifted uneasily as he watched Lumo and Meera don the robes. The fabric draped smoothly over Lumo's frame, fitting him like a glove, while Meera's figure was somewhat lost in the voluminous garment, the excess fabric pooling at her feet like a puddle after a rainstorm.

“They look convincing,” Lumo remarked, adjusting the hood of his robe.

Meera tugged at the sleeves of her robe, trying to adjust the fit. “Convincing? I look like a ghost that got stuck in a curtain.”

“Oh, I know! Why don’t you just drift along and say you're here for unfinished business,” Lumo chuckled.

Meera shot him a playful glare. “Very funny, but seriously, what do you think?”

“I won’t lie, you look ridiculous. But, they'll have to do,” Lumo replied.

“Yeah, yeah. All right, let's go over the plan one more time before we head to the shrine.”

“Agreed. We need to minimize any risks.”

“Okay, so first we need to get into the shrine. Surely, they will have some security measures at the entrance. Cernunnos, remember the name.”

“Right. That’s their god,” Lumo confirmed. “I hope they don’t ask us too many questions.”

If only the answer to all questions were dandelions, Lumo hoped in his mind.

"We're going to have to wing this one, Lumo. Once we're inside, we need to be as discreet as possible, avoiding any unwanted attention. We only gather information first. We need to stay close and keep our wits about us. If we spot Oliver and the others, we need to formulate a plan to save them later. No rushing in, agreed?"

Lumo agreed with minimal eye contact.

"Oh, and I think it's best we leave our weapons here. They might get suspicious if they spot your sword," Meera added.

Lumo nodded reluctantly.

"Gus, you're going to be waiting for us outside. These robes are too small for you. Besides, you'd attract too much attention."

"Okay, Meera," Gus mumbled.

As Lumo and Meera finalized their preparations, Gus fidgeted nervously, his hands clenching and unclenching at his sides.

"Do you need anything else? Any help from us?" Chief Vaida's voice startled them, as he appeared from behind.

"Th—Thank you, Chief Vaida," Lumo responded. "We're just going to scout the area today. We will report what we find later."

"All right, just remember to make it back before dusk," Chief Vaida cautioned.

"Hmm... looks like it's a moonless night tonight," he mumbled.

***

Lucius, Serena, and their entourage of armed guards arrived at the broken bridge. As Lucius surveyed the obstacle before them, it became clear that crossing the river without Serena's help was not possible, at least not without further delay.

Lucius nodded toward Serena, and she stepped forth with her staff raised high.

"Stand back," she said.

With a wave of her hand, she chanted her spell.

From soil to sky, let vines align,

Forming a bridge, in nature's design.

As she spoke, the ground trembled beneath their feet, and tendrils of green energy snaked out from the earth. Numerous vines burst forth from the ground. With a flick of her wrist, Serena moved her staff toward the direction of the broken bridge. As if on cue, the vines gushed forth in that direction, twisting and intertwining within the frame of the old bridge. With each passing moment, the bridge grew sturdier, the vines weaving together to form a solid path.

The armed guards watched in awe as Serena's magic worked its wonders, transforming the broken bridge into a sturdy path across the river. With a final flourish, Serena completed the spell, and the bridge stood firm, ready to bear the weight of their passage.

Lucius nodded approvingly.

"All right, men! Let's go," he shouted as the group rode on.

***

As Lumo, Meera, and Gus approached the shrine, they found themselves standing at the base of a towering mountain, its rugged cliffs rising ominously into the sky.

Nestled within the heart of the mountain was the shrine itself, its entrance carved seamlessly into the rocky facade.

In front of the entrance was a vast circular clearing, encircled by a ring of towering stone pillars. Each pillar was marked with a weathered appearance, bearing the weight of countless ages. Moss and ivy clung tenaciously to the pillars, as if nature itself sought to reclaim them.

As Lumo, Meera, and Gus stood at the threshold, they couldn't help but feel a sense of trepidation wash over them, knowing that they were about to enter a world shrouded in mystery and danger.

Spotting the entrance ahead, Lumo motioned for the group to proceed.

"Gus, I think you should wait here. If all goes well, we should be back in an hour or so."

"But what if..." Gus mumbled, his voice trailing off.

"If we don't make it before evening, you should head back to the safety of the village. Got it?"

Gus nodded as he watched Lumo and Meera move cautiously toward the entrance. The entrance to the shrine was lit with torches along the sides. A solitary cultist, cloaked in the same robes they wore, stood not far inside the entrance.

As they approached, Lumo and Meera lowered their gaze, hoping to pass unnoticed by the solitary cultist standing guard. But as they neared, the cultist dropped his crescent spear in their path, blocking their way forward.

Lumo took a deep breath.

"All hail Lord Cernunnos," he tried saying in a strong voice, but his voice caught in his throat and came out like a frog's croak.

The cultist's eyes narrowed slightly, but he returned the greeting with a curt nod.

"All hail Lord Cernunnos. Haven't seen you here before."

"We're new to the order. We are here to pay our respects to our lord and to partake in the rituals," Lumo said, hoping his words sounded convincing.

"Initiates?" The man scratched his head. "I don't recollect hearing about new members."

Lumo glanced at Meera, exchanging a subtle nod before turning back to the cultist. "We were initiated in secret, known only to our most trusted brethren."

The cultist's gaze shifted between Lumo and Meera. "You bear the robes of the faithful, but..."

"But what? Surely you wouldn't question the judgment of our superiors," Meera interjected. "Or do you dare to doubt the wisdom of our leaders?"

The cultist hesitated, clearly conflicted by their assertive response. Sensing an opportunity, Lumo pressed on.

"The time of our cause is nearing. We are here to fulfill our duties as loyal followers. Look at us, brother. Do we appear as outsiders to you?"

For a moment, the only sound was the faint crackle of torches and the distant murmur of unseen voices within the shrine. Finally, after what felt like an eternity, the cultist let out a slow, measured breath. His hand tightened around the shaft of his crescent spear. And then, with a deliberate motion, he raised the weapon blocking their path, his gaze lingering on Lumo and Meera with a mix of suspicion and wariness. With a slight nod, he gestured for them to proceed into the shrine.

"Go on then," he said gruffly. "But remember, the sanctity of the shrine must be respected. Any misstep will not be taken lightly."

As Lumo and Meera cautiously passed the cultist, they couldn't help but exchange a relieved glance, silently acknowledging their success so far. Lumo's lips twitched with a hint of amusement. With a sense of triumph, they stepped through the entrance of the shrine, leaving the looming figure of the guard behind them.

With cautious steps, they passed through the corridors of the shrine, the cool darkness enveloping them like a shroud. As their eyes adjusted to the dim light, Lumo and Meera found themselves in a spacious antechamber, its walls adorned with intricate carvings depicting scenes of ancient rituals and offerings to a horned deity. The deity's imposing figure loomed large in the center of the carvings, its form half-human, half-beast, with antlers protruding from its head and eyes that seemed to pierce through the stone itself. Despite the ominous aura that emanated from the carvings, there was a strange beauty to the depiction of the horned deity, its presence commanding both fear and awe in equal measure.

As they ventured deeper into the shrine, the antechamber gave way to a series of winding corridors, leading to more such antechambers. Eventually, they came upon an antechamber unlike any they had encountered before. In one corner of the room, iron cells resembling cages stood in stark contrast to the intricate carvings that adorned the walls. The cells exuded an aura of confinement and despair, their bars rusted and worn from years of use.

Were these the cells meant for the Cwn Annwn? Lumo wondered. *No.* The shackles attached by chains to the walls indicated these cells might have been used for imprisoning humans, although they appeared to be empty. Lumo and Meera pressed on, apprehensive as they navigated the endless, twisting corridors.

As they approached the next chamber, Lumo and Meera froze at the sight before them. A group of cultists knelt around an altar, their heads bowed in reverence, completely unaware of the intruders. With a shared glance, they silently slipped past, careful not to draw attention. Finally, they arrived at what appeared to be the corridors leading up to the main chamber. The distant echoes of activity grew louder with each step they took. Peering cautiously around a corner, Lumo and Meera caught glimpses of cultists moving about the corridors purposefully.

As they continued discreetly, they eventually found themselves in a large chamber, its ceiling stretching high above them. The expanse of the chamber was vast, easily capable of accommodating a hundred people. In the center of the chamber, a large square-shaped cutout in the floor caught their attention, filled with what appeared to be water, its murky surface shimmering softly in the torchlight. Four towering pillars stood at the corners of the square, reaching skyward to the very ceiling of the chamber, clearly bearing the load for the massive chamber.

At the far end of the chamber, a large altar bearing a statue of their god stood against the back wall. The statue itself was slightly larger than human-sized. Cernunnos was sculpted in a seated posture, his legs crossed as he held a curved ivory blowing horn to his lips, as if calling for something.

As Lumo and Meera took in the scene, they noticed a group of cultists moving about the chamber, each engaged in various tasks. Some were sweeping and mopping the floors. Others were scurrying about, preparing for something, their voices murmuring in hushed tones as they made final preparations.

Lumo and Meera watched in silence, their senses on high alert as they observed the bustling activity around them. It was clear that they were now in the heart of the shrine, surrounded by the faithful who served the mysterious deity worshipped within its walls.

Suddenly, a cultist emerged from the back of the chamber. His gaze swept over them, his expression stern as he addressed them.

"What are you two doing idling about?" he demanded, his voice sharp with authority. "Go mop that area over there. We have no time for idle hands in the service of Lord Cernunnos."

Lumo and Meera exchanged a quick glance, their expressions guarded yet compliant. They knew they couldn't risk drawing attention to themselves. They moved quickly to obey the cultist's command, picking up mops and buckets without protest.

As Lumo and Meera diligently mopped the designated area, they couldn't help but steal furtive glances at the other cultists bustling about the chamber. Lumo discreetly edged closer to a group of cultists who seemed engrossed in their tasks. This group of cultists appeared to be arranging candles and incense decoratively at the base of the altar.

With practiced nonchalance, he started mopping the area around the altar, all the while straining to overhear their conversation.

"The Lord appeared in my dreams last night," one cultist murmured in awe.

"Really? You are truly blessed then!" another cultist exclaimed. "Please, what did he say to you?"

"That he was pleased with my devotion. It was... surreal to be in the presence of the divine," came the hushed reply.

"I, too, have felt his presence in my dreams," another cultist whispered, his gaze fixed on the statue of their god. "His words echo within me, guiding my steps and fortifying my resolve."

In their fervor, a cultist's elbow knocked over a flask of oil, sending it tumbling to the stone floor. The sharp scent filled the air.

"Brother Sven, what are you doing?" one cultist gasped, jumping back as the oil crept toward the candles.

"Watch out, the candles!" yelled another.

A burst of fire erupted, catching the hem of one cultist's robe. His eyes widened in terror. "I'm on fire!" he shrieked, flailing his arms wildly.

Panic erupted. Cultists scrambled about, only adding to the chaos. Amidst the flurry, one hapless cultist, slipped on the wet floor Lumo had been mopping. With a yelp, he careened into another cultist, sending them both tumbling to the ground in a clumsy heap.

"Get off me, you oaf!" the second cultist growled, trying to push the other away.

They scrambled to their feet, only to slip and slide in the puddles left behind by Lumo's hasty mop job, while others flailed about in a futile attempt to regain their balance.

"Fire! Fire!" another cultist shouted.

The collision set off a domino effect as candles toppled from their stands, igniting the area further.

"We're all going to burn!" a terrified cultist wailed, arms flapping like a panicked chicken.

"Quick, put it out!" another screamed.

Through the chaos, Lumo darted forward with a bucket of water, narrowly avoiding the flailing limbs of his fellow cultists. With a swift motion, he doused the flames, extinguishing the immediate danger and eliciting a chorus of relieved sighs from those nearby.

As the flames subsided, a man of authority strode forward with purpose. Small flushed circles appeared on his cheeks as he surveyed the scene before him.

"What in the name of Lord Cernunnos is happening here?" he demanded.

One of the trembling cultists, his robes still smoldering, stammered out an explanation of the mishap. Before he could finish, the man's expression darkened with fury. With a swift motion, he raised his hand and delivered a sharp slap across the face of the hapless cultist.

"You fool!" he thundered. "Your incompetence endangers us all!"

As the cultist cowered under the man's wrath, Lumo couldn't help but feel a twinge of sympathy mixed with amusement at the dramatic scene unfolding before him. However, he knew now was not the time for laughter.

"Clean the area, and be more careful. Tonight is of utmost importance. Any more slip-ups, and it's off to the gaols," the man in charge bellowed before departing.

As the chaos settled, Lumo quickly made his way over to the cultist who had been slapped. Extending a hand, he helped the shaken man to his feet, offering a reassuring smile despite the tension lingering in the air.

"You all right there?"

The cultist nodded, still visibly shaken from the ordeal.

"Don't worry, accidents happen," Lumo offered, trying to lighten the mood.

The cultist let out a frustrated sigh.

"Accidents, yes, but it's always Sven, isn't it? That clumsy oaf seems to attract trouble like a magnet," he grumbled. "And yet, it's always someone else who ends up paying the price for his carelessness."

Lumo let out a chuckle, but the man's stern expression remained, his jaw clenched as he bit the inside of his cheek in displeasure. Sensing the tension, Lumo quickly apologized.

"Sorry, I didn't mean to make light of the situation. But, yes, that Sven; always so clumsy. Perhaps a few lashes would knock some caution into him. Or at least keep him out of trouble for a while."

The cultist's lips twitched. "Indeed, maybe that's what it'll take... Thanks, friend. I appreciate the help. I'm Cedric."

"Lumo. Pleasure to meet you, brother," Lumo replied.

The tension eased and Lumo offered to help Cedric with restoring the decorations for the altar. As they worked, Lumo spoke, "So, tonight is an important night. I'm quite looking forward to it."

"You are?" Cedric quizzed.

"Well, of course... It is an important night," Lumo said, forcing a smile that didn't reach his eyes.

"Yes, yes, you're right." Cedric nodded. "It is a bit sad, but it must be done, for the greater good. After all, it's the will of Lord Cernunnos."

His brief interaction with the man had revealed his human side to Lumo, yet Cedric's words raised a red flag in Lumo's mind, reminding him that he was dealing with the same people responsible for the disappearance of his friend, amongst others. Lumo had to get more information.

"Err, would you mind reminding me of what is expected of us tonight?" Lumo asked.

"You mean the verses?" Cedric retorted. "We simply chant the verses in unison as the sacrifices take place. The leaders will take care of the rest."

Lumo's heart skipped a beat at the mention of sacrifices. The word echoed in his mind, sending shivers down his spine. He tried to maintain his composure, but inside, a wave of fear washed over him. *Sacrifices?* he thought, his mind racing. *But what kind? Animal sacrifices, right? It must be animal sacrifices.* Yet, a nagging doubt gnawed at him, whispering the possibility of something far more sinister. *Could it be...* The thought sent a chill through his veins, but he had to remain calm.

"Yes, um, the verses. I'm afraid I might have forgotten some part," Lumo said, coolly.

"Oh, we could go over the verses once we're done here."

Just then, Meera approached Lumo from behind.

"Brother, could you help me with something," she said, tapping Lumo on the shoulder.

"Not now, Mee—err, sister..."

"Please, it will only take a second."

Lumo shared a quick glance at Cedric.

"Go, I think I got this," Cedric replied, as he busied himself with the finishing touches of the altar.

Lumo joined Meera as they moved out of earshot of the cultist.

"Meera, I was about to—" Lumo began.

"They're planning to sacrifice people tonight," Meera said grimly.

Lumo's heart sank at Meera's revelation. His worst fears had been confirmed.

"Are you sure?" he whispered.

"Positive. I heard these people talking. Remember, the chieftain said it's a moonless night tonight. They're going to be sacrificing all those people, tonight!"

"So, what do we do now?" Lumo's voice came out a little strained.

"We can't head back to the village now, there's no time. We have to try to free those people."

"But how? We don't even know where they're keeping the captives," Lumo said, frustrated.

"There must be more holding cells somewhere. We just have to find them," Meera reasoned.

"Okay, yes. I've built a rapport with one of these guys. Maybe I can get more information."

"All right, you do that. But be careful not to raise suspicion. There are too many of them. Meanwhile, I will try to do some more digging myself," Meera instructed.

Heading back to the altar, Lumo spotted that the altar decorations were nearly complete.

"I apologize, brother. All done, I see."

"Oh, that's quite all right," Cedric replied, adjusting the final candle. "Now then, shall we go over the verses?"

"Um, I think I remember all the verses now, but there is something else I wanted to ask you about. Something you said earlier."

Cedric raised an eyebrow.

"I couldn't help but think back on what you said, about it being sad to sacrifice all those people. I think you're right; it is sad. I wish there was a way to get my head around it now, maybe if I could see all those people and talk to them; give them some words of comfort. You know, for closure."

Cedric's expression softened slightly, but he remained guarded. "Oh, I'm not sure if that's possible. The fated must already be... prepared for the ritual," he replied cautiously.

Lumo's eyes narrowed, his mouth forming a slight frown as he tried to piece it together.

"I mean, you could probably see them, but I doubt you could talk to them," Cedric added.

"Ah, I think that might be enough," Lumo said, maintaining his facade of concern.

"Very well. If it brings you peace, brother, they're being held down there," Cedric gestured toward a darkened passage.

"Thank you, brother," Lumo said gratefully.

Lumo quickly huddled back to Meera with the newfound information.

“Meera, I found out where they’re kept. This way.”

Lumo and Meera cautiously made their way down the dimly lit passage, their hearts pounding in their chests. As they rounded a corner, their eyes fell upon a horrifying sight. Rows of captives—men, women, and children, not bound by chains, but adorned in eerie, ritualistic garments—sat motionless like statues in a tiny chamber.

Lumo's breath caught in his throat, his hands trembling involuntarily as he beheld the sight before him. The faces of the captives, once filled with life and vitality, now gazed into nothingness, their eyes vacant and hollow as if their very souls had been drained. He felt a surge of dread knotting in the pit of his stomach, the weight of the truth bearing down upon him with suffocating force.

“What’s wrong with them?” Meera whispered.

Lumo could now understand what Cedric meant when he said he couldn’t speak to the fated. These were not merely victims awaiting sacrifice; they were souls robbed of their agency, trapped in a waking nightmare from which there seemed to be no escape.

“They’re under some kind of spell, maybe,” Lumo replied, the voice still caught in his throat.

As they moved closer, they could see the faces of the captives more clearly. Lumo’s eyes widened in horror as his gaze fell upon one of the faces.

“Amelia!” he gasped, the name tearing from his lips in a desperate cry, the sound echoing through the chamber.

In an instant, Meera's hand shot out, clamping firmly over Lumo's mouth, her eyes wide with urgency as she silenced his outburst.

Lumo's heart raced as he felt the weight of Meera's hand pressing against his lips, the sound of his own panicked breaths thumping loudly in his ears. With a nod, he looked at Meera, silently promising to stay quiet.

In that tense moment, a faint rustling reached their ears, sending a shiver down Lumo's spine. He realized his outburst had not gone unnoticed, his blood running cold with the sudden realization of their peril.

Without a moment's hesitation, Meera pulled Lumo away from the place, her movements swift and purposeful as they retreated back to the safety of the main chamber. Lumo followed her lead as they hurried through the dimly lit passage.

“That was close. What were you thinking?” Meera scolded once they were back in the main chamber.

“Meera, that's Amelia! H—How?” Lumo responded, his voice still trembling with shock.

“I know, but we almost got caught. You need to control your emotions, Lumo.”

Lumo nodded, but his throat felt dry as he swallowed hard, trying to steady himself. His trembling demeanor did not escape Meera's notice; it was evident that Lumo was deeply shaken by the revelation.

“Just to be clear, when was the last time you saw her?” Meera's voice cut through.

Lumo blinked, the fog in his mind lifting slightly as he focused on Meera's words.

“I think the last time was back in the dungeon… yeah, that's it. I remember telling her to do whatever it took to pass the information to…” His eyes went round. “Lucius.”

Meera observed Lumo's shaken state. She knew they couldn't afford to dwell on the shock of the moment; there were bigger things at stake.

"Lumo," she said firmly. "We'll deal with that later. Right now, we have a mission to focus on. We need to stay sharp and keep moving forward."

"R—Right. What do you think we should do now?"

"I'm afraid trying to free the captives is out of the question for now. But there is something else, though."

"What?"

"Earlier, I was able to find out a bit more about the ritual itself. It's going to be tonight, but more specifically within the midnight hour. I overheard them saying the midnight hour was crucial," Meera began. "If we can find a way to disrupt the ritual such that they miss that window..."

"We can delay the sacrifices until the next moonless night," Lumo completed her sentence. "That'll give us enough time to find reinforcements and save them."

"Right. I think the next thing we should do is gather as much information as we can about the ritual. We'll split up and keep conversing with these lesser-ranked cultists. Just make sure not to draw any suspicion, though."

As Lumo and Meera agreed on their next move, they continued observing the cultists going about their tasks, taking mental notes of their routines and interactions, hoping to glean any additional information that might aid them in their mission.

***

Come evening, Lumo and Meera met again at the same spot.

"Any luck?" Meera asked.

"I found out from Cedric about this one guy—High Priest Marachi. He's the guy conducting the ceremony," Lumo replied.

"Did you see him?"

"No, Cedric mentioned they should be arriving a few hours before the designated time."

"They?"

"I think there are a few more guys, including their leader. But I couldn't straight up ask him for the leader's name now, could I? Not without gathering suspicion," Lumo clarified. "What about you, did you find out anything interesting?"

A grin appeared on Meera's face as she explained.

"Yes, for one thing, these guys are meticulous. From the preparations to the way the ritual has to be carried out, each step has to be done perfectly. One misstep and they'd much rather postpone the entire thing."

"I know that already, how is that going to—" Lumo began.

"Let me finish," Meera interrupted. "So, even the artifacts they use in the ritual are oddly specific. I found out about this one artifact that is crucial for their ceremony."

"What artifact?"

"Actually, the answer was staring us right in the face, Lumo," Meera said with a chuckle.

"Meera, enough with the riddles," Lumo said, losing patience.

"Okay, okay, it's the Horn of Cernunnos," Meera said, gesturing to the statue.

Lumo's gaze followed Meera's gesture, settling on the imposing statue of Cernunnos blowing from the horn. He cocked his head, trying to make sense.

"That horn?" he asked.

Meera nodded. "Yes, that's right. The horn is a crucial part of their ritual. It's not just a ceremonial object; it's meant to collect, um… you know."

Lumo blinked blankly.

"The blood... of the sacrifices."

Lumo's eyes widened as he stared at the statue again. "Wait, you mean..."

"Cernunnos isn't calling from the horn... he's drinking from it. The horn is a vessel," Meera replied with a large grin.

Meera's revelation hit Lumo like a bolt of lightning.

"Okay, so let's get the horn and run. We can't waste any more time," Lumo said.

Meera shot him a wry smile. "Yeah, let's just waltz up to the statue, grab the horn, and sprint out of here," she quipped.

"But why not? What's stopping us? I can create a distraction while you grab the horn."

"It's not that simple, Lumo," Meera said, shaking her head. "How can we be sure that's the real horn? It could be a replica for all we know."

"But if we steal it now, won't the cultists' reactions tell us if it's real?"

"Yes, but you're forgetting one thing. We still need to get out of here. If we do it now, they're going to be on high alert looking for us, and even if we do get out, what if they have a backup plan?" Meera explained. "We need to wait until they are busy with the ritual itself. When we spot an opening, that's when we try to steal it. Besides, remember the goal here. We need to postpone the ritual so they miss their window."

"Hmm... all right, so all we do now is wait."

Meera nodded with a rough smile.

***

CHAPTER 14

As midnight approached, the cultists shifted around in nervous anticipation. Lumo and Meera, disguised among the congregation, observed with bated breath as the atmosphere grew increasingly charged with anticipation.

Suddenly, a hush fell over the chamber as High Priest Marachi made his entrance, flanked by a group of figures cloaked in black robes. Lumo and Meera exchanged a knowing glance, recognizing the distinct aura that surrounded the newcomers. These were no ordinary members; they were the inner circle, the ones who held sway over the fate of all who stood before them.

High Priest Marachi's face bore the weathered lines of age, his angular jawline obscured by a large, scraggly white beard that cascaded down to his chest. Bushy and unkempt eyebrows framed his deep-set eyes, surrounded by dark circles. Strands of white hair peeked out from beneath the folds of a voluminous hood. In his weathered hand, he gripped an intricately carved staff topped with a crystal orb. The flickering light from nearby torches reflected off the orb's smooth surface, casting an iridescent glow that seemed to absorb the room's energy.

As Marachi and his retinue took center stage, the other cultists gathered around to listen. Lumo and Meera huddled in amongst the group, anxiously waiting for what was to come.

Marachi raised his hands, his voice resonating with a solemn authority. "My brethren," he began, his words carrying across the chamber. "The time is upon us. Tonight, we stand on the threshold of greatness, poised to fulfill our sacred duty."

His words were met with murmurs of agreement from the gathered cultists, their fervor rising with each passing moment.

Taking a brief moment of pause, Marachi turned toward one of the other figures behind him. The hooded figure stepped forward. With a subtle gesture, she lowered her hood, revealing a woman of striking beauty and undeniable power.

"My brethren, before we begin, it is my honor to present to you our glorious leader, Hierophant Lilith."

As Lilith stepped forward, her presence commanded attention. She exuded an aura of confidence and power, her every movement deliberate and commanding. Her long, flowing ebony hair cascaded down her back, framing her face like a dark halo. Adorning her neck hung a pendant with a ruby-red gem at its center. Crimson-colored lips parted as she addressed the gathered cultists, her voice smooth and melodious, yet carrying an underlying tone of authority.

"Dear brothers and sisters," Lilith began. "Tonight, we stand united in our purpose, bound by our unwavering devotion to the divine. I extend my deepest gratitude to each and every one of you for your unwavering faith, for it is your dedication that has brought us to this pivotal moment."

Her piercing gaze swept across the crowd, acknowledging each member with a nod of approval.

"Tonight marks the beginning of our journey toward fulfilling our sacred duty," Lilith declared. "Together, we shall take the first step toward a new era of power and enlightenment."

"It is... unfortunate that some among us have faltered in their belief," Lilith continued, her tone tinged with subtle disappointment. "But rest assured, my brethren, that we have dealt with such matters swiftly and decisively. Our ranks are now purified, strengthened by the resolve of the faithful."

A murmur of agreement rippled through the gathered cultists; their fervor reignited by Lilith's words. She smiled serenely, her crimson lips curling into a knowing grin.

"Let us now raise our voices in supplication to the divine. Together, let us offer our prayers and praises to our lord who guides our path."

With Lilith leading the chant, the cultists' voices swelled, echoing off the stone walls of the chamber.

All hail Lord Cernunnos,
Blessed be your name!
All hail Lord Cernunnos,
In your honor, we acclaim!
All hail Lord Cernunnos,
Lord of life and death.
All hail Lord Cernunnos,
With every final breath!

As the cultists repeated the same verse again and again, Lumo and Meera, who had initially started lip-syncing, found themselves drawn into the rhythm of the chant. In an effort to maintain their guise, they echoed the words of praise with growing conviction, their voices becoming indistinguishable from the fervent throng.

As the chanting reached a crescendo, Lilith's gaze turned toward Marachi, her expression unreadable yet filled with purpose. With a subtle nod, Lilith signaled to Marachi, who swiftly disappeared into the shadows of the chamber. Moments later, he reappeared, leading a line of captives who awaited their grim fate with stoic resignation.

The gathered cultists watched in rapt attention as the sacrifices were unveiled, their gazes fixed upon the solemn procession. Lumo and Meera, hidden among the throng, felt a surge of apprehension as they realized the gravity of what was to come. The midnight hour was drawing near, and with it, their window of opportunity to disrupt the ritual and seize the Horn of Cernunnos.

Lumo cast a fleeting glance at Meera. They both knew that they had to act swiftly, but they also needed to wait for the perfect moment amidst the chaos of the ceremony. Time was running out, and they had to find the opening they desperately sought before it was too late.

As Marachi took center stage, a solemn aura enveloped the chamber. The prisoners stood in rows just in front of Lilith and him, wading in the murky waters. Each captive appeared to be in a trance-like state, their eyes glazed over as if they were disconnected from the reality unfolding around them. Their movements were slow and robotic, as if they were being guided by an unseen force, compelled to follow the commands of their captors without question.

Lumo’s and Meera’s gazes shifted to the statue where the Horn still stood, undisturbed. With a quick exchange of a glance, Meera quietly slipped through the crowd, edging closer to the altar where the Horn rested. Lumo also purposefully moved to the back of the crowd, his gaze darting around as he searched for a way to divert attention away from the altar.

Before Lumo could finish formulating the plan, a sudden commotion erupted at the entrance. As he turned around to spot the disturbance, his eyes widened in shock. A group of guards barged in, their presence commanding attention as they swiftly made their way into the chamber. At the front, two guards marched with stern faces, leading the way. Behind them walked none other than Gus, looking obedient as he followed. The reason for his obedience became apparent as two more guards flanked him, holding their spears to his back.

"What is the meaning of this?" Lilith barked.

"We caught an intruder loitering near the entrance," one of the guards explained.

Lilith's lips twitched as she addressed Gus.

"Who are you?"

"I—I'm Gus, Gus the glu..."

"Silence!" Lilith thundered. "Why are you here?"

Gus hesitated, his eyes darting nervously around the room as he struggled to find the right words.

"I asked you a question," Lilith bellowed.

As Gus's eyes scanned the room, searching for Lumo and Meera, Lilith's gaze followed his, her expression rife with realization. She turned her attention back to the gathered cultists.

"Brothers and sisters," Lilith began, her voice dripping with disdain, "It pains me to see that whenever we are close to fulfilling our duty, we are always interrupted by the forces of evil, such as these intruders."

Her words sent a shiver through the chamber as the cultists exchanged uneasy glances.

"This man is not alone," Lilith continued. "His comrades are hiding amongst us, lurking in the shadows like cowards, seeking to thwart our sacred mission."

The cultists murmured amongst themselves, their apprehension mounting as they scanned the crowd, searching for any signs of treachery.

Lilith's voice reverberated through the chamber. "Now is the time to reveal yourselves, you traitorous scum!" she declared, her eyes blazing with righteous fury. "Step forward and face the consequences of your betrayal, or suffer the wrath of Lord Cernunnos!"

The cultists shifted uneasily, casting nervous glances at one another as they awaited the response to Lilith's call. Lumo and Meera, hidden among the throng, had their hearts pounding with apprehension.

As the tension in the chamber mounted, Lilith's gaze swept across the crowd, her eyes ablaze with determination.

"Very well. If they will not reveal themselves willingly, then we shall flush them out like rats from their hiding places!"

With a cruel smirk, Lilith turned her attention back to Gus, her eyes gleaming with malice. With a murmured chant, Lilith concentrated her hands in front of the necklace, channeling dark energy into the air. Slowly, wisps of shadow materialized, swirling around her fingers like ethereal serpents. As her incantation grew in intensity, the shadows coalesced into dark tendrils that snaked their way toward Gus, ensnaring him in a web of darkness.

Gus let out a choked cry as the tendrils tightened their grip, squeezing the air from his lungs. His body contorted in agony as Lilith's spell wracked him with pain, each twist and turn amplifying his suffering.

Everyone watched in horrified silence as Lilith's dark magic consumed Gus. With Gus writhing in agony under the grip of Lilith's dark magic, she turned her gaze back to the crowd. Her voice resonated through the chamber, cutting through the air like a razor.

"This is your last chance. Reveal yourselves, or this man dies!"

As Gus's tortured cries echoed through the chamber, Lilith's lips curled into a cruel smile, reveling in the power she held over him. With each passing moment, his resistance weakened, his will crumbling under the relentless onslaught of pain and fear.

Lumo felt a surge of guilt and desperation wash over him as he watched Gus suffer at Lilith's hands. He couldn't bear to see his friend harmed because of their mission. Despite the risks, he knew he had to act. With a heavy heart and a sense of resignation, Lumo stepped forward from the crowd, his hands raised in surrender.

"Stop, I surrender."

Lilith's gaze narrowed as she studied Lumo, her expression one of thinly veiled contempt.

"You? You're just a boy," she scoffed, her voice dripping with derision.

Lumo stood his ground, his resolve steeling against Lilith's disdain.

"What is your name?" she demanded.

"Lumo," he replied defiantly.

"And does Lumo have a last name?"

"I—I'm an orphan," Lumo admitted, his voice faltering slightly.

Lilith's lip curled into a sneer, but before she could speak again, Lumo interrupted, his voice steady despite the fear roiling inside him. "You have my friend... Oliver."

A hush fell over the crowd as Lilith's eyes widened in surprise.

"Prince Oliver?"

"He was taken by your followers. I came here to find him. Please... release Gus," Lumo pleaded.

Lilith's nostrils flared, her features twisting into a mask of anger.

"So, you seek to defy us and rescue your precious prince," she spat, her voice dripping with venom. "How noble."

Without warning, Lilith lowered her hands, and the tendrils of dark energy surrounding Gus receded, releasing him from their grasp. Gus collapsed to the ground, gasping for air as he struggled to regain his strength.

"Are you alone?" Lilith asked.

"Yes," Lumo replied, meeting her gaze head-on.

"Lies!"

"No, it's true. It's just me."

Lilith studied Lumo for a brief moment.

"Very well. I see you people need more persuasion," Lilith continued, her eyes gleaming with malice. "You shall suffer the same fate as your friend."

Lilith concentrated her hands once again in front of her chest and began murmuring chants under her breath. However, before she could finish, another loud commotion erupted from the direction of the entrance. Lilith's concentration was abruptly disrupted as her gaze shifted toward the area, her eyes shifting around in confusion.

The sound of heavy footsteps reverberated through the chamber, growing louder with each passing moment. Suddenly, the source of the disturbance became clear as Lucius, accompanied by his army of royal guards and Serena, marched boldly into the chamber.

Lucius, Serena, and a few guards pushed through the sea of cultists, who parted to let them pass. Behind them, the remaining guards fanned out, forming a formidable barrier that effectively sealed off any escape routes.

Lilith's temple veins throbbed as she took in the sight before her.

"We come in the name of the king," Lucius declared.

As Lucius stepped forward, his gaze inadvertently shifted to find Lumo amidst the crowd. He was shocked.

"You!" he exclaimed, his voice sharp with disbelief. "I knew it! You had to be responsible."

Lilith, sensing Lucius' contempt, took the opportunity to intervene, her voice dripping with false sincerity.

"Thank Lord Cernunnos, you have arrived. We have just now discovered the presence of traitors in our midst."

"No, wait! These are the people responsible for the abduction of Prince Oliver and the other people in the village," Lumo pleaded.

"This is absurd," Lilith pretended. "There have been no abductions. We are simply followers of the lord, gathered here to pray."

"That's not true!" Lumo exclaimed, pointing toward the prisoners. "Look over there, those are the prisoners!"

All eyes shifted toward the prisoners.

"They're no prisoners; they are part of our sacred order," Lilith lied.

"That's a lie! Look, Amelia is here! She was abducted from the castle after—" Lumo stopped mid-sentence.

As Lucius shot disdainful stares at Lumo, Lilith continued. "Amelia is one of our new followers; they all are. Amelia, dear, could you tell us why you are here?"

"I am here to serve the will of Lord Cernunnos," Amelia said softly, her gaze fixed on Lilith. "I have found enlightenment and purpose in our sacred order, and I willingly offer myself to the divine cause."

"See, she is no prisoner."

"T—This is..." Lumo stammered. "S—She is under their spell."

"Is there no end to your lies?" Lilith scoffed.

Lucius, finally having had enough of their arguments, spoke. "It's not our business if someone wants to pursue their religious beliefs."

Lumo could not believe it. Lucius's words hit him hard, and the sense of reason within him disappeared for a moment.

"You!" he snapped. "You are responsible for her abduction. You were the last person she spoke to before her disappearance," he said, fingers pointed toward Lucius.

For the first time in his life, he had stood up to the Lord Knight. Lucius's lips quickly downturned at Lumo's accusation, his jaw tightening with controlled anger. He regarded Lumo with a cold, steely gaze, his features betraying no hint of guilt or remorse.

"You dare accuse me?" he retorted, his voice laced with barely contained fury. "I have no hand in her disappearance, nor do I tolerate baseless accusations from insolent peasants like you."

Lilith, seizing the opportunity to further discredit Lumo's accusations, interjected with false sincerity.

"Indeed, this boy has been lying through his teeth ever since we caught him. There is nothing he will not say to save his own skin."

Lucius's disdain for Lumo was evident in every line of his face. He addressed the cultists with authority.

"Hand over this troublemaker. We will deal with him accordingly."

As Lilith agreed with a wry grin, the cultists, ever loyal to their leaders, obeyed without question, surrounding Lumo and Gus and leading them toward Lucius. As Lumo found himself at Lucius's mercy, desperation clouded his thoughts. He turned to Serena, his voice pleading.

“Please, you have to listen to me. If we don't stop them now, those prisoners will be sacrificed within the hour. You have to let me go; we can't let them get away with this.”

Serena, who had watched the exchange unfold the entire time with her usually unreadable expression, spoke in a calm voice.

“You’re Lilith Folsham, aren’t you?”

“Oh, excuse my manners. I’m Hierophant Lilith Folsham,” Lilith introduced.

“I heard about you at the academy, years back. You’re the one who went crazy and created the ruckus.”

Lilith’s grin quickly turned serious.

“Lucius, perhaps we should consider what Lumo is saying,” Serena suggested tentatively. “If there's even a chance that these accusations hold truth, we can't afford to ignore them.”

“Serena, please, you know me. You know I wouldn't make these claims lightly. These people, they're planning something dark, something far worse than we can imagine. They're going to use that horn to collect the blood of the sacrifices. We have to stop them before it's too late,” Lumo pleaded, gesturing to the statue.

As Lucius and Serena’s eyes darted to the statue, their expressions turned to one of confusion.

“What horn?” Lucius scoffed.

Almost instantly, Lumo’s eyes widened as his gaze turned toward the statue. However, another person there had a far worse realization. Lilith, who had turned to spot the Horn, only to find it missing, thundered in fury.

“THIEF!” she bellowed.

As Lilith's accusation rang out through the chamber, Lumo felt a surge of panic grip him. His mind raced, frantically trying to make sense of the situation. Then, amidst the chaos, a realization dawned upon him. Meera, his ever-resourceful companion, had managed to steal the Horn of Cernunnos right from under their noses.

A chuckle bubbled up from Lumo's throat, quickly growing into full-blown laughter. It was a laugh born from the absurdity of their predicament, from the sheer audacity of Meera's feat, and from the knowledge that, against all odds, they still had a fighting chance.

"Guess you can't complete your ritual now."

Lilith's gaze shifted between Lumo, Serena, and Lucius, her rage growing until she could contain it no more.

"Enough of this! Now you die! NOW YOU ALL DIE!"

The cavern erupted into chaos as the cultists in the black robes fanned out behind Lilith almost instantly. A sudden flash lit the darkness—a large bolt of fire hurtled toward Serena, trailing wisps of smoke. Her heart raced as she planted her staff firmly into the ground, fingers tightening around the cool wood. She murmured a swift incantation, her voice steady as energy surged through her staff. A shimmering barrier erupted at its tip, crackling as it met the fiery bolt head-on. The impact exploded into harmless sparks.

Across the cavern, chaos reigned. Cultists hurled fire spells at the guards, fierce flames erupting in the dim space The guards scrambled for cover, shields raised just in time to deflect a torrent of energy. The sharp crack of spell collisions echoed like thunder, mingling with the clang of weapons. Guards grunted as they staggered back, struggling to regain their footing against the relentless assault.

Lucius brandished his mithril sword, its surface glinting as he swung defensively, deflecting incoming spells. Amidst the crossfire, some cultists ran helter-skelter; not all were spellcasters.

In the midst of the chaos, Lilith raised her arms, dark energy coalescing in her palms. She unleashed a massive beam of shadow aimed directly at Lumo. But before it could reach him, Serena lunged into its path. Their magical energies collided, unleashing a blinding flash that illuminated the cavern with shifting shadows. Lumo stood frozen, eyes wide, as he watched the two powerful figures locked in battle, energy surging around them.

In the corner of his vision, Lumo caught sight of the prisoners, standing eerily still, their vacant gazes as if the chaos around them was a distant storm they couldn't feel.

"We have to help the prisoners," he declared.

"Go," Serena shouted, still locked in battle with Lilith.

Lumo and Gus sprang into action, rushing to aid the mesmerized prisoners. As they guided the bewildered captives to safety, they were assailed by desperate cultists attempting to thwart their escape. Lumo managed to dodge a fire spell that came in his direction, but he was unsure if he would be able to dodge the next one. Just then, Meera, emerging from the shadows, quickly dispatched one of the attackers with a massive hit to the back of their head with the Horn in her hands.

As Lucius adeptly deflected yet another onslaught of incoming spells, it became increasingly evident that the tide of battle was turning against the cultists. Seeing their plans unraveling, Lilith signaled Marachi, who began chanting a dark incantation.

O' Houn-vas Annun, vyrae enarth malis,
Faer vethan sorun, vithran akthal vithran thalis.

As he raised his staff high into the air, the orb at its tip pulsated with ominous black energy. As Marachi's voice rose in intensity, the air hummed with dark energy. From the depths of the murky waters, there arose the dreaded Cwn Annwn—spectral guardians of the abyss. Their forms were twisted and ethereal, blending seamlessly with the shadows that enveloped them. Each Cwn Annwn bore the semblance of a large hound, but their features were far from mundane. Their eyes burned with a fiery glow, illuminating the darkness around them with an eerie luminescence. Their fur, if it could be called such, seemed to ripple and shift like wisps of smoke, as if they were not wholly of this world but rather beings of pure darkness given shape. With each step, they left behind trails of ethereal mist, marking their passage with an otherworldly energy that belied the malevolent intent burning within their spectral hearts.

One of the hounds descended upon a guard with savage ferocity, its jaws snapping hungrily as it tore into flesh and armor alike. The unfortunate soldier barely had time to react before he was overwhelmed by the unearthly force of the creature's assault, his screams drowned out by the cacophony of battle. Another hound set its sights on a fleeing cultist. With a swift and deadly grace, it pounced upon the hapless worshiper, its spectral form engulfing him in a maelstrom of darkness.

As the relentless waves of Cwn Annwn continued to pour forth from the murky depths, Lumo, Gus, and Meera exchanged desperate glances, realizing the dire threat posed by the ongoing summoning. With a sense of urgency burning in his voice, Lumo called out to Meera and Gus above the chaos.

“We have to stop Marachi!”

Without hesitation, Gus charged toward Marachi, intent on wrapping him in a crushing bear hug. But just as he closed the distance, a cultist unleashed a searing fire spell. Meera spotted the fiery projectile racing toward Gus.

"Gus, watch out!" she shouted.

Gus's eyes widened as he spotted the firebolt zooming toward him. He tilted his body slightly to the left, and the firebolt streaked past his head, narrowly avoiding his face and singeing a few hairs of his beard.

With swift determination, Meera sprang into action, her movements fluid and precise as she closed the distance between herself and Marachi. With a calculated leg sweep, she brought the High Priest crashing to the ground, disrupting his spell and effectively halting the further summoning of the spectral hounds.

As the battle raged on, Lilith's gaze shifted toward Lumo and Gus, who were hastily ushering the prisoners toward the exit. A feral glint of fury gleamed in her eyes.

"No! No one escapes!" she thundered.

With a snarl of determination, she began chanting a dark spell toward Lumo, Gus, and the fleeing prisoners.

Cimora zalrithun, thanor enarth drel,
Ath oram tharn xenrak il zylth,
Khora thaloraeth rathul vael elosir,
Ithrazar thalora nabi tos likhun thulnara.

Serena instantaneously moved to intercept Lilith, her staff raised in an attacking posture. But before she could unleash her magic, two black-robed cultists surged forward, their own spells intertwining with Serena's in a violent clash of opposing forces.

As Lilith's spell materialized, a dark beam of energy came streaking toward Lumo and the group, finding its mark in the hapless form of Amelia. The searing blast struck her squarely in the back, eliciting a gut-wrenching scream of agony from the young woman. Lumo's attention, focused on their desperate escape, was abruptly torn away by the heart-wrenching sound, his eyes widening in horror as he witnessed the cruel fate befalling Amelia. Her anguished cries reverberated through the chamber for agonizing moments until finally, her lifeless body came crashing to the ground. Lumo, paralyzed by the harrowing scene unfolding before him, could only release a primal scream of anguish and despair.

"AMELIA, NO!"

In the meantime, Meera, having bested Marachi, had found herself in a predicament of her own. One of the Cwn Annwn stood face to face with her, its teeth gnarling at her with venomous intent. Time seemed to stand still as the creature readied itself to attack, inching ahead slowly, one paw at a time.

As Lumo watched in terror, witnessing poor Amelia succumbing to her plight, his attention snapped back to Lilith, who was preparing for another attack. As he realized what was about to happen, his earlier paralysis melted away, replaced by a fierce determination. Lumo observed with dread as the next spell hurtled toward Gus. With no time to think, Lumo's body surged into action, propelled by instinct and desperation. In a display of sheer bravery, Lumo lunged forward, intercepting the spell with his own body.

As the spell struck Lumo's body, agony engulfed him like a tidal wave, his senses overwhelmed by searing pain. A primal scream tore from his lips as pain seared through every fiber of his being.

At that moment, Lumo saw flashes of the life he had lived. Memories of his time with Oliver, the king, Lucius, Serena, Amelia, and even Madam Tissuré flashed before his eyes, each memory etched with bittersweet clarity. Amidst the pain and turmoil, there were also glimpses of new beginnings, of friendships forged in the crucible of adversity. Images of Lily, Bart, Meera, and Gus appeared in his mind, their faces slowly dissolving into the darkness that threatened to consume him.

But just as the light in his eyes seemed to fade away, something remarkable happened.

BLAST!

From Lumo's writhing form erupted a surge of dark energy, an unexpected counterattack.

The force of Lumo's release sent Lilith staggering backward, her hands flailing for balance as she fought to regain her footing. However, Gus, who stood closest to Lumo at the time, bore the brunt of the blast. With a startled cry, he was launched backward, his body hurtling through the air before crashing into the unforgiving stone wall with a sickening thud. As the blast reverberated through the chamber, a powerful shockwave rippled outward, shaking the very foundations of the cavern. Cracks spiderwebbed across the surface of one of the ancient stone pillars, weakened by the force of the explosion. With a deafening rumble, the pillar crumbled, large chunks of stone cascading down to the ground below.

Lilith, her eyes wide with shock, struggled to maintain her footing as the ground trembled beneath her. She stumbled backward, nearly losing her balance as debris rained down around her.

The explosion occurred just as Meera was locked in a tense standoff with the menacing Cwn Annwn. The blast caused the creature to turn its head abruptly toward the source before turning back to Meera. With a snarl, the creature poised itself to lunge; however, a massive chunk of rock, dislodged by the earlier explosion, came crashing down from above. With a thunderous crash, the stone collided with the creature, smashing it beneath its colossal weight. Meera, her heart pounding with adrenaline, watched in astonishment as the creature was vanquished by the unforeseen turn of events.

Amidst the chaos, Lumo stood at the epicenter of the explosion, his chest heaving as he struggled to regain his breath. Sweat beaded on his brow, his body trembling from the exertion of the unexpected release of energy.

As Serena rushed to Gus's side, she extended a hand to help him up.

"Are you all right?" she asked.

Gus winced as he rose to his feet, leaning heavily on Serena for support.

"I'll be fine," he replied through gritted teeth.

Meera swiftly moved toward Lumo, assisting him in steadying himself. Lumo, still exhausted, could not utter a word.

"C'mon, Lumo," she said softly, yet urgently. "We need to get out of here. This place is falling apart."

Lumo nodded weakly, allowing Meera to wrap his arm around her shoulder for support.

As the prisoners hurriedly made their escape, Lilith and Marachi seized the opportunity to retreat, their forms disappearing into the darkness of a swirling portal. With a frustrated growl, Lilith cast a final glance back at the chamber before vanishing from sight.

"This isn't over, Lumo," she hissed, her voice echoing faintly through the chamber. "We will meet again."

Meanwhile, Lucius and the surviving guards, battered but unbowed, withdraw from the chamber.

"Fall back, men!" Lucius commanded.

As the last of the guards filed out of the chamber, the once-stalwart pillars groaned under the weight of impending collapse. With a deafening roar, the chamber crumbled, stone and debris raining down like a torrential downpour. The ground shook violently, sending tremors rippling through the very air. Dust filled the air as the ceiling came crashing down with an earth-shattering impact. Its descent was swift and merciless, sealing off the entrance to the shrine. With the chamber now nothing more than a labyrinth of rubble and ruin, the shrine lay hidden, its secrets safeguarded by the unforgiving embrace of the earth.

***

As the group emerged from the crumbling ruins of the shrine, the air was thick with swirling dust, catching in their throats and stinging their eyes. Lucius squinted against the haze, his hands instinctively reaching out to shield his face. He surveyed the ragtag assembly gathered before him, their figures obscured by the billowing clouds of debris.

Meera stood by Lumo's side, her arm wrapped around his waist, offering him support. Lumo, still struggling from the ordeal, was in a clearly disoriented state, his steps faltering and his complexion paler than before. Gus limped beside Serena, his footsteps faltering with each painful shuffle. The guards, their numbers halved from earlier, appeared battered and bruised, their once pristine armor now dented and scratched. Many of them bore the marks of the skirmish etched across their weary faces. Some limped slightly, favoring injured limbs, while others clenched their weapons tightly, their knuckles white with exertion and adrenaline. The prisoners, no longer under the influence of the mesmerizing spell, looked around with wide eyes, taking in their surroundings with astonishment. Some rubbed their eyes in disbelief, as if trying to shake off the remnants of the enchantment that had clouded their minds for so long. Others murmured among themselves as they struggled to make sense of the situation unfolding around them.

"Is everyone okay?" Lucius asked.

No words were said, but the absence of words indicated no one assembled there had any serious injuries.

Taking a deep breath to steady herself, Serena turned to face Lucius, her voice firm yet tinged with weariness.

"We need to talk."

Lucius's jaw clenched as he regarded Serena, his expression guarded.

"We've failed, Lucius," Serena continued.

"This is a disaster. And it's all thanks to him," Lucius said with gritted teeth, half pointing a finger toward Lumo.

"Wait, you are still blaming Lumo after all that happened?" Meera spoke in disbelief.

Serena stepped forward, raising a hand. "Lucius, those people escaped, and we know now that they're responsible for everything."

"Responsible for what? We were here looking for the assailants who captured the prince. Sure, those guys were up to no good, but I did not see our prince anywhere, did you?" Lucius said, staring into Serena's eyes.

"Those guys are responsible," Meera argued. "Lumo confronted them before, and they did not deny it."

"Lumo? The same guy who was responsible for causing the collapse and in turn helping these murderers escape? Hah," Lucius scoffed.

"Look, we need to focus on what the next step is; blaming Lumo will not help," Serena stated, trying to be the voice of reason.

"You dare say blaming will not help, especially since the brat blamed me for Amelia's disappearance back then?" Lucius said in anger. "You have got to be joking, Serena. It's pretty clear to me that Lumo has a hand in all this."

"That's not true. Lumo is innocent," Meera pleaded.

Lumo remained silent, his normally quick retort absent as he leaned heavily against Meera, his breaths shallow and labored. The color drained further from his face, his features drawn with exhaustion and pain.

"Can you prove it?" Lucius retorted.

Meera began explaining as best as she could. She explained their entire journey from the dungeon to the shrine, how they came to know of Malikoth and the cult, eventually discovering the whereabouts of the cultists from Kael.

"…And so, we finally ended up infiltrating the shrine with the robes we got from Gideon's house. You can ask his wife; our story will check out."

As Lucius absorbed the details Meera put forth, his expression softened slightly.

"Very well, we will surely ask this person from the village to see if you tell the truth. But for now, the three of you must come back with us to the castle," Lucius replied.

"Guards," he commanded.

"You're taking us as prisoners?" Meera questioned.

Lucius gave a barely perceptible incline of his head.

"But after all I explained, you still don't believe us?"

"I'm simply taking the precautions to ensure we get to the bottom of this the right way."

Just as the guards closed in to capture the trio, Lumo, still disoriented from the harrowing experience, faltered in Meera's grasp, his body swaying dangerously before collapsing with exhaustion.

"Lumo, are you okay?" Meera yelled as she struggled to hold his body from collapsing to the floor.

"Let me see," Serena said, stepping forward.

"He's running a fever," she ascertained, placing the back of her palm to Lumo's forehead.

Muttering a quick incantation, she touched Lumo's forehead, the warmth of her healing magic spreading through him, soothing his fevered skin and easing the tension in his body.

"The fever is gone for now, but he needs to rest. Perhaps… it's best if Lumo were to stay with me," she said, her gaze directed at Lucius.

"No, I cannot allow it," Lucius spat.

"Lucius, I know of your apprehension, but surely you trust me, don't you?" Serena spoke. "Let him accompany me, and when this is all over, I will make sure he is returned safely to you. Besides, I am intrigued at what happened back in the shrine, and I'm sure Sylvanus can shed some light on the matter as well."

Lucius, who normally conceded to Serena's logic, would not budge this time.

"I'm sorry, but—"

Before Lucius could complete his sentence, the screech of a hawk above his head disrupted his attention. He held out his arm and the hawk descended promptly on it. Grabbing a piece of parchment tied to the hawk's feet, Lucius then let the hawk fly away.

As he read the contents of the parchment, his eyes widened ever so slightly.

Dear Lucius,

Please hurry back to the castle as soon as you can. We have news that the king of Ophidonia is expected to pay us a visit.

Warm Regards,
Archibald.

"Is everything okay, Lucius?" Serena asked.

"I—I must head back to the castle," Lucius replied.

After a brief moment of thought, Lucius continued.

"Very well, Serena. I shall trust you with the boy for now, but I want him back at the castle when you return. This is far from over."

"I assure you, he is my responsibility. Thank you for your trust."

"All right, men, let's get the villagers back to the safety of the village. We can rest there for a bit before heading back," Lucius commanded.

As the group collectively headed back to the village, the rugged landscape was cloaked in darkness. The night sky stretched endlessly above them, devoid of any lunar light, with only the occasional wisp of cloud drifting lazily by.

***

CHAPTER 15

Lumo slowly blinked his eyes open, the dull ache in his head pulsating with each beat of his heart, like an offbeat drummer with a personal vendetta. He found himself lying on a rough rush mattress atop a wooden cot in a small, dimly lit room. The prickly fibers of the mattress poked at his back, adding to the discomfort he already felt. Rubbing his temples, he pushed himself upright, wincing at the throbbing pain that shot through his skull. With a groan, he swung his legs over the edge of the cot and stood up, swaying slightly as he regained his bearings.

Making his way to the door, Lumo stepped out into the main room of the chieftain's house. The aroma of savory food greeted him, wafting tantalizingly through the air, and he followed his nose to the source, finding Meera and Gus seated at the table, plates of steaming food in front of them.

"Hey, look who's up!" Gus exclaimed, waving at Lumo.

"Good to see you finally awake. How are you feeling?" Meera greeted.

Lumo managed a weak smile in return. "Like I've been trampled by a horse."

As he settled into a seat at the table, his eyes scanned the room for familiar faces.

"Where is everyone?"

"Lucius and the guards left already," Meera replied.

"They left?"

"Yeah, back to the castle. Seems something came up."

"Huh, but I thought…"

"Maybe Lucius isn't all that bad, Lumo. Anyways, it was Serena who persuaded him," Meera said as she took a hearty bite of a succulent piece of salted pork.

The main door swung open and Serena, along with the chieftain, entered the room.

"Lumo, how are you feeling?" Serena asked, spotting Lumo.

"I've been better," Lumo shrugged.

Serena exchanged a concerned glance with Meera before turning back to Lumo.

"You took quite a hit back there. But you're lucky to be alive."

Meera leaned forward. "Do you remember what happened?"

Lumo shook his head, his memories still muddled and fragmented. "The last thing I remember is... spotting the attack from Lilith," he began, his voice trailing off as he struggled to recall the events. "And then jumping in front. But after that, it's all just... hazy."

His eyes widened as his thoughts raced to their mission

"Meera, where's the horn?

"I'm sorry. I lost it in the chaos," Meera replied.

"What about the prisoners? Are they safe?"

Before anyone in the room could answer his question, Lumo's gaze drifted into the distance.

"Amelia… is she…"

"I'm sorry, Lumo. Unfortunately, she didn't…" Meera finally replied. "But, hey! We saved the villagers."

A half-hearted smile appeared on Lumo's face.

"What about Lilith? And the others…"

"They, um, got away…" Meera admitted. "But we managed to thwart their plan, and Lucius and the guards know whom to pursue now. This is good, Lumo."

Lumo clutched his head, trying to soothe the pounding headache that muddled his thoughts. Meera recounted the events that had unfolded, and Lumo stared wide-eyed, absorbing each detail.

"I—I did that?" Lumo stammered.

"I'm sure you have a lot of unanswered questions, Lumo. So do we, but we'll get to that in time," Serena spoke. "You should get your strength first and eat something."

"The entire village got together to prepare the delicious meals in front of you, travelers," Chief Vaida chimed in. "They're eager to meet you all."

Lumo looked up at the chief, who was beaming with happiness.

"Thank you, chief," Lumo responded warmly.

"It's us who should be thanking you. Please dig in," Chief Vaida soothed.

Lumo's stomach rumbled at the mention of food, reminding him of just how hungry he was. Without hesitation, Lumo reached for a piece of crusty bread, tearing off a generous chunk and dipping it into a bowl of rich, savory stew.

"There are warm baths prepared as well if you are interested."

"Oh, yesss!" Meera jumped with joy. "I'm going first."

After devouring the hearty meal, Lumo felt invigorated, his spirits lifted by the warmth of the food and the hospitality of the villagers. With Chief Vaida's words about the warm baths still ringing in his ears, Lumo eagerly accepted the offer, feeling a wave of relief wash over him at the thought of soaking away the aches and pains of their recent ordeal.

As Lumo emerged from the comforting embrace of the bath, feeling refreshed and rejuvenated, he and his companions gathered outside the chief's house. The scene in the village was markedly different this time. Where once the village appeared desolate and abandoned, it was now bustling with gathered villagers. Beth and her husband were already there, as was Isolde and pretty much the entire village.

"Ah, Lumo, you remember Beth. Her daughter, Lotte, was one of the captives. She wanted to thank all of you for rescuing her daughter," Chief Vaida announced as Lumo joined the group.

Beth's daughter stood beside her, a young woman in her teens with expressive blue eyes and a cascade of chestnut curls. She smiled appreciatively as Beth thanked Lumo and the rest of the group.

"We are truly indebted to you; you have no idea," Beth said, tiny tears trickling down her cheeks.

Lumo's eyes drifted ever so slightly toward Lotte. A mild blush ran across his cheeks.

"There's no need for thanks," Lumo said sheepishly.

"Oh, but you saved me; you saved us all," Lotte insisted.

The other villagers murmured in agreement.

Meera, who had been observing Lumo and Lotte, quickly stepped in.

"On behalf of all of us," Meera interjected, her lips tightening imperceptibly. "Thank you, everyone, for your kind words. We're just grateful we could help reunite your family."

Isolde promptly stepped forth, carrying a bundle of food items. "For your journey," she said as she handed the bundle to Meera.

Meera's lips barely twitched. "Isolde, I'm sorry we couldn't find..."

"That's all right..." Isolde forced a smile. "He's been gone a while now. I had my doubts if he'd even be there."

After an awkward pause, Serena's voice broke through the silence. "We should be leaving now."

"Where are we going then?" Lumo asked.

"Veridia," Serena replied. "Let's go."

Lumo shot a glance at Meera. Meera filled Lumo in on the stipulations at which Lucius had let them go.

"I knew there was something amiss," Lumo noted.

As they readied their horses for the journey, Gus mounted a sturdy draft horse. Though the knights had departed, Gus had managed to borrow the horse earlier, ensuring it was strong enough to bear his weight with some effort. The group then moved toward the village border, with the entire village following them to bid farewell. As the villagers watched them depart, Lumo, Meera, Gus, and Serena rode off, the clip-clop of hooves fading into the distance.

***

A few hours after the group departed the village, they slowed down. Serena signaled a halt as she looked around at the surroundings. Arriving at a fork in the road, Serena surveyed the two diverging paths stretching before them, one leading toward the mist-shrouded expanse of Veridia and the other winding its way toward the sand dunes of Isara.

"This way," she informed, pointing toward the path that veered off to the left.

"So why are we going to Veridia again?" Lumo asked, nudging his horse closer to Serena's.

Serena glanced over. "We're meeting an old friend of mine."

"From Harbridge?" Lumo tilted his head, curious.

"No." Serena's gaze drifted ahead. "Well, he was my mentor, but not at the academy."

"Your mentor? I don't think you've ever mentioned him before," Lumo said, raising an eyebrow.

Serena's lips curved into a wistful smile. "He's not just any mentor. Sylvanus is... well, he's different."

"Different how?" Meera piped up from behind, her head popping between them as she tried to keep pace.

"For starters, he was the Imperial sorcerer before I took over."

"Before you?" Lumo's eyes widened as he adjusted his grip on the reins. His horse gave a little snort, sensing his surprise.

"Long before I even began my training," Serena clarified, brushing a loose strand of hair away as she spoke. "He was arguably the best sorcerer there was."

"He must be quite knowledgeable then," Lumo opined. He hesitated, frowning thoughtfully before adding, "Wait, how is it that I've never heard of him back at the castle?"

"It was decades ago."

"He must be quite old then," Meera remarked.

Serena gave a slight tilt of her head. "Unconventional… is what he is. Sylvanus has this deep understanding of the natural magic that exists, and he was never afraid to experiment, within reason."

"Sounds like quite the character," Meera added.

"He is," Serena agreed, a hint of fondness in her voice. "But he's also one of the wisest and most powerful magic practitioners I've ever known. If anyone can help us understand what Lilith is up to, it's him."

There was a glint in Lumo's eyes when Lilith's name came up.

"That reminds me," he began. "Back at the shrine, you said you knew Lilith. I saw the look on her face when you mentioned her from the academy."

"I never really knew her," Serena recounted. "She had left the academy before I joined, but I had heard stories of her. You've seen her magic? It's dark. Not many are attuned to darkness."

"But you mentioned something about her going crazy."

Serena nodded solemnly. "Indeed. Lilith was dangerous even before she practiced dark magic. I remember hearing about this one time when they had to evacuate an entire wing of the academy because she had used a void spell. But I think what drove the academy to banish her was that she was delving into forbidden realms of magic, especially the gateways between worlds."

"Like when those hounds were summoned," Meera added.

"Exactly. The academy tried to rein her in, to guide her toward more ethical paths of magic, but Lilith was relentless. Her reckless pursuit of power knew no bounds, and her actions endangered not only herself but everyone around her. At least that's what I heard."

"Did, um, Sylvanus know her… personally, I mean?" Lumo asked.

"I'm not sure. He was never the chatty type, at least when it wasn't about magical discussions. We could talk for hours on end about magic, but never about people."

"But you think he knows something..."

"I'm sure he does," Serena bet.

"Then there's hope of finding Oliver," Lumo mumbled.

"Gus, you all right back there? You've been awfully quiet," Serena called out.

"I'm fine," Gus thanked.

"He's like that," Meera crooned.

"All right, I think there's a clearing up ahead. We can stop there for a quick moment; then we have to pick up the pace," Serena announced.

As they approached the clearing, the dense canopy above them gradually gave way, allowing slivers of golden sunlight to filter through the trees. Serena led the way, her horse deftly navigating the winding path until they emerged into a small meadow bathed in sunlight. Flowers of vibrant colors, some of which Lumo had never seen before, dotted the landscape.

Serena dismounted first, followed by Lumo, Meera, and Gus. The air was cool and crisp, carrying the scent of pine and earth. The horses whinnied softly, enjoying the brief respite from the journey.

Lumo stretched his arms above his head, relishing the sensation of his muscles loosening after hours in the saddle.

"Feels good to stretch my legs," he remarked, glancing around the peaceful clearing.

Gus remained silent. He was busy admiring the butterflies.

"It's beautiful here," Meera murmured.

"The Veridian border isn't far from here, but you can already see the subtle influence of the realm," Serena remarked.

As the group took in the tranquil beauty of the clearing, Lumo and Meera sat next to each other in the gentle swaying grass.

"So that Lotte girl was cute. You like her, eh?" Meera teased.

Lumo's cheeks blushed quickly at Meera's remark.

"No, no. It wasn't like that..." he defended; his cheeks still flushed with embarrassment.

"Really? Because it looked like you two were getting along pretty well," Meera continued, raising an eyebrow and folding her arms.

"We barely talked. She was just thanking us."

"Thanking us? Or thanking you? She seemed pretty focused on you," Meera pressed.

Lumo rubbed the back of his neck, looking for the right words. "She's nice, but I wasn't... I mean, she's just a friend."

Meera smirked, though her lips tightened imperceptibly. "Just a friend, eh? Well, I don't believe you."

Lumo met her gaze, his blush deepening. "I swear, Meera. It's nothing like that."

Before Meera could respond, their peaceful respite was abruptly interrupted by the distant sound of rustling leaves and snapping twigs.

"What was that?" Meera whispered, her hand instinctively moving toward the hilt of her dagger.

Lumo's instincts immediately went on high alert, and he exchanged a wary glance with Meera.

From the trees at the edge of the clearing, the group spotted a pair of glowing eyes fixed on them.

"We've got company," Lumo muttered, his hand inching toward his sword.

Serena stepped forward, her expression tense but composed.

"Stay calm," she instructed.

Moments later, the source of the disturbance revealed itself—a majestic stag with magnificent antlers emerged from the shadows, its silvery hide catching the sunlight in a mesmerizing display.

"It's just a stag," Lumo breathed a sigh of relief.

The creature regarded them with an intelligent gaze before turning and disappearing back into the trees.

"Phew, I thought it was one of the hounds," Meera remarked, still recounting her encounter with one of them.

"Not in this daylight, but we can never be too careful," Serena reckoned.

After a few minutes of rest, Serena announced that it was time to move. The group set off on their horses toward the border.

As they neared the Veridian border, the scenery changed. The trees became denser, the colors brighter, and an odd energy filled the air. Serena rode ahead, clearly excited. When they finally crossed into Veridia, it felt like stepping into a painting come to life. The air was redolent with the sweet fragrance of blooming flowers, intermingled with the earthy scent of the forest floor. In the distance, the melodic chirping of birds and the gentle rustling of leaves created a symphony of sounds that echoed through the verdant landscape.

"I thought there'd be guards at the border," Lumo remarked, even as he looked around wide-eyed.

"First time here, Lumo?" Serena asked.

"It's my first time, just about anywhere," Lumo chuckled.

Serena forced herself to smile.

"Veridia has been one of our oldest allies, and as such, there was never a need for border control," she explained.

"Well, it's beautiful..." Lumo observed. "So, about this Sylvanus person. How far from here?"

Serena remained silent for a few seconds before she spoke.

"We're going to the Everglades. The dryads there should shed some light on his whereabouts."

"You mean you don't know where he lives?"

"Sylvanus disappeared a while ago. But I'm confident he's here," Serena affirmed.

***

The group rode on for a few more hours. The dirt roads wound their way through a mostly dense forest landscape, with towering trees looming overhead and thick undergrowth carpeting the forest floor. The midday sun barely had any bearing, thanks to the dense canopy above. Despite the time of day, the forest remained cool and shaded, with a gentle breeze rustling through the leaves, carrying with it the earthy scent of moss and damp soil. It was a stark change from the hot, sunny weather of Avalora. They made a few more stops at the few-and-far clearings in between, stopping for food and water. Finally, they arrived at a crossroads.

A sign read:

To the West: The Everglade Forest

To the East: Avalora

To the North: The Elderine Forest (Beware)

To the South: Leafcrest Keep

"Stay sharp, we're entering Everglade soon. No more stops here on," Serena announced as they rode past the crossroad.

Lumo was relieved to have Serena there. The thought of venturing into unknown lands on his own was daunting, to say the least. He couldn't help but wonder if he'd ever have the courage or knowledge to navigate such terrain without her guidance.

***

As the sun disappeared, the forest grew darker. They kept riding through the evening, guided by the stars.

"Something's been following us," Meera, with her keen senses, noted.

Serena did not appear to be visibly threatened.

"Keep moving."

They moved swiftly and silently through the forest, on alert to every snapping twig and rustling bush. Meera had camped in forests before during her time on the run. She thought back on all the times she had to camp out when she was moving from location to location. She would manage it without worry, but this was different. It was as if every move of theirs was under someone's scrutiny.

As they ventured deeper into the Everglade forest, the dirt road narrowed considerably, and the group had to follow in a single file. Soon, they arrived at what appeared to be a glove.

"Stop," Serena signaled.

As they looked around, the area seemed desolate, save for the sound of birds chirping from the trees and then that too stopped.

"What are we…" Lumo began.

"Shhhh!" Serena cut him off as her eyes scanned the area.

Just then, a voice rang out from the trees, causing the group to startle.

"Who dares trespass in our domain?" it demanded, its tone sharp and commanding.

"We mean no harm," Serena called out, her voice steady despite the tension in the air. "We seek only answers."

There was a moment of tense silence before another voice, much softer than the earlier one, spoke.

"Humans are not welcome here. You must leave."

"We're looking for Sylvanus," Serena announced.

"Did you not hear what we said? Leave," the first voice commanded.

"Wait a moment, Zinnia. She said Sylvanus," the second voice spoke.

"Know your place, Meliae," the first voice thundered.

"We're not leaving till we get our answer," Serena declared. She pulled out her pendant and held it up high on display.

The voices disappeared and silence filled the air.

"Sylvanus isn't here. You have your answer," the voice belonging to the one known as Zinnia finally spoke.

"Do you know where he is?" Serena pressed.

"Maybe we do, maybe we don't. Why should we help you?"

Serena took a deep breath, steadying herself before responding to the skeptical dryads. She knew she needed to choose her words carefully if she hoped to gain their cooperation.

"We understand that humans have not always been kind to your kind," Serena began, her voice calm yet earnest. "But Sylvanus is not like other humans. We need to find him. You owe it to him."

"You're not Sylvanus; we owe you nothing," Zinnia drawled.

"That's true. But something dark threatens our realm, of which Sylvanus is part; of which you are part," Serena implored.

"Gaia protects us. Our kind has never intervened in the matters of the human realm. And we don't intend to start now."

"Zinnia, I sense earnestness in her. Maybe we should just tell her..." Meliae began.

"Enough, Meliae!" Zinnia bellowed.

"Leave now, humans, while we allow it," she snarled.

Serena's shoulders slumped slightly as she exchanged a resigned glance with her comrades. Despite her best efforts, it seemed that convincing the dryads was proving to be more challenging than she had anticipated. With a heavy heart, she realized that she might have hit a dead end in their search for Sylvanus.

Sensing Serena's disappointment, Lumo dismounted his horse, his expression determined yet empathetic.

"I... may not understand your reluctance to trust humans," Lumo began, his voice carrying a sincerity that resonated in the quiet forest. "But please, hear me out."

Serena's hand rose gently, a silent yet firm gesture signaling Lumo to pause. She knew that Lumo's words were heartfelt and well-intentioned, but she also understood the delicate balance they were treading with the dryads. The last thing she wanted was to infuriate the dryads. Dryad magic was in a different league altogether, and she knew it. Besides, they were at a serious disadvantage in the forest.

"It's all right, Serena," Lumo said, turning to her. "I may not know of the history between humans and dryads, but I know that these beings must feel empathy like we do."

"My friend... was abducted by these people who seek to unleash something dark into our world. Along the way, we have already lost people we knew," Lumo continued, his thoughts drifting to Amelia's death. "And I know this is not the end. More lives will be lost if we do nothing."

"I do not ask of you to intervene in our matters, nor do I ask for any favors that will threaten your existence. My friends have already risked their lives for me, and perhaps I can never truly repay the debt," Lumo said, turning to Gus and Meera.

"Rest assured, I can never ask anyone else to do the same. I only ask for your understanding. Please, just point us in the right direction to Sylvanus. He holds the key to uncovering critical information. I implore you."

As Lumo's heartfelt plea echoed through the forest, the air seemed to grow still, every word hanging in the air. Then, from the ancient trees, figures materialized, their forms gradually emerging from the bark and foliage as if woven from the very essence of the forest itself.

The first to reveal herself was Zinnia, her features stern, resembling the Oak tree from which she emerged. Beside her stood Meliae of the Ash, her demeanor gentler, her presence exuding a sense of quiet resilience. A few more dryads emerged from the nearby trees, surrounding Lumo and the group.

Zinnia walked up to Lumo, and as she stood face to face, Lumo could only look up to meet the gaze of the towering dryad. With a swift motion, her gnarly fingers wrapped around Lumo's throat as she lifted him up. Serena, Meera, and Gus watched in horror as Lumo struggled to breathe, choking in anguish. Before they could fully react, Zinnia pushed her face closer to Lumo's and she inhaled deeply, her nostrils flaring as she took in Lumo's scent. Lumo's breaths came in ragged gasps, his face contorted in pain and confusion. Then, with a swift and unexpected motion, Zinnia released her grip on Lumo's throat, allowing him to crumple to the ground, gasping for air.

As Lumo lay there, clutching his throat and struggling to regain his breath, Serena, Meera, and Gus dismounted their horses, anticipating an assault. Meliae, however, appearing concerned, inched forward slowly, raising her hands as if gesturing them to stand down.

"You smell like him," Zinnia growled.

As Lumo finally regained his breath on the forest floor, Meera stepped forth, helping him to his feet.

"Why did you do that?" she demanded, her eyes narrowing at Zinnia.

Zinnia's expression remained impassive, her gaze unwavering.

"We needed to be sure," she replied.

"Sure of what?"

"That he was not like the others."

Before Meera could respond, Meliae interjected, her voice soft yet firm. "Zinnia, perhaps it is time to consider their request."

Zinnia's eyes flashed with irritation, but she nodded reluctantly.

"Very well. But know this: our assistance does not come without a price."

"What do you want in return?" Lumo croaked, his fingers instinctively reaching up to soothe his bruised throat.

With a slow, deliberate voice, Zinnia explained. "Years ago, Sylvanus came to us with a proposition. In return for sanctuary within the forest, he vowed to keep the creatures of Elderine at bay..."

"...Not that we couldn't do it ourselves. Do you know why we allowed it?"

Lumo shook his head ever so slightly.

"They're pests, the creatures of Elderine. Offering one inconsequential human refuge meant we wouldn't have to deal with those mewling creatures. I have to say, though, he has done a fairly satisfactory job until now," Zinnia declared, her arrogance shining through. "Lately, his endeavors have proven... unfulfilling."

"Tell me..." Zinnia paused.

"Lumo."

"Tell me, Lumo. Do you think we owe Sylvanus anything?" She straightened, folding her arms across her chest. "Nay, it is he who owes us."

"I don't understand," Lumo's brows twitched. "What are you asking of us?"

"Ask of you, hah," Zinnia scoffed. She waved a hand dismissively, turning her gaze to the trees as though the very woods shared her scorn. "Go find out what plagues him and either ask him to hold up his end of the bargain or leave our forest."

"Is that it?" Lumo questioned, narrowing his eyes slightly.

"Oh no, that wasn't the price; that was just an obligation. Sylvanus's lacking attempts have allowed for a particularly vile creature to rampage through our forests; something we would have seen long before if we hadn't left it to him. You need to take care of the creature for us."

"What creature do you speak of?" Serena interjected.

"The Lindwyrm," Zinnia groaned.

"Nasty creatures, their kind. With that nasty venom they spit, they ought to be killed in infancy lest they become a bother."

Lumo looked at Serena, hoping for more insight.

"I'll fill you in later," Serena said. Her gaze shifted back to Zinnia as she agreed. "We will take care of the creature, you have our word, but we must see Sylvanus first."

"Meliae will lead you to him," Zinnia rasped. "But remember this: fail to deliver, and your kind will never be entertained henceforth."

"I promise," Lumo stepped forth, determined.

"Go on then," Zinnia directed before stepping back into the tree. The other dryads, as if on cue, did the same, except for Meliae, who stood there with a genuine smile.

"Please follow me," she said gently.

Lumo and the group mounted their horses obediently, trailing after Meliae's graceful form as she led them deeper into the woods.

"You have to forgive Zinnia…" Meliae's words broke the silence, her tone tinged with regret. "For her rudeness."

"Tell me about it. That was rude, wasn't it?" Meera muttered, his gaze shifting between Lumo and the rest.

"She can't help it. It's in her nature," Meliae continued.

"What really happened though? Between humans and dryads?" Lumo asked.

"It's complicated, Lumo," Serena chimed in. "But I have to say, I was a bit rattled myself. I always thought Sylvanus was their friend. He always spoke so fondly of them and their magic. This pendant which he gave me, he claimed, came from the dryads," she said, her fingers tracing the contours of the pendant.

"Indeed," Meliae replied thoughtfully. "It was a gift from us. We dryads occasionally impart gifts, if we see fit."

"But then, what's with the hostility?" Lumo quizzed.

"Humans and dryads have co-existed for ages," Meliae spoke with warmth. "A lot has changed with the passage of time, including our dynamics with humans. Please, do not misunderstand. Some of us have absolutely no problems with your kind."

"Some, however, like Zinnia," she whispered, "see the encroachment as a threat to our existence. Her nature will not allow her to see any other way. There's nothing you can do about it."

"It's still rude," Meera commented.

"I apologize, young ones. I can assure you, I bear no ill will toward your kind or Sylvanus for that matter. I always found him... amiable."

Despite the tension lingering from their encounter with Zinnia, there was a sense of relief among the group in knowing that not all dryads harbored animosity toward humans.

With a quiet flick of her wrist, Meliae encouraged the group to continue. After a short burst of silence, Lumo finally broke the quietude.

"So, this Lindwyrm," he began, his gaze directed at Serena. "Something we can handle? Or..."

"It won't be easy," Serena mumbled.

"Of course not," Lumo remarked dryly.

"It's an ancient creature and it can be quite formidable. Perhaps with Sylvanus's help..."

"What kind of creature is it?" Meera chimed in from the back.

"It's a serpent-like beast, but it's capable of wreaking havoc on anything in its path."

"Must be a huge creature then," Meera commented.

"It depends, but it can grow to great lengths. Meliae, do you know how big it is?" Serena questioned.

"The Lindwyrm? I'm sorry, I haven't seen it yet," Meliae confessed.

"This way," she guided, her hand gesturing toward a path on the right. "Please follow the path. I will be with you along the way."

With a soft rustle, Meliae disappeared into the embrace of a nearby ash tree. Yet, as they rode in silence, the occasional glimpse of Meliae flitting between the trees served as a reassuring beacon, guiding them onwards through the tangled maze of the forest's depths.

***

Night came swiftly and departed just as swiftly as it had arrived. The group had camped overnight without any worry, for Meliae had assured them of their safety in her realm. As the first light of dawn filtered through the trees, the travelers stirred from their sleep. With a sense of purpose renewed, they broke camp and resumed their journey through the ancient woods.

Following Meliae's guidance, they navigated the forest's winding paths, the horses' hooves muted by a thick carpet of fallen leaves. After hours of steady progress, the trees began to thin, allowing shafts of golden sunlight to pierce through. Ahead, through a break in the foliage, they glimpsed a small cottage nestled within a grove. It looked like an extension of the forest itself—woven branches and moss-covered logs blended seamlessly into the wild surroundings, while the scent of earth and pine filled the air.

Serena's search was almost over, and with that, the possibility of things returning to sanity finally seemed not so out of reach. Lumo too felt a sense of excitement in meeting Sylvanus. He could only imagine what he looked like—an old man with white hair and a beard, wise and knowledgeable like Serena had portrayed him.

“This is where he lives,” Meliae said softly.

They approached with a mix of excitement and unease. Serena reached for the door, her hand trembling slightly. It creaked open, revealing Sylvanus—but not as Lumo had imagined. Sylvanus appeared frail and gaunt, his head bald, skin pallid, and his eyes clouded with a weariness that seemed to seep into his very bones.

“S—Serena... I did not expect to see you here,” he murmured, his eyes widening at her sight.

Serena's heart clenched at the sight of her old mentor in such a state, while Lumo felt a pang of sympathy for the man. Meera and Gus too looked on with concern on their faces.

“What has happened to you, Sylvanus?” Serena said softly.

Sylvanus's lips curved into a tired smile. “I fear... I have grown weak.”

“How did you find me?” he asked.

Meliae’s graceful form in the back gave him his answer.

“Oh, I see,” he said wearily. “Do you want to come in?”

“You don’t look so good. Are you all right, Sylvanus?” Serena inquired.

“Not really,” Sylvanus replied, his face tightening with discomfort. “But you’re here for something. Why don’t you...”

Before Sylvanus could complete his sentence, his eyes drifted to Lumo, Meera, and Gus, his eyes widening and his steps faltering slightly. Big Gus had that effect on people.

“You are?” he asked, his lips twitching painfully.

“They’re with me,” Serena confirmed. “It’s all right, Sylvanus.”

“Please come in,” Sylvanus gestured.

As Serena, Lumo, Meera, and Gus prepared to enter Sylvanus's home, Meliae quietly disappeared into the forest. Sylvanus motioned for them to take a seat, his weary eyes scanning each of their faces with a mixture of weariness and curiosity.

Serena hesitated for a moment before taking a seat opposite Sylvanus. With a steadying breath, she met Sylvanus's gaze, her voice soft yet resolute.

"It's been a while. What was it—fifteen years?" she asked.

"Give or take."

"I see now why the dryads mentioned you've been failing in your duties, Sylvanus. You know, they asked us to tell you to leave their forest if you couldn't carry out your end of the bargain."

"What are they going to do, throw me out? I wouldn't worry about them," Sylvanus snickered. "They appear tough, but it's just a facade. Lovely creatures, those dryads."

"Why don't you tell me why you are here?" Sylvanus offered.

"I need your help," Serena began. "The king is gravely ill, and I fear his condition is linked to a poison that threatens the stability of our realm."

She relayed the recent chain of events to him, and Lumo's mind wandered briefly to the questions that lurked in his mind—*What were the cult planning to do with Oliver? How could they save him?*

"Oh, dear. I suppose this was inevitable," Sylvanus sighed, having heard Serena's story.

"Sylvanus, what do you know?" Serena queried.

Sylvanus closed his eyes, and as he held his breath, the entire room looked at him with worry and anticipation etched across their faces.

"There is no easy way to say this," Sylvanus grunted. "But you must let things play out as they will."

"What?" Lumo and the rest gasped in unison.

Sylvanus's eyes wandered shamefully to the floor, and he lowered his head.

"You mustn't intervene..."

"W—What do you… is this a joke?" Lumo blurted.

"I'm sorry," Sylvanus gulped.

Lumo appeared to be in a state of utter disbelief.

"You're sorry? Why don't you try putting that in a sentence? I'm sorry, but the king needs to die; I'm sorry, but the forces of evil must win. What's wrong with you?" Lumo lashed out.

Serena observed Sylvanus silently, even as a furious Lumo kept raging. Something was clearly troubling him. She gestured for Lumo to stop, and Meera instinctively rushed to his side, trying to calm him down.

"Why'd you leave?" she asked in a slow, calm voice. "All those years ago; why come here?"

Sylvanus got up and moved silently toward a wall. As he contemplated in deep thought, a tense silence enveloped the room.

"I had to," he replied, finally.

Serena got up and moved toward Sylvanus. Clutching his hands with affection, she gazed into his eyes.

"Sylvanus, why don't you tell me what's really going on? You can trust me with anything; you know that, don't you?"

Sylvanus's lips curled into a rough smile, yet his guilt betrayed him, and he looked away for a moment. Serena, however, kept on pressing.

"Is it this sickness? Is that why you left?" she asked softly.

Sylvanus shook his head.

"Does it have to do with the king then?"

Sylvanus nodded with an unspoken "Yes."

"What does it have to do with the cult?" she prodded gently.

"Everything..."

Serena watched as Sylvanus appeared deeply conflicted. She let the silence marinate for a minute.

"Fine, I will tell you everything," Sylvanus finally spoke. "But you must promise not to interfere in the matters of the cult. Promise me."

"I cannot promise you that, Sylvanus," Serena replied. "But I promise to understand without judgment."

Sylvanus sighed deeply. "I know. Had to try though."

"Look, I will tell you everything, but all I can ask is—when you know the truth, please don't hate me."

***

CHAPTER 16

As Lucius and his men rode through the entrance of the castle, the Ophidonian ship stood in the courtyard, signaling that the king of Ophidonia had already arrived.

Lucius dismounted and quickly made his way to the great hall where Archibald awaited him. The atmosphere was tense, the usual hustle and bustle of the castle replaced by an uneasy stillness.

Archibald's brow furrowed as he greeted Lucius. "You've returned just in time," he said, his voice hushed. "I assume you got my message."

Lucius nodded. "He has arrived, then?" he asked.

"Yes, a while ago. He's been asking questions about the prince."

"What about the king? Does he know?"

"Not yet. But I sensed that he was getting to it. I deflected the matter."

Lucius's heart sank at the news. It was as he feared—their kingdom's vulnerabilities laid bare before a foreign ruler.

"Where is he now?" Lucius asked, trying to mask his concern.

"In the throne room, with Marcus and the other nobles. I've asked Marcus to refrain from talking about the king and change topics if it came to such. Come, we must speak with him at once. Oh, and we mustn't let him know about the king, I need not stress this..."

"Of course," Lucius affirmed.

They hurried to the throne room, where the king of Ophidonia stood conversing with Marcus and the other members of the court. His imposing figure and steely gaze commanded attention as he surveyed the room. King Caelumyth of Ophidonia was the type of man who made most men shrink in awe, not because of his size but because of the aura he exuded. An aura of a ruler who would command respect with his mere presence, his eyes gleaming with an intensity that seemed to pierce through the soul, and his voice resonating with a power that could sway nations with but a whisper. His broad shoulders and regal bearing spoke of a lifetime of leadership. With a mane of silver hair cascading down his back like a waterfall of moonlight, and a face weathered by years of rule yet bearing an undeniable air of dignity and authority, he was a sight to behold, a true embodiment of royalty and power.

As Lucius and Archibald approached, King Caelumyth turned to greet them.

"Captain Lucius." King Caelumyth lifted a hand in a subtle wave. "It's been a long time."

Lucius forced a polite smile. "Indeed it has, Your Majesty."

Caelumyth's keen eyes darted toward the empty throne, his gaze lingering for a moment before returning to Lucius. "I've heard about the prince. I came to offer support."

Lucius's stomach churned with unease. *How much did the king of Ophidonia know?*

"We are facing challenges, Your Majesty," he admitted reluctantly. "But rest assured, we are doing everything in our power to address them."

Caelumyth's lips curved into a thin smirk.

"I see," he murmured, his tone inscrutable.

"I trust you have the situation under control, then, Captain Lucius."

Archibald interjected hastily. "Of course, Your Majesty. Our kingdom may be facing temporary setbacks, but we remain steadfast in our commitment to stability and prosperity."

"Well, then. I hope you don't mind if I speak to Reginald myself. I assume he is sick..."

Lucius's eyes widened in horror, a flicker of panic betraying his stoic demeanor.

"...Out of worry for his missing heir."

Lucius's expression relaxed a bit and he forced another polite smile.

"Prince Oliver's disappearance has caused all of us quite the distress. As for His Majesty King Reginald, he is currently unavailable."

"Oh, did he not get news of my arrival?"

"We've relayed the information, but I have to apologize on behalf of His Majesty; that he may be unavailable to meet you this time."

"That's a shame," Caelumyth uttered.

Archibald stepped in once again. "We are terribly sorry for the news, Your Majesty... err, how is Princess Seraphina faring? She must be distraught, having witnessed the event firsthand."

"She was, but she is my blood," Caelumyth gloated. "She will be all right. Thanks for your concern."

"Well then, it appears my arrival has been untimely," he remarked.

"Oh, no no, Your Majesty, you are always welcome," Archibald apologized. "Our alliance has always been a cornerstone of stability and prosperity."

"Yes, it has," Caelumyth replied, a subtle smirk appearing on his face. "Please, let me know if you need our assistance with anything."

"Thank you, Your Majesty." Archibald nodded. "Please stay for dinner. His Majesty would be most displeased if you didn't."

"Another time, perhaps. I must head back to Ophidonia. I will await better news. Perhaps Reginald can join us back in Ophidonia at a more convenient time."

"As you wish, Your Majesty." Archibald bowed. "Again, we are truly sorry you had to visit all this way for nothing."

"Oh no," Caelumyth smirked once again. "It was not for nothing. I'm happy to know that your kingdom is in… capable hands."

Lucius's chest tightened, a brief tremor running through his fingers, but he hid it behind a carefully measured bow.

King Caelumyth inclined his head in acknowledgment before turning to leave the throne room. His departure was swift, his regal form disappearing through the grand doors as if he were a specter vanishing into the night. Archibald followed closely.

Lucius watched silently as the ship disappeared beyond the horizon, a knot of worry tightening in his chest. King Caelumyth's visit had been a stark reminder of the precariousness of their situation, and the challenges that lay ahead. Though they might have dodged the situation with tact, an unsettling feeling gnawed at his mind, like a splinter he couldn't quite reach, about the whole interaction.

***

The group gathered around, anxiously waiting for Sylvanus to reveal the secrets he held closely. Lumo had never been so anxious in his entire life. Ever since he had left the castle, his mettle had been tested, and yet there was something so indescribably unsettling about this moment. When Sylvanus had asked them not to intervene in the grand scheme of things, his first reaction was anger, yet in the moments leading until now, his anger quickly turned to a deep-rooted fear. *What if there really was nothing they could do?*

Sylvanus stood before them, his gaze distant yet focused, as if he were peering into the depths of his own memories. Finally, he spoke.

"Avalora has always been peaceful, has it not?" he said, taking a deep breath. "No famines, no droughts. Even the neighboring kingdoms of Ophidonia and Veridia have had their fair share of disasters, yet Avalora has always been spared."

"It's not a mere coincidence, you know."

The group listened intently as Sylvanus continued.

"It started eons ago, perhaps more than a few thousand years in the past. Avalora was much smaller back then. Avalorans faced unimaginable trials. Wars with the neighboring kingdoms were frequent, and natural disasters ravaged our land, testing the resilience of our people in ways you cannot fathom. Our ancestors did not have it easy; I tell you, even with the discovery of magic."

"The cult you now know as the Cimmerian Order has existed for longer than you can imagine, perhaps under different names throughout the ages. I do not even know who started it, but I am aware that it was a wizard who dabbled in the forbidden arts—a man whose name has been lost to time."

"This man was the first to discover the dark realm. It was said that he communed with a being of immense knowledge—an entity known as Cernunnos."

Lumo and Meera exchanged quick knowing glances.

"The being imparted unimaginable knowledge and power to the wizard, and eventually he was able to amass a large following where they worshipped Cernunnos as their god."

"There was a lot of pushback against the cult from the kingdom, but the cult's power was growing beyond comprehension. The kingdom declared the cult's magic as forbidden and there was so much bloodshed," Sylvanus lamented. "And then something changed."

"What happ—" Lumo began.

"Shhhh!" Meera cut him off.

"I do not know what caused the cult's expansion to cease, but they disappeared from the public eye. You will barely find any references in the history books, I'm sure," he said, turning to Serena.

Serena furrowed her brow, concern and intrigue clouding her features.

"But I know this," Sylvanus continued. "Somehow the monarchy was influenced to the point that a pact was made."

"What pact?" Serena asked.

"And it has worked! The cult is now in hiding and it has never been more peaceful. No natural disasters, no wars, no unnecessary bloodshed," Sylvanus exclaimed.

"What pact, Sylvanus?" Serena repeated.

"E—Every thousand years, the royal bloodline would be purged. Th—That was the pact," Sylvanus revealed, his lips trembling as he spoke.

Sylvanus's revelation plunged the room into a suffocating silence, stifling all speech and leaving the group suspended in disbelief. Lumo's heart sank as dread washed over him, his knuckles white from clenching his fists. Serena, Meera, and Gus too were at a loss for words as they struggled to make sense of the implications. The peace they had known, the stability they had taken for granted, now lay tainted by the dark shadow of a millennia-old pact.

"That's... that's impossible," Lumo stammered, his voice barely above a whisper.

"It's true. Only the members of the royal bloodline and the highest order of the cult are aware of the pact."

"The last time the bloodline was purged was a thousand years ago, and I'm afraid it is that time again," Sylvanus wailed.

"But, then… it means that His Majesty knew?" Serena inquired, her thoughts focusing on the present.

"Do you see now, why you mustn't intervene? This is inevitable," Sylvanus declared.

"Does… Oliver know?" Lumo asked, his face pale with disbelief.

"I'm not sure, young one. But I don't think it matters, considering he will be… the last of the bloodline," Sylvanus said with some hesitation.

Lumo was seized by a shock that reverberated through his senses, freezing him in dread. Meera, equally stunned, managed to steady herself and reached out to gently grasp Lumo's hand.

"Lumo, are you okay?" she asked, her eyes filled with uncertainty.

Unable to contain himself, Lumo stormed out of the room. Meera and Gus watched nervously as Lumo darted out of the room with quick steps. They rushed outside, behind him. Lumo stood in the open air, breathing heavily, frantically struggling to comprehend the truth.

"Lumo," Meera said gently, approaching him from behind.

Meera could spot a single tear running down Lumo's cheek as she approached his side. She quickly huddled in front of him and hugged him tightly. Gus too approached from behind, extending his arms to encircle both Lumo and Meera in a comforting embrace. As the group stood in a solemn embrace, the sound of birds and trees rustling in the wind created a moment of silent reprieve.

"This is a lot to take in," Meera spoke softly, as they disengaged. "Will you be all right?"

"None of this makes any sense," Lumo mumbled.

"Actually, it makes perfect sense," Meera reckoned, her tone gentle. "Amelia's disappearance; the notion that someone from the castle was involved; the ease at which the event transpired. It's all so clear now. The king knew."

Lumo looked at Meera with a profound expression.

"All this time, we blamed Lucius, but it was really just part of the king's plan and this... pact," Meera continued.

Lumo could not believe what he was hearing. Part of him didn't want to believe. Yet, it was true. Sure, there were a few unanswered questions. *Why would the king want it to be made public? Was that part of the pact too?* The king seemed like a rational man, and being part of a cult-pact seemed like the last thing he would agree to*, so why would he?* And yet, as Lumo pondered, something hit him. He remembered the words that the king had spoken to him. He had asked him to save Oliver.

"No," Lumo said, with a fierce look.

Before Meera could react, Lumo spoke once more.

"I refuse to believe it. His Majesty asked me to save Oliver... when I visited him after the attack. If he believed in this—pact, then why would he ask me to save Oliver? There is something much bigger at play. I simply refuse to believe it."

Meera and Gus watched Lumo, their lips pressed into thin lines of concern.

"Will you stand with me?" he asked, his gaze fixed on Meera.

"You know I will, Lumo." Meera's eyes met his, steady and sure.

As Lumo turned his gaze toward Gus, he too bobbed his head in agreement.

Lumo pushed open the door to re-enter the house. Serena appeared to be in a deep conversation with Sylvanus. They turned their heads toward the door as Lumo barged in.

"Serena, what if… the king didn't agree with the pact?" he announced.

"Lumo, I…" Serena began.

"Hear me out, please," Lumo pleaded. "His Majesty has been poisoned, has he not? Why would the cult poison him if they wanted to kill him? Surely, there are swifter ways to end a life, unless maybe this was… unintended."

"That's…"

"Serena, I paid His Majesty a visit in his chambers, after he was poisoned," Lumo went on. "He asked me to save Oliver. I don't believe that he agreed to this. We have to save him at all costs."

Lumo briefly described the manner in which he had entered the king's room and how the king in his weakened condition had asked Lumo to save Oliver.

"We can know the truth only if we save the king," Lumo declared. And after that, if still…" he gulped.

A moment of silence filled the room as Serena pondered in solitude.

"Sylvanus, what do you know about the poison?" Serena asked, with a determined stare.

Sylvanus sighed heavily as his gaze returned to the floor.

"Serena, this isn't—" he began.

"You asked me not to hate you," Serena interrupted. "I understand your motivations thus far, Sylvanus. But if you turn a blind eye now, then I can never forgive you."

Sylvanus lifted his head, meeting Serena's haunting gaze.

"Help me find a cure for this poison. If His Majesty asks me to stand down, I will do so in a heartbeat," she vowed.

Hope returned to Lumo's heart as he heard Serena's words. He looked at Sylvanus with bated breath.

Sylvanus finally spoke after a moment of thought, albeit reluctantly. "The poison was delivered by an arrow, you say? Tell me about the king's condition."

"Pale and feeble. Darkened veins. Appears to be a slow poison of some sort," Serena replied. "I was able to slow the flow even further with magic."

"Tell me, the area where the arrow penetrated, was there any necrosis or swelling around the area?"

"Both," Serena answered.

"Hmm... I see, and difficulty in breathing too, I presume?"

"Yes," Lumo interjected, remembering the difficulty with which the king spoke. "And he coughed violently too."

Sylvanus hummed quietly. After a brief pause, he spoke. "The poison likely comes from the venom of a serpent, but this is no ordinary serpent. Knowing the cult, I have to assume that the poison isn't from a creature of this realm. That's why your healers aren't able to cure him."

"A serpent..." Lumo repeated.

"That's just my opinion, I could be wrong."

"But, then... all right, let's assume for a moment it is a serpent as you say. What do we do? How do we counteract the venom if we don't know what creature it is?" Lumo quizzed.

"It's true. Creating an antivenom hinges on obtaining the venom from the very creature, but unless you can track down the cult and compel them to cooperate, I see no alternative."

"I don't think we have that much time," Serena said. "It could take days, maybe weeks, and I'm unsure whether the king will survive that long."

"There has to be another way," Lumo muttered. "Please, Sylvanus, think."

Sylvanus gazed into the distance, the room thick with unease as everyone held their breath.

"There may be another way..." he finally said. "But it's a long shot."

"What?" Lumo and Serena spoke at the same time.

"If we manage to procure a venom, an exceptionally potent one, we could attempt transmutation alchemy to synthesize an antidote."

"That's possible?" Lumo asked.

"There is a challenge, though. It lies in its effectiveness; it may not completely neutralize the poison, but if it works it could prolong the effects of the venom to a great extent."

"What are we waiting for, then?"

"There is a risk," Sylvanus explained. "It's also possible that the antidote itself could... kill the king."

Serena felt the implications of Sylvanus's words. It was not an easy decision to make, but they really did not have a choice at this point.

"I think... it's worth a shot," Serena mouthed, reluctantly.

"You don't happen to have any venom lying around, do you?" Lumo asked sheepishly.

Sylvanus shook his head.

"We might get it in the potion shops at Leafcrest," Serena declared.

"The venom needs to be exceptionally potent. Procuring it from a shop would be exceedingly rare," Sylvanus opined.

"What about the... Lindwyrm," Meera chimed. "Serpent-like creature, spits venom, the dryads said."

Lumo's eyes widened at Meera's suggestion.

"Meera, that's a great idea!" he exclaimed. "Well, would that work?" He turned toward Sylvanus, a glimmer of hope in his eyes.

"Lindwyrm? Yes, I suppose the venom from a fully grown Lindwyrm would be perfect."

"Then it's settled, we go slay the creature, get the venom, and come back here. That'll fulfill our promise to the dryads as well; sound all right, everyone?" Lumo checked.

But before the group could respond, Sylvanus spoke, his voice heavy with concern. "Wait, no, you can't..."

"Why not?" Lumo asked, with curious eyes.

"The creature is extremely dangerous. You could die; you all could die," Sylvanus said.

Lumo's determination wavered for a moment as he considered Sylvanus's words, but he quickly pushed the doubt aside.

"Well, we have Serena with us. I have total faith in her abilities."

"Even so, if you're referring to the creature that I suspect dwells on the outskirts of the Everglade, I doubt Serena's magic alone will suffice," Sylvanus asserted.

"But Serena once saved me from a Bonnacon with a sleep spell. Surely, she can put the Lindwyrm to sleep. If it's a distraction she needs, then me and Meera can help. Even Gus here is magically gifted," Lumo argued.

"Serena, what do you say?"

"I've never really gone against one, to be honest. We've only learned of the creature in training, but it was all theoretical," Serena said.

"Well, we did promise the dryads, so it's not like we have a choice," Lumo countered.

"Serena's magic is powerful, but even she cannot guarantee the creature's defeat on her own," Sylvanus explained. "And as for Gus, what magic do you possess?"

Gus shifted uncomfortably under Sylvanus's scrutiny, his eyebrows twitching.

"I can make bubbles," he admitted, the gap in his teeth revealing itself.

Sylvanus smiled awkwardly as if unsure if Gus could help.

"What about you, Lumo? And you, Meera?" he asked.

"I'm skilled with a sword," Lumo replied. "And Meera here is exceptionally swift-footed, and I've seen her throw a dagger unlike anyone before."

Meera grinned half-heartedly as Lumo praised her prowess.

"The Lindwyrm's skin is extremely thick, armored if you will. Swords and daggers cannot penetrate it. It's resistant to most forms of magic too. Perhaps, the creature's only weakness is fire," Sylvanus revealed.

"I have no control over fire magic," Serena admitted, her voice tinged with resignation. "Sylvanus, can't you..."

"No," Sylvanus cut her off. "I'm afraid my magic days are long gone. Unless you can find someone with mastery over fire magic, taking down the Lindwyrm may be impossible."

"Serena, I thought you were the royal sorceress. Doesn't that mean you need to master all forms of magic?" Meera asked.

"It doesn't work that way," Sylvanus explained. "Every user is innately attuned to certain elements. Wind, water, fire, and earth—those are the four primary elements. Light and Darkness—those are the primordial elements. Magic is a combination of elements, and we sorcerers apply concepts to these combinations as we channel our magic. Take a shield, for instance. To create a wind shield, we compress the air into multiple layers and reinforce them with light."

"My magic is a combination of wind, earth, and water, while I draw upon the primordial form of light," Serena shared. "Sylvanus was probably the only sorcerer I knew who could use all forms. He was truly gifted."

"So, then there's no way you can manipulate fire?" Lumo asked.

"Darkness and fire go hand in hand. Those who are inherently attuned to dark magic can use the destructive power of fire. I'm afraid I cannot do this," Serena confessed.

A sudden hush fell upon the room, and then Serena spoke again.

"There may be a way, though… I cannot create the fire. But perhaps if there was a source, I could use wind magic to direct the fire."

"Then, that's it!" Lumo exclaimed. "I and Meera can be in charge of creating the fires, and perhaps you can use it to destroy the creature. Gus can use his bubbles to distract the creature."

"That sounds… plausible," Serena said. "What do you say, Sylvanus?"

"It's a risky endeavor. I would ask you not to risk your lives. Perhaps there are other ways we can think of."

"What other way?"

"I don't know," Sylvanus grumbled.

"Well, then. If there is no other way, then we should get to it. Anything else we need to know about the creature?" Lumo inquired.

"The creature is quite intelligent. It can be wildly unpredictable. We need to be on our toes. This will take some teamwork," Serena detailed.

"Right." Lumo nodded.

***

After a brief respite, the group prepared to resume their journey to confront the dreaded creature. Lumo and Meera gathered rushes for makeshift torches, while Gus collected familiar ingredients for his bubble concoctions. Outside the house, Serena noticed Sylvanus emerging, closing the doors of his abode behind him. A satchel hung across his torso, and he leaned on his wooden staff, which doubled as a walking stick.

"You're coming with us?" Serena asked. "Are you sure? You don't appear to be in the best of conditions, Sylvanus."

Sylvanus offered her a reassuring smile, though it was tinged with weariness. "I may not be as spry as I once was, but I still have knowledge and experience to offer. Besides, I cannot stand idly by while you brave the dangers of the Elderine alone."

"Very well," she conceded. "But promise me you'll take care of yourself. We cannot afford to have you become a liability out there."

With Sylvanus now part of their expedition, they set off, the sound of their horses' hooves on the dirt path marking the passage of time as they traveled for hours through the forest.

As they neared the edge of the Everglades, the scenery changed noticeably from the lush greenery of the Everglades to the eerie and foreboding landscape of the Elderine. The air grew thicker, heavy with moisture, like a damp blanket draped over them, and the ground became marshier beneath their horses' hooves, resembling a sponge soaked to its limit. Tall, twisted trees with hanging moss cast eerie shadows, like skeletal fingers reaching out, and the occasional distant call of a strange creature echoed through the dense foliage.

"This place gives me the creeps," Meera muttered, casting a wary glance around her.

"Keep your wits about you, everyone," Serena called out.

As they forged ahead, the air seemed to weigh heavily upon them, rife with anticipation and tension. Suddenly, Sylvanus held up a hand, signaling for the group to stop.

"We're getting close," he whispered, his eyes scanning the surrounding terrain. "We should leave our horses here."

Lumo took a steadying breath, his senses on high alert as they cautiously advanced on foot, their eyes darting nervously from side to side. And then, they spotted it.

There, slithering through the murky waters ahead, was the unmistakable form of the Lindwyrm. Its serpentine body coiled sinuously, scales glistening in the dim light. Each scale was as large as a shield, overlapping to create a protective armor. A pair of massive, muscular arms ending in razor-sharp claws hung at its sides, capable of rending flesh and crushing bone with ease. Despite its serpentine form, the Lindwyrm possessed a presence that was distinctly draconic. The Lindwyrm's size was nothing short of awe-inspiring, dwarfing any ordinary snake or creature of the marshlands.

"By the gods," Meera breathed, her voice caught in her throat.

Lumo's heart raced as he took in the sight before him, the enormity of their task looming large. But he squared his shoulders, determination shining in his eyes.

"We've come this far. Let's finish what we started."

***

CHAPTER 17

As Lumo and the group watched from the safety of the trees, the Lindwyrm appeared to be moving with purpose through the marshy landscape. Its sinuous body undulated gracefully as it slithered between the trees. At times, it seemed to be hunting, its keen gaze scanning the surroundings for any signs of prey. Other moments found it pausing to investigate something on the ground, perhaps a scent or a sound that piqued its interest. Occasionally, the Lindwyrm would stop and raise its head, flicking its forked tongue out to taste the air, as if searching for something specific.

As they observed the creature's behavior, a sense of unease settled over them. Nevertheless, Lumo quickly outlined the plan. He and Meera would ignite the trees to create a ring of fire around the Lindwyrm, while Gus utilized his bubble magic to distract it. Serena would keep a distance and direct the flow of fire toward the creature.

"Remember, once you set fire to the trees, stay clear and move away," Serena deadpanned.

Lumo and Meera quickly ignited their torches and spread out. Although it seemed like a straightforward plan, fate would have other plans for them. The marshy terrain meant the trees were too damp to catch fire.

"It's too wet," Lumo said as he tried applying fire to one of the trees.

"Keep trying. Move on to the next tree," Meera suggested.

As Lumo and Meera struggled to ignite the damp trees, their frustration mounted with each failed attempt. The marshy terrain seemed determined to thwart their efforts, resisting the flames and smothering the fire. Despite their best efforts, only a few trees caught fire.

As the fires eventually grew in intensity, the Lindwyrm's attention was swiftly diverted. It turned its head, spotting the fire, and hissed loudly.

It was time for Gus to work his magic. He stepped forward, consuming a few berries he had gathered before. With an enormous belch, large bubbles started emanating from his mouth. The bubbles moved rapidly toward the creature and popped near its eyes. The Lindwyrm writhed in pain, stopping in its tracks.

"Fascinating!" Sylvanus exclaimed, wide-eyed. "You seem to be creating bubbles with wind and water, yet the properties of the bubbles come from what you ate. Are those wildfire berries?"

Gus appeared to be fully concentrating. He kept belching. Serena took the opportunity to cast her magic. She raised her staff and began chanting her spell.

O zephyrs fierce, in strength and might,
Enwrap the flames, guide them in flight.
With breezes keen, let fire ignite,
Upon the serpent cast its bane, its blight.

As Serena's incantation filled the air, a gust of wind swirled around her, responding to her command. The zephyrs twirled, coalescing into a cyclone of elemental energy. With a final motion of her staff, Serena directed the swirling winds toward the flames, wrapping the fire in a whirlwind of air and guiding them with precision toward the Lindwyrm.

Gus's bubble magic had proved effective in distracting the Lindwyrm, momentarily diverting its attention away from Lumo and Meera. But even as the creature's focus shifted, it appeared to be aware of what was happening. Almost instinctively, it could sense the fire hurtling toward it. With a hiss of defiance, the Lindwyrm lashed out with its massive tail, sending a powerful wave of murky water that clashed with the gust of fire. Water met fire in a clash of elements, creating a sizzling explosion as they collided mid-air. Instantly, the intense heat of the flames caused the water to evaporate in a billowing cloud of steam, obscuring the battlefield in a thick shroud of vapor.

Serena was caught off guard. She fought to steady her focus, aware that the Lindwyrm's cunning move had upended their plans. Gus looked around in confusion, not able to see where he could direct his bubbles. Lumo and Meera continued with their job, lighting more trees for Serena. But they were not prepared for what was to come.

A loud rumble erupted from within the mist, increasing in intensity as it headed straight toward Meera. Heart racing, she strained to see through the thick vapor. Suddenly, the mist parted, and something hurtled at her with terrifying speed. Instinct took over—she lunged aside, feeling the rush of air as the threat whizzed past, brushing her skin with displaced mist.

After narrowly dodging the oncoming threat, Meera finally had a moment to catch her breath and assess the situation. With trembling hands, she pushed aside the lingering mist and peered through the dissipating vapor.

And there it was.

In the clearing ahead, Meera spotted the creature transformed into a formidable sight. Swallowing its own tail, it had coiled into a rolling wheel. The sight sent a shiver down Meera's spine as she realized the extent of the creature's cunning and adaptability.

The creature pivoted and charged again, rolling through the marsh with relentless speed. This time, Meera was ready—she sprang up, weaving through the undergrowth as the creature shot past and vanished into the mist.

Scanning the ground, she found her torch, now sodden and useless. She realized what the Lindwyrm was trying to do.

"Lumo, watch out! It's trying to douse the fires," Meera shouted.

Lumo was nowhere in sight.

"What?" Lumo shouted back.

The rumbling sound disappeared as Meera circled her way toward Lumo.

"Lumo... the Lindwyrm... It's fast... and it's going... for the fires," Meera said, puffing and panting as she approached Lumo.

Lumo, still confused, cast unsure glances around. As the duo peered into the mist, attempting to discern the creature's whereabouts, Meera urgently gestured for them to retreat from the haze. As the duo back-stepped away from the mist, they heard the sound of water splashing. The Lindwyrm had likely reverted back to its original form and was splashing water all around in an attempt to extinguish the fires. And then, in an instant, Lumo caught sight of the creature's tail whip out of the mist and come straight toward them. Reacting instinctively, he crossed his arms in a defensive stance, but the tail struck him with a thunderous force, sending him sprawling backward even as the torch went flying out of his hands. Meera narrowly dodged the tail thanks to Lumo taking the full brunt and she spotted it slither back into the mist. With no time to think, she rushed in Lumo's direction.

"Lumo, are you all right?" she yelled.

Lumo lay on the ground, his breaths coming in ragged gasps.

A loud hiss pierced the air as the Lindwyrm emerged from the swirling mist, its serpentine form slithering menacingly toward the hapless duo, venom dripping from its gaping maw.

As the creature prepared to attack, they heard the words, "Earth wall!"

Serena boomed at the top of her voice, and a towering mass of earth erupted from the ground standing between them and the creature. A barrage of bubbles came flying toward the creature and popped near its head, causing the creature to hiss out in agony and disappear back into the mist.

"Hurry, this way," Sylvanus said, appearing out of nowhere. As he and Meera helped Lumo to his feet, they quickly retreated and regrouped.

As the group gathered, their faces were etched with exhaustion and frustration. Lumo appeared to be still nursing his bruises from the Lindwyrm's assault.

"Serena, what do we do now? The fires are out," Meera spoke.

Gus let out a frustrated sigh, his hands empty of berries.

"I—I'm out of berries. Can't make any more bubbles."

"We've hit a dead end," Serena hollered.

But just as despair threatened to engulf them, Meera's eyes caught something peculiar in Lumo's gaze.

"Lumo, your eyes..." she began, her voice trailing off as she took a closer look.

Lumo blinked in confusion, reaching up to touch his eyes. His eyes were pitch-black, cornea and all. And then, they slowly faded back to their usual color.

"What about them?" he asked, puzzled.

Meera's brow furrowed in thought as she recalled Serena's earlier words.

"Darkness goes hand in hand with fire," she murmured, her mind racing with possibilities.

"Lumo can use dark magic!" she exclaimed with wide eyes, turning toward Serena. "Serena, what if... Lumo can create the fires we need."

Serena hesitated, her expression guarded. "That's... absurd," she said. "We don't know the extent of Lumo's abilities or how to control them."

"But, there's no other way," Meera argued.

"There's no time," Sylvanus said. "We have to retreat first."

"I agree," Serena concurred.

"No, wait," Lumo objected. "Teach me how. We're here already."

"Lumo..."

"Please," he cut her off.

Serena sighed, relenting to Lumo's determination.

"All right, Lumo, focus. Do you remember what went through your mind the first time you unleashed the dark magic? Close your eyes and focus."

Lumo closed his eyes and focused his thoughts. He tried to recollect the events that led up to it. He remembered jumping in before Lilith's attack hit Gus, and he tried to remember what transpired next.

"I—I remember..."

"Yes?" Serena mouthed.

"Nothing..."

"Darn it, Lumo," Meera squealed.

"This is hopeless; it's all so hazy," Lumo said.

Sylvanus stepped in, still a bit reluctant about the plan. He planted his staff in the ground in front of Lumo.

"Hold on to this staff. Lumo, you need to visualize fire in its truest form. You can try to tap into your anger. Let the rage build within you as you try to focus on the visualization," he coached. "This isn't the right way to learn, but I always found the strength when I focused on a particular emotion."

Lumo closed his eyes once again, his mind drifting back to moments of intense anger. He tried to visualize a burning fire, its flames dancing vividly in his mind's eye. Memories flooded his thoughts, all fueling the fire of his rage. The memory of Lucius's disdainful sneer sent a surge of fury coursing through his veins. The countless times he had been belittled and scorned replayed in his mind, each insult stoking the flames of his indignation. He remembered the anger he felt when Lucius had defended Lilith in the shrine and even the time when Sylvanus had asked them to step down. Yet, despite his efforts, the emotion failed to translate into tangible power.

"Still nothing," he sighed.

Meanwhile, the mist had slowly dissipated, and the Lindwyrm was seen hissing loudly in the distance. Serena rushed forward, raising her staff and uttering an incantation under her breath. She summoned towering walls of earth to encircle the creature, trapping it inside. The creature lunged forward, and the group could hear the sound of its claws tearing through chunks of earth, even as Serena kept summoning more walls.

"What do you mean nothing? Did you try tapping into your anger?" Meera sneered.

"I did. Nothing. Any other tips, Sylvanus? Getting kind of desperate here…" Lumo's voice trailed off.

Lumo's words sparked something in Meera's mind instantly.

"What did you say?"

"Um, I said I tried but got nothing," Lumo replied.

"No, after that," Meera mumbled. "Lumo, what if it isn't anger?"

Lumo raised an eyebrow.

"What do you mean?"

"The first time your power erupted, that was when you jumped in front of Gus to defend him, wasn't it?" Meera continued.

"Yeah?"

"And even now, when the Lindwyrm attacked you, I saw the darkness in your eyes. Perhaps the emotion you need to tap into isn't anger; perhaps it's something more primal... Perhaps it's…"

"…Desperation."

Lumo blinked as Meera mentioned the word. He closed his eyes the third time and focused his thoughts, trying to visualize the flames. He remembered the helplessness he felt when he saw Amelia's lifeless body lying on the ground, her once vibrant spirit extinguished by Lilith's cruelty. The memory of jumping in front of Gus, his body acting on instinct to protect his friend despite the overwhelming odds, sent a surge of emotion coursing through him. The memories of what happened after came rushing back to him. He recalled the faces of his friends disappearing from his mind as Lilith's attack threatened to engulf him. Oliver's face flashed before his eyes, a reminder of the stakes they were fighting for, the lives they were risking to protect. The sensation of power surged within him, raw and untamed. With a deep breath, he channeled his emotions, letting the despair and desperation fuel his resolve.

And then, it happened.

A sudden burst of energy erupted from within him, manifesting in a towering mass of dark purplish-crimson-hued fire igniting on the ground before him.

"Lumo, stop," Sylvanus called out. "You need to control the flow of mana, or it will engulf us all."

Lumo opened his eyes, releasing the grip on the staff and stumbling back as he witnessed the fire burning on the ground. Meera and the others instinctively moved back, trying to clear the space.

"Serena, this is your chance," Meera shouted. "Lumo, get back."

Serena's eyes widened as she spotted the towering mass of dark fire that Lumo had summoned. With a quick gesture of her staff, she began chanting her incantation once more, her voice echoing through the clearing.

...Upon the serpent cast its bane, its blight. As the last syllables escaped her lips, she motioned her staff toward the swirling flames, commanding the whirlwinds to encircle them.

The Lindwyrm had almost broken through a portion of the wall, and as the last pieces of the wall came crumbling down, bringing the creature into full view, Serena directed the whirlwind straight toward it. The creature hissed loudly, lunging forward through the gap in the wall, venom still dripping from its fangs, and the gust of fire struck the Lindwyrm head-on, engulfing its serpentine body in a blaze of searing heat. The creature's deafening cry echoed through the marshland.

As the flames consumed the Lindwyrm's serpentine body, its scales crackled and hissed, releasing plumes of acrid smoke into the air. The once sleek and formidable creature now writhed and contorted in agony, its movements becoming increasingly erratic as the inferno tightened its grip. With a final, desperate lunge, the Lindwyrm attempted to break free from the flames' embrace, but its efforts were in vain. Its weakened form faltered, and with a deafening hiss of defiance, it collapsed to the ground in a heap of smoldering scales and charred flesh.

"It's down!" Meera jumped. "I can't believe it! We did it!"

She turned toward Lumo, who still couldn't get over the fact that he had channeled his magic intentionally for the first time.

As the Lindwyrm's struggles subsided and it lay still, Sylvanus moved forward with purpose. He lifted one side of the creature's mouth with his staff, revealing the charred fangs covered in ash.

"Oh dear, the fire has destroyed the venom," he said.

Meera and Lumo looked on with dread as Sylvanus explained. The fire had indeed incinerated all traces of the venom.

"We need to cut open this part here. There should be some venom still underneath," Sylvanus continued. "Meera, could you…"

"Uhm, yes," Meera said as she knelt down, gripping her dagger in her hand.

Lumo too moved forward, almost unsheathing his sword to help, but Serena stopped him.

"Not you. You're coming with me."

As Lumo cocked his head, Serena continued, "We need to find its nest. It should be close. Follow me."

Lumo followed Serena as they moved purposefully in search of the creature's nest. As they followed the marshy path deeper into the forest, the ground squelched beneath their feet. Soon, they reached a clearing where the air was heavy with the stench of decay.

"There," Serena said, pointing toward a gigantic mound of earth covered in thick, thorny vines.

As they drew closer, the mound revealed itself to be a massive, twisted nest woven from the roots of trees and lined with mounds of decaying vegetation.

Lumo's heart raced with excitement as he peered into the depths of the nest, expecting to find the creature's eggs lying within. But instead, his gaze fell upon something far more unexpected.

TREASURE.

Glittering jewels, gleaming gold, and shimmering artifacts lay scattered amidst the decaying vegetation. Lumo could hardly believe his eyes as he took in the sight, his mind reeling with the possibilities.

"We have to tell the others! We can't possibly carry all of these ourselves," Lumo exclaimed.

Serena placed a firm hand on Lumo's shoulder, her expression grave.

"Lumo, we cannot take any of this treasure. Believe it or not, it's the very reason for the Lindwyrm's existence," she explained. "Desire, when left unchecked, can lead to greed, which corrupts the soul."

Lumo frowned, struggling to comprehend Serena's words.

"But how..."

Serena sighed, her gaze turning toward the glittering hoard.

"This treasure represents everything the Lindwyrm once desired. It coveted wealth above all else, hoarding its treasures and letting its greed consume it until it became the monstrous creature we faced today."

"So... the Lindwyrm was once human?" Lumo asked.

"Yes, Lumo. And we cannot let the same fate befall us or anyone else. I need your help covering this mound so no one can discover it again."

As Lumo reluctantly agreed to help cover the mound, a sudden glint of light caught his eye, drawing his attention to a particular object within the hoard. Shielding his eyes from the blinding reflection, he moved closer to inspect the intriguing find. There, amidst the glittering treasure, lay a sheathed sword unlike any he had ever seen before.

Within the hilt of the sword lay embedded a mesmerizing gemstone, its facets catching the light and casting prismatic hues across the clearing. The crossguard was fashioned into elegant curves, suggesting a blend of functionality and artistic finesse. Lumo's breath caught in his throat as he reached out tentatively, his fingers brushing against the cool metal of the sheath. With both hands, he carefully drew the sword from its scabbard, marveling at the blade's exquisite craftsmanship.

As Lumo drew the sword from its sheath, the blade revealed itself to be equally extraordinary. It bore a mirror-like polish, reflecting the ambient light with a mesmerizing clarity. Etched along its length were ancient runes, their meaning lost to time but radiating an aura of power and mystique. Despite its apparent age, the blade appeared sharp and pristine, hinting at the craftsmanship that defied the passage of centuries. A soft hum filled the air, resonating with a strange, otherworldly energy, and Lumo could feel the power coursing through the sword, its presence seeming to pulse with a life of its own.

"Lumo, drop the sword," Serena's voice cut through the air, sharp and commanding.

Startled, Lumo blinked, tearing his gaze away from the mesmerizing blade to meet Serena's stern expression. His hand trembled slightly as he unknowingly released his grip on the sword, allowing it to fall back into its sheath with a soft clink.

"Sorry, I got carried away," Lumo murmured, his cheeks flushing with embarrassment.

"Remember what I said. We do not want the same fate to befall us."

"Yes, you're right," Lumo agreed. "It's just that... it's almost as if it was calling out to me."

"Greed has a way, Lumo, of twisting even the noblest of intentions. We must resist its temptations, no matter how alluring they may seem."

"Serena, what if... I promised to return the sword... once we've saved Oliver. Do you think I can have the sword then?"

"Lumo, I..."

"I won't break my promise. I'll return it once we've saved Oliver. You can make sure I do."

Serena forced a smile as she gave in reluctantly. "All right, but remember, this is a solemn oath and everything else stays buried."

"I agree," Lumo said, his features betraying no emotion as he picked up the sword.

As they worked together to conceal the treasure, Lumo felt a sense of purpose wash over him. This journey was about more than just finding Oliver—it was about facing the darkness within themselves and emerging stronger for it.

Once the mound was covered and hidden from sight, Lumo and Serena stood back, surveying their handiwork. With one last glance at the buried treasure, Lumo and Serena turned away, returning back to the group.

Meanwhile, Meera and Sylvanus had managed to carefully dissect the charred remains of the Lindwyrm in an effort to extract its venom.

Working in tandem, Meera and Sylvanus extracted the venom with utmost care, ensuring not to spill a single drop. From his satchel, Sylvanus produced an earthen gourd and carefully stored the venom.

Sylvanus inspected the gourd with a satisfied glance, ensuring it was sealed tightly. "Looks good."

Serena and Lumo joined them just in time. With Sylvanus leading the way, the group made their way back to the safety of his home. Along the journey, Lumo found himself lost in thought, contemplating the implications of his newfound discoveries and the role he was destined to play in the unfolding events. Lumo's mind buzzed with questions and uncertainties. But one thing was certain: the journey was far from over, and the trials that lay ahead would test not only his strength but also his resolve.

***

Deep within the shadowy corridors of the cult's hidden stronghold, Lilith paced restlessly. As she moved with silent grace, she turned her attention to a group of shadowy figures kneeling before her. Lilith's voice was a low, commanding whisper as she addressed them.

"Any news of them?" she asked, her tone betraying no hint of emotion.

The informants bowed their heads respectfully, their faces hidden beneath dark hoods. One of them spoke.

“They have been spotted,” he murmured. “They seek refuge in the home of the one known as Sylvanus.”

“That fool? What are they up to?” Lilith boomed.

“My apologies, glorious leader. I could not lurk in the Everglades for long. The dryads are too watchful,” the informant replied.

“Very well. They can’t hide there forever,” Lilith echoed. With a dismissive wave of her hand, Lilith turned away from the group of informants, who disappeared into the shadows.

Nearby, Marachi observed the exchange with keen interest. As Lilith's attention shifted to him, Marachi bowed respectfully.

“They betrayed us, Marachi,” Lilith fumed. “How could he do this? ...Never mind. What news do you bring?”

“The king still lives, my lady,” Marachi replied, his tone deferential.

“Excellent,” Lilith smirked, a glint of malice in her eyes.

“What do we do about the boy?” Marachi asked.

Lilith's gaze narrowed, considering the question for a moment before responding with a chilling certainty.

“Send Malikoth,” Lilith declared, her tone brooking no argument.

“As you wish. All hail Lord Cernunnos,” Marachi bowed before turning away.

***

Night had fallen as Lumo and the rest arrived at Sylvanus's house.

“I’m hungry,” Gus mumbled, his stomach rumbling loudly.

"Please help yourselves. There's plenty of food inside," Sylvanus said.

After a hearty meal, the group was ready to settle in for the night. Exhausted, they slept peacefully, the worries of the day fading away. A few hours past dawn, they were already awake, eager to head back to Avalora.

"How long will this take?" Lumo asked.

"A few hours," Sylvanus said. "I need to let the venom rest after transmuting it. I'll need some help."

"Aw, shucks! Well, how can I help?" Lumo asked.

"Not you, the big guy."

"M—Me?" Gus mumbled.

"Mmhmm..."

"All right then, I'm going to head outside for a bit," Lumo said.

Meera was already out in the backyard, and Serena was nowhere to be seen.

"What are you up to?" Lumo chimed.

As Lumo moved closer, Meera turned back to greet him, and Lumo saw Sylvanus's staff in her hands. Thin lines appeared on his forehead as he moved closer.

"Oh, nothing. Watching you yesterday, I was thinking to myself, maybe I should give some time studying the arts. I mean, I know I have the potential for it. I was speaking to Serena earlier, and she told me to try it out."

"T—That's great." Lumo smiled. "Yes, I remember you telling me that you can use the memory stone. I'm sure you can do it, Meera."

"I'm trying, but it isn't working for me," Meera tittered.

"Well, keep trying," Lumo chuckled.

"By the way, that new sword, where'd you get it?"

"Uhm, found it in the forest, near the Lindwyrm's nest," Lumo replied sheepishly.

"It looks good."

"It's perfectly balanced too," Lumo said, unsheathing the sword and attempting to stab the air.

"You've got moves, Lumo," Meera praised.

"Yeah. All thanks to my training with Oliver." Lumo gave the air a quick, confident slash with his sword.

"You don't say," Meera drawled. "Just be careful. That sword looks like it might fetch a good price."

"Oh, It's more than just a sword." Lumo beamed. "Here, look."

He held it in both hands, facing directly upwards. He closed his eyes gently and began focusing. Within moments, the sword pulsed with energy, and it erupted into flames. But these flames were larger and more intense than before, towering high into the air with a dark purplish-crimson hue.

Overwhelmed by the sudden surge of power, Lumo's grip faltered, and the sword slipped from his hands, clattering to the ground with a resounding clink.

"Still need to work on controlling it though," he laughed nervously, a hint of embarrassment coloring his cheeks as he ran a hand through his hair.

"I—It's amazing," Meera exclaimed. "How'd you figure out that you can use it that way?"

"You know, I'm not really sure. It's as if the sword was telling me I could."

"The sword spoke to you?" Meera asked, with raised eyebrows.

"No—I mean, I don't know. I really can't explain it… I just hope it's not cursed," Lumo quipped.

"Now where'd Serena go off to?" he asked, looking around.

"She said she had to collect some ingredients for Sylvanus."

"I see." Lumo gave a thoughtful glance.

Inside the house, Sylvanus was busy with the process. A tiny portion of the house contained a workbench full of beakers and tubes. Sylvanus poured the venom carefully into one of the beakers.

"All right, Gus. These are some of the items I need to add to the venom to transmute it," Sylvanus said, pointing to a few items on the table. "But they need to be converted into different forms first. It would take too long if I were to do it with alchemy. Luckily, I have you."

"How do I do that?" Gus asked.

"You, my friend, have a unique ability. I noticed it earlier. You were able to transform the wildfire berries into their most potent form and infuse them into your bubbles. That's precisely what I want you to do with these Nightshade berries and Moonflower nectar. Don't worry, they're harmless to you."

"So I just make bubbles?"

"Yes, just consume those and direct the bubbles in this tube. If my assumption is correct, I will be able to extract the most potent versions of the ingredients as the bubbles condense."

"Do I eat them one at a time or together?"

"Either way works," Sylvanus replied calmly.

Gus nodded eagerly, his eyes lighting up with anticipation as he reached for the Nightshade berries. As Gus consumed them, a sudden grimace contorted his face, betraying his initial enthusiasm.

"Whoa, these berries are a bit bitter."

He hurriedly reached for the Moonflower nectar, gulping the liquid down in one go.

"Ah, that's so much better." He exhaled with relief.

With a contented smile, he savored the combined flavors of the ingredients, relishing their unique tastes and textures.

"Mm, they're quite good together—mm."

With his usual belch, he manipulated the essence of the ingredients, channeling them into bubbles. Each bubble shimmered with a faint, ethereal glow, carrying within it the essence of the raw ingredients in their most potent form. Sylvanus watched with keen interest as Gus's bubbles coalesced and condensed inside the tubes into which Gus directed the bubbles.

"Perfect!" Sylvanus exclaimed, as he carefully adjusted the apparatus, ensuring that each bubble was captured precisely.

The door swung open, and Serena entered the room.

"I couldn't find it," Serena announced.

"What? But we need it," Sylvanus said, turning to her.

"Need what?" Gus asked.

"Mandrake root. I'm afraid it's crucial to stabilize the transmutation. Without that, this won't work."

"What do we do now?" Serena asked.

"You may get it in a tonic form at the potion shop at Leafcrest. It's popularly called Mandragora tonic."

"Wait, Mandra...gora. Is this it?" Gus mumbled, pulling out the tonic Maebh had given him for his sore throat.

As Gus pulled out the tonic, Sylvanus inspected it. "The brown color suggests this is it. Where'd you get it?"

"The Apo... Apo...the... um, the herbal shop in Avalora."

"That's great," Sylvanus said. "Let's just hope this is the right stuff."

Sylvanus added the tonic to the mix, stirring the beaker gently. Once the mandrake had been fully incorporated, Sylvanus stepped back, his gaze focused on the beaker before him.

"And now, we wait."

***

CHAPTER 18

In the war room, Lucius stood at the head of the table, his expression grave as he gazed at the map spread out before him. Archibald stood beside him on the right. The door swung open, and Marcus entered the room.

"Well?" Lucius asked.

"He's not there, but we found someone else who might know of his whereabouts," Marcus replied.

Marcus quietly signaled a few guards, and they retreated from the room, re-entering a few seconds later. Walking in front of them was Moose.

"Where is he?" Lucius demanded.

Moose appeared stoic as he replied, "I've already told your men, he's away on some business."

"Cut the horseshit." Lucius scowled. "You know where Kael is. It'd be best if you come clean now."

"And I've told you already. He's away."

Lucius appeared frustrated at Moose's response.

"Look, this isn't about the gambling den, all right? We just need to ask him some questions."

"Yeah, right," Moose smirked.

"You know the peasant boy… err, Lumoquin, don't you?" Lucius sighed. "You led him to the village at the border earlier. This is about that matter, all right? We just have a few questions for Kael about this… Malikoth person."

Moose's expression softened slightly. He was hesitant whether to believe Lucius or not. His first instinct reminded him that no guard nor knight was to be trusted, yet Lucius appeared to be honest.

"I will pass on your message. But I cannot convince him to come. That's all I can say on this matter."

"Now, listen here, you worthless scum," Marcus growled. "You seem to have forgotten who you're dealing with. If you think for one moment that you can play games with us, you've got another thing coming."

"Oh, yeah? What are you going to do about it?" Moose sneered, towering over Marcus with his broad shoulders squared and arms crossed defiantly across his chest.

Marcus shrank in his stead for a minute, but Lucius quickly intervened.

"That's enough, Marcus."

"Just tell Kael we wish to speak with him," Lucius said, turning his attention toward Moose. "You're free to go."

Moose scoffed in response. Just as he turned to leave, he clenched his fist and pretended to take a step toward Marcus, causing him to take a step back as a reflex. With a sneer, he exited the room.

***

As Lumo and the group sat around the table, the mood was one of weary relief. The successful creation of the antidote had lifted a great burden from their shoulders, yet Lumo's mind was anticipating their journey back and what awaited them at the castle—the truth. His mind wandered to questions about the cult.

"Did you know Lilith?" he asked Sylvanus, out of the blue.

"A little," Sylvanus replied, taken aback for a split second. "They tried recruiting me many years ago."

"Into their cult?"

Sylvanus pressed his lips together. "They were quite relentless. Kept hounding me."

"So that's why you left," Serena noted.

"It was the only way." Sylvanus exhaled softly.

And then Serena remembered something.

"Sylvanus, when I visited your cottage back at Honey Grange, I met an old man there, your neighbor. He said something about a lad… who died."

Sylvanus's eyes widened at Serena's words. He shied his eyes away.

"I'm sorry, Serena. I do not wish to talk about it, please."

"Very well, Sylvanus. But if the cult is responsible…"

"Please… stop," Sylvanus protested.

Noticing Sylvanus's demeanor, she stopped pressing further, and a pause filled the air.

"Well, this is awkward," Meera commented.

"I think… we should head back. Our work here is done," Serena suggested.

"I'm coming with you," Sylvanus declared.

"Back to Avalora?"

"You'll need my expertise in administering the antivenom. I cannot have this weigh on your conscience. If Reginald doesn't make it, the responsibility will be mine alone," Sylvanus grimaced.

"Besides, it's not like the dryads will miss me, right?" he jested.

As the conversation settled into uncomfortable smiles, the group gradually gathered their belongings, preparing for the journey back to the castle. Sylvanus carefully packed the vial containing the newly created antidote, ensuring it was secured within his satchel. With their preparations complete, the group set out from Sylvanus's home.

***

"It should be this way," Sylvanus pointed.

As the group began their journey home, amidst all uncertainties, one thing was certain: on their journey back, they would pass through the dryad grove.

"Oh, great! We get to meet the charming Zinnia again," Meera commented.

"Zinnia is an excellent leader," Sylvanus defended. "Without her, much of this forest would be encroached upon already. Even when the wildfires rage through the forest, it's her solemn duty to rally the dryads to aid with the restoration."

"Have you known her long?" Lumo asked.

"I've known her ever since I was a young mage, but dryads are immortal beings. Zinnia, in particular, has lived for millennia, if not longer. I can only imagine the things she has seen through the passage of time."

"You mean they don't die like us?"

"Dryads are bound to the trees of their birth. As long as their trees thrive, so do they, enduring through the ages."

Lumo gave a soft hum of understanding.

A few hours later, they arrived at the dryad grove. Zinnia, Meliae, and the other dryads appeared as they entered the grove.

"It seems our unwelcome visitors have returned," Zinnia remarked with a thinly veiled tone of disdain. "Have you fulfilled your promise?"

"The Lindwyrm is no longer a threat," Lumo announced.

Meliae, standing beside Zinnia, maintained a respectful silence; however, her smile showed how pleased she was—how they all were.

"Hello, Zinnia," Sylvanus greeted.

Zinnia's stoic expression remained unchanged, although her head bowed imperceptibly.

"Are you leaving our forest?" she said, her tone betraying a touch of guardedness.

"Isn't that what you wanted?" Sylvanus grinned mischievously.

"Hmm..." Zinnia grunted.

"Tell me about the Lindwyrm," she continued. "Is it dead?"

"It is. Serena took care of it," Lumo spoke.

"Me? You're being too modest, Lumo. Without your magic, it would not have been possible."

Lumo smiled sheepishly. "Let's just say it was a team effort, then."

Zinnia shared a knowing glance with Meliae, who stepped forward promptly.

"Zinnia and I agree you should have this gift as a token of our appreciation," Meliae announced, holding in her hands an intricate wooden staff with a golden topaz gem embedded within its head. "It's fashioned from the branches of our own trees."

"Go on, Lumo. It's yours," Serena prompted.

"Me? I already have this," he said, gently tapping his new sword.

"I think Meera should have it."

As all eyes turned to Meera, she hesitated, her gaze flicking to the staff in Meliae's hands.

"You'll need it if you want to practice magic, won't you?" Lumo proposed.

She stepped forward reluctantly. Accepting the staff from Meliae, she stared at it for a moment, appreciating the craftsmanship. She moved her fingers along the contours of the delicate patterns carved along its length.

"Thank you," she said, clutching it tightly.

"Use it well," Meliae said kindly.

After a brief moment, the group departed silently, their footsteps blending with the murmurs of the forest as they made their way toward the road leading to Avalora. The dryads watched in silence, their ethereal gazes following the travelers until they disappeared from view. As the forest reclaimed its tranquility, a subtle sigh seemed to ripple through the leaves, a whisper of farewell carried on the gentle breeze.

***

A few hours later, as the group journeyed back along the forest path, Lumo's eyes wandered to the signboard at the crossroad.

"I wonder what Leafcrest is like?"

"Leafcrest? Oh, it's the largest human settlement in Veridia," Sylvanus explained. "It's truly a magnificent city, if that is what one prefers. I prefer the forests any day, though."

"Is it like Avalora then?" Lumo asked.

"Indeed," Sylvanus concurred. "You'd think the name indicates the city is a blend of nature and human artisanship. On the contrary, the city is more urban than one can imagine."

"Really?" Lumo exclaimed.

"Perhaps it started out deserving of its name, but I suppose over time, we humans have discovered what truly works for us. Who knows?"

"Have you been to Leafcrest, Meera?" Lumo asked.

"Ughh, don't ask. I'm not exactly welcome there."

"Why, what'd you do?"

"I told you not to ask, didn't I?" Meera maintained. "But if you must know—I stole stuff and got caught far too many times."

"Some master thief you are," Lumo sneered.

"Hmpff."

"I really miss their festivals, though," she crooned.

"What kind of festivals?"

"They have a bunch of them. The annual Harvest Festival, the Grand Summer Carnival, and a few more in between. It's quite beautiful, really. The streets, they really come alive," Meera explained.

"They have the best honey-roasted pork," Gus chimed, his mouth drooling with saliva.

"Wait, Gus, you've been there too?"

"I was born there..." Gus smiled. "My Ma and Pa still live there."

"Well, it seems I'm the only one who hasn't been there," Lumo grumbled.

"Maybe, when this is all over, we can go there together," Gus remarked, gently rapping the index finger of both hands together. "Ma and Pa will be happy to meet you."

"You bet," Lumo chirped.

Lumo's thoughts were still lingering on the idea of Leafcrest when suddenly, a chill breeze swept through the trees, causing the leaves to rustle ominously. Lumo's senses prickled with unease, and he instinctively tightened his grip on his sword.

"I don't like the feel of this," Lumo muttered, glancing warily at the dense foliage surrounding them.

"Something's not right," Serena murmured.

Before anyone could react, a shadowy figure emerged from the underbrush, its eyes gleaming with malice. Malikoth revealed himself, inching forward slowly.

Malikoth's voice cut through the silence of the forest. "I see you are out of the Everglades," he remarked, his voice cold and authoritative, betraying no emotion.

Lumo's jaw clenched as he locked eyes with the sinister figure.

"Malikoth," he uttered.

Serena stepped forward promptly.

"You're making a grave mistake, Malikoth," she declared, gripping her staff tightly.

"You know who I am? Intriguing! Then perhaps you should also know that I'm not alone," Malikoth boomed.

Before long, more figures materialized behind Malikoth—at least a dozen hooded figures. Among them stood the menacing mime who had bested Serena earlier, grinning widely with malicious intent.

Meera swiftly drew her daggers, one in either hand. She still didn't know how to use magic. Gus, too, went on alert.

"Easy now," Malikoth spoke. "We just want the boy. The rest of you need not get hurt."

"Like hell!" Meera retaliated.

"Where is Oliver?" Lumo demanded.

"Oliver's whereabouts are none of your concern. Your only priority should be that of your companions. Come quietly with me and they may live," Malikoth said.

Lumo glanced at his friends, who betrayed no sign of yielding.

"We won't let you take him. Avalora will not bow to your threats," Serena reiterated.

"You underestimate the power of the Cimmerian Order. We will take what we desire, with or without your cooperation," Malikoth sneered.

"Then you will have to go through us," Serena countered.

"So be it!"

"Take the boy alive," he announced calmly to his brethren.

Serena, however, had no intentions of defending this time. She was certain this wouldn't go down quietly, and to top it, they were clearly outnumbered. She knew she had to go on the offensive.

"Gust of wind!" she shouted at the top of her voice.

Slashing her staff, she summoned a draught of wind, which caught the assailants by surprise. Malikoth evaded the attack at lightning speed. It was as if he disappeared into thin air and materialized somewhere else. Many of the assailants were sent flying backward, whereas the mime stood silent, his palms facing Serena as if leaning against an invisible wall.

Lumo, sensing the urgency of the situation, drew his sword even as a few surviving assailants spread out, encircling the group. He took up a battle-ready stance, his eyes locked on their enemies, his muscles tense with anticipation.

Meanwhile, Malikoth's voice echoed through the trees, taunting them with their outnumbered status. "You are but a handful against our might."

As Serena's attention was diverted, she felt a sudden tug on her staff. With a sinking feeling, she realized that the mime had once again summoned an invisible rope, attempting to wrest her weapon from her grasp. This time, however, Serena refused to go down without a fight.

"Oh no, you don't!"

With fierce determination, Serena planted her staff firmly on the ground and pushed with all her strength, driving the lower end of her staff into the earth.

"Earth, part beneath me!" she shouted as she drove the staff further into the earth.

The ground trembled and cracks spiderwebbed out from the point of impact, snaking their way toward the mime, who struggled to maintain his footing on the unstable ground. As the cracks spread, the invisible rope that had ensnared Serena's staff vanished, causing the mime to stumble backward in surprise. With a quick sidestep, he narrowly avoided falling into the growing chasm. The assailants near the mime, who were ready to launch their fire spells, lost their balance, their spells faltering. A few of the hurled bolts of fire went flying in different directions.

"They're using fire spells!" Lumo announced.

Gus knew exactly what he needed to do. He pulled out a flask filled with water and began gulping it down. With a large belch, he summoned bubbles of water that shimmered around the group. With full concentration, he began directing the bubbles in the path of the fiery spells. The bubbles effectively blocked the fire spells, fizzing out and keeping the group from harm's way. Serena, too, went on the defensive with the sheer number of spells coming their way.

"Meera, we need to cull their numbers," Lumo directed.

"Right," Meera nodded.

Just as Lumo and Meera prepared themselves to engage with the cultists in physical combat, Malikoth revealed himself. As Malikoth emerged from the shadows, his presence sent a shiver down their spines. His dark aura seemed to suffocate the surrounding air, and his eyes gleamed with malicious intent as he surveyed the scene.

Without hesitation, Malikoth mumbled a spell and shadowy tendrils snaked from his own shadow toward Lumo and Meera. Meera quickly threw a dagger in Malikoth's direction, but Malikoth lunged sideways, narrowly avoiding the dagger. The shadowy tendrils merged with Lumo's and Meera's shadows, rooting them in place, and then made their way upwards, wrapping around their limbs, binding them tightly, and rendering them immobile.

"Can't move," Meera grunted as she struggled to free herself.

Lumo had no choice. He closed his eyes and focused. The sword went ablaze, its dark fire towering in the sky.

"Control the flow of mana, Lumo," Sylvanus shouted. "Concentrate."

Lumo focused harder, and the dark fire indeed subsided, shaping it into a controlled inferno that danced along the length of his sword. As the flames grew brighter, they seemed to react with the shadowy tendrils binding them. Slowly but surely, they unravel, their grip loosening on Lumo and Meera's limbs. With a final surge of determination, Lumo exerted his will, pushing the flames to their limit. The shadows shattered, dissipating into wisps of darkness that faded into nothingness.

Free at last, Lumo and Meera stumbled, their bodies trembling from the exertion of the ordeal.

Meanwhile, as more of the assailants recovered from their previous ordeals, the intensity of fire spells coming toward the group increased. Gus and Serena struggled with the defense.

"Uh, I'm running out of bubbles," Gus gasped.

As Serena looked around with horror in her eyes, it really seemed as if this was their end unless she did something. With no time to lose, she launched a counteroffensive.

"Shield your eyes," she ordered.

Lumo, Meera, Gus, and Sylvanus quickly raised their arms to shield their eyes as Serena raised her staff high in the air.

By sun's bright grace, let brilliance embrace,

Shroud foes in blinding light, truth in its blaze.

As the words left her lips, a blinding ball of light erupted from the tip of her staff, radiating with an intensity that illuminated the entire forest. As the light spread, it washed over the assailants, blinding them with its dazzling brilliance. Their movements faltered, and they staggered back, their hands flying to shield their eyes from the searing brightness. Within the glow of the light, their forms appeared as mere silhouettes, their features obscured by the intense illumination. Hindered by the sudden onslaught of light, they stumbled and groped blindly, disoriented and vulnerable in the face of Serena's powerful magic.

"This is our chance," Serena said.

As Lumo and Meera opened their eyes, they witnessed many of the assailants appearing dazed. They closed the distance, taking out the attackers one by one.

Serena slashed her staff, shouting, "Ice shards!" The shards took out many of the cultists with chilling precision. A silent scream of agony seemed to emanate from the mime's expressionless mask as a sharp shard found its mark, piercing his arm. Despite his inability to vocalize his pain, his contorted features and the way he stumbled to the floor were as subtle as a marching band in a library, speaking volumes to everyone present.

As the tide of battle turned in favor of the heroes, it became clear that this was a thorough victory. Malikoth, however, was called the unbearable for a reason. Relentless, he summoned his most terrifying power yet. Dark tendrils, like insidious serpents, slithered from the shadows, seeking their prey. With a predatory precision, they homed in on Gus, finding purchase upon his form.

In a horrifying display, the tendrils snaked their way up Gus's body, coiling around him like a suffocating shroud. They slithered into his mouth, silencing any protest, his eyes widening at the ordeal, and then, they claimed dominion over his will. Gus stood frozen, a mere puppet in the hands of Malikoth, his eyes vacant and devoid of warmth. The group watched in horror as their friend was transformed before their eyes, his once jovial demeanor replaced by an eerie stillness.

As Gus stood motionless, the group was stunned into silence, grappling with the unnerving sight before them. They exchanged bewildered glances, unable to comprehend the sudden shift in their companion.

Gus, meanwhile, lunged forward with an unnatural swiftness, catching Serena off guard. With a forceful shove, he sent her sprawling backward, the impact knocking the staff from her grasp. She tumbled several feet away, her breath stolen by the sudden assault. Gus then turned his attention toward Lumo, his gaze empty and devoid of recognition.

It became clear now. Their dear friend had become a weapon, a vessel of Malikoth's malevolent influence. Lumo’s sword was at the ready, but this was his friend, the very person he had risked his life to protect earlier. As Gus lunged forward once again, Lumo had no choice but to evade him.

"Gus, it's me!" Lumo shouted.

However, Malikoth was in complete control of Gus. Gus pivoted slowly and charged again at Lumo. Playing a game of cat and mouse with Gus, Lumo grew increasingly apprehensive. It felt like a human facing off against a bear—daunting and relentless. Gus, being the big guy that he was, took his sweet time to pivot. Lumo used these moments to observe Malikoth's behavior, noting that he appeared thoroughly focused on controlling Gus.

"Meera... do something about Malikoth," Lumo directed.

Meera turned her attention toward Malikoth, who indeed stood with unwavering focus as he exerted his control over Gus. She noticed the belt that hung around Malikoth's waist. It was a sturdy metal belt with a dark onyx jewel embedded in the centerpiece.

"I know what to do," she mumbled.

Summoning all her skill and precision, Meera gripped her dagger tightly. With a swift and practiced motion, she launched the dagger toward the center of Malikoth's belt, aiming directly for the jewel. The dagger soared through the air, guided by Meera's unwavering aim. As it struck its mark with a resounding impact, a crack echoed through the forest, and the jewel shattered into countless shards, casting a brief flash of light.

With a triumphant cry, Meera's actions shattered Malikoth's control over Gus, freeing him from the shadowy grasp that had ensnared him. As the tendrils dissipated, Gus stumbled forward, his eyes slowly regaining their clarity as he shook off the remnants of Malikoth's influence.

"Gus, is that you?" Lumo asked nervously.

"Uhm, yes... I don't know what happened," Gus replied.

"Thank heavens."

Malikoth was in shock as he surveyed the damage to his belt. He looked around, confused and disgusted at the same time.

As victory seemed within their grasp, a new threat emerged from the chaos. The injured mime, fueled by fury and desperation, launched a relentless assault. Trees splintered and fell, cut cleanly in two by an unseen force, as the group watched in horror. Amidst the chaos, Sylvanus's keen senses detected the telltale signs of an invisible blade, its lethal edge cutting through the air, although the mime clearly had problems controlling it with his injured arm. With a sinking feeling in his heart, he knew that their enemy wielded a weapon of unimaginable danger.

Before Sylvanus could warn the others, Malikoth's voice rang in the distance. "No, the boy must be taken alive."

The mime's response, however, was a defiant gesture, a silent rejection of Malikoth's authority. With a smirk playing across his lips, he raised a single middle finger.

As Sylvanus heard Malikoth's call, it became clear—the mime was targeting Lumo. With Serena's staff still out of her reach, Sylvanus knew he was the only thing standing between the mime and Lumo.

Sylvanus summoned his last ounce of strength, calling upon the last remnants of magic that coursed through his veins. With his staff in hand and muttering a spell under his breath, he conjured a barrier of shimmering light, its radiant energy forming a protective shield in front of him. As the mime's invisible blade came slashing forward, it clashed against the barrier, briefly shimmering into view and revealing its lethal nature in a flash of silver.

As Sylvanus struggled to fight the impending assault of the blade, he felt his force weakening. Despite his valiant efforts to maintain the barrier, the sheer force of the blade proved too much to withstand. With a deafening crack, the barrier shattered under the relentless assault, sending Sylvanus reeling backward, his body bathed in the fading glow of magic. Lumo watched in horror as Sylvanus went flying beside him. Gus, who was behind Lumo at this point, caught Sylvanus as he landed, but it was too late. Sylvanus was clearly injured.

"Sylvanus!" Serena cried.

Reacting quickly, Serena grabbed her fallen staff and sent forth a gust of wind, throwing the mime backward.

"Retreat!" Malikoth shouted as an inherently unstable swirling dark void materialized behind him. The few remaining cultists rushed in, as did the mime, who struggled with his foothold.

"Serena, do not let him escape!" Lumo screamed.

Serena did not need to hear anymore. With a swift motion, she chanted the words of power, calling upon the very essence of nature to heed her command. Vines erupted from the forest floor, moving swiftly toward Malikoth and binding him in place before he could disappear.

Lumo dashed forward with unparalleled speed, his sword held firmly in his grasp. With a resounding strike, he delivered a powerful blow to Malikoth's side with the back of his sword, sending him sprawling to the ground in stunned silence.

As the dust settled and the last echoes of conflict faded into the air, the group stood victorious, although it did not feel like a victory.

Serena rushed to Sylvanus's side, who lay on the ground, his form haggard and broken, his breaths shallow and labored. Sylvanus's chest bore a gaping wound, a jagged tear in his flesh that oozed red and hinted at the severity of his injuries. She knelt beside him, her hands trembling as she reached out to touch his battered form.

"Sylvanus," she whispered with a choked voice.

Sylvanus managed a weak smile, his eyes flickering with fading light.

"I... I did what I could."

"Stay still, don't move," Serena directed as she moved her staff to cast a healing spell.

"No. It's... it's my time. I can feel it."

Tears welled in Serena's eyes as she cradled his head in her arms, and perhaps for the first time, the usually stoic sorceress appeared to be in deep emotional turmoil.

Sylvanus's gaze met hers, his eyes filled with a quiet acceptance.

"You... you must carry on... Save the k..."

Before he could finish his sentence, with a final, labored breath, Sylvanus's eyes fluttered closed, his form growing still. Serena's tears fell freely as she held him close, the weight of his sacrifice heavy upon her heart. In that moment, amidst the quiet of the forest, she knew that they had lost more than a comrade—they had lost a friend, a mentor, a guiding light in the darkness.

Lumo had rushed back to Serena's side, and he fell silent as he saw Serena holding Sylvanus's lifeless body.

"Sylvanus..."

Serena wiped the tears from her eyes and, with a cold, determined look, she directed, "We need to get him back to Dryad's Glove; it's what he would have wanted."

"Serena, are you all right?" Lumo asked.

"Now is not the time, Lumo," Serena said, her voice cold and distant.

Lumo surveyed the scene, taking in the numerous bodies of their fallen adversaries.

"What about all the other bodies? Do we..."

"Does it look like I care?" Serena's voice thundered.

As a tense silence settled over the forest, Meera quietly approached Lumo, placing a hand on his shoulder and motioning for him to follow.

"Come, I'll help you bind Malikoth," she said.

***

CHAPTER 19

"That was pretty insensitive of me," Lumo broke the quietude as they journeyed back to the Dryad's Glove.

"It was an inappropriate question, yes," Meera mumbled. "But you weren't wrong. It was just bad timing. Relax."

Lumo offered a soft grunt.

Meera and Lumo had managed to bind Malikoth tightly with her rope. They made sure his belt was stripped off, as were the countless shards that fell off. Serena appeared quiet, lost in her thoughts, and Lumo let her be.

The rest of the journey was quiet. A while later, they arrived at the Glove. Zinnia and Meliae appeared as Serena and the others came into view, bringing Sylvanus's lifeless form on horseback.

Zinnia moved forward slowly. Her expression displayed the turmoil she faced in her mind. Meliae, too, was stricken with grief.

"Is he..."

Serena and the others had their heads lowered as if unable to respond. Zinnia had her answer.

"How did this happen?" she asked, her gaze fixed on Sylvanus.

"We were ambushed," Serena replied. "Sylvanus fought bravely, but..."

Zinnia's eyes narrowed as she turned her attention to Malikoth.

"Was it him?" she demanded, her voice a low growl of anger.

Malikoth was awake but silent. Not a word of protest escaped his lips.

Lumo explained what had transpired. "This is the threat I spoke of earlier. The cult will not stop at anything to achieve their purpose in the name of their god, and believe me, this won't be the last unless we put an end to it."

Zinnia pondered. She moved quietly closer to Malikoth. "What god do you serve?"

The fury in her eyes was evident, yet Malikoth continued to maintain his defiant silence.

"I'm speaking to you, vile creature," she bellowed.

As Malikoth continued ignoring her with a disgusted look on his face, Lumo detailed the specifics they had encountered at the shrine and the deity they worshipped.

"Cernunnos..." Zinnia repeated, with a perplexed look on her face.

She quietly retreated a distance away, and a few of the other dryads followed her. They spoke something in secret. Zinnia appeared to be in a deep conversation with the rest of them. Before long, she reappeared in front of the group.

"What do you know about Cernunnos?" she asked.

"Not much," Lumo replied. "We know the cult seeks to vanquish the king's bloodline, but we really don't know much more about their plans and this god of theirs. What do you know of him?"

"The god they worship, Cernunnos, is one of the primordial deities."

"Primordial, you mean... before time?"

Zinnia nodded solemnly. "He is darkness incarnate... We need to commune with Gaia. We shall lay Sylvanus to rest."

Gus dismounted his horse with some effort and carried Sylvanus down from the horse. As Meliae stepped forward, she tenderly cradled Sylvanus in her arms, accepting him from Gus with a silent solemnity.

Together, they carried Sylvanus's body to a sacred grove within the Glove, where they laid him to rest beneath the sheltering boughs of the ancient trees. With trembling hands, Serena carefully placed the pendant Sylvanus had given her back onto his chest. Each movement was slow and deliberate, as if she were reluctant to let go. As she released the pendant, she leaned forward, pressing a gentle kiss to Sylvanus's forehead.

"May you journey well, my friend," she whispered.

As the group stood in silent reverence, Zinnia spoke, her voice resonating with solemnity. "May the earth embrace him, and may his spirit find peace. Gaia, please guide this soul to eternal rest."

With a soft rustling, the soil seemed to part of its own accord, enveloping Sylvanus's body in a cocoon of earth and foliage. In a mesmerizing display of magic, Sylvanus's form sank, gradually melding with the earth until he disappeared from view, becoming one with the sacred grove.

With a final farewell, the group bid Sylvanus farewell.

***

Departing the Dryad's Glove once again, they rode silently several hours into the evening, stopping at the village for the night. Chief Vaida and the others were happy to see them. Meera kept a keen watch on Lumo and Lotte, and it seemed as if Lumo was very much wary of Meera's scrutinizing gaze the entire time, although she said nothing. He tried to keep it casual. Besides, a lot of the group's attention was diverted to making sure Malikoth did not escape. Malikoth did not even try.

They encountered Isolde again, who had heard about the ambush and was worried her husband Gideon might have been among the assailants. Meera quickly laid her suspicions to rest.

They rode onwards to Avalora the next day. Not much was said about the transpired events during the entire trip, but the tension had dissipated over time. Lumo tried to get more information from Malikoth on the day; however, Malikoth's lips remained tightly sealed.

As the day progressed, Serena's demeanor was back to her usual self, and Lumo was more apprehensive about the future than the past. He did have a new sword to practice with, and every time they stopped, he would practice a bit more, trying to gain control over the fire. Meera would join him in the practice bouts, trying to summon her own magic, all in vain. Gus's stomach rumbled more often, prompting the group to take more frequent breaks. Eventually, though, they did make it back to Avalora.

Lumo's heart pounded in his chest as they approached the castle gates. He could only guess what fate awaited him under Lucius's mercy. As they entered the castle gates, they were met with the gaze of a few guards, who noticed their prisoner. They instinctively went on guard; however, Serena motioned for them to go at ease.

"I must see Lucius," she said.

"Err, yes, madam sorceress. He's been in the war room more frequently these days," one of the guards informed.

With a quick tilt of her head, Serena entered the castle courtyard along with the rest. A few squires promptly took charge of the horses, leading them to their stables. Serena led the way. Lumo had a firm grasp of Malikoth's bindings as they continued their way into the castle.

Just then, Archibald came into view.

"Serena, you're back," Archibald greeted.

His gaze shifted immediately to Malikoth, and a glint of fear shone in his eyes. Malikoth's eyes, too, met Archibald's, but they showed no fear, only contempt.

"You've captured him. T—That's excellent news. Lucius is in the throne room. This is perfect timing."

"Perfect timing for what?"

"Come, you'll see," Archibald said.

As Serena and the others entered the throne room, Lucius stood with authority, with Marcus beside him. In front of him stood Kael in his usual elegant suit. Moose stood by Kael's side, casting a watchful eye on Marcus throughout, while Marcus wore a slightly daunted expression, evidently affected by Moose's presence. The combination of Kael and Moose standing next to each other would have been comical given any other time—Moose being almost 6'4" and Kael being the opposite at around 4'6"—but the discussions were serious.

"I've told you everything already," Kael reiterated.

Their attention was quickly diverted as Serena and the others stepped into the room with Malikoth.

"E—Elion…" Kael mumbled as his eyes fell on Malikoth.

"I don't go by that name anymore… father," Malikoth declared after a pause.

That was the first time Malikoth had said anything since his capture.

"Serena, how did you…" Lucius's voice trailed off.

As Serena related the incident, Lucius listened intently. Kael's eyes, however, widened in shock. He knew what his son was capable of, but to hear it firsthand unsettled him deeply.

"I'm sorry to hear about Sylvanus. May he rest in peace," Lucius offered.

"Well, it seems you are no longer needed," Lucius admonished, turning to Kael.

"What are you going to do with him?" Kael asked.

"Isn't it obvious? We're going to get the information we need about Prince Oliver, and if he refuses to cooperate... that's something one can only imagine."

"Elion, please. Tell them everything. I beg of you," Kael pleaded.

"Stop calling me that," Malikoth growled.

"You should listen to your father," Lucius warned.

Malikoth, however, spat in defiance. "You're going to have to kill me. My dedication to our cause is unwavering."

As the conversation appeared to conclude to a stalemate, Serena promptly stepped forward.

"This can wait, Lucius. We have urgent matters to tend to first. Any improvement on His Majesty's condition?"

"I'm afraid not. It's getting worse."

"Then there's no time. We were able to procure an antivenom thanks to..." her voice wavered, "Sylvanus."

"We need to go now."

"Impossible," Malikoth mocked. "The poison comes from a creature not of this realm. You will never be able to cure him."

Serena's expressions displayed her uncertainty. Lucius, sensing her demeanor, spoke up.

"Is it true? Are you sure the antivenom will work?"

"No," Serena mumbled, her gaze wandering to the floor.

"Tell us how to cure him," Lucius growled in fury, his hand instinctively reaching out for the handle of his sword.

"Never," Malikoth hissed.

"Lucius, this antivenom was specifically created by Sylvanus," Serena imparted. "Although he was unsure of it, he would never have concocted it if it did not have promise. It's our best chance, given we are running out of time."

Archibald quietly moved forward with concern. "I beg to differ. I don't think we should risk it, Lucius. We can compel him to divulge the information."

Lucius's grip on his sword relaxed as he pondered the next course of action.

"We have no choice, Archibald. Serena is right; we are running out of time. We will have to trust her judgment."

"Guards, send this man to the dungeon," Lucius condemned. "…And his father too."

Throughout the conversation, Lumo had refrained from speaking until this moment.

"Wait, Kael is innocent. Why are you…"

"Boy, you and I have an entirely different score to settle. Unless you want to join them as well, you will watch what you say," Lucius commanded, cutting him mid-sentence.

"But he's right," Meera chimed. "Kael is innocent."

"Perhaps so, but Malikoth seems to respond to him. We will do whatever it takes to get the information we need."

"Then you're no different from them," Lumo retorted, a look of defiance in his eyes.

Lucius stared with a bewildered look, momentarily taken aback. As Marcus and a few guards stepped forward to take custody of Kael and Malikoth, Moose advanced defiantly.

"It's all right, Moose. Don't get involved," Kael intervened, accepting his fate. Despite the dire circumstances, he had harbored a faint hope of reaching his son during their time together, no matter how daunting the task.

"I knew it was a mistake trusting you," Moose grunted, his gaze locked with Lucius's.

As Moose reluctantly stepped aside, Marcus moved forward proudly, as if claiming victory from their earlier confrontation.

"Keep a close watch on them," Lucius commanded as Marcus and a few guards led Malikoth and Kael in chains to the dungeon.

"Let's get on with it, then. No time to lose," Lucius announced.

***

As Lucius led the way to the king's chambers, the guards at the entrance quickly stepped aside, allowing the group to enter.

"Not you three," Lucius declared, his words directed at Lumo, Meera, and Gus.

"Lucius, it's all right. They risked their lives to get the antivenom. I think they deserve to be here," Serena clarified.

Lucius's face grimaced in reluctance, but he gave in.

As everyone gathered around the king's bedside, they took note of his frail form. He had lost a lot of weight. His cheeks were pallid and sunken, revealing the bony outline underneath the skin. The poison had snaked its way across the veins in his neck to just beneath his jawline. The king was barely breathing but alive, albeit unconscious. The healers were promptly called in.

"This is the antivenom," Serena said, pulling out the concoction and handing it diligently to one of the healers, an elder among the group. As the healer uncorked the vial, a thick fume of dark green smoke escaped its neck. The smell was putrid and foul, filling the room instantly.

"Does it need to be mixed with something?" the elder healer asked.

"No, just administer it orally."

"Very well," the healer murmured.

"Wait, Lucius, are you sure about this?" Archibald advised once more.

"Go on," Lucius directed the healer with authority.

As one of the healers carefully lifted the king's head, the elder healer carefully held the vial to his lips, ensuring the liquid entered the mouth without spilling. With some difficulty, they managed to orally administer the antivenom to the king.

As everyone watched with bated breath, a tense silence enveloped the room. Within moments, the king's arms and legs convulsed with violent spasms. There was a wisp of agony on his face as his wrinkles appeared more prominent. His breathing became more violent, and agony turned to horror as the black poison began creeping across his cheeks, seeping into every vein on his face.

As the onlookers watched with horror, it seemed as if things had truly gone wrong.

"I knew this was a mistake! We're going to lose him," Archibald exclaimed.

Lucius turned to Serena with a helpless look on his face.

"Steady his limbs," Serena directed without turning to meet Lucius's gaze.

The healers wrestled with the king's thrashing limbs, their efforts barely enough to contain his violent spasms. For a harrowing moment, it seemed as though the convulsions would never cease. But eventually, they stopped. With a final long, hard breath, the king's body went limp. The king had stopped breathing.

“NO!” Lucius screamed in despair as the healers released their grip on the dead king’s limbs.

Serena closed her eyes, lowering her head. She knew this was a possibility. This was precisely the scenario Sylvanus had sought to prevent by insisting on administering the antidote himself. All hope was lost.

But just then, a sudden gasp shattered the silence. The king's chest heaved with the effort of drawing breath.

“No, he’s still alive!” Lucius’s exclamation rang out with renewed hope.

The room fell into a tense silence, eyes fixed on the king. Slowly, the poison seemed to fade, its dark color receding inch by inch. The king’s face, though still pale, showed signs of life returning. The antivenom had begun its work. A collective sigh of relief filled the room, quickly followed by cheers of joy as the realization sank in. The king was alive.

“Shhh,” the elder healer hushed.

Recognizing the sensitivity of the situation, the gathered members piped down.

“His Majesty needs to rest,” the elder healer croaked. “One of us will be monitoring his condition the entire time, but perhaps it’s best to clear the space.”

“Right, we should vacate the room,” Lucius announced.

One by one, each member quietly exited the room in a silent procession, their faces reflecting a peaceful expression as hope was restored.

***

Back at the cult’s stronghold, the mime and a few of the defeated cultists stood in front of Lilith, with Marachi by her side.

“What is he trying to say?” Lilith quizzed Marachi.

The mime shook his head in disbelief. He tried again to reenact the events that had transpired.

First, he pantomimed the action of lassoing Serena's staff, his hands mimicking with a pull and push how he had attempted to wrestle control of the weapon from her grasp. Next, he depicted the ground parting beneath his feet, his body swaying and trembling as he acted out the sensation of the earth splitting apart beneath him, a look of exaggerated shock and disbelief on his face.

Then the mime recreated the scene of Malikoth's binds ensnaring their enemies, holding himself tightly with both hands and thrashing about. As the mime continued his performance, he mimicked Lumo brandishing his blazing sword, his hands flickering with imaginary flames, eventually fizzling out into feeble sparks.

Mimicking Serena's blinding light, he stumbled around blindly, bumping into imaginary obstacles and tripping over his own feet. With a wince of pain, the mime then mimicked the shard of ice striking his arm, his face contorting in mock agony.

Next, he depicted the moment of Malikoth's control over Gus. He stiffened his limbs and moved around robotically. The mime then recreated the scene of Meera's dagger shattering Malikoth's belt, his hands gesturing dramatically as he portrayed the shattering of the jewel.

Finally, the mime acted out the moment of his own rage, thrashing both fists in the air and gesturing an invisible blade only to have it shattered, and then he fell back comically as if trying to explain Serena's gust of wind knocking him back. As the mime concluded his performance, he acted out the final moment of the battle, running toward the swirling portal with exaggerated strides.

"What?" Lilith asked with a befuddled look.

The mime waved his hand with a sigh as if saying, "Never mind."

"Where is Malikoth?" Lilith inquired.

The mime simply shrugged.

Lilith's brow twitched as she held three fingers to the middle of her temple, as if at wit's end.

"Can someone please tell me what happened to Malikoth?" she boomed, her voice echoing loudly.

"We were defeated in battle, glorious leader. Malikoth never made it back," one of the defeated cultists finally spoke.

With an exasperated expression, the mime threw his hands up in the air, palms facing upward, and let out an exaggerated sigh. Then, with a dramatic sweep of his arm toward the cultist, the mime nodded vigorously, as if to say, "Exactly! That's what I've been trying to convey all this time!"

"Hmm... I see. It seems they might have defeated Malikoth then," Lilith concluded.

"What if he has been captured?" Marachi asked.

"Capturing Malikoth? Highly improbable. He would never yield without a fierce struggle."

The mime caught hold of one of the sleeves of his tunic with his hand and slowly pulled his other arm into the tunic. He pointed to the hanging sleeve promptly.

"Disarmed... I think he means Malikoth was disarmed," Marachi suggested, even as Lilith stood blank-faced.

The mime snapped his fingers and bobbed his head enthusiastically with a smile, happy that someone had finally understood what he wanted to say.

"If he has been captured, they could compel him to..."

"Malikoth is loyal to our cause. His capture will do them no good," Lilith cut Marachi off.

"There are always ways, milady. You know this better than anyone. If he has indeed been captured, we must silence him."

"You will do no such thing. Let me think for a moment," Lilith said as she pondered.

"Perhaps… this will work in our favor, Marachi," she spoke after a moment.

"What do you mean, milady?"

"They will come for their… prince. If Malikoth breaks, he will lead them right to us. If not, you know what has to be done."

"I understand, milady." Marachi grinned wickedly.

The mime scratched his head in confusion as Lilith quietly withdrew from their midst.

***

CHAPTER 20

A few days had passed. Malikoth was in the dungeons with Kael, and Lucius had made sure the security was tightened, leaving nothing to chance. He had let Lumo be on the condition that he would not intervene in any of the affairs of the throne. Lumo was free to go.

Meera who had been pardoned for the time being, was now under the watchful training of the sorceress. Though still a bit of an outsider, the castle's new arrangements were giving her a second chance. Lumo had seen her a few times in passing, and though he hadn't had a chance to talk much, it was clear her path had taken a different turn from her past as a thief.

Lumo stepped into the castle courtyard, feeling the weight of his earlier trials lift from his shoulders, if only for a moment. He took a deep breath, savoring the scents of the various flowers lining the space.

He wandered further in, running his fingers over the familiar grooves of the stone balustrade, letting the moment sink in. The sound of the bubbling fountain filled his ears—a comforting melody he had known his entire life. He was finally home.

"Back at last," he muttered, a weary smile tugging at his lips as he strolled past the courtyard, reaching the training grounds.

"Oi, Lumo!" a cheerful voice called from across the yard.

Lumo turned to see Eamon, one of Lucius's knights who often trained with them, striding over. Eamon was as broad-shouldered as ever, his blonde hair tousled from whatever rigorous training he'd been engaged in.

"I see the dungeons couldn't hold you for long," Eamon teased.

Lumo chuckled, shaking his head. "They made it far too boring in there. I had to get out."

Eamon leaned in with a crooked grin. "Well, I'm sure we can fix the boring part."

"What's the wager this time?" Lumo shot back.

Eamon's eyebrow quirked, clearly entertained. "Your pride versus mine. Let's see if your blade is as quick as your tongue." Without waiting, he tossed Lumo a wooden practice sword from a nearby rack.

Lumo caught the sword and tossed it back with a dismissive flick of his wrist. "A wooden sword? I don't think so." He reached for his real blade and unsheathed it in one smooth motion. "If we're going to spar, I'll need something with a bit more weight."

"Oh, this'll be fun." Eamon laughed heartily.

Eamon lunged forward with a sharp thrust, his own sword coming down hard toward Lumo. Lumo parried the blow, the impact of steel ringing out sharply through the courtyard. The sound drew a few glances from nearby squires, but the two combatants were entirely focused on each other.

"Too slow, Lumo!" Eamon teased, pushing the attack with a flurry of blows.

Lumo's boots churned the dirt as he danced back, deflecting each blow. Eamon's attacks came fast and relentless, driving him on the defensive.

"Come on, Lumo!" Eamon urged, easily blocking Lumo's counterattacks. "You're moving like you've still got shackles on! Come on, show me something real."

Lumo's brow furrowed as he jabbed and swiped, but Eamon's defenses were unyielding. His sword rang against Eamon's with every failed strike, pushing him to rethink his next move. Before he could adjust his approach, Eamon twisted his blade, knocking Lumo's aside with a swift flick.

"You had an opening," Eamon remarked, lowering his sword but keeping it unsheathed. "Why didn't you go for the disarm when I overextended?"

Lumo exhaled sharply, frustration tightening his jaw. "I—" he hesitated, glancing down at his sword. "I haven't quite mastered that move yet."

Eamon studied him for a moment, then let out a soft chuckle. "Still struggling with it, huh? You'll get there. But remember, hesitation is what gets you killed out there."

Lumo walked over, retrieving his fallen sword before sliding it back into its sheath with a quiet snick.

"I know," he muttered. "Just need to get the hang of it."

"Good," Eamon said, clapping him on the back with a grin. "Because next time, I won't be going easy on you."

Lumo wiped the sweat from his brow, still catching his breath. "You know, I fought a bunch of people earlier and I felt I was able to deal with them rather proficiently, but sparring with you… You're just too fast for me and it looked so easy."

Eamon gave a half-hearted shrug, brushing dirt from his tunic. "It's nothing, really. Just the usual stuff."

"Well, at least Lucius made a smart choice when he put you in charge of the training," Lumo remarked.

Eamon chuckled dryly, his smile more of a twitch. "Yeah, well... Lucius always trusted me. But you know how it is. He's got his favorites. Marcus—" he paused again, as though unsure if he should continue. "Marcus is the one who really gets his attention. Feels like he's Lucius's brother more than I ever could be."

Lumo's eyes narrowed slightly. "What do you mean by that?"

Eamon glanced toward the wooden dummies, his gaze distant. "Nothing, just... Marcus always seems to be the one who gets the credit. I'm just another knight in the company, you know?"

Lumo wasn't sure if it was the tiredness from the sparring or something else that made Eamon's words carry a certain finality.

Before Lumo could respond, a figure appeared at the edge of the training ground. It was Meera, her footsteps quick as she made her way toward him.

"There you are," she said, a hint of urgency in her tone. "I've been looking all over for you."

"Oh, hey. Meera. What's going on?"

"Lumo. We need to go," Meera said.

"Where to?"

"The king has been asking for you."

Lumo's heart skipped a beat. "He's awake?" Lumo asked, a glint of happiness in his eyes.

"Yes, let's go."

Lumo hesitated for a moment, glancing back at Eamon, who had already turned to walk toward the training rack, resuming his duties with his usual focused intensity. Eamon gave him a brief, silent nod.

Lumo gave him a quick smile, but there was no time for more. He turned back to Meera. "Lead the way."

***

Lumo and Meera rushed to the king's chambers.

"His Majesty is busy," said one of the guards manning the entrance.

"We've been asked to come," Meera spoke.

"Wait here," the guard said, exchanging a glance with the other guard.

The man disappeared inside and quickly reappeared.

"All right, you two may enter."

As Lumo and Meera cautiously entered the chamber, they witnessed the king in his bed, surrounded by Lucius, Archibald, Serena, and a few healers. The king's condition was much better than what they had witnessed; the color in his face was almost back to normal. All traces of the poison seemed to have disappeared, visibly at least. He appeared to be smiling and discussing matters with Lucius and the rest.

King Reginald's gaze shifted to Lumo as he entered. "Lumo, please come," the king gestured.

"Your Majesty, how are you feeling now?" Lumo asked, taking a bow.

"Still alive." The king smiled appreciatively.

"Lucius, I wish to speak to the boy alone. Could you clear the room, please?"

The healers promptly walked out of the room, as did Archibald and Serena. As Serena left, she motioned for Meera to follow her. Lucius, however, stayed back.

"Your Majesty, in the interest of your safety, I suggest I should stay back here," he said.

"I'll be all right, Lucius. Please wait outside." The king shot Lucius a look.

"Yes, My Liege," Lucius said reluctantly. He cast a wry glance at Lumo before stepping outside.

As the doors closed behind them, Lumo cautiously approached the king's bedside.

"Please take a seat," the king gestured.

Lumo settled onto a nearby stool, his nerves tingling with anticipation.

"Serena told me everything you did. You put yourself at risk for me."

"It was my duty, Your Majesty."

"Please don't take this the wrong way, Lumo. I appreciate what you did, but you really shouldn't have."

A confused look spread on Lumo's face, but he quickly remembered what Sylvanus had said. In fact, it was all he had been thinking of. This was the moment of truth.

"Then it's true. The pact," he murmured, lowering his gaze.

King Reginald's eyes widened. "Y—You know of the pact?"

"Sylvanus told us."

"Who else knows of it?" the king asked, a worried look spreading on his face.

"Serena and my friends," Lumo confessed. "We haven't told anyone else; I swear. We wanted to verify it from you, Your Majesty."

The king's jaw clenched, his gaze shifting momentarily to the window as he exhaled slowly. "What exactly did he tell you?"

"That the cult and the kingdom have a pact. Every thousand years, they would..." Lumo croaked, his voice caught in his throat.

"Boy, speak up!" the king boomed, unable to contain his emotion.

Lumo flinched, his back straightening instinctively. "That you have a pact with the cult to end your bloodline," he said, looking the king in the eye.

"What else?"

A perplexed look spread on Lumo's face. "That... Prince Oliver would be... sacrificed; the bloodline would be purged."

"Is that all he said?" the king asked, still worried.

"Yes," Lumo replied as he studied the king's expression. A sense of relief seemed to wash over the king.

Lumo's mind churned with unanswered questions. *How could the king be so calm after what he had said about Oliver? What else did Sylvanus not tell them?* It was clear to him that the king was withholding information, something that he clearly did not want anyone to know. Lumo had a tough time framing his question in the midst of the monarch, yet he steeled himself. He had questions only the king could answer.

"I don't understand, Your Majesty. I don't believe for a moment that you would be all right with the cult sacrificing your own son, and yet you somehow seem relieved. Is there something you are not telling us?"

"Lumo, listen to me. You are to forget everything that has been told to you and stop pursuing this matter."

Lumo, however, would not back down.

"Your Majesty, my friends and I risked our lives to fight the cult. Sylvanus died fighting the battle. You cannot ask us to just forget everything."

"Be that as it may, you will stop right now or else..."

"I know you will send me to the dungeons," Lumo replied with a disappointed look. "But I still don't understand; if you didn't want me to intervene, if you truly believe in this pact, then why would you ask me to save Prince Oliver? None of this makes any sense," Lumo said.

"I said no such thing," King Reginald declared.

Lumo's face was flushed with disbelief, but he put aside his doubts to ask the one question that truly mattered. *Did the king believe in the legitimacy of the pact?*

"Do you believe in this pact? That Oliver must die?" he asked calmly.

"Lumo, I'm going to say this one more time. You are to forget what has been said."

"No," Lumo said defiantly. His heart hammered like a frantic woodpecker as he stood up to the king.

"First the truth. Sylvanus said we are not to intervene in the matters of the cult. That Oliver must be sacrificed. Do you believe in this?"

As the king looked back with a stern expression, Lumo immediately averted his eyes. He realized he had crossed a line.

"Your Majesty, I saved your life. I think I deserve the answer. You have no idea how restless I have been to uncover this truth. Please, I beseech you," he pleaded.

The king's expression softened. With a deep breath, he began, "The pact is true. Sacrificing Oliver brings peace to our kingdom. It's his destiny."

"One final question, and when I have this answer, I will pursue it no further. Why did you ask me to save Oliver?"

"I never asked you to save Oliver," King Reginald said, his gaze lowered.

"Your Majesty, perhaps you don't remember it. After the attack..."

"I remember everything... I never asked you to save Oliver," the king reiterated, his voice louder this time.

Lumo could not believe it. *Had he heard it wrong?*

"But you did," he pressed. "When I visited you after the attack. You asked me to save your bloodline. Why would you—" he stopped mid-sentence.

Lumo's eyes went round, reacting to the one thought that went through his mind at that moment, something he had never even thought about.

"Y—Your bloodline. You asked me to save your bloodline. Oliver... isn't your blood, is he?" Lumo asked, his voice getting caught in his throat.

King Reginald fell silent.

"Is it true? Oliver isn't your real son?" Lumo asked, searching for the truth in the king's eyes.

A single tear ran down the king's cheek. He did not even need to say it. Lumo knew.

"Who, then?"

"All right, that's enough. I've answered all your questions. No more," the king stated firmly.

A heavy silence filled the room.

"This pact is meaningless... I will not stand by idly and let Oliver be slaughtered for no reason," Lumo declared.

"You can and you will," the king spoke with authority. "Or you will be confined to the dungeon."

"You may confine me to the dungeon, Your Majesty, but you will never silence me. Or perhaps, to save your true heir, you will have another innocent life taken—mine."

Lumo had indeed come a long way from being the boy who could not even stand up to the Lord Knight, and yet here he was, challenging the king.

King Reginald's gaze softened as he spoke. "You do not understand the burden I carry. I've raised Oliver as my son. Do you think it is an easy decision to make?"

"What I don't understand is the irrationality behind it. T—This pact, it's supposed to save our kingdom, isn't it? And yet sacrificing Oliver, who isn't even your blood, makes it moot. What happens when the cult finds out? I can save Oliver; we can destroy this cult. Isn't that the right course of action?"

"And what if you perish while trying?" the king countered.

"Why does my life matter? Isn't doing what is right above everything else? Isn't that what being just is about?"

"Lumo, everything I have done is to prevent this very outcome. I cannot have you intervene."

"Why not?" Lumo pressed.

"Because YOU ARE MY TRUE SON," the king echoed.

Lumo was dumbfounded at the revelation. He had no words to counter. He did not even have any thoughts. He simply stared, frozen with disbelief.

"You are my son and my blood... Oh, Sylvanus, what have you done?" the king mumbled.

As Lumo kept studying King Reginald's expression, one thing was evident: the king wasn't lying. He could see it in his gaze, which never left the floor.

"H—How is this possible?" Lumo murmured.

The weight of the truth settled heavily upon Lumo's shoulders, causing him to slump slightly in his seat. He ran a hand through his hair, his fingers trembling with each pass, as if trying to grasp hold of the shattered fragments of his reality.

"When you were born... I knew it was the only way to save your life. I had you switched with..." the king's voice trailed off.

"But I remember when you brought me to the castle... who was it that..."

"Sylvanus," King Reginald mumbled. "He took custody of you as a child. I had ordered him to leave the castle and raise you… till the cult pursued him. It was no longer safe for you to stay with him after that. That is when I had you brought to the castle."

As Lumo kept ruminating on all the truths that lay bare before him, they all started to make sense. Sylvanus's apprehensions with Lumo battling the Lindwyrm, the kindness the king had shown him his entire life, and even the reason why he was imprisoned in the dungeon—the king was making sure no harm would befall him when it was certain that Oliver would be in harm's way.

"I don't know how to process all this," he broke his thoughts.

"I never wanted you to know," King Reginald said. His voice wavered as he spoke, the words tumbling out in a broken cadence. "Not until…"

"Oliver was dead?"

"Until you were old enough to understand."

His gaze remained fixed on Lumo, pleading for understanding yet braced for rejection.

"Lumo, you are my blood. When Lavinia died, I made a promise to her, to keep you safe. If you endanger your life, everything I have done will be meaningless… I know, to you, I may seem like a cruel man, but I'm just a father who has been trying to protect his son."

Lumo's reaction spoke volumes, though no words escaped his lips. His silence was laden with unspoken questions, his inner turmoil evident in the way his hands clenched and unclenched at his sides. Despite his efforts to maintain composure, the tumultuous storm of emotions raging within him threatened to consume him whole.

"Promise me, son," King Reginald spoke. "Promise me, you will let things be."

"I—I need some time alone," Lumo said, rising from his seat and moving toward the door.

"Lumo, please…" King Reginald said as he struggled to get up, trying to stop Lumo from leaving.

"Lumo…"

Lumo stopped at the door, casting a sidelong glance over his shoulder, his gaze meeting the king's helpless eyes. He left without a word.

***

Outside the king's chambers, Lucius, Archibald, Serena, and Meera gathered, waiting anxiously for Lumo to come out. As Lumo resurfaced through the doors, all eyes turned to him. Lumo, however, was least interested in acknowledging anyone. He seemed to be arguing with his own thoughts.

"What'd he say?" Meera asked.

"Nothing," Lumo muttered as he quietly walked away.

Lucius, who seemed suspicious of Lumo's behavior, quickly peeked inside. He found the king sitting on his bed, deep in thought, with a somber expression on his face.

"Everything all right, Your Majesty?" Lucius asked.

King Reginald slowly lifted his gaze to meet Lucius's eyes.

"Yes, Lucius. Everything is as it should be… I'm going to rest for a while. Please see to it that I'm not disturbed."

"Yes, Your Majesty," Lucius said, disappearing behind closed doors.

Meanwhile, Lumo had already walked away from the group. Not knowing what to do with the information he had just uncovered, he wandered aimlessly through the castle corridors. He had just been shaken to his core, and nothing he could do would help him understand what his future meant for him. *Was he meant to save Oliver after all?* It seemed like the right thing to do. It seemed like the only thing he wanted to do until this point. But this new information had far-reaching implications. *What use was this information to him now anyway? He couldn't just let Oliver be sacrificed and later reveal to the kingdom that he was the true prince all along.* Nothing made sense. Sure, the king was only trying to protect his own blood, but this wasn't about the king; this was about him.

As he wandered the empty corridors, his feet had a mind of their own, perhaps used to the same routine he had followed all those years, and unknowingly he found himself at the threshold of his quarters, the same place where he would retire after a hard day's work. He pushed open the door, and the familiar scent of lavender greeted him, wrapping around him like a comforting embrace. The worn table, the worn book, the extinguished candle, and all the mementos he had collected all stayed as they were. Nothing had changed.

He sank onto the worn bed, the familiar creaking sound echoing in the quiet room. Running a hand through his hair, Lumo closed his eyes, seeking solace in the tranquility of his humble abode. He tried to shut out every thought from his mind and find the peace he had always felt after a hard day's work. Tough as it was, eventually, he drifted off.

"Troubled, are we?" a deep voice spoke to Lumo, echoing with an otherworldly resonance.

Startled, Lumo's eyes fluttered open, darting around the room, searching for the source of the voice. His hand instinctively went to the hilt of his sword. His fingers tightened around the familiar grip, ready to draw the weapon should the need arise to defend himself against this mysterious intruder.

"I am here," the voice continued, faint and resonating from the very essence of the sword itself.

Lumo's eyes narrowed, his gaze fixated on the sword as if searching for any sign of trickery or illusion. The voice was unlike anything he had ever heard before, both mesmerizing and unsettling in equal measure.

"What... what are you?"

"I am you," the voice spoke softly.

Lumo's breath caught in his throat as he struggled to comprehend what he was hearing. *Was he dreaming?* He pinched himself, and he felt the pain of it. He looked outside the window of his room. Everything seemed normal.

"Unsheathe me," the sword commanded.

Without the need for further prodding, Lumo complied. As he held up the sword, he saw his own reflection in the blade.

"You see, I am right here," the reflection spoke back, its voice growing stronger.

"H—How is this possible?"

"You are asking the wrong questions," his reflection replied.

"What do you want from me?" Lumo asked, his voice steadier this time.

"I am but you. What do you want, Lumo?" the reflection spoke in a horrifying tone that sent shivers down Lumo's spine.

"I don't know."

"Oh, but you do. Think, Lumo. What must you do now?"

"I must save Oliver… right? It's the right thing to do."

"Righteousness… intriguing. But, what if you didn't?" the reflection countered seductively.

"Let Oliver die? No, I can't do that."

"If Oliver lives, you can never become the king to the throne."

"I don't want to be king. I can never become the king either way. What do I do—just announce to the kingdom that I was the true heir all along?"

"No one has to know," the reflection grinned.

"T—That's absurd," Lumo stammered.

"If Oliver dies, the throne is up for the taking. It doesn't have to be an heir."

"Oliver… is my friend. He would have saved my life if this was the other way around."

"Are you sure about that? Would Oliver willingly give up his claim to the throne?" the reflection questioned, trying to tempt Lumo.

Lumo's mind wavered with doubt, but he persisted.

"Oliver would give his life if this were him."

"And what about the life that was lost already, Lumo?" the reflection said.

That's right, Sylvanus had died protecting him. He had known that Lumo's life mattered above his own. But Sylvanus was at the end of his lifespan anyway.

"Sylvanus was…"

"I'm not talking about Sylvanus," the voice interrupted. "Are you not forgetting someone else?"

"Amelia…" Lumo's eyes went round.

Lumo had completely forgotten that Amelia's death was the indirect result of what the king had sought to achieve. He had no more doubt that Amelia was sentenced to die by the king for uncovering their agenda. The king had indeed gone to great lengths to save Lumo, silencing anyone who knew.

“No one must know, Lumo; especially not your friends. You know what will happen to them if they know, don’t you?” the reflection spoke. “Or perhaps you will go against your father?”

Lumo had no words to counter. His mind was a tumultuous whirlwind of uncertainty.

“Which will it be? Kill your own father to save Oliver? Or let Oliver die to save your friends?”

Lumo's eyes widened in shock, his heart pounding with the weight of the choices laid before him.

“I sense a powerful force within you; within us. We are destined for great things, together. We can rule all of Avalora and perhaps even more... It’s only possible if Oliver dies.”

Lumo's mind reeled with the weight of those words, the implications echoing in his thoughts as he stared at the shimmering blade in his hand. Could he really consider such a dark path? Lumo couldn't shake the sword's voice, its temptations lingering like a stubborn shadow.

As Lumo was lost in thought, grappling with the newfound revelations swirling in his mind, a soft knock echoed through the room, breaking the heavy silence.

“Lumo, you in there?” Meera’s voice came from behind the door.

Startled, he swiftly sheathed the sword, concealing its unsettling presence as best he could. As the door creaked open, his eyes darted to Meera, who stood in the doorway.

“I thought that was you,” Meera spoke.

“Err, yes. I was just resting a bit.”

“Who were you speaking to just now?”

“No one. I was just speaking to myself.”

“Out loud?”

"Y—Yes, just trying to wrap my head around something…" Lumo confessed. "Did you follow me?"

"I was worried. You seemed tense."

"No, I'm just a bit tired. Maybe I'm coming down with something," Lumo lied.

"Oh, I see. Well, did the king say anything about…"

"Err, no. We didn't get to that part," Lumo lied again.

"But time is against us, Lumo. We need to…"

"I know," Lumo cut her off. "To be honest, the king was still a bit weak. And I think I might have had a bit too much cider at lunch; didn't want to create a ruckus. We need to approach this with tact. He is the king after all," Lumo said sheepishly.

"Ah, all right," Meera conceded, though her expression betrayed a lingering sense of unease. "Is that what you were talking to yourself about then?"

"Yes, precisely! I was trying to figure out the right way to discuss the matter without making Lucius throw me out of the room midway," Lumo lied, his attempt at humor falling flat in the face of Meera's scrutiny.

"Perhaps later, though. I'm going to rest for a bit and think this through if it's all right with you."

"Sure," Meera agreed, though her gaze lingered on Lumo.

As Meera quietly exited the room, closing the door behind her, Lumo's gaze wandered back to the sword. The sword remained silent. It had already said all it needed to say. It was up to Lumo to make a decision.

***

CHAPTER 21

Lumo had not known when he fell asleep. The night had come and gone. When he woke up, he still wondered if he had dreamt it all. The last thought that went through his mind was, *were his friends safe?* It did not matter if it was true or not, whether the sword really had spoken to him or not; one thing had been revealed to him: his enemy and his father were one and the same.

Lumo looked outside the tiny window of his room that allowed just enough of a glimpse of the castle courtyard. He could see Meera already practicing with Serena.

I wonder if Serena has spoken to the king yet? he thought.

He rushed downstairs to meet them. Meera had finally managed to at least summon a gust of wind, which he could see as he approached them.

"Wow, that was impressive," he exclaimed.

Meera turned back to meet Lumo's gaze. A tiny bead of sweat trickled down the side of her forehead as she replied, "Thanks. I see you're up. Feeling more rested today?"

"Err, yes." Lumo rubbed the back of his neck. "Meera, um, yesterday… did you visit my quarters?"

"Boy, you really did drink too much cider, didn't you? And here I was worried you were hiding something." Meera chuckled.

"Oh, haha. Sorry, I suppose I was a bit out of it yesterday." Lumo smiled sheepishly.

"About the matter… with the king. I will speak to him today," he said, his expression turning serious.

"Well, there's no need for that now."

"What do you mean?"

"You didn't hear? It seems King Reginald is already rallying the troops. They are planning a rescue mission for the prince. You were right, Lumo. The king wasn't in on the plan all along," Meera explained.

"He is?"

What is the king playing at? Lumo wondered.

"Indeed. And here's some more good news—it seems Malikoth finally broke, and they know where the cult's stronghold is."

Lumo blinked, trying to wrap his head around Meera's words.

"Wait, so, did the king speak to anyone… Serena?"

"He held a council earlier, Lumo," Serena shared. "We could not speak privately, but His Majesty's intentions seemed clear: do whatever it takes to save Prince Oliver."

"I see," Lumo said, lost in thought.

"You don't seem particularly thrilled," Meera mouthed.

"No, no, I am," Lumo refuted, trying to muster a smile. "So, where is this stronghold, did they say?"

"They're apparently holed up in the old castle of Rochfell. Lucius is sending scouts to confirm as we speak," Serena divulged.

"Rochfell…"

"Yes. That castle has remained unoccupied for centuries now. It's quite the distance from here too, so I can see how they could be using it to their advantage to stay hidden all this time."

"Any idea of their numbers, then?"

"We aren't sure, but I can tell you this—laying siege to that castle is going to be one hell of a task. Let's just hope it doesn't come to that," Serena replied.

"Hmm," Lumo mumbled. He still couldn't figure out what the king really intended to do. Surely, he couldn't have changed in the one day that they spoke. There had to be something more to this. As he pondered, his thoughts went to Malikoth and Kael. Meera had mentioned he broke. It seemed too convenient. Skepticism had snuck under Lumo's skin like a persistent itch, making him question everything.

"All right, what's going on? Spit it out," Meera probed, noticing Lumo's departure from their conversation.

"Huh?"

"You're obviously thinking about something; might as well tell us."

Lumo wanted to lay bare the truths, but he was still worried about the safety of his friends.

"Nothing, I was just thinking about Kael," Lumo deflected. "Now that Malikoth has revealed the information, has Lucius ordered his release?"

"I don't think so. Maybe, once the scouts have confirmed, he will let him go."

"That makes sense." Lumo gave a small, contemplative hum. "Um, Serena, do you think there's a chance I can see Kael? I mean, the guy did help us. It seems unfair to him that no one should care."

"Lumo, you know Lucius. The only reason you two have been spared is because of your valuable contributions thus far. But, I honestly doubt he will extend the courtesy. I suggest you let it be for the time being."

"Fine," Lumo said as he turned back to go inside.

"Where are you going?" Meera called out.

"I'm going to get something to eat."

The day slipped away swiftly. Lumo tried to get more access to the king's affairs, yet Lucius had made sure he was forbidden entry to the court. Meanwhile, the king remained ensconced in discussions throughout the day, his court a hub of activity. Lumo could see the movements of guards scurrying in and out of the castle, between the armory and the war room. Yet, despite the flurry of activity, Lumo found himself kept in the dark. Such secrecy was commonplace in the days preceding Oliver's disappearance. He was merely a prince's attendant back then, but now, armed with the knowledge of his royal lineage, Lumo found the exclusion gnawing at his sanity.

It wasn't just about being of royal blood, either. In the past few days, his entire world had been upended. He had been thrust far beyond his comfort zone, confronting monstrous creatures and facing dangers he never imagined. He could have sworn if the Bonnacon had invaded now, he would have been able to burn the deluge of fiery feces mid-air. And here he was, back to being disregarded altogether.

Was this the king's new strategy? To keep him at bay while he handled matters independently? Perhaps the king never intended to save Oliver. Maybe he's planned it so they would all die together at Rochfell.

***

The good news finally came through a few days later. The scouts had sent a pigeon confirming the hideout of the cult.

"How many?" King Reginald asked as Lucius unfurled the note.

"A few hundred," Lucius replied. "At least that's what the scouts report."

"Seems like a small number," King Reginald remarked. "Surely not all of them are magic wielders. How many can we assemble in this short time, Lucius?"

"Perhaps five thousand."

"I see. And how many do we have ready to leave right away?"

"Perhaps five... no, seven hundred cavalry."

"Serena, Marcus, are you ready to depart?" the king inquired.

"Yes, Your Majesty," Serena and Marcus replied in unison.

"Excellent. Serena, Marcus, and I will leave for Rochfell immediately. We can't waste any more time. Lucius, I expect you to gather the rest of the army and arrive with reinforcements should the need arise," the king ordered.

"Yes, Your Majesty," Lucius replied. "Although it may take us about a day."

"Please do it immediately," King Reginald commanded.

Lucius bowed in agreement.

"Archibald, you will take control of matters in our absence," King Reginald motioned.

"Of course, Your Majesty," Archibald bowed.

As the king dismissed the court, he interrupted Lucius once more.

"One more thing, that boy, Lumo... What is he up to?"

"The peasant boy? Keeping out of trouble, for now," Lucius said with a shrug. "Had him running some trivial errand outside the castle—figured it'd keep him out of everyone's hair for a bit."

"Hmm... I see. All right, carry on."

"Yes, My Liege," Lucius nodded as he turned to leave.

***

An hour later, Serena, Marcus, and the rest of the regiment, led by King Reginald, stood at the castle gates, poised to depart. King Reginald, clad in resplendent armor polished to a mirror shine and adorned with the regal crest, stood at the vanguard, exuding an aura of authority and resolve. His voice thundered above the bustling preparations, each command reverberating off the ancient stone walls like a herald's trumpet. The regiment—a sea of polished armor and focused faces—buzzed with anticipation. The sound of clinking armor and the soft rattle of weapons filled the crisp morning air.

Restless horses pawed the ground, their impatient snorts punctuating the atmosphere with puffs of warm breath. With a rallying cry that could rouse mountains, King Reginald spurred his charger into motion, leading the procession through the open gates. The castle walls echoed with the thunderous stomp of hooves, while thick clouds of dirt and dust billowed up from the well-trodden path, swirling around the regiment like a hazy shroud.

Lucius waved them farewell, his fist tightly clenched against his chest as a sign of salute. He busied himself with the preparations for the reinforcements.

***

It was late evening. The castle grounds were chaotic, with the movement of guards shuffling in and out.

"What's happening?" Lumo murmured.

"Something is going on. Excuse me, I'm going to find Serena," Meera said, excusing herself.

Meanwhile, Lumo had finally decided; not what he intended to do in the grand scheme of things, but to not stand idly by while the king carried on with what he thought was his nefarious plan. He had to be a part of it.

Spotting Lucius in the castle courtyard, he approached him cautiously.

"Sir Lucius, may we speak?"

"Not you again?" Lucius muttered, barely masking his irritation.

"I've heard about the cult's hideout from Serena. Are you—"

"Stay out of it," Lucius cut him off, almost ready to walk away.

"What about Malikoth... and Kael? What do you intend to do with them?"

"That's none of your concern." Lucius scowled, walking further away.

"Then perhaps you are not interested in the truth."

Lucius stopped in his tracks, turning around.

"What truth?"

"Do you remember Amelia?" Lumo asked.

"The maid?"

"Aren't you curious how she ended up at the cult's shrine earlier?"

Lucius's eyes narrowed. "What are you going on about?"

"Remember, back at the shrine... I blamed you for Amelia's disappearance."

"As if I can ever forget your insolence." Lucius's scowl deepened.

"Well, I'm ready to believe you weren't a part of it. But doesn't it raise a question in your mind? If not you, then who?"

"Go on," Lucius directed, his eyes trying to read Lumo's face for any signs of deceit.

Taking a leap of faith, Lumo related the incident that Amelia had once confided in him.

"You're lying," Lucius rebutted.

"Am I? Didn't you see her at the shrine? She died that day. Someone sought to silence her."

Lucius pondered Lumo's words. "A traitor... within the castle? Follow me. We have to find Archibald and relay this information to the king," Lucius declared.

"No, wait! The truth is that there is a traitor, but we don't know who. Surely, you don't want to report incomplete information to the king," Lumo lied.

"What are you suggesting?"

"Malikoth," Lumo replied. "He is the only person who can tell us the truth."

"Hmm... there is some premise in what you say."

"Let me come with you," Lumo said.

"Fine," Lucius grunted.

Together they walked toward the dungeon. As they ventured into the depths of the dungeon, a heavy silence enveloped the corridor, broken only by the echo of their footsteps on the cold, stone floor. Lumo's mind flashed back to the thick, musty scent he had encountered not too long ago, a scent that permeated the corridor, mingling with the cold, damp air. The guards, upon spotting Lucius, immediately snapped to attention, their postures rigid with alertness.

Lucius wasted no time, his voice cutting through the heavy silence like a blade.

"Where are the prisoners?"

"Through there, Sir," one of the guards promptly replied.

The other guard immediately recognized Lumo, and a sense of panic spread across his face. He hastily tried to mask it, but in his rush, he turned away too quickly and almost banged his head against the wall, stumbling back. He quickly recovered.

Passing through the dungeon door, Lucius and Lumo's eyes fell upon Malikoth, confined to a cell at the very end. Malikoth's condition spoke volumes—the bruises, cuts, and new injuries on his face told a grim tale of relentless interrogation and brutality. It was evident that no expense had been spared in the quest to extract information from him.

"We have some questions for you," Lucius declared, stepping closer to Malikoth.

Malikoth did not answer.

Lucius clenched his jaw. "Did you hear me, scum?"

Frustrated, Lucius's eyes darted around the dim chamber until they landed on one of the guards.

"Where is his father?" he demanded.

"I'm here," Kael's raspy voice echoed from a nearby cell.

Lumo turned toward the voice, his breath catching. Kael's face was gaunt, bruises blooming along his jaw and arms. Lumo's brows drew together, concern etched into his features.

"If he hasn't spoken yet, you should understand the extent of his will," Kael said, his words slow and deliberate.

"What are you talking about?" Lucius snapped. "He's already revealed the cult's location."

"T—That's not possible," Kael replied, his voice trembling as he spoke. "I've been right here the entire time. He hasn't spoken a word."

Lumo had guessed as much. His intuition was right. *This was the king's plan after all.* He also knew Lucius would never have believed him without him revealing his real identity, and even then, there was a high likelihood that Lucius would have shot him down.

"Did the king inform you of the cult's hideout, then?" he directed his question at Lucius.

Lucius hesitated, his jaw tightening. He glanced to the side, fingers twitching slightly as if weighing his words. "No... It was... Marcus," he finally admitted.

Lumo's breath hitched, eyes widening. *Marcus?*

Malikoth's sinister laughter echoed through the silence that permeated the air. "It seems you cannot even trust your own men."

Lucius looked on in dread as Malikoth finally spoke. Lumo too was lost for words.

"Well, there's no point in staying quiet anymore. It seems our leader has decided already on what must happen. Go ahead, ask me this question of yours, Lord Knight," Malikoth taunted.

Lucius's nostrils flared as he took a sharp breath, his fingers tightening into fists. His entire frame seemed to tense, every muscle coiled as if ready to launch himself at the bars.

"Come on, Lumo. We need to go," Lucius said.

It was the first time he had acknowledged Lumo by name, and it made Lumo pause.

"Wait," Lumo turned to face Malikoth. "I have a question."

Lucius shot him a warning look, but Lumo pressed on. "I know you plan to sacrifice Prince Oliver; when and where? Surely he's not at Rochfell."

"Hah," Malikoth scoffed. "Soon... and you're mistaken, he's at Rochfell, all right."

"'Soon' is not an answer; answer the question," Lucius commanded, taking a step forward.

A wicked grin stretched across Malikoth's face. "The veiling of the moon... just a few days from now. If you truly care about saving your precious prince, you'd better hurry."

"Let's go," Lucius said, his boots thudding heavily against the stone floor as he moved toward the dungeon door. Lumo hesitated, glancing back at Kael, still slumped in his cell.

"What about Kael?" Lumo asked. "He's innocent in all this."

Lucius paused, exhaling sharply. "Fine, I'll have him released."

As Lumo and Lucius hurriedly stormed out of the dungeon, they came across Meera, who stood near the large fountain in the castle courtyard. Lucius quickly excused himself as he took a moment to communicate with some of the guards.

"Lumo, where have you been? I've been looking all over for you," Meera declared as she spotted him.

"Sorry, Meera. I was in the dungeon."

"Dungeon... well, I just thought you should know; Serena has already left with the king."

"Left? Where? Rochfell?"

"Indeed, they left earlier, apparently," Meera confirmed.

"But Lucius is still here," Lumo said, his brow furrowing as he glanced at Lucius.

"It seems Lucius is gathering reinforcements to depart later. Darn it, why didn't she tell us?" Meera complained.

As Lucius joined them, he had an unreadable expression on his face. "It's done. Kael will be released in the morning."

"Lucius, His Majesty… has he left with Serena already?" Lumo asked.

"I'm afraid you're right. Marcus was with them too. They left this morning."

"Darn it!" Lumo exclaimed. "Lucius, we have to follow them. You know the truth. I'm worried that they are heading into a trap."

Lucius stood still, his posture rigid as he ran a hand over his face, trying to suppress his own rising tension. "I know… I've been rounding up reinforcements. I understand your concern, but if I leave now, then there is no one to lead these men. We can depart at dawn and try to make up for the time lost."

"No, I know these people and what they are capable of. I'm afraid it may be too late."

"What do you suggest, then?" Lucius asked.

"Meera and I will leave immediately and try to find them. Can we count on you to follow?" Lumo took a step closer.

"No effort will be spared, Lumo. Go," Lucius directed.

"Did he just call you… Lumo?" Meera mumbled to herself.

"Meera?" Lumo nudged her urgently.

"Er, yes?"

"You coming?"

"Wait, what is going on?" Meera replied, confused.

"Come on, I'll fill you in," Lumo said, pulling her by the hand.

***

"What! Marcus… is the traitor?" Meera exclaimed as they rode side by side into the night.

"Yes, keep up," Lumo said, noticing the slack in her speed. "Believe me, Meera. I can't tell you yet, but the rabbit hole runs much deeper."

"What can't you tell?"

"In time, Meera. For now, just trust me. We need to focus first on catching up to them. Serena's life is in danger."

"Serena? I think they are all in danger if what you said is true."

"Indeed, there's no time to waste," Lumo said, tugging at the reins of his horse.

***

Deep in the recesses of the Rochfell Castle, Lilith gathered a group of elite cultists, including Marachi.

"It seems they have already left the castle, milady," one of the cultists spoke with a sinister undertone. "The king leads the army along with brother Marcus and the sorceress. They should be here in about five days."

"Excellent. What about the boy, Lumo? Is he with them?"

"No, milady."

"Hmm... I see. Never mind, he will come."

"Another thing, milady; it seems the Lord Knight is rallying a regiment of at least five thousand men as reinforcement. They should arrive a day later."

"Pointless, but let them come," Lilith smirked. "After all, the more eyes, the better, right, Marachi?"

"Indeed, milady." Marachi grinned.

"Is he ready?" Lilith inquired.

"He will be."

"Good... that is good. The time is near, Marachi. Have you sent word to them?"

"All is going according to plan, milady," Marachi confirmed.

"Excellent. All hail Lord Cernunnos," Lilith chanted.

"All hail Lord Cernunnos," the rest of the cultists chanted in unison.

***

"Lumo, we can't go on like this. We have to stop for the night," Meera suggested.

"We have to catch up to them," Lumo countered.

"Well, we can't do it like this. The horses need to rest. If we end up over-exhausting them, it will take us that much longer to catch up."

Lumo pondered Meera's words, glancing at the sweat-drenched flanks of their weary horses. They had been traveling non-stop for hours, and the animals were flagging.

"Fine, we'll find a clearing and camp it out there," Lumo said, reluctantly.

A few minutes later, they arrived at a clearing where they stopped. Lumo tethered the horses to a nearby tree, patting their necks reassuringly. Meera set up camp, creating a bonfire that crackled and sparked in the growing darkness. The warm air had disappeared, giving way to cool breezes that would make one shiver and make sleeping that much more difficult if not for the fire's comforting warmth.

"Do we even know if we're going in the right direction?" Meera asked as she rubbed her hands against the warm fire.

"I think so… Lucius told me we need to head north till we arrive at the Skelian Highlands. We might have to ask for directions after that. It's going to be a long journey for sure."

"Well, all right. So…"

"So?"

"So, this is the part where you tell me that thing you said earlier; the thing that you said you can't tell me." Meera's eyes gleamed with curiosity.

"Err, I still can't tell you."

"Why not?" Meera pressed, leaning forward.

Lumo sighed, "I just can't, all right?"

"But why? What's the big secret?" Meera asked, her curiosity unwavering.

"Well, it's complicated," Lumo replied, his breath sharp as he leaned back. "What about you? There are lots of things you've never told me. Do you see me pressing for those?" he added, trying to keep his tone even but failing.

Meera's expression turned serious. "What do you want to know?"

"Um, you can start by telling me your story."

"My story..." Meera repeated.

"Yes. If you want to know my secrets, you have to give up some of yours. How'd you end up being all by yourself?"

Meera sighed deeply. "All right," she began, drawing a deep breath. "My father was a drunk; used to gamble a lot too. Most days we had trouble having a single square meal, and yet there he was, getting sloshed at taverns across town. Word is he had run up quite the tab."

"Was he abusive?" Lumo whispered gently.

"Mother used to fight with him a lot; sometimes it got physical. She always protected me though. She was a good mother, at least that's what I thought."

Lumo listened intently, careful not to say anything insensitive.

"Eventually though, it broke her. One night while I slept on an empty stomach, I remember hearing them arguing loudly in the other room, louder than the grumbling of my own stomach. I remember trying to drown out the sounds by covering my ears. Before long, the sounds had stopped."

"When I woke up the next day, my mother had disappeared and my father lay on the floor, dead."

"Oh my goodness," Lumo exclaimed softly. "How old were you?"

"About ten, I suppose… I think she panicked and ran."

"That must have been traumatic," Lumo remarked.

"Tell me about it."

"Did they find her after?"

"No," Meera sighed. "I've been on my own since. The Debtmasters reclaimed our house, and I was out on the streets. Started out begging for scraps, but you know what I found out, Lumo?"

Lumo looked into her eyes, waiting for her to continue.

"People don't care about anyone but themselves, and that's the truth," Meera murmured, her voice filled with a quiet bitterness. "I mean, my own mother; why didn't she take me with her? Didn't she care enough for the safety of her own child?"

Sadness filled Lumo's eyes and he gripped Meera's hand empathetically.

"After that, I had to turn to stealing for a living. And that's my story, pretty much."

"That's… harsh. I'm sorry," Lumo said.

"You know, Lumo, earlier I said it was rough for you to not even know your parents. I take it back. I think you're better off," Meera said, with a shrug.

Lumo managed a rough smile, one corner of his mouth lifting reluctantly.

"Now, you go. Tell me about this secret," Meera remarked, her eyes searching his.

"Fine. I suppose I owe you this much..." Lumo began. "Remember that day His Majesty and I convened in his chambers?"

"Go on."

"Well, His Majesty pretty much admitted that the pact exists."

"What? Really?" Meera's eyes widened.

"Yes," Lumo confirmed. "We know that Marcus is a traitor, but to be honest, Meera, I think our king is in cohorts with them. What's worse, I'm worried this is all an elaborate scheme by him. I think he plans to end his life, Oliver's, and pretty much everyone else's at Rochfell... all in the name of this pact that is supposed to save the kingdom."

"Gosh, that's..." Meera began.

"Uh-huh... hard to take in, I know," Lumo completed her sentence.

"So, that's what it was about that day. So you were lying," Meera deduced.

"Umm, yes, sorry." Lumo brushed his hair.

"But, Lumo, didn't we agree to stand down if the pact was true?"

Lumo froze, his mouth parting slightly as he stared at Meera. He had indeed agreed to stand down if the pact was true. But Meera did not know about the irrationality of the pact given he was the true heir, and for the time being, he did not want her to know either. His thoughts went into overdrive trying to find another way to explain it.

"Err, true, but we didn't agree that so many people must die. We have to save them."

"Y—Yes, of course, you're right," Meera agreed. "We should find Serena first. I don't think she knows about it either, or she would have told us. If we are to save all those people, I think she is our best chance."

"Right." Lumo met Meera's eyes.

A quiet moment passed between them.

"Well, we'd best be sleeping. We need to wake up early if we are to catch up to them," Meera suggested.

Lumo exhaled lightly, settling down. "Goodnight, Meera," he said as he curled up beside the warm fire.

***

CHAPTER 22

"Wake up, Lumo." Meera shook him. "Wake up."

"Huh? What? Is it morning already?"

"Lumo, the horses. They're gone," Meera informed.

"What?"

Lumo got up hurriedly, scanning the area. The horses had indeed disappeared. *Had he forgotten to tether them properly?*

"I think someone took the horses," Meera added.

Lumo hurriedly checked for their other belongings. Meera still had her staff, and his own sword was still dangling at the side.

"I don't understand; all our other stuff is here."

"Common thieves, maybe. Darn it!" Meera squealed. "What do we do now? We're in the middle of nowhere."

"Umm…"

"You think we should wait for Lucius and the rest?" Meera asked. "They did say they would leave at dawn."

"I don't think that's such a good idea. I think he is gathering a large army, which includes foot soldiers. I doubt he will be able to reach us before nightfall, and we were riding at a fairly fast pace; at best, he should be here by dusk."

"Fine, then we have no choice but to keep walking," Meera resigned. "Let's hope we come across a settlement or someone who can help."

***

A couple of hours had passed since they began their journey along the north road. The path stretched out before them, a ribbon of well-trodden earth cutting through the landscape. The road was remarkably straight, with only the occasional fork veering off into unknown directions. On either side, massive meadows unfurled like vibrant green carpets, lush with grass that swayed gently in the breeze. The meadows stretched for acres upon acres.

As they continued on foot, the long north road stretched endlessly before them, disappearing into the distant horizon. Lumo was particularly apprehensive, knowing that walking like this could defeat their entire purpose. With no other choice, they trudged onward.

A half-hour later, they arrived at a very prominent fork in the road, heading toward the east. There were no signboards, but the track marks of wheels veering toward the fork hinted at a possible town or trade post ahead.

"I think we should take this road," Lumo announced.

Meera, too, had noticed the signs. "I think you're right."

Taking the road to the east, they journeyed onward.

Another half hour later, they could see signs of life. The empty, grass-filled meadows had transformed into vast fields of corn and pumpkins.

"Not too much further, Meera," Lumo remarked dryly. "I think this is some sort of farmland."

"I see that," Meera replied curtly. Hours of walking had left her feeling slightly irritable.

A few minutes later, as they approached a solitary post at the road's corner, a large plaque came into view, dusty and worn out, likely unchanged for years. The plaque read, "Greenfield Meadows."

"Wait, this name sounds familiar," Lumo remarked, trying to recollect where he had heard it before.

Meera wondered too, and then it struck her. "Lumo, this is where Robert said he's from!" she exclaimed in excitement.

"Oh, that's right," Lumo said, jumping in realization. "This is good. Maybe we can catch up after all if we can borrow their horses."

"Right." Meera nodded. "Let's ask around for Robert's house."

As they continued, the road beneath their feet gradually shifted from dirt to cobblestone. Small cottages with thatched roofs and colorful gardens appeared, each one exuding a welcoming charm. Children played in the streets, their laughter mingling with the distant clatter of carts and the hum of village life. Farmers and townsfolk went about their daily routines, tending to their chores and chatting amicably. The scent of fresh bread wafted through the air from a nearby bakery, mingling with the earthy aroma of tilled soil and blooming flowers.

Lumo and Meera continued walking, their eyes scanning the village for any sign of familiarity. Eventually, they approached an older woman who was sweeping her porch, her face lined with years of hard work and wisdom.

"Excuse me," Lumo called out politely. "We're looking for Robert's house. Could you help us?"

The woman paused her sweeping and looked up, her eyes crinkling into a warm smile. "Of course, young ones. I assume you mean Robert and Helen. Their house is just down the road a bit, near the old mill. Can't miss it—big red door with a brass knocker."

"Thank you," Meera said gratefully.

The woman waved her hand dismissively. "No trouble at all. Just follow the road past the bakery and turn left at the mill. You'll see it."

Lumo and Meera thanked the woman again and continued on their way. They followed her directions, passing the bakery with its enticing aroma and the mill with its large, slowly turning wheel. Soon, they spotted the house she had described—a charming cottage with a bright red door and a shiny brass knocker.

"Here it is," Lumo said, relief evident in his voice.

Meera's eyes brightened; her earlier irritation forgotten in the excitement of finding Robert's house. Lumo stepped forward and knocked on the door. They waited, anticipation building as footsteps approached from within.

The door creaked open, and a familiar face appeared. Robert's eyes widened in surprise and then lit up with a warm smile.

"Lumo, Meera! What brings you here?" he asked, stepping aside to let them in.

"It's a long story," Lumo began. "But we need your help."

As they stepped inside, Lumo and Meera were greeted by the cozy warmth of Robert's home. The interior was quaint and welcoming, with wooden beams overhead. The scent of freshly baked bread lingered in the air, mingling with the faint aroma of herbs and honey.

"Please make yourselves at home," Robert urged, closing the door behind them.

A sturdy wooden table occupied the center of the room, adorned with a vase of wildflowers. Lumo noticed the shelves lining the walls, filled with umpteen books; more books than he had ever seen in his life. If he hadn't known better, he could have easily mistaken their home for a library. Robert hadn't been wrong about Helen's penchant for reading.

"Helen is out back tending to the bees," Robert explained, gesturing toward the back door. "She's been working on expanding our hives this season."

He then walked to the back door and opened it, calling out, "Helen! We have visitors! Come meet Lumo and Meera!"

A moment later, Helen appeared in the doorway.

"Lumo and Meera, you say?" Helen asked, a smile spreading across her face. "It's lovely to meet you both. Robert has told me about you."

Lumo and Meera returned her smile warmly.

"Likewise, it's good to meet you, Helen," Lumo replied. "You know, if it wasn't for your help earlier, we would never have discovered the things we did. We have you and Robert to thank for it."

"Oh, that's quite all right. We were all worried about that ourselves, but after Robert told me you were taking care of the matter, I let it go. Besides, not much we simple folk can do."

Robert guided them to the wooden table, motioning for them to sit. "Please, have a seat. Can I get you something to drink? Perhaps some honey tea?"

"That would be wonderful," Meera said.

As Robert busied himself with preparing the tea, Helen joined them at the table, her presence warm and welcoming.

"So, what brings you to our humble home?" she asked.

Lumo exchanged a glance with Meera before speaking. "We're on a bit of a mission, and we could use your help. We've been traveling for a while, and we need some assistance to catch up with someone."

"Of course, we'll do whatever we can to help. Tell us more about what you need."

Robert returned with steaming cups of honey tea, placing them before Lumo and Meera. "Here you go. Now, tell us everything," he said, taking a seat beside Helen.

Lumo took a sip of the tea, savoring its warmth and sweetness before beginning their tale. Unsure of how much detail to share, he briefly recounted their journey, the challenges they had faced, and the disappearance of their horses.

"And so, we were about to journey to the castle of Rochfell, to catch up with Serena. But, we were stranded, unfortunately."

"Oh, you poor dears. That must have been quite a walk," Helen rasped.

"It was tiring, indeed," Meera explained. "But we have no time to lose. Time is of the essence. We were wondering if there's any chance we could borrow a couple of horses."

"Ah, I can lend you my horse. But it's just the one. Is that okay?" Robert asked.

"I suppose it'll have to do. Thanks," Meera said.

"By the way, Helen, Robert told us what an avid reader you are; we can see that's clearly true," Lumo remarked, his gaze sweeping over the shelves brimming with books.

"Oh, thanks," Helen chuckled appreciatively. "Life can get a bit dull around here. One does what one can to stay busy."

"She's quite the historian, too. Ask her anything about Avalora, and she'll tell you. Go on, tell them, Helen," Robert urged, smiling proudly.

"Oh, come now, Robert," Helen blushed, waving her hand playfully.

"Please, do tell us something interesting, Helen," Lumo encouraged.

"All right, you know our castle at Avalora? The stones used there were actually sourced from the kingdom of Rochfell, ages ago. Back then, as you probably know, Rochfell was a separate country, and the then king, King Clifford Brighton, had generously donated the stones carved out from the Hamburg Mountains. Isn't that fascinating?"

"Err, yes. Fascinating indeed," Meera replied, trying to mask her boredom.

"Wait, Brighton? Is he related to our king?" Lumo inquired.

A playful grin appeared on Helen's face as she replied. "Indeed, he was a great-great...great ancestor of King Reginald."

Lumo lost count of the number of times Helen said: "Great." He smiled in return, but he was clearly intrigued by Helen's revelation.

"Was there a war then? Between Rochfell and Avalora? I mean, how did they end up merging?" he asked.

"Surprisingly, no. It was a peaceful surrender. The then king of Avalora, King Geoffrey Omond, had apparently gotten sick, and with no living heir, they strategically merged the kingdoms of Avalora and Rochfell. Another one of King Reginald's ancestors then assumed responsibility for the merged kingdom."

"That's quite interesting."

"Oh, yes. History can be so fascinating," Helen chuckled. "If you are interested, I can tell you a whole lot more. Do you want to know about the southern trade post of Avalora?"

"Err, perhaps another time, Helen. We are in a bit of a hurry at the moment," Meera replied.

"Oh, of course," Helen nodded. "Sorry, I get carried away sometimes. Robert here keeps telling me that."

"No, no. It's quite all right," Lumo replied sheepishly. "We... just really need to get to Rochfell as soon as possible."

"So, I take it you two will not stay for lunch then?" Robert asked.

"Can't, unfortunately," Meera replied.

"Next time for sure, though." Lumo smiled appreciatively.

"All right, then. Let me go get the horse ready. Meanwhile, if you two want to freshen up, the privy is at the back," Robert said.

"Thanks," Lumo and Meera replied in unison.

After freshening up, Lumo and Meera rejoined Robert at the front of the house. As Robert adjusted the saddle on a sturdy, chestnut-colored horse, he looked up and gave them a warm smile.

"I trust you both are ready for the journey?" Robert asked, tightening the girth strap securely.

Lumo bobbed his head. "This is a fine horse, Robert."

"His name is Bramble," Robert replied, patting the horse's neck affectionately. "He's strong and reliable, perfect for the roads you'll be traveling."

Meera stepped forward, reaching out to stroke Bramble's velvety nose. "He's beautiful. Thank you, Robert. We'll take good care of him."

Robert chuckled. "You're welcome. You've both got a long way to go. Here you go," he said as he handed the reins to Lumo, who took them with a firm grip.

"Oh, that reminds me. Do you perhaps know how far it is to the Skelian Highlands from here?" Lumo asked.

"At least a two-day ride from here," Robert replied. "But it's a fairly easy route till there. It gets rough after that since the terrain is mostly mountainous, but don't worry; Bramble here will see you through safely."

"Thank you, Robert. We owe you much," Lumo said sincerely.

"Nonsense," Robert replied with a dismissive wave of his hand. "Just promise me you'll be careful out there. The roads can be unpredictable."

"We will."

Robert then proceeded to check the saddlebags, ensuring they were securely fastened and well-stocked. "I've packed some provisions for you—dried meat, bread, cheese, and a large flask of water. It should last you for a few days."

Lumo opened his mouth to thank Robert again but caught himself. "Th—" he began, then smiled sheepishly and nodded instead.

With one last check of the stirrups and a final pat on Bramble's flank, Robert stepped back. "All right, then, you're set. Safe travels, and may the winds be ever in your favor."

Lumo mounted Bramble first, then extended a hand to help Meera up behind him. Settling in the saddle, they both looked back at Robert, who stood watching them with a proud, albeit concerned, expression. Helen stood beside him, her hands clasped in front of her.

"Goodbye, Robert, Helen," Meera called out.

"Goodbye, and good luck," Robert responded, lifting his hand in a parting gesture.

With a gentle nudge from Lumo, Bramble started forward, his hooves clopping rhythmically on the cobblestone path as they set off on their journey.

***

CHAPTER 23

They could no longer ride as fast as before, especially with both of them on a single horse. But with a steady pace, Lumo and Meera traveled well without any major hiccups. They took the bare minimum breaks needed, and when they camped at night, they made sure to camp further away from the main road, careful not to lose Bramble to more thieves. Robert would have killed them.

It had been two days since they journeyed north. As Lumo and Meera approached the Skelian Highlands, the landscape around them transformed. The gentle, rolling meadows gave way to a more rugged and untamed terrain. The road gradually climbed, winding through rough patches of forests. The air grew cooler and crisper as they ascended, carrying the fresh, invigorating scent of pine and earth. The path became narrower and more winding, flanked by rocky outcrops and thickets of brambles and wildflowers.

As they emerged at the top, the true majesty of the Highlands unfolded before them. Jagged peaks and craggy ridges rose dramatically against the sky in the distance. Below the peaks, lush valleys stretched out, blanketed in wild grasses and vibrant gorse. Crystal-clear streams flowed through the valleys, while waterfalls cascaded from rocky cliffs, their mist shimmering in the sunlight.

In the distance, patches of dense, dark green forests dotted the landscape, interspersed with open moorlands covered in purple heather and golden broom. Rocky plateaus offered sweeping views of the surrounding countryside, where one could see for miles in every direction. The sky above was a vast expanse of blue, occasionally punctuated by fluffy white clouds that drifted lazily.

"Breathtaking, isn't it?" Lumo exclaimed.

"You can say that again," replied Meera.

As they journeyed deeper into the Highlands, the landscape around them became increasingly rugged and confusing. The road they followed branched off into multiple narrow paths, each one winding through rocky terrain.

"Well, looks like the easy part is over," Meera remarked, gesturing at the confusing path in front of them. "Where do we go now?"

"Look there," Lumo announced, pointing to a signboard in the distance.

Relief quickly turned to frustration as they approached closer. The signboard had clearly not been maintained. One of the signs had chipped off, leaving only the word "Roc."

Lumo assumed it was Rochfell, but for all he knew, it could have meant Rockfall, a treacherous stretch where the cliffs often crumbled. The other signs, too, pointed in directions that seemed nonsensical, with one even pointing directly into a thicket with no visible path.

"Let's try this way," Lumo declared.

"Lumo, wait. It's this way for sure, look at all the tracks," Meera refuted.

"There are a lot of tracks heading this way too," Lumo argued. "My instinct tells me we should head this way."

"Well, I hope you're right," Meera caved in.

Taking the path to the left, they traveled for a few more minutes. The path wound through large rocky overpasses for a while before opening up to a small, rustic village nestled in a valley. At the heart of the village stood a weathered-looking tavern with a wooden sign creaking ominously in the breeze. The building's exterior was rugged, with darkened wood and small, grimy windows that gave off an uninviting air.

"The Golden Loch," read the signboard.

Outside the tavern, Lumo's sharp eyes caught sight of a group of horses tied to a post. Among them were two familiar ones. He nudged Meera, who nodded, recognizing them immediately.

They dismounted and secured Bramble before pushing through the tavern's heavy door. Inside, the atmosphere was dim and tense, with a few patrons scattered around the room. The murmur of low conversations mingled with the occasional clink of mugs. Lumo and Meera made their way to the bar, where a grizzled bartender was polishing a glass.

Lumo leaned in, lowering his voice. "Excuse me, we're looking for the people who came with those horses outside. Can you tell us who?"

The bartender eyed them warily. "How should I know?" he replied curtly.

Lumo and Meera exchanged a glance. Apparently, not all bartenders were as friendly as Bart.

Taking matters into his own hands, Lumo spoke out loudly. "Who are the people with the horses outside?"

The murmur of conversations died down as the tavern patrons turned to look at him. From a corner table, a gruff voice responded, like a dog guarding a particularly juicy bone, "What's it to you?"

Lumo and Meera turned to see a group of about six rough-looking men glaring at them. The one who had spoken, a man with a glass eye, stood up and sauntered toward them.

"We recognized two of those horses outside," Lumo stated firmly, his hand resting on the hilt of his sword. "They were stolen from us, and we want to know who took them."

The man laughed harshly. "Stolen? Finders keepers, I say. Those horses are ours now."

Lumo stood his ground, his eyes flashing with anger. "We just want the horses back. But if you keep stealing from people, you're going to cause more trouble than you can handle."

"Are you threatening us? He's threatening us, boys," the glass-eyed man sneered.

"No, we just want you to understand what you've done. Do you understand how much you have set us back?"

The tension in the room thickened as the other thugs rallied behind the man. Both groups sized each other up.

"Looks like we've got ourselves a problem, boys." The man let out a harsh laugh.

Before the confrontation could escalate further, the bartender stepped forward, raising his hands.

"Hold on a minute," he barked. "They're just kids. Look, if it's indeed their horses, give them back. No need for bloodshed in my tavern."

The glass-eyed man spat. "Oh, it's too late for that. Besides, didn't you hear what they just said? They said they don't just want the horses back; they also want to make us pay. They came looking for trouble, and trouble is what they will get."

"We didn't say that," Meera said, glancing around the room as if seeking confirmation from the others nearby.

"Yes, you did. We all heard it," the man argued.

"No, we didn't." Meera's voice stayed firm, though a hint of irritation crept in.

"Yes, you did."

"No, we didn't."

"Yes, you did." The glass-eyed man stomped the floor, his voice turning gravelly as he glared at them, his glass eye bulging, almost ready to pop from its socket.

The man leaned in closer, his breath sour as he snarled, his hand twitching toward his side. But before he could take another step, the bartender moved between them, arms crossed, blocking the man's path. "If you're planning to continue, you'd best be handling your matter outside, or you'll have the entire village on your backs," he warned.

The glass-eyed man looked around, his single good eye darting all over the place.

"Hmpff," he grunted as he walked past Lumo and Meera. "See you two outside."

As Lumo and Meera watched the men disappear out the front door, the bartender turned to them. "You should leave out the back door."

"No. We're going to see this through," Lumo replied firmly.

Casting a glance at Meera and nodding together, the duo headed outside where the men waited for them, knives and swords at the ready.

"That's a fine horse you've got there. Looks like we've got another one, boys." The man laughed maniacally.

Lumo drew his sword with a swift motion. "We're not letting you get away with this."

The glass-eyed man lunged forward, slashing with his sword. Lumo parried the attack and countered with a thrust that forced the man back. Meera, quick and agile, circled around, trying to flank the other thieves. Two of the men charged at Lumo simultaneously, forcing him to defend himself from both sides. He ducked under a wide swing and brought his sword up, grazing one attacker's arm.

Meera, meanwhile, had no problems subduing the other three. With a slash of her staff, she summoned a gust of wind that knocked all three men to the ground.

The glass-eyed man looked around in dread as almost all of his friends lay squirming on the ground. Now furious, he roared and charged at Lumo once more. Lumo saw an opportunity to use the move he had practiced for so long. He lifted his sword high in a deliberate block, feinting a momentary opening. As the glass-eyed man swung at the feigned weakness, Lumo dropped into a low stance, attempting to hook his sword around the man's wrist. The man attempted to block, but his defense was clumsy. Lumo's sword clanged off the man's defense and hooked the air rather than the man's wrist.

The glass-eyed man blinked and tilted his head. "What are you doing?"

Lumo, momentarily flustered by the failed execution, quickly improvised. He pressed his advantage with a forceful push, sending the glass-eyed man sprawling to the ground. As the man tried to scramble back up, Lumo placed the tip of his sword at his throat.

"Enough!" Lumo commanded. "Call off your men."

Seeing their leader defeated, the remaining thieves hesitated and then slowly backed away, dropping their weapons.

"All right, all right," the glass-eyed man wheezed. "You win. Take the horses. Just let us go."

Lumo withdrew his sword but kept it at the ready. "No. You don't understand how important it was for us to get to

Rochfell quickly. Your thievery has set us back. You're going to be handed over to the authorities now."

Panic flashed in the man's good eye. "Wait, Rochfell? The castle? I know a quick way to get there. Let us go, and I'll help you."

"Lumo, we can't trust this guy," Meera said as she moved closer.

"No, really. I can help you," the man insisted. "Look, if you're here already, it means you've taken the wrong route. You've traveled here from Avalora, right? The road to the right would have been straighter, which means you don't really know the way. But I do. And I know a shortcut too. You will easily shave off a day's ride going my way. Just let us go, and I'll help you."

Lumo exchanged a glance with Meera, who looked skeptical but resigned.

"Fine. Tell us about this shortcut."

"I can't tell you, but I can show you the way. It goes through a hidden ridge."

"Lumo, I really think we shouldn't trust him," Meera whispered.

"What choice do we have?" Lumo whispered back.

He turned to the glass-eyed man. "We are going to give you a chance, but know this: if you try to deceive us, I will not hesitate to use my sword. Lead the way."

"Deal. I'll show you the quickest path. You have my word."

Lumo kept his sword ready as the man stood up slowly.

"Follow me," he said, a hint of relief in his voice.

Lumo sheathed his sword and mounted Bramble. Meera climbed onto one of the reclaimed horses, while the glass-eyed man mounted the other. Once at the edge of the village, the man started riding toward a narrow, almost hidden path leading out of the village.

Lumo and Meera exchanged one last glance, then followed, keeping their guard up. They knew they couldn't trust the man, but they had little choice if they wanted to reach Rochfell in time.

"I'm Garrett. I assume you're some sort of knight, then. Why do you wear those commoner garbs though?" Garrett asked, eyeing Lumo's attire.

"What?"

"Well, you are a knight, aren't you? Or at least a squire. There's no way a commoner has moves like those. And the girl is obviously a sorceress."

Meera beamed with pride.

"Lumo… and this is Meera. I think it's best we keep the assumptions to a minimum," Lumo said firmly.

"Hey, woah. All right. Just trying to make conversation," Garrett said, raising his hands in mock surrender.

The trio rode in silence for a few hours.

"How much further? I've seen no ridge yet. You'd better not be—"

"Almost there," Garrett replied curtly.

As they rode on, the landscape changed. The path grew narrower and more uneven, weaving through dense thickets and patches of rocky ground.

"Just a bit further," Garrett said, glancing back at Lumo and Meera. "We'll cut through this forest and come out on the other side. From there, it's a straight shot to Rochfell."

The forest was dense and dark, the pine trees towering high above them. The ground beneath the horses' hooves was a mix of soft earth and occasional rocky patches, making the ride challenging but manageable. Lumo kept his eyes on Garrett, ready for any signs of deception. The forest was eerily quiet, the only sounds being the crunch of hooves on the forest floor and the occasional rustle of leaves.

"Why are you really helping us, Garrett?" Meera asked, breaking the silence. "You're not exactly doing this out of the goodness of your heart."

Garrett sighed. "I see, you still don't trust me. I know what we did was wrong. Stealing those horses... it wasn't personal. We were desperate. This land hasn't been kind to us, and we thought we could make a quick escape with them. But I see now that we caused you more trouble than we intended. Besides, I'm not looking to get myself killed or thrown in a dungeon. Helping you is my way out of this mess."

Meera sympathized with Garrett. After all, she knew exactly how harsh life could get. Lumo, though, remained silent, his grip on Bramble's reins tightening. His mind was focused on one task—getting to Rochfell.

After another hour of riding, they finally emerged from the forest onto a narrow ridge that overlooked a vast, desolate valley. The landscape was bleak and lifeless, with barren hills and a dry, winding riverbed. The air was thick with an eerie silence, as if all life had long since abandoned this place. In the far distance, the crumbling spires of Rochfell Castle could be seen, their once-glorious structure now a haunting silhouette against the dim evening light.

"There," Garrett said, pointing toward the castle. "We follow this ridge down into the valley, then cross the riverbed. It's the fastest way. If we head this way, we will be able to arrive at Rochfell Castle in no time."

Lumo's gaze lingered on the spires of the Castle. "All right, let's move. We need to reach Rochfell as quickly as possible."

They descended the ridge carefully, the path steep and treacherous. Lumo stayed close to Meera, ensuring her horse didn't lose its footing. The air grew cooler as the sun dipped lower.

As they crossed the valley floor, they urged their horses into a trot, heading toward the riverbed. The sound of wind rustling through the barren landscape grew louder as they approached the dry riverbed, wide and filled with cracked earth and scattered stones.

Once on the other side, they continued toward Rochfell, the castle growing larger with each passing minute. Lumo felt a surge of hope; they were finally nearing their destination.

As the light continued to fade, the surrounding landscape grew even more desolate. Twisted, leafless trees dotted the barren hills, and patches of dead grass added to the somber atmosphere. The castle loomed ominously in the distance, its dark outline fading against the night sky.

"I suggest we make camp here for the night," Garrett said, pointing to a small grove of gnarled trees just off the road. "Tomorrow we take the ridge heading up to the castle, and I will have finally kept my word."

"Fine," Lumo said as they dismounted. They led their horses into the grove, the trees offering some shelter from the biting wind. The ground was hard and uneven, but they managed to find a relatively flat spot to set up camp.

Lumo and Meera gathered what little wood they could find, starting a small fire that cast shifting shadows on the twisted trunks around them. As the fire crackled to life, Lumo turned to Garrett, his expression stern.

"You're going to stay on that side. I suggest you keep your distance. If you get too close, I'll consider it an act of aggression."

Garrett raised his hands in a placating gesture. “Understood. I’ll stay over here,” he said, moving to the opposite side of the fire.

The three settled in, the night air growing colder.

“You get some sleep, Meera. I’ll keep an eye on him,” Lumo said, positioning himself so he could keep one eye on Garrett, his back against a tree, sword within easy reach.

The fire cast a warm glow, but the atmosphere remained tense.

Garrett broke the silence, his voice cautious. “So, why are you heading to the Rochfell Castle? It’s not exactly a popular destination these days.”

“We have our reasons,” Lumo replied.

“Fair enough. I just thought it might be something I should know, considering I’m helping you get there.”

“We don’t owe you any explanations. Just lead us there, and you’ll be free to go.”

Garrett sighed. “All right, all right. No need to get defensive. I’m just trying to understand what I’ve gotten myself into.”

“Like I said, get us there, and you’re free to go. You got yourself into this by stealing our horses and then trying to kill us,” Lumo retorted. “Remember that.”

“I get it,” Garrett resigned.

Lumo fixed his gaze on Garrett, not once looking away.

As the night wore on, Meera slept peacefully while Lumo slept sitting up, his sword resting across his lap. Garrett kept to his side of the camp, making no attempt to approach.

At one point, Garrett looked over at Lumo, a thoughtful expression on his face. “You know, trust goes both ways. I could have tried to run, but I didn’t.”

Lumo’s eyes narrowed. “And that’s supposed to earn you points?”

"Just saying," Garrett replied with a shrug. "I'm trying to make things right."

Lumo didn't respond. He wasn't ready to trust Garrett, but he couldn't deny the man had a point. For now, all they could do was get through the night and hope that the morning would bring them closer to their goal.

***

As dawn broke, Lumo, Meera, and Garrett prepared to break camp. The castle loomed closer now, shrouded in morning mist and an eerie silence that promised both challenge and revelation.

"Let's move quickly," Lumo said, his voice firm with resolve.

Garrett nodded. "We're almost there. This way."

They mounted their horses and continued along the path.

A couple of hours later, they approached the ridge that led them to higher ground. They climbed steadily, with Garrett leading the way. As they neared the top, Garrett slowed his horse and turned to Lumo and Meera.

"This is as far as I go. The castle is just ahead. You'll find a narrow path leading directly to one of the gates."

Lumo looked toward the castle, then back to Garrett. "All right. You've held up your end of the deal, Garrett. You're free to go."

Garrett paused for a moment before speaking. "Before I go, there's something I need to say."

"Go on," Meera said.

"Look, I know how we got off on the wrong foot. I hope after this you can forgive me for my actions. Clearly, whatever this mission of yours is, it's bigger than anything I've been a part of."

"We forgive you, Garrett." Meera glanced at Lumo.

"Oh, and if you need an ally, you can reach me at Valtarra. My comrades and I were headed there, hoping to find some decent jobs."

"Valtarra?"

"Yeah, the town in the mountains. My brother lives there, and he seems to be doing fine. If you're ever there, just ask for the Dusseldorf twins."

"We will keep that in mind," replied Meera.

"Thanks, and do you mind if I keep this horse?" Garrett asked sheepishly.

"You may." Meera smiled

"Lumo," Garrett addressed.

"Garrett," Lumo replied.

Garrett gave a grateful nod, then turned his horse around and retraced the path. Lumo and Meera watched him for a moment, ensuring he was truly leaving. Once Garrett was a good distance away, they turned their attention back to the imposing structure before them.

Rochfell Castle stood right ahead, built seamlessly into the rugged face of the mountain. Its stone walls, weathered by time and elements, seemed to grow out of the rocky landscape. Towers and turrets jutted from the mountainside; their peaks crowned with crumbling battlements. Moss and ivy clung to the stones, giving the castle an air of forgotten grandeur, like an aging bard still clinging to the trappings of former fame.

The gate, a massive wooden structure reinforced with iron bands, stood slightly ajar, blending into the mountain's natural crevices. A narrow, winding path led up to it, bordered by jagged rocks and sparse, windblown trees.

Lumo took a deep breath, his eyes scanning the castle for any signs of movement. "This is it, Meera. We're finally here."

Meera's grip tightened on her staff. "I hope we aren't too late."

***

CHAPTER 24

Lumo and Meera stood at the edge of the narrow path, gazing up at Rochfell Castle. The morning mist clung to the air, shrouding the ancient fortress in a ghostly veil. They had expected to see the king's army surrounding the castle, but the landscape was eerily quiet.

"No sign of the king's forces," Lumo muttered, his brow furrowing in concern.

"You're right," Meera agreed. "So we were able to get ahead of them after all."

"Looks like it." Lumo exhaled lightly.

"So, do you think we should wait for them?"

"I don't know, Meera. I think they should be here soon, but something doesn't feel right."

"Why do you say that?"

"This place looks deserted. Shouldn't we have seen some signs of activity by now?"

As Meera took note of the situation, she realized Lumo had a point. If the cult had indeed holed up in the castle, and Marcus and the king were leading the men for slaughter, it seemed like the cult would be well prepared or at the very least show themselves, unless maybe they weren't here at all.

"Lumo, what if... they're not in there? What if this is some kind of ruse?"

"W—What do you mean?" Lumo asked.

"I mean, what if we were only led to believe they are here?"

"Unlikely," Lumo mumbled. "Malikoth said Oliver is at Rochfell. I think he was telling the truth. Although, I agree we shouldn't dismiss the possibility. I think we should go in first."

Meera's eyes sharpened with resolve. "You're right. Let's go."

As they approached the gate, Lumo pushed it open slowly, the old wood creaking under the strain. The gate swung inward, revealing a dark, narrow corridor beyond.

The air inside was damp and cold, filled with the scent of mildew. Lumo and Meera exchanged a glance, then stepped through the gate. They moved carefully, scanning the area for any signs of danger. As they ventured deeper into the castle, the narrow corridor opened into a vast, dimly lit hall. Tall columns lined the walls. The floor was strewn with debris. Old, tattered banners of Rochfell, once emblazoned with the insignia of a proud lion, now hung limply from the ceiling, their faded motifs barely clinging to their former majesty.

"I don't think anyone is here," Meera whispered.

Lumo nodded, his hand resting on the hilt of his sword. "Stay alert."

They continued through the hall. The silence was oppressive, broken only by the faint sound of their breathing and the occasional drip of water from the ceiling. As they reached the far end of the hall, they found a set of stone stairs leading downward.

"Looks like it's this way," Lumo said, gesturing to the stairs.

As they descended cautiously, the stairs led them to a lower level of the castle, a warren of narrow passages and dark chambers.

"Seriously, what is up with these dark passages all the time? Do all cults have a thing for creepy hallways or something?" Meera remarked, pouting as she spoke.

Lumo chuckled softly, despite the tension. "Seems to be a common theme, doesn't it? Just stay close. We'll get through this."

They moved deeper into the passage, but the darkness became almost impenetrable. Meera squinted, trying to make out the walls and floor ahead, but it was no use.

"It's too dark to see anything," she said.

Before they could do anything about it, they heard a soft click. Meera had stepped onto an uneven stone that pressed down gently.

"Lumo, I think I just stepped on someth—"

"Aaaaaaah!" Lumo and Meera shouted as the floor beneath them gave way with a loud crack. They plummeted into darkness, landing eventually with a hard thud, the impact knocking the wind out of them.

"Damn it," Lumo cursed, scrambling to his feet. "Meera, are you okay?"

Meera groaned, pushing herself up. "I'm okay. This place is full of surprises, huh?" she muttered, rubbing her shoulder.

"You can say that again."

"This place is full of surpr—"

"Not literally, Meera."

Meera sighed dramatically, putting her hands on her hips. "And here I thought you finally got a sense of humor."

"It's still too dark," Lumo mumbled as he pulled out his sword. The sword went ablaze, lighting the area and revealing the pit they had fallen into.

The floor was littered with skeletons and debris, and the air was thick with the stench of decay. Meera instinctively covered her mouth with her sleeve, her eyes watering from the odor.

Meera shuddered, her eyes scanning the grim scene. "We need to find a way out of here."

Lumo responded with a head bob, then held his glowing sword high to better illuminate the pit. As they moved cautiously through the debris, he spotted a torch bracketed to the wall, the wood still intact despite the years.

"Over there," Lumo pointed. "Let's light it."

Carefully holding the sword to the torch, Lumo lit it, and the torch flared to life.

"How big is this place?" Lumo called out, eyeing the vastness of the room.

"What is this place, anyway? Some kind of dumping ground?" Meera asked.

"No, I think it's a pitfall. Castles use them to trap and slow down intruders," Lumo explained.

"Ughh, judging by all these bones on the floor, I don't think people really got out of them."

"Perhaps, or maybe just the unfortunate ones," Lumo remarked, glancing at the high, crumbling walls. "Anyway, we're clearly not going back the way we came in… unless you can use your wind magic to lift us back up there."

"Sure, yes, I can definitely summon the wind, but I hope you don't mind being skewered by all these bones and other debris," Meera replied.

"Let's go, this way then. Here, you take the torch," Lumo suggested, handing Meera the torch.

They carefully made their way through the pit, stepping over the skeletal remains. They eventually came to the other end of the pit.

"There's no exit," Meera remarked. "Don't tell me we're stuck down here."

"No, wait. There has to be a way. Let's look for hidden doors."

As Meera moved the torch, inspecting the walls closely, a draft of wind blew across the fire, causing it to waver slightly.

"Did you feel that?" Meera asked.

Lumo grunted in acknowledgment. "There must be a hidden passage behind. Keep looking."

They continued their search, feeling along the walls for any sign of an opening. And then, Meera noticed a stone with a slight elevation. Carefully, she pushed the stone down and heard a soft click. A section of the wall slowly shifted, revealing a narrow passageway hidden behind it. Dust filled the air, causing Meera to cough.

"Nice work, Meera," Lumo said, peering into the newly revealed passage.

"Thanks. Let's hope this leads us out of here," Meera replied, lifting the torch higher to illuminate the path ahead.

They squeezed through the narrow opening, finding themselves in a winding, cramped corridor. The walls were rough and uneven, and the air felt even damper and colder, if that was possible. The torch struggled to stay lit as Lumo and Meera made their way through the passage.

"Stay close," Lumo whispered.

After several tense minutes of navigating the narrow corridor, Lumo and Meera found themselves at the opening of what appeared to be a larger room.

"Here, this is—" Lumo began and immediately stopped mid-sentence. "Oh, no! We're back at the pit."

"Damn it!" Meera squealed. "What do we do now?"

"Don't lose hope. Getting out won't be easy, but I'm sure there's a way. We've likely entered some sort of labyrinth designed to trap us down here. We just need to find the way out. Let's go."

***

Lumo and Meera had been trapped for a few hours, desperately trying to escape their predicament. Meanwhile, the king and his army had arrived at the front entrance to Rochfell Castle.

"Glorious leader, the king's army has arrived at the entrance," one of the cultists informed Lilith as she gathered with Marachi and the others in the inner sanctum.

"Good, let them enter the castle. We need to delay them until the veiling tomorrow."

"But there has been a development," the cultist said, shifting nervously.

Lilith stared without a word, waiting for what the man had to say.

"The pit, glorious one. It appears to have been triggered already."

"What? How is that possible?"

"It seems a couple of intruders have snuck in. They must have found another way; none of our brethren have left their posts, and they were watching the main path the entire time."

"Go find out who it is," Lilith demanded.

"Yes, glorious one." The cultist bowed and disappeared from view.

"What do we do about the king, milady?" Marachi asked.

"We need to delay them, Marachi. What about our friends?"

"They're already on the way; they should be entering the tunnels soon."

"Good. Make sure the king's army is well met at the entrance."

"Understood," Marachi said.

"And, Marachi... no more setbacks."

"Yes, milady," Marachi replied before storming out.

***

Outside, King Reginald and the rest of the army approached steadily.

"Halt! Positions!" King Reginald commanded with authority.

Flanked by Marcus and Serena, the king stood at the forefront, with the rest of the cavalry forming three rows behind him, all facing the castle.

"This place looks deserted, Your Majesty," Marcus observed, scanning the ominous structure.

Within moments, the cultists seeped out of the main gate, with Marachi and the elite cultists leading the way.

"Never mind," Marcus commented, a slightly befuddled look on his face.

Marachi, the mime, and a few cultists inched forward on foot, while the king, Marcus, and Serena trotted forward on horseback. As the two groups met at the center, it was Marachi who spoke first.

"Your Majesty, it's an honor to have you here. I'm High Priest Marachi; we have been expecting you."

"I'm sure you have," the king said. "Where is my son?"

"Your son? Oh, you mean Prince Oliver? Is that why you are here?" Marachi sneered mockingly.

"Stop playing games. I'm here to claim my son. Hand him over."

"Now, now, Your Majesty. Please be reasonable. Besides, we had a pact, remember?"

"What pact?" Serena quizzed, a look of surprise on her face.

"Oh, I'm sorry. Maybe I was mistaken; His Majesty doesn't regard pacts. Perhaps that's why Oliver… I mean, Prince Oliver, is here in the first place."

"What are you…?" the king began.

"You thought we wouldn't know? We know everything. But never mind, this changes nothing. Prince Oliver will die. He has to."

"Enough!" Serena fumed. "Unless you wish for bloodshed, hand over the prince now."

The mime pretended to be scared, cowering and trembling in mock fear.

"I think you and I both know this, sorceress; bloodshed is inevitable as it stands," Marachi declared. "…Unless you wish to do this the old way, our champion against yours? Of course, I will understand if you are scared of losing."

The mime enthusiastically pointed to himself, bobbing his head as if saying he was their champion.

"Didn't you hear what His Majesty said? We're not here to play games. Hand over Prince Oliver," said Serena.

"Oh, come now. Don't be like that. All right, I'll sweeten the deal here. You pick any one of our brethren out there, and you can still present your champion. If we lose, you get Prince Oliver without unnecessary bloodshed, but if you lose, you turn back immediately. Sounds like a good deal, doesn't it?"

With a deft flick of his hand, the mime brushed off his disappointment, his expression shifting seamlessly from frustration to nonchalance.

Serena's mind wavered with doubt, but the possibility of a peaceful victory seemed too tempting to resist.

"Your Majesty?" Serena turned to the king.

"Marcus here will represent our champion; you may call on your best melee fighter," King Reginald replied.

Marachi began laughing maniacally.

"What's so funny?" Serena asked.

"Well, now that it's decided, you must turn back as per our deal."

"What are you going on about? The deal was that our fighters would engage in one-on-one combat," Serena argued.

"Oh, but don't you see? You've already lost... Brother Marcus?"

"Brother?" Serena mumbled in surprise.

Before anything else could be said, Marcus slowly trotted his horse forward and stood beside Marachi, facing the king with a sly grin on his face.

"You traitor!" King Reginald bellowed.

The king's roar of betrayal echoed across the field and an uneasy murmur spread among the cavalry. The tension in the air was palpable, a fuse waiting to be lit.

Marcus's sly grin widened. "Did you really think I would stay loyal to a king who breaks pacts?" he taunted. "Your reign ends here, Reginald."

King Reginald's eyes blazed with fury. "You will pay for your treachery, Marcus. Cavalry, prepare to charge!"

Before the command could fully register, Marachi raised his hands, and a dark, swirling mist formed around his hands.

King Reginald, sensing the imminent danger, barked out, "Fall back! Regroup!"

Serena and the king quickly retreated to their original positions, forming a tight defensive line.

Marachi and his cultists did the same, retreating back to their fortified positions near the castle gates. The battlefield now lay between them, a no-man's-land charged with tension.

King Reginald unsheathed his sword. "Archers, at the ready!" he commanded.

Arrows were nocked and drawn, ready to release a deadly volley. Serena's grip on her staff tightened as she chanted a protective spell, a shimmering barrier forming around the king and his immediate guard.

Marachi's voice cut through the tense silence. "Now, show them the true power of our dark lord, whose magic flows through us!"

With a wave of his hand, several cultists stepped forward, chanting incantations. Suddenly, fireballs hurtled through the air toward the king's forces, trailing dark smoke.

"Shields up!" King Reginald shouted. The knights raised their shields, but the impact of the fire spells was devastating, sending men sprawling and breaking the formation.

"Archers, fire!" the king commanded.

The archers let loose their arrows, a deadly rain aimed at the cultists. Many cultists fell, pierced by the swift shafts, but those adept in magic conjured shields of fire, melting the arrows mid-air or deflecting them harmlessly to the ground. The mime stood next to Marachi, protecting himself and his immediate allies with an invisible wall.

"Hold steady!" Serena yelled, casting a counter-spell to protect her side, even as more fire spells came hurtling toward the army.

King Reginald scanned the battlefield, his strategic mind racing. "Red Company, form up! Prepare to charge!"

The cavalry from the Red Company quickly regrouped, forming a tight, disciplined line, and raced ahead.

Meanwhile, Marachi's elite cultists continued their assault, weaving dark spells that summoned shadowy tendrils from the ground, which ensnared and crushed the king's cavalry. Horses reared and neighed in panic as the dark magic sapped their strength and sent riders toppling.

As the advancing cavalry fell to the battlefield, Marcus and the cultists armed with crescent spears stepped forward, promptly engaging the fallen warriors.

"We need to disrupt their spellcasters!" Serena shouted.

"Green Company, form up and prepare to charge. Blue Company, take the right flank and target their spellcasters!" King Reginald commanded.

"On it!" The Blue Company broke off, charging toward the right flank, aiming to outmaneuver the cultists and strike at their less protected spellcasters.

Marachi saw this and snarled. "Protect the casters! Don't let them through!"

He sent his elite guards to intercept the Blue Company, while he himself began a grand incantation.

Faer il oram, Enar ithrak il zarvoth,

Nythir vael thalvohkhal aag,

Norith thalrath

A massive vortex of dark energy began taking shape in the sky.

"Brace yourselves!" Serena warned.

The vortex churned with an eerie, otherworldly glow, its dark tendrils reaching out like grasping fingers. Lightning crackled and danced along its edges, casting eerie shadows on the battlefield below. As the vortex grew larger, its ominous presence seemed to suffocate the very air around it, instilling a sense of dread in all who beheld it. The vortex unleashed a storm of dark lightning bolts, striking indiscriminately across the battlefield, causing chaos and confusion among the king's ranks.

"Serena, you need to do something about that vortex!" King Reginald shouted amidst the thundering roar of the battlefield.

"Right!"

Raising her staff high, she began chanting a spell to counterattack the vortex.

By Zephyr's breath, I summon winds of might,
To stand against the dark in fervent fight.
In counter-spin, their force shall tightly bind,
A tempest born, to break the dark's confine.

As Serena's chant echoed across the battlefield, the winds responded to her call, swirling and gathering momentum. A tempest was brewing, born from Serena's invocation and fueled by the boundless energy of the winds. Around the dark vortex, a swirling maelstrom took shape, its form mirroring the opposing rotation of the dark vortex. The winds intensified, swirling around the dark vortex in counter-rotation. The winds howled and whipped at the dark energy, destabilizing its form further.

Serena could feel the elemental power surging through her, the winds obeying her command with fierce determination. With the vortex teetering on the brink of collapse, Serena turned her attention to harnessing the sunlight. Raising her staff higher, she directed her focus skyward, seeking the radiant energy of the sun.

So shine, O sun, with all your might, be bright,
And scatter darkness with your piercing light.
From heavens high, let one pure beam descend,
To aid in battle, darkness to amend.

A beam of sunlight pierced through the clouds, aimed directly into the eye of the vortex. There was a blinding flash of light as the dark energy collided with the brilliance of the sunlight-infused beam. Then, with a deafening roar, the vortex collapsed in on itself, imploding with a force that sent shockwaves rippling across the battlefield. Dark tendrils dissipated into nothingness, leaving behind only a lingering echo of their malevolent power.

King Reginald, now confident, rallied his men. “Archers, provide cover fire! Green Company, advance on the left! Yellow Company with me! Charge straight at their center!”

The cavalry archers continued to rain arrows on the cultists, while the main cavalry force, led by Reginald himself, charged forward with a thunderous roar, their lances and swords raised in attacking positions.

Despite the cultists' devastating magic, the king’s disciplined troops advanced steadily, their numbers and training beginning to turn the tide.

Marachi, sensing the shift in momentum, called out to his followers, “Do not falter! Draw upon the power of the dark lord!” His voice carried an almost hypnotic influence, reinvigorating the cultists.

Suddenly, a thick, black fog seeped from the ground, spreading across the battlefield and reducing visibility. The king's forces struggled to maintain formation as the fog enveloped them. Cries of confusion and disarray echoed through the ranks.

“Hold your positions!” King Reginald commanded, but his voice was drowned out by the clamor. The cultists used the cover of the fog to launch a counterattack, their dark spells crackling through the haze and striking down unsuspecting soldiers.

Serena knew she had to clear the fog if there was any chance of regaining the edge. Raising her staff, she uttered a chant to use more wind magic to clear the fog. The winds howled and pushed against the fog, but the dark magic was resilient. Though Serena managed to thin the fog, it still clung stubbornly to the battlefield, providing the cultists with an advantage.

As the fog swirled around the king's forces, its insidious effects became evident. Soldiers stumbled and faltered, their movements sluggish and their vision blurred. Some rubbed their eyes vigorously, trying to clear the haze that clouded their sight. Others swayed on their feet, their limbs going limp as if drained of strength. Horses threw riders off their backs, neighing and stamping in dread.

A knight near King Reginald dropped his sword, his eyes wide and unfocused.

"Mother, what are you doing here?" he muttered, looking around in confusion.

Another soldier fell to his knees, clutching his head as if in pain, his face contorted in bewilderment.

"Focus, men! Hold the line!" Reginald shouted, but the mesmerizing fog dulled their senses and eroded their discipline. Warriors who had been steadfast moments before now moved erratically, their coordination shattered.

The cultists, sensing their advantage, pressed their attack. Dark spells flew through the air, striking down soldiers who could no longer defend themselves effectively. The battlefield was a scene of chaos, with the king's forces caught in the grip of the mesmerizing fog.

Realizing the dire situation, King Reginald called out to his commanders, "All Companies, fall back and regroup! Form a defensive line!"

The soldiers pulled back, trying to reform their ranks despite the disorienting effects of the fog. Their movements were slow and uncertain, but they managed to create a semblance of order.

The numbers had thinned on both sides, ranged battles continuing through the day. All the ranged casters had retreated to the castle walls, gaining an advantage, despite their fewer numbers. The battle raged on into the evening, with both sides locked in a fierce struggle.

“Your Majesty, night approaches. We will be at a serious disadvantage,” Serena said, remembering Marachi could summon the Cwn Annwn at night. If that were to happen, they would have no chance.

“We should fall back and wait for Lucius and the reinforcements,” she continued.

King Reginald's face tightened with frustration. “All units, fall back! Retreat!”

The soldiers, despite their weariness and the confusion caused by the fog, obeyed the command with disciplined efficiency. They slowly withdrew from the battlefield, maintaining a defensive formation to protect their retreat.

Marachi watched them retreat with a smug smile, his dark eyes gleaming with malevolent satisfaction.

“Yes, run while you can. The night belongs to us.”

***

CHAPTER 25

The labyrinth seemed endless, its twisting passages and echoing corridors confounding Lumo and Meera at every turn. They had been trapped down there since the first light of day, and now, as night fell, their frustration grew.

Lumo wiped the sweat from his brow, peering down yet another shadowy corridor. “There’s got to be a way out.”

Meera had heard Lumo say that all day. She had given up responding after a while, feeling hopeless.

Throughout the long hours, they had tried everything they could think of. Each time they found a new entrance by pressing down hidden stones embedded in the floor and walls, the old ones would close, sealing them back into the maze that eventually led them right back to the pit. They mapped out their paths by scraping marks into the dirt-covered walls with small stones they found on the ground.

“And we’re back.” Lumo sighed as they found themselves once more at the pit. He moved to the wall to add the new markings to their map. As Lumo finished adding the newly discovered route, he stepped back to observe the map.

“This is hopeless. I can’t believe we can’t figure this out,” he mumbled.

“Thank goodness you accepted it, finally,” Meera remarked.

"Oh, come now, Meera. Look at it this way, at least we're alone down here. I mean, there could have been some death traps or worse—monsters."

"I don't know which one's worse though," Meera commented. "I'm tired. My feet hurt, my back hurts, and my head is pounding. This place is a nightmare. And those skeletons? Those people probably died of boredom before anything else."

Ignoring Meera's rambling, Lumo turned toward the map again.

"So, all these paths are dead ends..." Lumo traced his fingers along the map.

Meera continued to ramble, "I mean, who builds a labyrinth with no exits? What kind of sadistic mind thought this up? I'm so hungry, and the air down here is so stale. I wouldn't be surprised if we run out of oxygen. And don't get me started on the dripping water. It's driving me insane. Drip, drip, drip, all day long."

Lumo squinted at the map, deep in thought. "And this area here seems a bit unexplored..."

Meera kept going, "Honestly, it's like this place is designed to mess with us. Every turn, every stone, it's all a cruel joke. We keep ending up back at this stupid pit. Why can't there just be a simple door? Like, right at the entrance. No, it has to be hidden and convoluted."

"Wait... what did you just say?" Lumo paused.

Meera huffed, "I said it's all a cruel joke, and there should just be a simple door right at the entrance, but no—"

"That's it!" Lumo exclaimed. "A door at the entrance!"

"What?"

"Meera, we've been so focused on the labyrinth and the pit, we haven't considered the possibility that the answer is much simpler. What if there's a door near the entrance that we missed?"

"No, come on, it can't be that simple, can it?"

Lumo nodded, a glimmer of hope in his eyes. "When we fell, we came this way and found this door that led to the maze, but what if…"

"We're going back to the entrance?"

"We're going back to the entrance. Come on," Lumo said, leading the way.

They headed back, across the length of the pit, stepping over the skeletons and debris again. Lumo was so excited at the possibility of escape that he didn't mind crushing a few bones on the way. Reaching the other end of the pit, they scanned the wall, looking for an exit.

"Here," Lumo jumped with joy, finding a dislodged stone.

They had become adept at locating hidden mechanisms. Lumo pushed the stone, and a small door creaked open. A sliver of light pierced the darkness, revealing stone stairs that ascended upward.

"Meera, you're a genius!" Lumo exclaimed.

"I am? I mean, of course, I am," Meera replied, smiling proudly.

Without thinking, Lumo pulled her into a tight hug. For a moment, they both froze, the closeness between them unexpected. Immediately, they disengaged in awkwardness.

"Umm, sorry," Lumo mumbled, visibly flustered.

"N—No, yeah, it's all right," Meera replied, her cheeks red as well.

Quietly, they stepped through the door and ascended the stone stairs, the light growing brighter with each step. Finally, they reached the top and emerged into a small, dimly lit chamber. They both took a moment to catch their breath, their eyes adjusting to the change in light.

Lumo turned to Meera, a smile spreading across his face. “We did it. We’re out of that nightmare.”

Just as they were about to step forward, a sudden noise behind them made Lumo turn. Before he could react, a heavy blow struck the side of his head. He crumpled to the ground, unconscious. Meera barely had time to gasp before she too felt a sharp pain at the base of her skull. Darkness engulfed her as she fell beside Lumo, both of them lying motionless on the chamber floor.

***

The night had gone by restlessly for the king's army. Campfires had smoldered in the darkness as soldiers huddled around them, whispering about the battle to come. Anxiety hung heavy in the air, and despite their exhaustion, few found solace in sleep. Serena had stood watch, her gaze fixed on the distant silhouette of Rochfell Castle. She had anticipated Marachi to unleash the Cwn Annwn, but surprisingly, the night passed peacefully.

As the first light of dawn crept over the horizon, a distant rumble echoed through the valley. The soldiers stirred, looking toward the source of the sound. A cloud of dust rose in the distance, growing larger and closer with each passing moment.

“It's them,” Serena murmured, a mix of relief and anticipation in her voice.

King Reginald, standing tall and resolute, offered a curt, approving gesture.

The rumble grew louder, and soon, the banners of Lucius's army came into view. Leading the formidable force, Lucius rode at the forefront, his presence commanding and inspiring. The sight of the massive army boosted the morale of the king's men, a collective cheer rising from their ranks.

Serena's eyes scanned the arriving soldiers, and she spotted a familiar face among them. Gus, with his imposing stature, rode beside Lucius. Her heart lifted at the sight.

"I hope you don't mind; I brought this guy. He insisted, really, and I couldn't refuse," Lucius said, half-smiling at Serena, while Gus had the widest of grins.

As Lucius dismounted, he approached King Reginald and took a knee.

The king clasped Lucius's shoulder. "Your arrival couldn't have been more timely, my friend. We were beginning to lose hope."

"You know you can depend on me, Your Majesty," Lucius replied.

Scanning the remainder of the king's forces, Lucius continued, "Marcus isn't with you... I assume he was made out?"

The king's eyes widened at Lucius's words. "You knew?"

"Only after you left, Your Majesty. It was Lumo's idea to confront Malikoth, which led us to Marcus's betrayal. Speaking of, where is Lumo?"

"Lumo?" the king muttered, a look of horror on his face.

"Yes, he rode before me. Wasn't he the one who informed you?"

The king turned to Serena. "Serena, did you spot Lumo yesterday?" he asked, panic in his voice.

"No."

"Oh, Lord. I hope it's not what I think it is," the king mumbled to himself.

"Lucius, prepare the army. We storm the castle within the hour," King Reginald commanded with authority.

"Yes, My liege."

***

With the morale of the army bolstered by Lucius's arrival, the soldiers formed ranks, their spirits high and their resolve unwavering. An hour later, the renewed force began their march toward Rochfell Castle with a collective purpose, their footsteps echoing like thunder through the valley.

Lucius rode at the front along with King Reginald, his voice carrying over the clatter of armor and the beat of hooves.

"Men of Avalora! Today, we march to reclaim our prince and our honor! Remember why we fight: for our kingdom, for our families, and for the future of Avalora!"

The soldiers responded with a resounding cheer. The sight of Lucius leading the charge, along with the banners of their homeland waving proudly in the breeze, filled them with renewed strength.

As they neared the castle, a sudden tension gripped the air. The morning mist, thick and swirling, obscured their view. But as they advanced, the mist thinned, revealing ominous silhouettes in the distance.

King Reginald's eyes narrowed, realization dawning on him.

"Hold," he commanded, raising his hand.

The army halted, their eyes fixed on the emerging shapes ahead. Slowly, the mist cleared, and to their astonishment, an enormous army came into view. Clad in dark armor and bearing the crest of King Caelumyth, the forces were already assembled, their ranks stretching across the mountainside and flanking the cultists who stood ready to defend their stronghold.

"What is Caelumyth doing here?" Lucius spoke.

King Reginald remained silent, his expression grave and troubled.

"They must have used the tunnels in the mountain to arrive, but why do they stand against us?" Lucius continued.

"Your Majesty?" Serena pressed, her eyes searching his face.

King Reginald, still silent, turned to Lucius and Serena. He knew why Caelumyth's army was there, but unable to divulge any information, he simply met their stares, his eyes heavy with unspoken knowledge.

"Your Majesty… Perhaps it's time to tell us the truth about this pact…" Serena implored.

"You know it already, Serena," King Reginald uttered.

"Know what?" Lucius asked, confused.

"I know part of it. The bloodline is to be purged, but I don't understand Caelumyth's involvement," Serena replied.

"Purged?" Lucius mumbled.

"It's obvious, isn't it? With my reign over, someone needs to take over the kingdom. The cult has likely struck a pact with Caelumyth."

"Take over? I don't understand…" Lucius continued.

"Lucius," Serena interjected. Lucius met her gaze, and she subtly shook her head, signaling him to stop pursuing it further.

"I never agreed to it, you know. But, this pact has been going on for millennia. But, no more; it ends here," King Reginald said, with fierce determination. "Serena, Lucius, do you trust your king?"

"Of course, Your Majesty," both of them replied.

"Then, today, no matter what, we save Oliver."

The king's words instilled confidence in both Serena and Lucius, soothing their troubled minds for the moment.

King Reginald drew his sword, lifting it high. "Men of Avalora, our destiny awaits! For the prince, for our kingdom, charge!"

Lucius and Serena, inspired by the king's resolve, echoed his battle cry, urging their horses forward. The soldiers, driven by the fierce determination of their leaders, surged ahead, their collective roar filling the valley.

With weapons drawn and banners flying, the king's army advanced toward Rochfell Castle, ready to face the cult and their newfound allies. The ground trembled under the force of their charge, the final battle for Avalora's future about to commence.

***

Inside Rochfell Castle, deep within its dark stronghold, Lumo and Meera stirred from their unconscious state. Bound in chains, they found themselves in a dimly lit chamber, the air thick with the scent of damp stone and old magic.

Lumo groaned, his head throbbing as he tried to shake off the disorientation. "Meera, are you all right?"

Meera blinked, struggling to focus. "I think so," she replied, her voice weak but steady. "Where are we?"

Lumo scanned their surroundings, his eyes narrowing as he took in the heavy iron chains binding their wrists and ankles.

"I think we're still inside the castle."

They both tugged at their restraints, the chains clinking loudly in the oppressive silence. Lumo strained against the iron, his muscles tensing with effort, but the chains held fast.

"It's no use," Meera said. "If only I had my staff."

Just as they were beginning to lose hope, the heavy door to the chamber creaked open. A figure stepped into the dim light, her presence exuding an aura of dark power and authority. Lilith smirked as she approached, her eyes glinting with malevolent delight.

"Well, well, what do we have here?" Lilith's voice was smooth and mocking. "Lumo, how delightful to see you and your girlfriend."

Lumo glared at her, his jaw clenched.

"Why don't you free us and see how delightful we can be?" Meera spat.

Lilith laughed, a sound that sent chills down their spines. "Feisty, isn't she? I love it! Let's see how long it lasts when she sees what's about to happen to you."

Lumo struggled once more in vain.

"Don't struggle so much. I will free you of your torment, but not before I thank you personally for arriving in the nick of time. The timing couldn't have been more perfect, really."

"You don't know the joy I felt when they told me you two had snuck into the castle. Oh, I love it when a plan comes together as perfectly as this," she continued.

"Are you done with your monologuing yet? Because I would love to have a crack at you… personally," Meera spoke.

"Not yet," Lilith's reply was curt. "I still have so much more to share. Your friend, Oliver, barely speaks much to me these days. I've been so lonely."

"Where is Oliver?" Lumo grunted.

"Oh, he's here. Would you like to meet him?"

Lilith turned toward the doorway. "Bring him out," she commanded.

The heavy door creaked open, and a single cultist stepped forward, his face hidden beneath a hood. He led Oliver, who appeared to be in a trance-like state, his eyes glazed and unseeing. Lumo and Meera's eyes widened in shock.

"Oliver, are you all right?" Lumo shouted.

Oliver remained silent, disjointed from reality.

Lilith smiled wickedly. "See what I mean? But I'm so glad you're here, Lumo. We have so much to discuss."

"What have you done to him?" Lumo demanded, his voice steady but edged with determination.

Lilith's smile widened, enjoying the sight of Lumo's turmoil. "Oh, come now. You've seen us do this before. Besides, it's all part of the ritual."

"Let him go. He's not the one you want."

"Oh, but he is," Lilith drawled.

"No, you don't understand, Oliver isn't—"

"The true prince? We know," Lilith divulged. "We know it's you. That's why I'm sooo happy. We can finally fulfill our promise to Lord Cernunnos."

"What?" Meera exclaimed, confusion spreading across her face like ripples on a pond.

"Oh, your girlfriend doesn't know, does she? Tsk tsk."

"He gave it away back at the shrine," Lilith explained, turning to Meera.

"You thought we wouldn't recognize the dark mark? You continue to underestimate us, Lumo," Lilith said, turning back to Lumo.

"If you know who I am, then let Oliver go," Lumo urged.

"Oliver has to die, unfortunately, thanks to your father."

"Thanks to my father? What are you—"

"The entire kingdom believes he's the true heir, dear boy. But look on the bright side, at least he won't die alone. You get to join him."

Lumo's eyes blazed with fury and desperation, but he resisted the urge to struggle against the chains. Instead, he took a deep breath, trying to keep his composure. He knew he had to think strategically, not let Lilith see his fear or anger.

"Why?" Lumo demanded, his voice steady but cold. "Why go through all this trouble? What do you gain from this?"

Lilith's smile never wavered. "What do we gain? Power, of course. The power to reshape the world in Lord Cernunnos's image. We tried doing it the right way, but the resistance was too much. So now we continue to spread the lord's influence, one kingdom at a time, growing slowly but surely."

"We have to stop this," Meera whispered.

"We will," Lumo replied.

"You are sorely mistaken. When Lucius arrives, he will put an end to your nonsense," he announced.

"Oh, he already has, and we are well prepared for him," Lilith laughed. "Our ally, Caelumyth, stands with us and is ready to engage them as we speak. Caelumyth, of course, will take over the kingdom of Avalora, and a millennium later, it will be someone else. There is no stopping this, Lumo."

Lumo snarled in response.

"Well, good chat. But I must leave you now. The veiling is soon, and I need to prepare."

"Watch over them," Lilith commanded the lone cultist standing nearby.

"Oliver. If your friend here tries to escape, do be a dear and take care of him, will you?" she barked before leaving.

Oliver stood steadfast, his eyes silently calculating Lumo's every move.

***

Outside, the clash of steel and the thunderous roar of battle filled the air as King Reginald's forces engaged with Caelumyth's army. The morning mist, now fully lifted, revealed the chaotic scene of swordsmen, archers, and cavalry locked in a fierce struggle for dominance.

King Reginald, astride his warhorse, led the charge. Beside him, Lucius commanded a squadron of elite knights, their armor gleaming as they cut through the enemy ranks.

The two armies met with a resounding crash, the front lines colliding in a violent storm of metal and flesh. Soldiers on both sides shouted battle cries, their voices mingling with the clash of weapons and the cries of the wounded. Arrows rained down from above, archers on both sides seeking targets amid the melee.

Amidst the battlefield, Lucius spotted a group of ranged cultists taking aim at their front lines. "Archers, to the left!" he roared. "Take them down!"

The Avaloran archers turned their attention to the threat, loosing arrows with deadly accuracy. The enemy fell one by one, their bodies crumpling to the ground.

Serena moved with grace and precision, taking out multiple enemies at once. Gus too unleashed a barrage of bubbles, incapacitating the enemy cultists, making them dance to his tune.

As the battle raged on, Lucius carved a path through the enemy ranks, his eyes scanning the chaos for the one face he knew he would eventually encounter. The moment came when he saw Marcus, standing tall in the Ophidonian armor. Lucius narrowed his eyes, his grip tightening on his sword. With a determined stride, he made his way toward Marcus, their gazes locking amidst the clamor of battle. The air between them seemed to crackle with tension, a silent acknowledgment of the betrayal that had brought them to this moment.

"So, it's true," Lucius said, his voice carrying over the sounds of combat. "You've fully embraced your role as a traitor."

Marcus smirked, his eyes cold and unyielding. "You always were too trusting, Lucius. Did you really think I would choose to follow a weak king and a dying kingdom?"

Lucius's grip tightened further, his knuckles turning white. "Avalora is not dying. It's people like you who are tearing it apart."

"You never understood, Lucius. Power is all that matters. Loyalty, honor—they're just illusions," Marcus said, raising his sword.

Lucius charged forward, their swords clashing with a resounding ring. "You were like a brother to me, Marcus. How could you turn your back on everything we stood for?"

Marcus parried the blow. "Because I saw the truth. Reginald's reign is over. Caelumyth offers a future where I can thrive."

The two warriors exchanged blows, their swords clashing loudly. Lucius fought with a fierce determination, each strike fueled by a sense of betrayal and a desire for justice. Marcus, on the other hand, moved with a cold, calculated precision.

"You're nothing but a pawn in their game," Lucius grunted, dodging a powerful swing. "They'll discard you the moment you're no longer useful."

"And you're a fool for believing in a king who can't even protect his own son."

Before Lucius could respond, a shadow loomed behind him. An enemy soldier raised his weapon, aiming for Lucius's back. Marcus smirked, his eyes darting to the impending attack, but before the blow could land, a flash of steel intervened. Sir Eamon had blocked the strike just in time.

"Lucius, watch out!" Eamon shouted, deflecting the enemy's attack.

Lucius turned, a mix of surprise and gratitude in his eyes. "Thank you, Eamon."

"We need to regroup!" Eamon urged, his eyes darting between Lucius and Marcus.

Lucius nodded reluctantly, realizing the battle was far from over. With a final glance at Marcus, he and Eamon fought their way back to the main force. The chaotic battle continued to rage around them, the clash of swords, the cries of the wounded, and the relentless onslaught of Caelumyth's forces filling the air.

***

Back inside the stronghold, Lumo and Meera were alone, only guarded by a single cultist. Oliver stood motionless; he only needed Lumo to make a move.

As Meera continued struggling against her chains, the cultist moved closer, urging her to stop.

"Please stop, or the consequences will be dire," he said, a tinge of empathy in his voice.

As the cultist moved closer, Meera couldn't shake the feeling that his face appeared familiar. She had seen him before, but she couldn't quite figure it out.

And then it hit her.

"Lumo," she whispered.

"What?" Lumo whispered back, not making any sudden movements.

"I think that's Gideon."

"Who? Oh. Ohhhh," Lumo's eyes went round. "Wait, are you sure?"

Meera continued observing Gideon's face, which peeked beneath his hood. She was sure this was the same person she had seen in Isolde's memories. The mole on his chin was a dead giveaway.

"I'm positive."

"Well, what difference does it make? He's one of them."

"Maybe I can convince him to help us," Meera said.

"And how are you going to do that?"

"I don't know. Let me try talking to him first."

As Lumo continued in a tense stare contest with Oliver, Meera called out to the man.

"You're Gideon, aren't you?"

Gideon's head snapped toward Meera, his eyes narrowing. "What are you talking about? M—My name is not Gideon."

"Yes, it is," Meera insisted. "We met your wife, Isolde. She told us about you."

"Isolde..."

"She misses you dearly, Gideon. She hasn't given up hope," Meera continued, her voice softening. "She's been waiting for you all these years."

Gideon's eyebrows twitched. "No. I can't go back. I made my choices. I have a purpose here."

"You've been brainwashed," Meera said, her tone urgent. "They manipulated you, turned you into someone you're not. Your life is with Isolde, not here."

Gideon shook his head, taking a step back. "You don't understand. My place is here, serving Lord Cernunnos."

Meera's heart raced, but she kept her voice steady. "Gideon… you have a son, you know."

Gideon's face contorted with confusion and disbelief. "A son? No, you're lying."

"I'm not lying. Isolde was pregnant when you left. She's been raising your son all by herself."

Gideon's breath hitched. He looked away, his gaze fixed on the ground as if searching for answers in the stones. "Even if it's true, my duty is here."

Meera took a deep breath. "Gideon, take this ring," she said.

"What are you—"

"Just take it," Meera insisted. "This isn't a trick. Put it on and hold my hand. I want to show you something."

Gideon hesitated, turning nervously toward the door, then stepped forward and pulled the ring from Meera's finger. He placed it on his own and held Meera's hand.

"Now close your eyes and shut out all thoughts. I want you to see the truth."

As Gideon closed his eyes, so did Meera, projecting the memories she wanted him to see. The memories flooded into his mind.

He saw Isolde clutching her stomach, standing at the doorway, waiting for Gideon to return. Her eyes were filled with hope and uncertainty, longing for the man she loved. The scene shifted, showing her holding their newborn son for the first time, her eyes brimming with tears of joy and sorrow.

The memories continued, revealing the sleepless nights Isolde endured, rocking their son to sleep, singing lullabies with a voice filled with love and exhaustion. He saw her comforting the child through his first fever, her worry palpable yet tempered by a mother's unwavering strength. The vision shifted to Isolde teaching their son to walk, her hands guiding him with gentle patience as he took his first wobbly steps.

Gideon witnessed the small victories of motherhood: Isolde cheering as their son spoke his first word, the pride in her eyes as he learned to read, and the joy of watching him play in the fields, his laughter a melody of innocence. He saw the struggles too—Isolde mending clothes, tending to their small garden, and working tirelessly to provide for their son.

As the boy grew older, Gideon saw him asking about his father. Isolde's eyes filled with sorrow, yet she maintained a brave face as she fabricated stories of him and how he had to leave on a very important mission.

When the memories finally ended, Gideon fell to his knees.

"I... I didn't know," he whispered, his voice breaking. "I didn't know she was pregnant. I didn't know... about our son."

"Now you do," Meera said gently. "You can still go back to them, Gideon. You can still make things right."

"I'm so sorry," he sobbed. "I'm so sorry... for everything."

"It's not too late, Gideon. Help us, and you can start making amends right now."

"I—I can't. It's impossible to leave. You don't know these people."

"Well... you don't know us," Meera grinned. "Help free us and we will make sure no one has to go through this again."

"How? He is standing guard," Gideon said, turning his head slightly toward Oliver.

"Get our weapons," Meera instructed. "Bring them to us, and we'll take care of the rest."

Gideon nodded, his resolve hardening. He moved swiftly to retrieve their weapons. He returned moments later, carrying Meera's staff and Lumo's sword.

"Thank you, Gideon," Meera said, taking her staff. "Now, get out of here as soon as you can. Leave the rest to us."

***

CHAPTER 26

They were now alone in the room with Oliver.

"Lumo, um..." Meera said softly.

"I'm listening," Lumo replied, his eyes on Oliver.

"Why didn't you tell me?"

"Tell you what?" Lumo frowned.

"About being the true heir." Meera shifted her weight. "Didn't you trust me?"

"It's not that, Meera." Lumo sighed. "Look, I will tell you later, all right? Now is not the time."

"Fine, but you owe me an explanation." Meera shot him a look.

Lumo grunted.

"Well, this is it, then. I'm going to use a spell to break our binds. When that happens, Oliver will charge at you. You need to handle him. Do you think you can do that?"

"I can." Lumo straightened himself. "Leave him to me."

"Lumo, I want you to remember something. He isn't in his right mind. You might hold back because you don't want to harm him, but don't forget your life is at stake here too. Of course, I will be here to intervene should—"

"No," Lumo exclaimed with conviction.

"You will not interfere. This is between me and him. Promise me you will not intervene."

"But—"

"No buts," Lumo interrupted. "Stay out of it. Keep an eye on the door. If anyone else tries to attack, I need you to stay alert and defend us."

"Why?" Meera pressed. "Why must I stay out of it?"

"Because this is my fight," Lumo replied, his voice steady. "Oliver is my friend, and this is something I need to do myself. I need to face him alone. I can't kill him, Meera. I have to find a way to subdue him without taking his life. And I can't focus if I'm worried about you getting hurt. Please, promise me you won't interfere."

Meera hesitated, then nodded. "Fine."

"Are you ready?" she asked.

"Yes," Lumo replied.

Meera took a deep breath, focusing her energy. Despite her chains limiting her movement, she managed to plant her staff firmly into the ground, mumbling an incantation under her breath. The air around them swirled, vibrating with magical energy.

"Hold still," Meera whispered. "This might sting a little."

The wind around them intensified, forming a circle of sharp, whirling wind. The sound was a high-pitched whine, like the keening of a thousand invisible knives cutting through the air. The blades of wind clanked against the iron chains, chipping away at them little by little until they finally shattered and fell to the floor. As the chains broke, fragments clung to their wrists and ankles, the edges of the wind blades nicking their skin.

Lumo flinched, and in that instant, Oliver's eyes snapped into focus, lunging forward with feral intensity.

"Here he comes!" Meera shouted, quickly moving to the side.

Lumo was ready. He pulled out his sword, instantly raising it to parry Oliver's vicious strike. The clash of metal echoed through the chamber, sparks flying as their blades met.

"Oliver, stop! It's me, Lumo!" Lumo shouted, hoping to break through the trance.

But Oliver's eyes remained cold and unseeing, his attacks relentless and precise, driven by muscle memory and reflex. Lumo's heart pounded as he parried another strike, his mind racing to find a way to subdue his friend without causing harm.

"Oliver, snap out of it!" Lumo pleaded, dodging a particularly aggressive swing. He countered with a quick strike to Oliver's arm, aiming to disarm rather than injure.

Oliver staggered but quickly recovered, his blade slashing through the air with deadly intent. Lumo blocked and parried, his movements fluid but cautious, constantly on the defensive. The room was filled with the sounds of their combat: the clash of steel, the clinking of chains, heavy breathing, and the scuffling of feet on the stone floor.

Meera stood at the side, her staff ready, eyes darting between Lumo and the entrance. She was tense, every muscle in her body screaming to help Lumo, but she held back, honoring his request. Her fingers tightened around the staff, her heart aching as she watched the two friends battle.

As the fight intensified, Lumo felt a familiar presence in his mind. His sword, which had been quiet all this time, finally began whispering to him.

"Lumo," the sword's voice echoed in his mind. "Unleash your power. Use the inferno within you. Claim your destiny."

Lumo gritted his teeth, trying to ignore the voice. "Not now," he muttered.

"Use the fire, Lumo," the sword insisted. "You can end this quickly."

"I will not do it!" Lumo screamed, trying to drown out the voice.

"What?" Meera called out, looking utterly lost. "You... you won't do what?"

"Do it," the sword urged. "Burn him down."

"No!" Lumo shouted, shaking his head. "Stop talking to me!"

"All right," Meera mumbled, still confused.

Oliver took advantage of Lumo's momentary distraction, lunging forward with a powerful strike. Lumo barely managed to parry the blow, the force of it pushing him back.

"USE THE FIRE!" the sword commanded.

With a roar of defiance, Lumo summoned the inferno, flames engulfing his blade. He swung the fiery sword with precision. The attack was merciless, yet Oliver managed to dodge it purely on reflex. The intense heat forced Oliver to retreat, his movements slowing as he struggled to defend against the blazing attack.

"Lumo, what are you doing?" Meera shouted.

Lumo snapped to attention, realizing his fire could potentially end Oliver's life. As he focused, the fire slowly subsided, leaving behind a reddish tinge on his sword.

Oliver quickly regained his speed and again went on the offensive, whereas Lumo continued on the defensive, blocking each one of Oliver's attacks. As Lumo kept defending, he found his defense faltering.

And then he remembered Lucius's words: "A shield may protect you, but it is the sword that wins the battle."

Lumo had to end the fight quickly. He remembered the move Lucius had taught Oliver, the one move he had tried but always failed.

The Iron Hook.

For all the times he had struggled in the past, this was the one time he had to use it more than ever. Maybe he couldn't use it perfectly, but he had to try.

Lumo took a deep breath, focusing intently on Oliver's movements. As Oliver swung his sword in a powerful arc toward Lumo's head, Lumo saw his chance. He lifted his sword high in a deliberate block, feinting a momentary opening. As Oliver committed to the attack, Lumo dropped into a low stance, bringing his sword swiftly down toward Oliver's legs.

Oliver, caught off guard by the sudden change, shifted his defense downward with mechanical precision. This was the moment Lumo had been waiting for. With a fluid sweep, he hooked his sword around Oliver's wrist, feeling the impact as the blade connected. In one swift, decisive motion, Lumo twisted his wrist sharply, flawlessly executing the move and leveraging his sword to dislodge Oliver's grip.

Oliver's eyes remained vacant as his sword was flung from his hand, arcing through the air before clattering to the ground. Without hesitation, Lumo followed through, pushing against Oliver's chest with his shoulder. The force of the push, combined with Oliver's unbalanced stance, sent him sprawling backward.

Oliver hit the ground with a thud, breathless and disarmed, his expression unchanged, staring blankly up at the ceiling. Lumo stood over him, sword poised.

"Now, Lumo!" the sword's voice echoed in his mind, more insistent than ever. "Finish him! With Oliver gone, the throne will be yours. You are the rightful heir."

Lumo hesitated, his grip tightening on the handle of his sword. The weight of the sword felt heavier as the temptation grew stronger, like a leaden anchor dragging him down. The room seemed to close in around him, the voices in his head becoming louder and more persuasive.

"Think of the power, the respect," the sword continued, its voice silky and enticing. "All that you have ever desired, within your grasp. Just one strike, and it's all yours."

Lumo's eyes seethed with inner turmoil. He looked down at Oliver, who lay defenseless and entranced by the cult's magic.

Lumo, no he whispered to himself, shaking his head, trying to clear the fog of temptation. "I can't."

"Yes, you can," the sword whispered seductively. "End it now. Claim your birthright!"

Lumo raised his sword, the fiery temptation roaring back to life within him. The blade glowed faintly, as if responding to his conflicted emotions. His muscles tensed, and for a moment, he felt himself teetering on the edge of darkness.

"Lumo, what are you doing?" Meera's voice cut through the haze, sharp and desperate.

Lumo turned to see Meera, her eyes wide with fear and confusion.

"Stop!" she pleaded, stepping closer.

The sword hissed in Lumo's mind, angry and insistent. "Don't listen to her. She doesn't understand. Mercy is a luxury the weak cannot afford. You're not weak, are you?"

"You deserve this. This is your destiny! Kill him!"

Lumo's hand trembled, his resolve wavering as he looked down at Oliver. The sword pulsed in his grip, its dark promise tugging at him, whispering of power. He hesitated, his eyes flickering with doubt, but the pull was relentless. His grip tightened, and with a fierce, steely look, he held the blade aloft, poised to strike.

"Lumo, no!" Meera's voice cut through the silence, desperation in her tone.

But Lumo's gaze was locked on Oliver.

"Gust of wind!" Meera chanted wildly, thrusting her staff forward. A powerful gust erupted from her, crashing into Lumo with the force of a storm.

Lumo was caught off guard. The blast of wind knocked him off his feet, sending him crashing to the floor, his sword clattering away from his grasp. The sharp impact jolted him back to his senses.

Meera rushed to his side, her eyes filled with concern. "Are you okay? I'm sorry."

Lumo looked up at her but then shied his eyes away.

"What happened back there?" Meera asked.

"I don't know..." Lumo shook his head.

As Meera stared intently, Lumo continued. "There's so much to tell you. I promise I will once we're through here."

"Fair enough," Meera said, extending a helping hand to Lumo.

Together, they hurriedly rushed over to Oliver's side. Before he could recover, Lumo delivered a slap to Oliver's face, shouting urgently, "Snap out of it now!"

The sharp slap seemed to jolt Oliver out of his trance. His vacant eyes slowly regained focus as he blinked, disoriented.

"Lumo, what are you doing here?" Oliver asked, looking around in confusion.

Lumo helped Oliver sit up. "Glad to have you back."

"Lumo, the cult; they're planning to kill me," Oliver said with a panicked expression.

"We know. We won't let them," Lumo said, glancing at Meera with a smile. "Now, hurry up, we need to go."

As the trio prepared to escape, Meera noticed Lumo hadn't picked up his sword.

"Lumo, your sword," she said.

Lumo stared at the sword, hesitant to touch it again. But he had made a promise to return it back from where it came. With their mission on the edge of completion, he decided he would fulfill his oath no matter what. He grabbed the sword and secured it within its scabbard. Together, they rushed through the door, one step closer to escaping.

***

Outside, the battle had ensued for a while, with heavy casualties on both sides. The battlefield was a chaotic scene of clashing swords, fallen soldiers, and desperate cries. The ground was stained red, and the air was thick with the metallic scent of war.

Somewhere on the battlefield, Marachi and his elite cultists were holding their ground, channeling fire and dark spells that cut through the ranks of Avaloran soldiers.

Amid the chaos, a sudden, unnatural darkness crept across the sky. The light dimmed, and a chill spread through the battlefield as the moon slowly moved in front of the sun. Gasps of alarm and awe rippled through both sides as the eclipse reached totality, casting an eerie twilight over the scene.

"The time has come, my brethren!" Marachi exclaimed, his voice carrying over the battlefield. "Embrace the power of the dark and crush our enemies!"

The cultists responded with renewed fervor, their spells brimming with dark energy.

Emboldened by the eclipse, Marachi started chanting his spell.

O' Houn-vas Annun, vyrae enarth malis,
Faer vethan sorun, vithran akthal vithran thalis.

A dark, swirling vortex formed on the ground in the distance, expanding and twisting as he chanted faster and louder. The vortex grew into a giant ball of void, an abyssal sphere that seemed to absorb all light around it.

From within the depths of the dark void, eerie, ghostly howls emerged. The air grew colder, and the ground trembled as the Cwn Annwn materialized, their eyes glowing with malevolent fire. The monstrous hounds surged forward, their ferocious attacks wreaking havoc on the Avaloran soldiers.

On the eastern ridge stood Caelumyth himself, clad in dark plate armor trimmed with golden edges. His pale violet cloak billowed behind him as he surveyed the battlefield from an elevated ridge.

"Advance the left flank. Box them in against the cliffside," Caelumyth ordered, his voice resonating like a cold bell. "And have the archers target their artillery. They must not breach our lines."

A lieutenant at his side saluted and relayed the commands, and within moments his army shifted like a well-oiled machine. The left flank surged forward, driving Avaloran soldiers into a narrow pocket. Screams echoed as blades found their mark, and arrows rained through the air, shattering Avaloran defenses.

Satisfied, Caelumyth strode down the ridge, mounted on his warhorse. A squadron of Avaloran knights, desperate to halt the advance, charged toward him. But Caelumyth's troops were prepared. At his signal, a wall of shields locked together with a resounding clang, the ground trembling as the two forces collided.

With a flick of his reins, he maneuvered his mount into the thick of battle, the beast's iron-shod hooves trampling any Avaloran soldier who strayed too close. His longsword gleamed dully under the eerie twilight cast by the eclipse as he struck down another knight with a precise, downward slash, the momentum carrying the wounded soldier into the dirt.

Far below, amidst the chaos, Lucius fought to stay focused, his gaze darting over the turmoil. He scanned the battlefield with growing desperation.

"Where's Serena?" he asked, cutting through an advancing foe.

"I think to the right," Eamon said, finishing off an enemy.

Lucius charged through the fray, dodging attacks and cutting down foes as he searched for Serena. Eamon followed. They finally spotted her, battling near the edge of the field, her staff whirling with wind and light magic.

"Serena!" Lucius shouted as he approached. "We need you to do something about those hounds!"

Serena glanced at the spectral hounds causing havoc among their ranks. "I need a moment!" she called back. "Cover me."

Lucius and Eamon stood guard around Serena, taking out all the attackers as she began her spell. She planted her staff firmly into the ground and closed her eyes, drawing deep from the earth's power.

"Lucius, this spell is intense. It will take massive amounts of mana, and I can do this only once. I will be an open target while I'm channeling this magic. I'm counting on you," Serena said.

"Do your magic, Sorceress. Leave the rest to us," Lucius replied.

Serena began her incantation.

From depths below and caverns deep,
Rise, protectors, in earth's keep.
For duty sworn and purpose true,
In soil and stone, I conjure you.

The ground trembled as Serena's incantation took hold. A low, rumbling hum resonated through the air, growing in intensity. Gigantic hands, fingers sculpted from solid rock, pushed their way through the ground, followed by massive, stony torsos and legs.

The Golems, three in number, each distinct yet united by their elemental origin, rose to their full height. Luminescent orbs of mystical energy flickered to life within the hollow sockets that served as their eyes.

The ground, now consecrated by their emergence, retained a faint luminescence, as if imbibed with the residual magic that birthed the Golems.

In unison, the Golems turned their attention toward Serena, their movements synchronized and purposeful. They stood as silent guardians, poised and ready for the next command from their summoner.

Serena pointed her staff toward the hounds, and the stone golems lumbered forward, their heavy steps shaking the ground. They met the Cwn Annwn head-on, their massive fists swinging with incredible force. The spectral hounds snarled and lunged, but the golems were relentless, their rocky bodies impervious to the hounds' ghostly bites.

The battlefield became a clash of titans as the stone golems and the Cwn Annwn battled fiercely. The Avaloran soldiers, heartened by the sight of their new allies, redoubled their efforts, pushing back against the cultists with renewed vigor.

"Stop her," Marachi snarled.

The mime who stood as Marachi's personal bodyguard charged toward Serena, Lucius, and Eamon almost dramatically. The mime's face was painted with a perpetual, unsettling grin. He knew he was no match for them all by himself, yet the sneaky villain had tricks of his own.

The mime raised his hands, and invisible walls appeared around him, bending and reflecting light in a way that made him nearly invisible behind them. The battlefield behind the mime was perfectly mirrored on the walls' surfaces, making it seem as though he had vanished into thin air.

Lucius and Eamon narrowed their eyes, scanning the area. "Where is he?"

Invisible blades and tripwires struck at them from seemingly nowhere. Eamon felt sharp stings as invisible blades cut through his armor, and he stumbled over unseen obstacles, struggling to maintain his balance.

Lucius swung his sword defensively, trying to anticipate the attacks, but the mime's constructs were unpredictable. The reflective walls distorted their view, and the invisible traps seemed to come from all directions.

"Serena?" Lucius called out.

"Don't move," Serena replied.

Serena knew the cost of engaging the mime—losing control of the Golems. Taking a deep breath, she closed her eyes, recalling her academy training in darkness, where she had learned to sense magic and trust her instincts.

Drawing on that training, Serena closed her eyes, shutting out the confusing reflections and the visual noise. As Serena focused on dealing with the mime, the golems crumpled to the ground, their stone bodies falling apart without her control. As the Golems collapsed into rubble, Serena heightened her awareness, feeling the earth's vibrations, the whisper of shifting air, and the hum of magic around her.

Focusing on the mime's movements, she gripped her staff, slamming it into the ground. A spike of solid rock shot up from the ground, piercing through the reflective wall and striking the mime directly through the chest. The illusion shattered, revealing the mime's shocked expression as he crumpled to the ground.

Serena stood over him, breathing heavily. Even as he fell, a twisted grin remained plastered on his face, a final act of defiance. At least he was victorious in stopping Serena, if only for a moment. Serena stared intently, content at having finally avenged Sylvanus's death. But she had overused her magic. She fell to the floor, weak but conscious, just as Lucius caught her.

"We need to get the sorceress back to safety," Lucius commanded, urgency in his voice.

With Serena's arm around Lucius's shoulder, they moved quickly. Eamon took the lead, clearing the way. They navigated through the chaotic battlefield, weaving through skirmishes and parrying attacks. Despite the ongoing conflict around them, they managed to reach a safer area behind their lines, where the Avaloran medics quickly took Serena in.

As Lucius turned to scan the battlefield, nothing seemed to have changed; the battle was still raging on. The battlefield was a tumultuous sea of chaos. Bodies littered the ground, a grim reminder of the high cost of this conflict. The Cwn Annwn continued to wreak havoc on the battlefield. All hope was dwindling.

***

Inside, Lilith marched hurriedly with a few cultists in tow. One of the cultists held the Horn of Cernunnos carefully.

Another cultist carried a sacrificial dagger, its blade glinting ominously. The third cultist clutched a weathered leather-bound grimoire, while another carried a satchel brimming with ritualistic herbs, and yet another carried candles and incense in his hand.

"Hurry, it has already begun," Lilith commanded.

They moved quickly through the dimly lit corridors, their footsteps echoing ominously. As they rounded a corner, they were abruptly confronted by Lumo, Oliver, and Meera. The escapees stood ready, determination in their eyes.

Lilith's eyes widened in surprise and anger. "How did you escape?" she demanded, her voice a hiss of fury.

Lumo stepped forward. "We're not as easy to kill as you thought," he replied coolly.

Oliver, now fully back to his senses, gripped his sword with the finesse of a well-trained swordsman.

"Your plans end here, you maniacs," he declared.

Without another word, Lilith raised her hands, dark energy pulsing at her fingertips.

"Attack them!" she commanded her cultists.

The corridor erupted into chaos. Meera faced Lilith, summoning her wind magic. Gusts of wind swirled around her.

"You won't win this time!" Meera shouted, launching a powerful wind blast, which Lilith countered effortlessly.

Meanwhile, Lumo and Oliver engaged the cultists. Oliver's movements were fluid and precise, each strike of his sword displaying his training. He parried a cultist's attack and countered with a swift slash, disarming his opponent.

Lumo, still hesitant to unsheathe his sword, deflected a blow and followed up with a powerful kick, sending the cultist sprawling. The cultist with the sacrificial dagger charged at him, but Lumo sidestepped and struck with the pommel of the sheathed sword, knocking the attacker out cold.

Seeing their comrades fall, two of the cultists turned to flee. "We need to warn Brother Marachi!" one of them shouted as they ran down the corridor.

Lilith, realizing her position was becoming precarious, intensified her attacks on Meera. Dark tendrils of magic clashed with Meera's wind spells, filling the corridor with flashes of light and shadow.

Oliver and Lumo quickly dispatched the remaining cultists, then turned their attention to Lilith.

"It's over, Lilith," Lumo said, advancing with Oliver by his side.

"You fools! You think you can defeat us? We are the Cimmerian Order!" Lilith bellowed.

With a sinister grin, Lilith raised her hands, dark energy swirling at her fingertips.

Enar ithrak il vylthar vas cimora,
Tharn zalrithari hadh vael maas,
Uthar khida,
Vael vyrae enarth zarvorak.

Tendrils of smoky darkness snaked out from her hands, condensing to the floor. The dark smoke seeped into the fallen cultists' bodies, their wounds beginning to emit a faint, ghostly glow.

The lifeless eyes of the cultists snapped open, now glowing with darkness. Their bodies twitched and convulsed, slowly rising from the ground with jerky, puppet-like movements.

"Rise, my brethren!" Lilith commanded, her voice echoing with malevolent power. The reanimated cultists, now puppets of her will, stood before her, ready to obey her every command.

Lumo and Oliver watched in horror as the undead cultists advanced toward them. Despite the deep wounds inflicted by their swords, the undead continued to move, their bodies held together by the dark magic coursing through them.

Oliver swung his sword with precision, slashing through the chest of one of the undead, but the smoke seemed to knit their wounds, closing with threads of darkness. They continued to advance, driven by Lilith's necromantic power.

"They just keep coming!" Oliver shouted, frustrated.

"Meera, we need you!" Lumo called out, trying to fend off another undead cultist.

But Meera had her own problems. She was locked in a duel with Lilith, who had the upper hand. Lilith's dark magic had grown stronger, fueled by the power of the eclipse. With a wicked grin, she summoned a torrent of shadowy tendrils, lashing out at Meera's wind shield. Meera struggled to maintain her barrier, but the relentless assault was too much. The tendrils pierced through the wind, shattering the shield and sending Meera sprawling backward.

"Meera!" Lumo shouted.

***

CHAPTER 27

As Lumo and the others battled Lilith inside, the escaped cultists ran out, frantically searching for Marachi.

"Brother Marachi," the cultists shouted, spotting Marachi.

Marachi had been channeling the void, with more hounds pouring out by the minute.

"I'm busy," Marachi said, turning to them.

"Brother, the prince and his friends; they've escaped, and they took out several of us. Milady is fighting them alone."

"What?" Marachi said, a look of dread on his face.

As Marachi looked onward with a decision to make, it was made for him. The eclipse ended, with the sun peeking slowly. The once-dark skies brightened, the oppressive darkness receding as the sun emerged from behind the moon. Gradually, the battlefield was bathed in a warm, golden light, dispelling the eerie twilight that had given the cultists their advantage.

Marachi stared at the sky with a look of bitter disappointment, realizing their plans were on the brink of failure. He stopped chanting and looked anxiously for Marcus.

"Where is Marcus? Inform him; he is needed inside," Marachi directed one of the cultists.

"Casters, follow me; we're going in," he continued, gesturing to a few cultists.

As the battlefield was restored to normal light, the Cwn Annwn howled in pain. The spectral hounds, once fearsome and relentless, writhed and twisted. Their ghostly forms distorted, unable to withstand the return of the sunlight. Their howls grew more agonized, echoing across the battlefield as their ethereal bodies started to disintegrate. One by one, the Cwn Annwn dissolved into wisps of dark smoke. The ground beneath where they had stood was left scorched and smoldering, a testament to their brief but terrifying presence.

The Avaloran soldiers cheered, their voices rising in triumphant unison, bolstered by the vanquishing of the otherworldly threat.

Amid the cheers, Gus spotted Marachi and his casters heading inside. His eyes widened in alarm, and he quickly turned to Lucius.

"Something is going on inside," Gus said.

"What's wrong?" Lucius asked.

"Those guys... they're, uh... con...congr— they're moving fast inside," Gus stammered, pointing frantically toward the group.

Lucius followed Gus's gaze. "Eamon, we need to follow them. Get a group of soldiers ready."

As Gus and Lucius pushed toward the castle entrance, their eyes scanned the chaotic battlefield, determined to keep Marachi and his cultists in sight. With a group of soldiers at their side, they fought through scattered pockets of resistance, pressing forward with urgency.

At the threshold of the castle, another group of cultists emerged, blocking their path. Eamon's sword was already in motion, cleaving through the first of the attackers. He turned to Gus and Lucius, his voice firm and commanding.

"Go! I'll hold them here."

Lucius hesitated for only a moment, his eyes locking with Eamon's. Then he nodded sharply, gripping Gus by the shoulder. "Come on!"

The two rushed inside, a handful of guards following closely at their heels. The sound of Eamon's battle faded as they plunged deeper into the castle. The echo of Marachi's retreating footsteps guided them down the winding corridors, their pace quickening with each passing second.

***

Meanwhile, Lumo, Oliver, and Meera had figured out how to defeat Lilith's undead minions.

"Go for their heads," Oliver shouted, swiftly dismissing yet another undead.

The dark smoke seeped out of their lifeless bodies like an unholy vapor, curling into the air before dissipating entirely. The puppets crumpled to the floor.

As the eclipse faded, Lilith's shriek split the air like a jagged blade. Her hands curled into fists as she glared at the trio.

"You've ruined everything!"

Lumo stepped forward. "It's over now, Lilith. Surrender peacefully, or there will be no mercy!"

Before she could respond, the heavy thud of boots echoed down the corridor. Marachi burst into the room, flanked by cultists who fanned out like a dark tide.

"Milady!" he cried, taking in the scene. "What happened?"

Lilith's lips curled into a feral snarl. "Get them!"

The cultists charged. Oliver and Meera found themselves increasingly outnumbered and overwhelmed. Lumo had no choice but to unsheathe his weapon again, igniting the sword ablaze with fire. Swords clashed, magic crackled, and the air pulsed with the acrid scent of burning essence.

Lumo and Oliver stood back-to-back.

"What do we do?" Oliver panted, deflecting a blow.

"We fight," Lumo growled. "We fight with everything we've got. This ends here, one way or another."

As the cultists closed in, Marachi's eyes locked onto Meera. Recognizing her as the primary threat with her wind magic, he moved quickly, his dark energy clashing against her spells.

"You'll be dealing with me now, little sorceress."

The room became a storm of howling gales and seething shadows. Meera pushed herself to the brink, summoning gusts that sent debris flying, but Marachi countered with relentless precision.

With Meera occupied by Marachi, Lilith silently turned her attention to Oliver. She focused her hands in front of her pendant, chanting an ominous spell.

Cimora zalrithun, thanor enarth vyran,
Ath oram tharn xenrak illythor,
Khora thaloraeth rathul vael elosir,
Ithrazar thalora nabi tos likhun thulnara.

Dark energy fizzed at her fingertips, growing in intensity.

"You will fall today!" she exclaimed.

Time seemed to slow for Lumo as he spotted Lilith targeting Oliver. His heart pounded, and a sense of dread washed over him. It was the same spell that had once taken Amelia's life. He knew he had to act quickly.

As he moved to intercept, a voice rang out from his sword.

"STOP!"

Lumo froze in his tracks, unable to move, as if an invisible force held him back.

Wide-eyed and helpless, Lumo watched as Lilith's chant reached its crescendo. He glanced around: Oliver was locked in a fierce battle with a cultist, narrowly dodging a deadly spell and swinging his sword with precision. Nearby, Meera was desperately fending off Marachi, her magical defenses barely holding against his relentless assault.

Lilith's chest heaved as she gathered the swirling darkness in her palms, forming a concentrated, malevolent sphere. Her lips curled into a feral grin, and her eyes burned with a dangerous light. With a sharp inhale, she thrust her hands forward, unleashing the surge of energy.

"Morah!" she screamed, her voice ringing with fury and triumph. The dark blast tore through the air, rippling with unrelenting force, its trajectory locked on Oliver.

In that split second, Lumo did not notice when Lucius had arrived with a group of soldiers. Lucius sprinted forward, his mithril sword raised high. The blast streaked toward Oliver like a streak of night-given form. With a fierce roar, Lucius swung with all his might, the blade colliding with the seething mass of darkness. The dark beam ricocheted into the corridor wall, exploding in a deafening roar.

The shockwave rippled through the air, hurling people off their feet. Smoke billowed as part of the wall collapsed, launching jagged debris in all directions.

Oliver blinked through the haze, his ears ringing. Lucius stood over him, extending a hand.

"Are you hurt?" Lucius's voice cut through the chaos like a lifeline.

Oliver clasped his hand, shaking his head as he staggered upright.

Seizing the moment, the soldiers burst into the area, quickly dispatching the remaining cultists with swift and decisive strikes. The air filled with the cries of the fallen.

Gus's eyes locked onto Marachi through the swirling chaos. With a thunderous roar, he barreled forward like an avalanche, crashing into Marachi with bone-jarring force. His massive arms coiled around him, muscles straining as he clamped down with an iron grip. Marachi thrashed and writhed, but Gus's hold was as unyielding as a steel vise, rooting the smaller man in place.

"Got you now!" Gus grunted.

"That guy is with us?" Oliver asked wide-eyed, as he watched the gigantic Gus squeezing the life out of Marachi. Lucius grinned proudly.

Lilith's gaze darted across the battlefield, her expression twisting from fury to dawning horror. Their plan had failed. Clenching her fists, she stumbled back, retreating into the shadows of the chamber.

Lucius turned to Lumo and Oliver, nodding with grim determination. "Let's finish this."

But before they could move to chase after Lilith, Lucius's face twisted in sudden pain. His instincts screamed too late, and a sharp, searing pain ripped through his back. He staggered forward, his hand tightening around the hilt of his sword as he fought to stay upright.

Lumo and Oliver froze as their gazes locked onto Marcus standing behind Lucius. In his hand was a stained blade, its length pressed firmly against Lucius's back.

Lucius gasped as he struggled to make sense of the situation. Slowly, he turned his head, his expression a mixture of pain and disbelief as his eyes met Marcus's.

"Marcus..." Lucius rasped.

He had been so absorbed in the chaos of the battlefield that he hadn't noticed Marcus slipping through the carnage behind him.

The tension hung in the air like a tangible weight, suffocating the space between them. Oliver's heart dropped into his stomach, his breath caught in his throat.

Lucius's hand trembled as he summoned what strength he had left. With a defiant cry, he twisted in Marcus's grip, his own blade finding its mark. The sword drove deep into Marcus's side, tearing through armor with brutal precision.

Marcus's eyes widened in shock, his lips parting in silent pain. He staggered back, collapsing to the ground without a word. Lucius's own knees buckled, and he collapsed.

"Lucius, no!" Oliver screamed, his voice breaking as he rushed to his side. He cradled Lucius's head in his lap, the trembling fingers of one hand pressed desperately against the wound. "No, no, no—you're going to be fine. Just hold on," he choked out.

Lucius coughed, his lips stained red. Lumo, now free from his paralysis, hurried to kneel beside Oliver. Lucius's gaze flickered between the two young men.

"It's... okay, Prince." His voice was barely audible.

"Lucius, stay with us," Oliver begged as he looked around for help.

Lucius's breath grew slower, shallower, and a deep weariness settled into his features. "I... won't make it," he murmured.

"Lucius, no! Don't leave us," Oliver cried, clutching his mentor's hand. "I can't do this alone."

Lucius's hand twitched, his fingers brushing weakly against Oliver's.

"Y—You're not... alone," he said softly, his eyes flickering toward Lumo, who was watching with quiet sorrow. "For what it's worth... I'm glad... you chose your companions well." A faint, pained smile tugged at Lucius's lips, a final expression of pride despite the agony.

Lucius's lips parted, and with great effort, he whispered, "You have to... finish this."

His eyes, full of fierce loyalty, flicked between Oliver and Lumo.

"Promise me... you'll protect our people."

"We will," Oliver vowed, tears streaming down his face. "We promise."

Lucius's eyes softened, a hint of peace settling over his features. With one final, labored breath, he closed his eyes, his body relaxing, as the last traces of life slipped away from him.

Oliver felt the world shatter around him. He held Lucius's lifeless body close, his chest heaving as the tears he'd tried to hold back poured freely. The deafening clamor of battle dulled to a distant roar, as though the world itself had paused to mourn alongside him.

"LUCIUS!" he cried out, his voice raw and broken.

Lumo stood still for a moment, his heart heavy with the loss of a man he had come to respect and admire. The bond between Oliver and Lucius had been forged through years of trust, and now it was shattered. He could see the pain in Oliver's eyes, the desperate, lost look that mirrored his own anguish. But there was no time to dwell.

With a deep, steadying breath, Lumo straightened himself. His grief would have to wait. Lumo's legs pushed him forward, his movements swift and determined as he sprinted down the corridor. His heart pounded in his chest. He rounded the corner just in time to see Lilith disappearing into a swirling portal, her expression a mixture of fury and defiance.

"Aluth thal cim thalrin, ethnor vyn vithran thor drael," she hissed before disappearing from view.

"NO!" Lumo shouted as he dashed toward the portal. But it was too late. The portal closed with a final, ominous swirl, leaving him staring at the empty space where Lilith had stood.

***

Outside the castle, the explosion shattered the uneasy rhythm of battle. Avaloran soldiers and cultists alike paused, heads snapping toward the castle as smoke poured from the newly gaping hole in its wall.

From a vantage point on the eastern ridge, Caelumyth's eyes narrowed at the sight. His lieutenant rode up beside him, his voice edged with panic.

"The castle wall is breached! Our ally leaders must be under attack!"

Caelumyth's gaze lingered on the column of smoke and the frantic movement of soldiers outside the castle. His mind worked quickly, calculating their odds. With the eclipse ended and their forces scattering, the battle was clearly turning against them.

"Sound the retreat," he ordered, his tone cold and final.

"But my lord—"

"The battle is lost," Caelumyth interrupted, his voice sharp. "We regroup and fight another day. Rally the men to fall back immediately."

The lieutenant hesitated for a fraction of a second before riding off.

Caelumyth turned his mount, his eyes hardening as he surveyed the battlefield one last time.

"Lilith," he muttered. "You'd better survive this."

Behind him, horns sounded the retreat. The serpent knights began pulling back, their dark banners receding like a shadow retreating before the light. The chaos of the battlefield shifted as Avaloran soldiers raised victorious cries, pressing forward against the retreating lines.

***

Lumo had reentered the corridor, his steps slow and heavy. Meera turned to him, her eyes brimming with hope, but the look on his face told her all she needed to know. His shoulders slumped and his fists were clenched tightly, his gaze dropping to the floor.

"She got away," murmured Meera.

Lumo's throat was too tight to respond. His eyes scanned the room, landing on Oliver still on the floor, clutching Lucius's body as if holding on would bring him back. The sight sent a pang through Lumo's chest, but he didn't approach. *What could he say?*

Nearby, Eamon stood frozen for a brief moment, as his eyes fell on Lucius's still form. His jaw tightened, and he took a halting step toward the fallen knight, his breath catching in his throat.

"Lucius..." he whispered.

For a moment, the chaos around him faded, and it was just the unbearable weight of loss pressing down on him. But the sounds of soldiers regrouping snapped him back to the present. He straightened, forcing himself to swallow his grief. There would be time to mourn later.

Eamon took a deep breath. "Secure the prisoner. Check the perimeter for any stragglers. We're moving out now!"

***

The retreat sounded like a death knell across the battlefield. Caelumyth's forces, their dark banners slowly fading in the distance, pulled back in disciplined formation. The serpent knights, grim-faced and battle-worn, retreated into the tunnels in perfect order. Even in the face of defeat, Caelumyth's army moved with chilling precision.

On the battlefield, the sight of the retreating army was a small victory, but one that King Reginald did not savor. His gaze swept over the chaos around him, his expression set in grim resolve.

"We've broken them," Reginald said, his voice carrying through the heavy air. His soldiers rallied behind him, their spirits lifted by the sight of the enemy's retreat. "Press forward! Take prisoners, and end this—today."

As the command echoed through the ranks, the Avaloran soldiers surged forward, cutting down scattered pockets of resistance and rounding up the fleeing cultists. Reginald's eyes never wavered from the retreating forces, his mind already turning to the next steps in securing the kingdom's future.

But just as his confidence seemed unshakable, a disturbance rippled through the ranks. Eamon emerged from the castle gates, his eyes hard, his steps grim. Behind him, Oliver and Lumo followed, their faces marked by exhaustion, sorrow, and something far darker—loss.

Relief flickered across King Reginald's face for a fleeting moment as he saw them, bruised and battered but alive.

Then, as Eamon drew closer, the unease in the air grew. In his hands, a bloodied standard bearer's flag hung limp, and behind him, soldiers bore a stretcher draped in blackened cloth. Whispers died as they caught sight of the lifeless form beneath the covering.

King Reginald's breath hitched. His gaze dropped to the stretcher, and a chill settled over him. He stepped forward, a sense of dread creeping into his bones.

"Eamon," King Reginald said, his voice rougher than he intended.

Eamon met his eyes, his own filled with a sorrow that even a king's resolve could not counter. Slowly, he lowered his gaze to the stretcher, where Lucius lay motionless. The ground beneath King Reginald seemed to shift, victory hollowed out by the weight of this loss.

Oliver, pale and trembling, approached his father. "Father..." he rasped, his voice thick with grief. He glanced at Lucius, the knight's death etched into his hollow expression.

Reginald remained silent for a long moment, his posture rigid, his face a storm of unspoken anguish. The weight of Lucius's sacrifice bore down on him, his pain manifesting not in tears, but in a smoldering intensity that burned like the fury of a hundred battles lost.

Lumo, however, had no such restraint. Standing beside Oliver, his jaw tightened, and his fists curled at his sides. His voice, when it came, was raw with anger. "This is your fault," he said, the accusation striking like a blade.

Oliver turned to him, startled. "Lumo—"

"No!" Lumo snapped, his focus pinned on the king. "You could have prevented this. All of it," Lumo growled.

Oliver could see the storm in Lumo's eyes, the raw emotion threatening to break free. He opened his mouth, but no words came.

Before the tension could erupt further, a commotion near the castle gates stole everyone's attention. A column of

Avaloran soldiers emerged, their boots ringing against the stone. At their center was Marachi, bound in heavy iron chains. Meera and Gus flanked him, their expressions hard and unyielding.

Marachi stumbled as a guard shoved him forward.

"Careful, brute," Marachi spat.

"Quiet," snapped the guard.

The soldiers marched Marachi to the center of the battlefield. Despite his disheveled appearance, Marachi held his head high, his defiance sharp as a dagger.

King Reginald's attention locked on him instantly, his grief giving way to fury.

"You," he snarled, his voice sharp enough to cut through steel. "How many lives have been destroyed because of your madness? How much blood stains those hands of yours?"

Marachi smirked. "More than you can count, Your Majesty. And your hands are no cleaner."

King Reginald's fist clenched, but Eamon stepped closer. "The remaining cultists are being rounded up as we speak, Your Majesty. Most have surrendered."

King Reginald didn't acknowledge him immediately, his gaze boring into Marachi with unrelenting hatred. But the news cooled his temper, if only slightly. He straightened, his voice commanding. "Secure him. And every one of his followers. They will answer for their crimes before the kingdom."

As Marachi was hauled away, King Reginald's posture faltered for a brief moment. A sharp pang seized his chest, and he instinctively clutched at it.

Oliver's eyes narrowed. "Are you alright, Father?"

Reginald straightened himself. "Yes. This... thing is persistent. But never mind." His voice was strained, though his gaze never wavered from the soldiers spreading across the battlefield, ensuring every cultist was subdued and accounted for.

The battle was over, but the war within their hearts was far from done.

***

Epilogue: A week later

Seven days had passed since the battle, and Avalora Castle stood shrouded in quiet mourning. The castle courtyard had been chosen to honor the fallen. Soldiers, nobles, and families of the fallen gathered in silence.

Simple caskets, draped in Avaloran banners, stretched across the cobblestones in perfect rows. Candles flickered in the cold breeze, their small flames braving the biting wind. At the forefront, Lucius's casket lay apart, with a single sword resting atop it.

King Reginald stood at the center of the gathering. At his side, Archibald held a scroll, though his posture suggested no need for the document. The words had long been prepared.

"Today, we stand in the wake of sacrifice," King Reginald announced. "These men gave their lives so that this kingdom may endure. Their courage will not be forgotten."

A murmur of agreement rippled through the crowd as the king bowed his head.

"And though we mourn, we must also honor their legacy by securing the future they fought to protect," he continued.

The crowd stilled as Archibald stepped forward. "Stability is not simply our duty—it is our strength. And today, we celebrate not only those we've lost but the promise of a brighter tomorrow. The prince has returned to us."

Oliver's stomach churned. His body tensed, the weight of the crowd's eyes pressing against him. He bowed his head slightly, but every muscle felt stiff, unnatural. The words of the king were a reminder of the lie he was now complicit in. His fingers fidgeted behind his back, though he forced a small, weak smile.

The truth had been revealed to him in the days since their return. Lumo had explained everything—the bloodline, the switch at birth, the crown that belonged to him. Weighty discussions with the king had followed, their outcome clear: the status quo would remain, at least until the war had settled.

Each word had settled into Oliver's mind like a foreign weight, something he couldn't escape. Beside him, the man who had been his ally, his friend—was the true prince.

And here he was, standing before the people, accepting the adoration that should be Lumo's.

Oliver's gaze flicked briefly to Lumo, who stood a step behind, his hands clasped in front of him and his head lowered just enough to seem reverent, though his expression betrayed nothing. He did not even flinch at the announcement.

The prince has returned.

It was true in the way a dulled sword still cuts.

Lumo didn't resent Oliver—not really. But standing there, knowing it was his own bloodline they were celebrating, felt like a slow-burning ache.

The crowd stood in silence, the weight of the king's words hanging in the air. Reginald's gaze swept across the fallen soldiers, pausing on Lucius's casket. For a moment, his eyes softened, but only for an instant. He raised his head and addressed the people again.

"Let their sacrifice be our reminder. We are bound by blood and duty, but more than that, by the resolve to protect what is ours. Their courage will guide us through the darkest of times."

The wind tugged at the banners above the caskets, their fluttering sound the only noise as the kingdom's final salute to those who had given everything.

King Reginald stepped back, his eyes briefly meeting Oliver's before shifting to Lumo. A brief flicker of hesitation passed between them. He turned to Archibald, who gave a subtle nod in return.

With a final bow of his head, King Reginald raised his hand in salute. "May their spirits find peace, and may we honor them by ensuring the future they died to protect."

The crowd responded in kind, a unified murmur of agreement spreading through the castle courtyard. As the last of the words faded, the crowd began to disperse, paying their respects before returning to their lives.

***

Lumo seemed withdrawn for the next few days. They had assigned a new servant to the prince. Lumo would often remain confined to his quarters, staring out the window and observing the stillness of the castle.

A soft knock was heard on his door.

"Hey, Lumo. You in there?"

Lumo didn't respond at first. He was still staring out the window

Another knock. "Lumo?" Meera's voice was soft, yet insistent.

With a slow exhale, Lumo finally turned away from the window, his gaze meeting the door. He hesitated for a moment before crossing the room and opening it to find Meera standing at the entrance.

"I brought you something," she said, lifting a small jug of apple cider. "I know you like it."

Lumo gave her a small, hollow smile, stepping slightly aside but not fully moving away from the door. "I'm not in the mood for a drink," he said.

Meera didn't wait for an invitation. She entered anyway, her eyes scanning the room as she set the jug down on his table. "Then what are you in the mood for, Lumo?" she asked gently.

Lumo shrugged, running a hand through his disheveled hair. "I don't know. Peace, maybe. Quiet." He turned back toward the window.

"Did you hear about Eamon? They're going to make him Captain, apparently," Meera said casually.

"I see," Lumo replied, his gaze still distant.

Meera moved closer, standing beside him and looking out the window with him. "You know, it's okay to feel lost sometimes. Even the strongest people do."

"I'm not strong," Lumo muttered. "Not anymore."

"You are strong," Meera insisted. "When you told me everything, I was shaken. I can't even begin to imagine what it's like for you. You've been through so much—and yet, here you are. That's strength, Lumo. It's not about having all the answers or being perfect. It's about what you do with everything you've been through."

Lumo turned his gaze back to her. "What do I do with it? I'm not sure I can do anything."

Meera remained quiet for a minute before breaking her silence. "Speaking of doing something, what are you going to do about that cursed sword? Didn't you tell me you made a promise to Serena to return it?"

Lumo stiffened at the mention of the sword, his jaw tightening involuntarily.

"I haven't forgotten," Lumo said quietly. "But I'm not sure what to do about it. I—I'm not allowed to leave the castle."

"So, you're a prisoner, eh? And since when has that stopped you, criminal?" Meera smirked.

Lumo gave a quiet, strained exhale, a ghost of a smile passing across his face. "Says the thief."

Meera arched an eyebrow. "Mast—"

"I know, I know," Lumo chuckled. "Thanks Meera... Anyway, what about you? Got any plans?"

"Oh, yeah! I've been meaning to tell you—I just never got the chance. Serena said she might be able to get me into... Harbridge! Can you believe it?"

"Amidst the chaos of war?" Lumo raised an eyebrow.

"Harbridge is untouched by the conflict—at least that's what Serena said. Well, she said she'd try. I guess I shouldn't get my hopes up just yet."

"Where is she anyway? I haven't seen her since we got back. She wasn't at the funeral either."

"She said she'd received a message from the Dryads and had to leave immediately."

Lumo tilted his head. "Zinnia?"

"The one and only," Meera smiled.

"Did she say anything else?" Lumo asked.

"Not really. Unless they've got her cleaning up more of the Elderine forests, she should be back soon."

"Hmm," Lumo murmured, his brow furrowing slightly.

Suddenly, the rapid pounding of hooves on stone echoed through the courtyard.

"There she is," Meera exclaimed, spotting Serena arriving on her horse. The horse skidded to a halt, and Serena swiftly dismounted, her cloak whipping around her as she came to a quick stop.

Serena instinctively turned her gaze towards Lumo's window. She gave them a hurried signal.

"I think she means us, Lumo. Let's go," Meera mouthed.

Lumo and Meera made their way past the corridor. They met Serena halfway, her breath coming in short, urgent bursts.

"Lumo," she gasped. "There's no time."

"Huh?" grunted Lumo.

"The Dryads," Serena panted, her eyes darting toward Meera. "I met with them. This isn't good."

Lumo's stomach tightened. "What happened, Serena?"

Her next words struck like a thunderclap.

"They said... the boy must die."

Lumo froze, his breath catching in his throat. "What boy?"

Serena's eyes met his. "You, Lumo. They mean you."

***

Acknowledgments

To Mentors and Guides

To Shivendra, thank you for guiding me through the labyrinth of storytelling. Your insights and unwavering encouragement transformed this dream into reality.

To Beta Readers and Editors

To my beta reader, Nikki, your feedback was a light in the dark corridors of revision. To my editor, Tiffany, thank you for polishing this story until it shone brighter than I could have imagined.

To the Readers

To you, dear reader, for stepping into this world I've created. Your willingness to journey alongside these characters means more than I can say. May their story resonate with you as it has with me.

Closing Words

This book exists because of the countless voices, hearts, and hands that shaped it. To everyone who walked this path with me, thank you. I am forever grateful.

About the Author

Nilesh Prabhu was born in Mumbai, India in 1986. From a young age, he showed a love for reading, particularly novels. At the age of eight, Nilesh began reading fantasy and mystery novels, which sparked a lifelong passion for the genre. After completing his education, Nilesh pursued a Master's degree in Finance, which led to a successful career in the financial sector.

Despite his busy schedule, Nilesh continued to read and write in his spare time, and he eventually discovered a talent for creating engaging content for children. Currently, Nilesh works as a part-time writer, using his creativity and love of storytelling to capture the imaginations of young readers.

When he's not working, Nilesh enjoys spending time with animals, particularly his beloved pets. He can often be found reading or writing his latest fantasy novel, or exploring the vibrant culture and cuisine of Mumbai.

Dear Reader,

If you want to know more about me and follow me for new updates on upcoming launches, you may scan the below QR code:

If you want to provide feedback on this book or sign up for email notifications on upcoming launches, you may scan the below QR code:

Also, if you haven't checked out my other book please check it out on Amazon.

Finally, please support the Author and review this book from where it was purchased.

Made in the USA
Las Vegas, NV
04 January 2026

38511167R00272